He sat in the ruins like an ownerless dog;
unable to pull himself together, walk away
and carry on with living. How long they
had been there he did not know. He saw,
and did not see.

Neither did he see where the child came
from, or how she came to be there. One
moment, it seemed, there was nothing in
the shadows under the broken staircase.
The next, a tiny waif shivering with the
cold. Afterwards it seemed to him
impossible that he could have hated her,
however fleetingly. Yet there she stood, a
child who had survived unhurt.

'You all right, honey?' he asked.

Also by Rhona Martin

GALLOWS WEDDING

and published by Corgi Books

Rhona Martin

Mango Walk

CORGI BOOKS

To R.E.L., remembering Madrid

MANGO WALK
A CORGI BOOK 0 552 11872 9

Originally published in Great Britain by The Bodley Head Ltd.

PRINTING HISTORY
Bodley Head edition published 1981
Corgi edition published 1981
Corgi edition reprinted 1982 (twice)
Corgi edition reprinted 1983

This book is set in 9½ on 10 pt. Melior

Corgi Books are published by
Transworld Publishers Ltd.,
Century House, 61–63 Uxbridge Road,
Ealing, London, W5 5SA
Printed and bound in Great Britain by
Cox & Wyman Ltd., Reading, Berks.

CONTENTS

ACKNOWLEDGMENTS

To Peter Ingram, restorer of gipsy
caravans, for his help and co-operation;
to the friends who provided specialised
information on telephones and the G.W.R.,
and who lent their 1950s newspapers,
almanacs and even diaries; and to the
late Josh White, who in 1956 was neither
too big nor too busy to help an unknown
writer to trace the words of a song.

'When I go,' he said, 'set light to this place and me in it. Don't let them bury me.'

'If that's how you want it, Pops.' Gaby stirred uneasily. 'You'll get me hung.'

'That's how I want it.' There was a silence in which she could clearly hear the broken-down pipe music in his chest. Then he murmured half to himself, 'It's what I should have done when your mother went. Now she can have me too.'

'Oh, Pops—' Gaby withdrew her hand with a little gesture of impatience. She hated sentimental talk, it made her squirm. Then she reminded herself that Pops was dying and replaced the hand.

'Just do like I say,' he said, wearily closing his eyes.

His fingers did not respond to her touch, they lay like charred sticks over the edge of the sheet. They were many shades darker than her own. She remembered inconsequentially being very small and thinking that when she grew up her hands would be pink like those of the adults. That was in the days of B.P. Before Pops. In the days of a shadowy presence, lost in time. She could hardly remember her, only the pale hands and a fall of hair, her image obliterated from her mind by Pops's descriptions of her, as if he had stolen her memory to feed his own obsessive love. She didn't begrudge him—it was all he had. When you thought of all those years without a woman...

'Was she really the only one you ever had?' she asked abruptly. She hadn't meant to ask it, ever. But now it had slipped out under her guard; she waited for the answer.

The old man smiled faintly under his skin, looking back across the years, assessing the others. 'No,' he said at last, 'just the only one I loved.'

Again he felt it, the quick convulsive twitch, the looking away, as if he had said something shocking. He had embarrassed her. You could talk about sex—but not love. Not so long ago it had been the other way around. Would there ever be a generation that could reconcile the two?

What did they really feel, the young ones now—what did Gaby feel? He knew her to be sexually experienced; now that the barriers were officially down a dark skin was a passport to anyone's bed. How many boys had tumbled her in the search for new sensation, had laid her and left her lonely in the cold hours of the morning...was this the price of the new freedom? He moved restlessly. Gaby smiled, a slow soft smile, and laid a hand on his forehead in a way that reminded him...drawing him back...

Poor Pops, she was thinking, his day is gone. He's lost in today's world, he doesn't understand it. The rules he had to live by are all forgotten now. It must have galled him—all that misery, all that sacrifice, to find in a few years' time he needn't have bothered. Only he would have bothered, inevitably, it was in his nature; no amount of saying it didn't matter would convince him. They told him he was inferior and he wound up believing it.

His eyes were on her now, troubled, as if she were still a child. 'You'll be all right?' came the faint question.

She said, 'You know me, Pops. I'm always all right.' They didn't put her down so easily; she bore her identity like a banner. She had said it once, at a party. 'Look, this is me, Gaby—second generation bastard, two millionth generation black. You want to make something of it? Come out in the dirt!' and they had warmed to her, laughing. But you couldn't say that to Pops, he would take the guilt upon himself. It wasn't always easy, knowing you were a part of that guilt. And yet, foreseeing a world from which his warmth was finally gone, she felt her throat constrict painfully. She wished there were a way to tell him what she felt. But the words were shabby and second-hand, they meant nothing any more. She picked up his weightless hand and held it warmly between her own. 'We've been happy, Pops,' she managed to whisper at last.

The skin about the tired eyes crinkled. 'That's for sure...' Yes, they had been happy. He had lived for so long now tranquilly with Gaby that the far-off days were fading from his mind, the beauty, the tragedy, the excitement leached out like colours from an old photograph, leaving only the shadow of what had been.

Looking back it all seemed so extraordinary, so distant; and it was all so long ago...

Part One

❧ ❧

Snakes in the Ocean
1940

"Snakes in the ocean, eels in the sea,
I let a red-headed woman make a fool out of me,
And it seems like I'm never gonna cease
My wandering.'

Traditional

I

Sam came round the last corner like a cat with its belly
to the ground. Running a few steps, then flattening his
back against reverberating masonry while a shower of
red-hot fragments and broken tiles cascaded from the
high roofs above. He had not survived six months on the
Atlantic run to be finished off in port by a falling slate.
The ground rocked and shuddered under his feet. Metal
whined upwards or downwards through darkness. The
air beat terrified wings about his head.

God damn her, he was thinking as he inched his way
along the pock-marked stone façade—God damn her, why
weren't they safely in the country? What possessed her
to bring the child back into this!

Something roared overhead with the din of an express
train and instinctively he threw himself down on his
face... his hand fell on something warm and fluffy. With

9

a shriek it broke from his grasp to go fleeing aimlessly down the deserted street, a matted dust-grey streak of terror. Poor beast... what did animals make of all this— what did anything make of it, animals or children with the innocence of animals... Georgia. He scrambled to his feet and pressed on. She would be frightened. And Nancy—he scarcely cared. Whatever she suffered she had brought upon herself.

A burst of gunfire overhead spattered the street with shrapnel and he sought the dubious shelter of a doorway. He wondered briefly about the people inside; it was hard to imagine anyone alive in this smitten city but he knew they were there in shored-up basements and cellars, crouched on the shivering stones, waiting for dawn to bring reprieve to those who lived to see it. If he pounded on any door he would be admitted, room would be made for him, the inevitable flask of tea produced... he sighed. In the safe light of day they passed him with empty eyes as if he were not there.

Things had warmed up quickly tonight. The sirens had begun their curious mating call as he got off the bus and before the last wailing notes had faded the guns had opened up and dangling flares showed the raiders meant business. In seconds all civilians went to ground and he was left to his urgent errand like the last man on Earth. A warden on duty shouted after him 'Take cover!' but he had yelled back "I'm going to my kid!' and kept on running. Once inside a shelter you were stuck there until the All Clear. The raid was concentrating over the docks. He thought momentarily of his ship but it no longer concerned him deeply. Forty pounds for the loss of his kit was the limit of his stake in it. He emerged from the doorway and pushed on.

Somewhere along the endless street a child woke and cried. He stopped, stood still, trying to make out through the din whether it was Georgia's voice. All the blinded windows seemed to be listening. But he could not tell, not with all Hell let loose up there. He wanted to shout 'Stop that racket, I can't hear!' And then he was hurling himself down the interminable street towards her, sobbing for breath, bellowing 'All right, honey, I'm coming,' hoping she would hear.

He heard the first of the stick of bombs drop. Then the second punctuated by Georgia's screams. The third rocked him to his knees and it must have been the fourth that did it. He felt himself dragged along the ground face downwards, his legs sucked from under him by the blast of the bomb whose explosion dazzled him. He was swallowed in blackness; he could not see, could not hear, could not move. For a moment he thought he had been hit. Then his vision slowly cleared.

As the last of the bricks and debris rattled back to earth around him he saw by the grey-green light of the flares a cavernous smoking hollow in the row of buildings like a jagged gap in a row of teeth. The screaming had stopped. In its place there was a sickening silence.

'Georgia,' he whispered, trying to press into use limbs which seemed not to belong to him. And then 'Georgia!'

He dropped his head on his arm and wept. When at last he got his shocked legs under him he lurched off drunkenly, hopelessly, towards the ruin.

How long he looked for her body he never knew, how many hours he spent in fruitless search and heavy labour among nameless rubble and still smouldering wood. But he found it in the end. To anyone else it would have been unrecognisable. But something in its attitude spoke to him, something indefinable told him that this had been his child. Once he had seen the remains of a rabbit run over by a tank; all that told it had been an animal were the shattered teeth, a few fragments of fur strewn up and down the road. Now he saw it again, painfully and against his will. He touched the matted mass that had once been hair and his hand came away sticky, darkened with something unfamiliar. He crawled away miserably to retch.

Slowly through his agony seeped the awareness of an anguish other than his own. Someone was moaning. The sound seemed to come from under his feet. Someone was buried—and alive. But not Georgia...he smothered the thought and started once more to dig, raking away debris and tearing at beams with hands already bleeding. He felt nothing, but he noticed that his left hand was not working properly. He looked about for help but there was none. A spectacular fire was raging in the next street and all the rescue workers would be there. Useless to shout— they would never hear him above the noise of the hydrants. He slogged on and at last uncovered a hand. It was a woman's hand, swollen, distorted, pathetically small in this wilderness of giants. The fingers were clammy and tried feebly to grasp at his.

He said, 'All right, we'll have you out,' but his voice was choked with dust and smoke and he could not be sure she heard.

She was pinned under a roofing beam and the remains of a kitchen table. He sweated and strained until he had released her head and shoulders. By then he knew he was too late. There was nothing to be done for injuries like these; he had seen such things at sea and knew too well what they meant. They were wounds for men in battle, not quiet housewives pottering at their sinks...he was too exhausted to feel anger. To feel anything.

She was trying to say something. Her lips moved without producing any sound. He knelt beside her, wishing he could ease her dying in some way. 'Yes...try again?' He bent his head down closer and recognised her in the reflected glow from the glaring sky; the woman from the flat below his own. He had seen her once or twice with a tiny girl who played alone on the dusty stairs. Nobody mixed with them, Nancy said, and quite right too—Sam cut her short. Poor woman, he was thinking now, dying with no one to care for her child. No one to search for it and see it safe. Was that what she was trying to tell him?

'Your child?' he prompted gently, and the taut face relaxed a little.

'...find her...' came the agonised whisper.

'I'll find her,' he soothed, 'not to worry.'

Most likely the child was already dead but the woman would never know. At least let her have the comfort of thinking someone was taking over from her. Let her slip away in peace. He waited, unwilling to leave her while she lived. He saw that she was straining to speak again, her ashen face sweating with the effort. He leaned down to catch the faint sound.

'...good...man...even if...' The words had taken the last of her strength. She was gone.

Even if...he was glad she had not finished that. Presently he would start looking for her child. Soon. For the moment he remained where he was, head on arms, too inexpressibly weary to move.

The sky began to lighten; the raiders had passed. Smoke and loss of sleep stung the eyes, the nostrils were soured by the acrid smells of charred and saturated wood. In the devastated quiet could be heard the soft sad tinkling fall of glass, the angry hiss of water turning to steam on white-hot masonry. As the city aroused itself and got to its creaking feet other sounds filtered through: the tired, hoarse voices of fire-fighters in the next block, the opening of a door as someone looked out to see the damage.

Sam heard it all, and did not hear. Everything he had cared for lay buried in this once familiar, now fantastic place. His child. His home, such as it was. Even Nancy...She might be here somewhere, he supposed. It was the first time he had thought of it—yet he did not want her to be dead. He felt a need to share the grief that was too much for him alone, to share it even with Nancy who despised him. Perhaps she too would find a need...He sat in the ruins like an ownerless dog; unable to pull himself together, walk away and carry on with living. Uniformed shapes moved about him in the gloom. How long they had been there he did not know. He saw, and did not see.

Neither did he see where the child came from, or how she came to be there. One moment, it seemed, there was nothing in the shadows under the broken staircase. The next, a tiny waif shivering there, two or three years old, silent as a ghost and chattering with the cold. Afterwards it seemed to him impossible that he could have hated her, however fleetingly. Yet there she stood, a child who had survived unhurt—and she was not Georgia. For a moment against which there was no defence, he hated...

He rose stiffly to his feet and covered the few steps between them. Gently he pushed back the straggling hair and even with her mouth full of thumb he could see whose child she was. What right had he, a grown man, to sit feeling sorry for himself?

'You all right, honey?'

She nodded gravely and held up her arms to him. He was stooping to lift her, had his hands under her armpits, when hurrying footsteps made him turn his head. A woman's high-heeled fluttering tread followed closely by a man's. The urgency in their beat caught his attention, their shadowy forms took shape, moving towards him down the pavement. As the faint light caught the fiery hair that had once set light to his senses, he knew. He reared up, murder in his heart. Nancy stopped dead, her hands flying to her mouth. As she did so the American sergeant behind her cannoned into her. Sam heard him say, 'Hey, what the hell!' before she grabbed his sleeve—

'Quick, run!'—and fled back the way she had come.

Sam took one lunge in her direction—and tripped over the child at his feet. They fell together on the bruising stones. She stared at him, bewildered, and then her face broke up and she began to howl. Her tower of strength had tumbled on her head; dismayed and desolate, she cried.

Sam let them go. He pulled her, still wailing, on to his knee and held her while the violence throbbed itself out of him, leaving him drained. He dried her tears on his own rough sleeve and tucked her inside his duffel coat. He owed her some warmth at least. She had stood between him and himself, saved him from committing God knew what. She lay against him quiescent, hiccuping; tickling her own face with the edge of her nightgown.

'Let's find you some breakfast,' he said, and felt the small head nod approval under his chin. When he looked, she was sucking her thumb again.

A voice behind him said, 'I see you found her?'

He turned to see the warden, his whitened steel helmet gleaming pale in the gathering light. He looked at him blankly.

A faint smile touched the circled eyes of the warden as he indicated the small face peeping out of Sam's coat. 'All right, is she?'

Sam concentrated with an effort. 'Yes, she's all right. Just needs some food.'

The man nodded. 'Mobile Canteen's not far away. Won't have much, but you'll get a hot drink. Just a minute'—as Sam turned to go—'I want your name.'

'McLeod. Sam McLeod.'

'McLeod, Sam,' the warden repeated it slowly, writing it down, 'and you lived here in Flat...?'

'Seven,' said Sam.

'And your daughter's name?'

'Georgia,' he said numbly. Why did they want the names of the dead...

'Anyone else in Flat Seven?'

'My wife,' he managed to keep his voice even. 'But she wasn't at home.'

The man looked sympathetic. But all he said was, 'I'd get the kiddie to bed if I were you. Got anywhere to go?'

Sam nodded, and as other figures began to take shape in the shadows he moved off. He wanted to get the child away before daylight betrayed her to a sight of what lay beneath that table. And for himself he had no wish to stay and hear the harsh shovels scraping into what was left.

He tramped the weary length of two streets in search of the canteen. His ragged nerves and cold stomach cried out for coffee, and morning was time for a child to wake and eat. Where had this one been all night that he had heard no sound from her? She could hardly have slept through it all. Unconscious, perhaps; he recalled uneasily that she had not yet asked for her mother. What was he to say to her, knowing what he knew...he gnawed at his lip as he walked, picking his way through rubble and over writhing lengths of hose with the little girl balanced precariously on his one good arm.

From everywhere rose the odour of destruction. Once he caught the menacing taint of gas escaping from a fractured main. Twice he was turned back by firemen because of the danger of falling masonry. Once, turning down a side alley, he found his way barred by a placard announcing baldly 'Unexploded Bomb'. No place for children, he thought; well, here was one who would sleep out of town tonight.

As if in reaction to last night's ravages a cheerful bustle of activity was breaking out around him. Housewives came to their doors in curlers and siren suits looking like middle-aged pixies in a variety of shapes, sweeping out glass and fallen plaster into the street and exchanging jokes he found it hard to understand. Shopkeepers hung out 'Business as Usual' signs and set about salvaging stock from flooded cellars and wrecked bins. It was hard to realise that none of them had slept. He glanced at his watch: the raid had lasted eleven hours. And in all that time he had not heard a single sound of panic, nobody had screamed, or run into the street.

At last he found the Mobile Canteen, an oasis of light now that blackout time was past, its steamy urns glittering a welcome through the knot of weary soot-grimed men in arm bands and steel helmets surrounding it. They too were grinning and exchanging quips. Maybe it was their way of coping with trouble, of cutting it down to size. Some folks sing, he thought; maybe some made jokes.

15

He edged his way to the counter where a tired-eyed woman in the green dress of the WVS was pouring tea without milk.

'Sorry, Civil Defence only,' she told him, 'I haven't got enough.' Then she looked again and pushed a steaming cup and a sandwich towards him. He thanked her and hitched a toe on the wheel of the vehicle, lowering his burden on to his knee.

She sat up and took notice at the sight of food. He gave her the sandwich. She took a laborious bite and handed it back to him. He had to agree. It only resembled a sandwich in that it was a different colour in the middle. Shore food was like that here and he marvelled that people managed on it. He had always brought food from the ship for...

'Thirsty?' he asked her.

She shook her head, thumped it twice against his shoulder as if she were pummelling a pillow and settled back to sleep.

'Sure?' he persisted, disturbed by her silence. He wondered if she had lost her power of speech. He would get her checked over once they reached the farm, get her bathed and rested and fed, find clothes for her from the caravan. She sighed and stuffed her thumb into her mouth, searching along the edge of her nightdress for the precise bit with which to tickle her face while she went to sleep.

He noticed two children sitting on a heap of stones; a girl about nine years old and the boy a little younger, clinging tightly to his sister's hand as if she were the last safe refuge in his world.

'What happened?' he asked the man next to him.

'Bombed out,' he was told. 'They're waiting to be taken to the Rest Centre.'

'Where are their parents?'

The man shrugged. 'God knows. They just wait. Perhaps they'll turn up, you never know.'

'And if they don't?'

His companion shrugged again. 'Council takes them, I suppose. They'll go into an orphanage, or maybe get billeted.' He glanced at Sam suspiciously, 'What's it to you, anyway?'

'Nothing,' said Sam. 'I just wondered.'

Sipping the hot unsweetened tea, he watched the two small castaways on their rocky perch. They seemed to

him more than anything like travellers lost on some be-
wildering journey not of their own devising, their past
shot away and their future unknown, unimaginable. Fearful to be a child, he was thinking, to be at the mercy of
any and every adult, to be forced to go anywhere they
chose to take you.

He glanced at the one on his knee, who was regarding
him with round grey eyes. He offered her the last of his
sandwich: she shook her head but the smooth cheek dim-
pled. He tried to smile back but it was so long since he
had done so that his face felt stiff. Drowsily, still with
her thumb in her mouth, she said, 'You've got crumbs in
your teeth.'

A policewoman had arrived and was taking charge of
the strays. She was kind and reassuring and armed with
sweets but the boy did not want to go. The unknown
destination was frightening, he wanted to stay in a familiar place and wait for his mother to come. He bawled
hopelessly. His sister added her persuasion and eventually they got him to his feet. She scrubbed at his tears
with her dress but they had undone her. Sam could hear
her sniffling, swallowing sobs; the pitiful sounds of a
child trying desperately to be a woman in a world that
no longer had time for children.

The policewoman moved off with a consoling arm
around each of them. After a few steps she stopped, and
called back over her shoulder, 'Are there any more?' She
looked pointedly at the little nightgowned girl.

Sam spoke without premeditation. 'No,' he said firmly,
lightly. 'This one's with me.'

2

When, long afterwards, he looked in search of that decision, he could not find it. In times when the future is

too chancy to be reckoned with, it tends to be disregarded: we live from day to day and leave it at that.

Sam, although he did not realise it, was himself in a state of shock: doing what he could to fulfill the moment's need and incapable of looking beyond it.

'This one's with me,' he said simply, and wondered about his chances of getting a taxi.

The canteen drove away, the little group dispersed, and ordinary people settled down to the dirty, slogging, back-breaking job of clearing up the mess.

He borrowed a safety pin and fixed up the left sleeve of his jacket to the right shoulder; it eased the swelling wrist a little but it still nagged like an aching tooth. He picked up the barefoot babe again and made for a telephone. The first booth he tried was out of order. He reported it at the next to a harassed operator and asked for the number of a taxi rank. He tried three taxi ranks but none of them would drive him out to the village.

'There's a war on,' they told him gratuitously, and without exception refused to go so far. Sam sighed. Who was getting the petrol, he wondered: since he had the dangerous job of bringing it in he would have thought it fair to be able to get a lift when he needed it...With the fourth he had slightly better luck.

'Look,' he said firmly, 'I've got a baby and a busted arm and I've just got to have a car.' He did not really think it was broken but it strengthened his case a little.

'Where have you got to get to?'

He told them.

'We can take you as far as the station.'

It would have to do. Waiting for the taxi, he reflected that he would need an extension of shore leave; the Old Man should be reasonable. He would have to have a day or two to get things straightened out. His twenty-four hours expired at four this afternoon: he must be back at the ship before then and if necessary sign off and collect his kit. But compassionate leave ought to be possible. They were still discharging cargo and would not be ready to sail.

The car arrived, shabby and paint-thirsty like everything in Britain at that time. The driver stopped but after a cursory glance did not get out to open the door.

'I haven't got all day,' he said tersely as Sam hesitated, hampered as he was. He contrived to open the door and

18

eased the pair of them inside, weary to death and aching in every bone. It was so long since he had relaxed that his spine had forgotten how to bend.

All too soon they reached the station and he had to struggle out again. The driver stood waiting for his fare on the pavement, making no attempt to help. Sam overtipped him but he did not smile and drove off without a word of thanks.

The Station Master thought there might be a train within the hour. It all depended on the damage up the line. There was nothing for it but to wait; he did so on a hard platform bench that dug ruts in his behind, wedged in between an elderly priest and a stack of shabby suitcases. His deadweight companion whimpered in her sleep, and he felt something seeping through the leg of his trousers.

Kids...he thought with a sigh as he shifted her carefully to the other knee. He should have thought of that.

An hour and a half later the train came slowly in, small, grimy, unheated and already full. He found a space in a corridor and jammed himself into it, his back braced against one bulkhead and his knees against the other, and somehow contrived to keep upright while the train rattled and coughed on its querulous way, stopping at every halt along the line.

At the end of twenty-seven interminable miles he crawled out on to a deserted platform. There was no transport of any description to take them the rest of the way; not even a farm cart that might have given them a lift. Sam set out to plod the eight miles from town, on through the village and down to the farm by the edge of the sea. It would have been a good place for a child to grow in. But Georgia had never seen it. Mrs. Bassett had told him yesterday that a red-headed young lady—would that be Mrs McLeod?—had come out to look at the caravan but had gone away again, not very pleased by the looks of it; but she hadn't had no little girl with her.

No, she had not been pleased. Did he expect her to live like a gipsy! Wasn't the tenement humiliation enough—she'd always been used to a decent home, a respectable neighbourhood—but there, what else could she hope for, married to him! She should have known—all her friends had warned her. Tight-lipped, he had told her that she didn't have to stay. She had stared at him,

19

green eyes glittering with tears, swept a contemptuous gesture towards their little daughter playing on the mat. How, she demanded passionately, could she ever go home to her parents—with that! That was when he had hit her. When shame overtook him he had tried to patch it up, but there was no warmth, no tenderness left to use. Just send me the money, she had said, and keep yourself out of my sight...And that was how it had been. What had passed between them would always be between them now. But he had gone ahead and bought the caravan, hoping that at least for Georgia's sake she would move out to it and keep her safe.

Well, he had been wrong. He had always been wrong about Nancy, all along the line. Maybe some day he would look back and laugh. But he had a long way to travel before then.

Lizzie Bassett was looking out of her kitchen window when he came stumbling towards her door. She panted to open it and stood there filling the doorway, a woman welcoming as a featherbed.

'Oh, my dear life...' she breathed, taking in the haggard young face, the pinned up sleeve, the hollow eyes red-rimmed under the dusty hair; the sleeping child. 'Oh, my dear soul, come in...'

Cooing and coaxing in her warm fruit-cake voice, she ushered him into her kitchen. It was firelit and clean and smelled of homebaked bread. She relieved him of his burden and eased him out of his overcoat, fussing about him like a mother hen.

He stood as one lost, surrounded too suddenly by warmth and sympathy, and abruptly reaction overtook him. Big as he was, he could have laid his head in her ample lap and wept. He fell into the large old-fashioned wicker chair and dropped like a stone into exhausted sleep.

He awoke in the wintry blue-grey afternoon, lit with a rosy glow from a dying fire. His jaw had dropped and he was snoring heavily. He sat up quickly and looked about in embarrassment, but he was alone except for his companion of the night before. She sat on the hearth rug, staring in fascination. She smiled at him, holding up the toy she was playing with for him to see. Then she scrambled on to his knee, lurching about unsteadily to get her balance.

'Steady,' he cautioned, checking her fall that menaced his injured arm. She looked at him, aggrieved. 'It's hurt,' he added by way of explanation.

She poked it very carefully with a finger; then pulled a face at the swollen wrist and got down again to the floor.

Mrs. Basset came in with a tray of steaming tea. 'I was having this in the parlour not to disturb you, then I heard you talking and thought you might like some.'

She poured it, hot, strong and sweet, in a homely kitchen mug, and he drank it gratefully.

'I sent my David with a message for the doctor,' she told him, 'I thought he ought to see that hand of yours.'

'You're very kind,' he said. He wondered who else would have taken that much thought for him.

'Oh well, if we can't help each other when there's trouble 'tis a bad job, I always say. Now have some more tea and then I'll cook you something. Dr Arthur will be here directly and he'll fix you up in no time.'

She bustled about, making up the fire, preparing a meal, and Sam watched her, thinking what a treasure her dead husband had left behind him. She was not beautiful, nor ever could have been; but she had a quality that mattered more: the art of making four walls a home, and the willingness to do it from the heart. Whatever Nancy had had to do was done grudgingly, a penance that she never forgave. He'd reminded himself you couldn't have everything—she was beautiful. God, how beautiful... and how she could melt...

'I must find this kid some clothes,' he said abruptly. 'There'll be some in the caravan.' He had taken them there himself last shore leave, new clothes for them both bought in peace-time New York, trying to encourage them to move in...

He fumbled through his pockets for keys but when he found them they were taken from his hand.

'You tell me where to look, I'll find them,' said Mrs Bassett. 'You're not going anywhere till you've eaten your meal and seen Dr Arthur.'

The thought of her running his errands disturbed him. 'I'm OK.' He struggled to rise.

Her large hand pushed him back into the chair, 'Oh

no, you don't—you stay where you are now, there's a good man.'

Sam grinned wryly. 'Pushing me around, eh?'

She broke into a rich countrywoman's giggle. 'I'll push you and ten like you!' and she went off into fresh paroxysms, coy as a schoolgirl. She scooped up the child and retreated from the room, her mountainous fat quivering and her face bright pink.

He felt better after a meal and a few cigarettes, and set about trying to ease the cramps from his legs. Lord, but he was stiff! Lord, Lord...

'Blast,' the doctor told him. 'You're lucky to be alive having been that close.'

A terse, quiet, grey-eyed man, he examined with pale strong delicate hands the useless arm, carefully flexing the joints while Sam set his teeth and sweated under his hair.

'Looks like a fracture,' he said at last. 'You'll have to get up to the hospital for an X-ray. Can you get there?'

'Guess I'll have to,' said Sam, his spirits sagging at the thought of the train. 'Can it wait?'

'No, it can't,' he was told. 'And you won't get an ambulance just for a broken arm. You should have gone to Casualty and joined the queue this morning.'

Sam said, 'I had the kid with me. I want you to look her over, she was in the house when it was hit. Must have been. She seems all right—only I don't see how she can be; I want to be sure.'

The doctor smiled, 'They're remarkably resilient.' He lifted her and sat her on the table. 'Let's have a look.'

He inspected her gravely from head to foot, tickled her so that she laughed, and said, 'Seems to be all right.'

He picked up the toy from the floor and said, 'What's his name?'

She looked at him, swinging a foot. Looked at the toy, then inquiringly at Sam.

'Bunny?' he prompted, and she whispered shyly, 'Bunny.'

The two men exchanged glances; the doctor said, 'And what's your name?'

The child looked from one face to the other, questingly, waiting for someone to supply the answer. She doesn't know, thought Sam. But surely she must know, it's the first thing any kid learns.

'Tell him your name, honey,' he urged gently; the small face clouded with doubt which turned to dismay as she grappled with the frightening discovery that she did not know her name. The corners of her mouth went down.

'Never mind,' he said swiftly, catching her up, and she buried her head against him.

'Mother?' mouthed the doctor across her shoulder.

Sam shook his head warningly. 'Dead,' he mouthed back.

'Amnesia,' said the doctor. 'In the circumstances, just as well. She seems to remember you, though.'

Again Sam shook his head. 'I was just the first person she saw after it happened.' And now, he was thinking, I'm the only one she knows; my face is the only one she can recognise. Christ, what a fate! He lowered her to the floor. 'Hey—what's the time?' Suddenly he had remembered. 'I got to get back to the ship!'

'Send a wire. I'll give you a certificate.'

'But—'

'You're no use to your ship like that. Take a trip off while you sort things out. Do you nothing but good.'

Sam hesitated, torn between the new responsibility he had taken on and the need to escape and lick his wounds; there was enough going on in the Atlantic to take any man's mind off his griefs. He said half-heartedly, 'My kit's still aboard. And I'd have to sign off and collect my Discharge Book...' He sighed. 'I'll have to go anyway.'

The doctor tossed his coat towards him. 'You can come with me. I'm going up by car with an empty seat—do the whole thing and have done with it.' He glanced at his watch. 'Get moving, I haven't got all night.'

Sam started to say, 'Are you sure—' but he was already out of the door and starting the car engine.

Sam struggled into his coat on his way down the path, the little girl whimpering and clinging to his legs, threatening to trip him.

'You stay here,' he said to her, 'I'll be back.'

She cried inconsolably, even after he handed her to Mrs. Bassett.

'There, there, my lover,' crooned the woman. 'You stay with Bassie till your dad comes back. You'll be all right, never fret. What's that you called her—"Honey"? There now, Honey, in we go and see what we can find...'

The sounds of her distress followed them faintly as

they drove away. His companion said, 'You will take that trip off? I don't need to tell you that child's in a bad way. She'll need all the love and comfort you can give her for a while.' He glanced beside him at where Sam sat silent. 'It'll help you, too. Take your mind off your wife.'

Sam looked at him dazedly, wondering how he knew. He nodded and said, 'I'll stay.'

They continued the journey in silence as darkness enveloped the monotonous road. Sam dozed uneasily as well as the nagging bone would let him; between half-waking dreams he thought of the new responsibility he had temporarily shelved in the Bassetts' kitchen. He had to be crazy to take on another child, one not even his own. Yet someone had to; and he would only be doing for her what he could no longer do for Georgia. He had no plans to be interfered with, no interests worth the name: in the numb hopelessness that succeeds shock he could think of nothing he wanted out of life. She had needs and wants and knew very clearly what they were. And she saw them—or thought she saw them—in him. Well, he could only do his best...He sighed, and turned restlessly in his seat.

'You all right?' came the voice beside him. 'You could have had some codeine.'

'I'm all right,' he answered automatically, and fell back into his reverie.

He would have to board her out when he went back to sea; Mrs Bassett was kind and motherly and would no doubt take care of her. Both she and the doctor had taken her for Georgia; they might as well go on thinking so. In that way she could be accepted, without trouble or argument, without painful probings into things only remembered by the dead. She would have a name, a background, a place where she belonged. He thought inescapably of the real Georgia, nameless and forgotten in the ruins of her home. But there was nothing he could do, nothing...there was not even enough left there to bury, and his heart turned sick at the memory. Forgive me, he whispered to the little splintered bones...

He drifted into a haunted sleep. In his dream he was strolling along a sunlit cliff, watching the gulls weaving over the beach below. The beach dropped further away as he walked, the path narrower and more unsafe until he was clinging to a perilous catwalk, thousands of feet

above the sea. Somewhere ahead a child was wandering heedlessly along the overhang—in dread, he shouted to her...

The sound awoke him. 'Ah—sorry,' he mumbled. But if the older man had noticed it, he said nothing.

A heavy fog had descended with the dusk; it crept up from the river and seeped between the houses, shrouding the wounded city in a damp grey blanket. People looked at it and at each other, observed cheerfully that there would be no raid tonight.

Sam passed long shapeless hours in corridors and waiting rooms, chain smoking, awaiting his turn for X-ray and for treatment. The overworked staff were still swamped with casualties from the previous night, yet they found time to dispense cups of tea, to ask if he had somewhere to spend the night. At last he was set and plastered, and told what he had already guessed: that in his hopeless quest he had worked for half the night with a double fracture. The bones were only cracked, they told him. He was one of the lucky ones...

It was late at night when they let him go. He decided to go to the ship and spend the night aboard. He left his taxi at the dock gates and made his way out to the oil wharf, feeling his way carefully through the fogbound blackness, reminded, as he slid his feet forward over the greasy cobbles, of how easy it was to slip over the side and never be seen again. This time last night he might have welcomed that. Now it was different: he had other work to do.

The Old Man looked sceptical as he listened to his explanation. Sam could see 'Hmm...wife trouble' written in his look. He had asked for shore leave so many times on that count. But the freshly plastered arm was there to support his application: it could not be disbelieved. 'Can you hang on till we get somebody else?'

'Only till the morning, sir. I'm sorry.'

The Captain looked at him piercingly with his old, experienced eyes.

'I see,' he said tersely, his suspicions unallayed. 'You'd better get a certificate off to the Company. All right, you can go.'

A pity about that one, he was thinking as Sam went out. A man was only as good as his wife, he couldn't give his mind to the job if he was always worried about what

25

he'd left behind him. Good worker too, and a decent lad on the whole. Well, they all went through it, one way or the other...

Walking from the station the next morning with his case in his good hand, his battered old guitar slung on his back, he heard a car pull up behind him.

'Get in,' called the doctor, holding open the door. 'How's the arm?'

'Fine.' he replied. A whole night's sleep had worked wonders with his spirits. He stowed his case on the back seat and piled the guitar on top.

'Musical?' His host raised a quizzical eyebrow.

Sam grinned. 'Well...I strum a bit. I'm not Segovia.'

'My wife plays the piano. I only know one tune—the National Anthem. That's only because everyone stands up.'

Instead of going down through the village to the farm they turned in at the driveway of an impressive grey stone house.

'Come in for a minute, there should be some coffee...' and he found himself in a spacious hallway, somewhat ill at ease.

'I forgot to ask your name?'

'McLeod,' said Sam.

'No, no, no—your first name.'

It was always the same, he thought, they always expect to use your first name.

'Sam,' he said, resignedly. To his surprise, the doctor held out his hand.

'Arthur,' he said, smiling. And then, 'Maggie!'

'Coming, dear,' came a voice from somewhere out of sight, closely followed by its owner, a pleasant-faced young woman a few years older than Sam. 'Oh—I'll get another cup—'

'Just a minute, first come and meet Sam McLeod. Our new neighbour down at the farm. Sam, this is Maggie.'

'Pleased to meet you, Sam,' said Maggie, and shook hands warmly as though she meant it. 'My, you have been in the wars!' There was a curious sweetness in her voice: it took him a few moments to identify it as Highland Scots. She was as gentle in her manner as her husband was brusque. They complemented each other—or maybe cancelled each other out. Her husband was abrupt to the point of rudeness, but behind it Sam sensed an

26

honest and kindly man, grown prematurely grey through worrying over other people's problems. Now, he tossed off the last of his coffee, glanced at his watch, and said, 'Can't waste time gossiping—come on, I'll drop you home.' He tapped Sam on the shoulder and went striding out to the drive.

Standing in the road outside the farm, watching his car disappear, Sam scratched his head. The little girl arrived with a thump against his legs and Mrs Bassett came lumbering after her.

'That sure is one strange fellow,' mused Sam.

Mrs Bassett said, 'You don't want to take no notice of what he says, got a heart of gold has Dr Colby. "Dr Arthur" they call him—well, that shows... but I never heard him speak anyone fair in all the years I've known him!"

'I like people like that. You know where you are with them.'

Lizzie Bassett smiled. 'Yes, well, he's one of the best. If you've got him on your side you'll be all right.'

Sam picked up his case, thinking, 'On your side...' why did she have to say that?

In the six weeks he was ashore, he acquired skills that would have astonished his shipmates.

He learned to tie hair ribbons, to launder petticoats, to darn socks which would almost have fitted on his thumb. Caring for a small girl was no great problem to him as the eldest of seven who had all helped to bring each other up. He had suspected that the only times Georgia had been bathed were when he was on leave. Nancy had said sulkily that she had 'something else to do'. He knew now what it was; he thought wryly, well, she could have her American, or whoever it was by now, he wished him joy of her.

His last communication from her came in the form of a bulky envelope. In it were Georgia's ration book and her National Registration identity card. He puzzled over them until he saw that Nancy had fallen into the same error as the others: in the darkness and the heat of the moment she had taken the little survivor to be Georgia. Clearly, she had washed her hands of them both... He looked at the documents in his hand. There seemed little point in sending them back, applying for another set identical but for the name. And he did not know that name; if he called the attention of officialdom to that—anything

could happen while he was at sea, she could be whisked away into some Home, back to the Blitz-torn city he had tried to save her from...It might be illegal to use Georgia's ration book...but who was to know? He put the cards back into the envelope and handed them without comment to Lizzie Bassett.

So it was Nancy who gave Honey to Sam; which was ironic, as things turned out. Officially she became Georgia McLeod, though to him she was always Honey: the name to which she answered and which saved him the pain of calling her Georgia.

She followed him at heel like a little dog and watched while he scoured the caravan one-handed, disinfecting against its stale shut-up smell and driving spiders into hasty exile. Soap and water revealed the ceiling as a minor work of art, romantic as a Valentine with scrolls and painted roses, while above the bed in the after end a foal frolicked among flowers. Panels of cut glass slid over this bed to form a miniature bedroom with a window of its own. The 'bed-place' the gipsies called it, said Lizzie, and the cupboard-like space on the deck beneath, the 'chavy-bed', for the children too young to sleep outside in tents. Honey always started the night in the chavy-bed. But she was a bad sleeper and all too often he woke to find an extra head on his pillow.

He kitted her out in Georgia's clothes, the frilled American dresses he had thought so pretty and which Nancy had set aside as needing too much ironing. He remembered how the baby face had fallen in disappointment...he wrenched his mind away. Only the shoes were too big. Georgia's feet had been large and strong like his own, feet that meant business, but this child's were small like her hands, delicately arched and developed beyond her years.

The straight silky hair that fell to her shoulders gave him something to think about. When he had washed the dust out of it with kitchen soap and dried it he found he could not control it. He brushed it vigorously in the hope of subduing it but his efforts had quite the opposite effect: it reacted by flying out in a cloud, floating about her head and crackling with defiant electricity, clinging to her face and getting into her food. Reluctant to cut it off, he imprisoned the lot in an elastic band and tied a ribbon over the top.

'Hey, that's cute!'

He chucked her under the chin and she smiled up at him happily.

She was a quiet, unobtrusive little thing, all too obviously accustomed to amusing herself without the aid of other children. She shunned the society of My David—which was no surprise to Sam, who found him a dull, pale, over-coddled boy, some years her senior, who had only to whine 'Mu-um!' to be given the top brick off the chimney. She was happiest pottering about the farm with Sam, straining up to hold his hand or a handful of his trouser leg, poking into this or that which did not concern either of them. She wanted to join in everything he did, whatever he was using she must have some and imitate. She was an amiable creature who gave no trouble—except at night.

The first night in the caravan, she ripped him from sleep by screaming frantically. For an instant, he was back in the darkened street—the screams were Georgia's—he flung himself out of bed, still dazed, and shook her—'Stop it, stop it, stop it—' before he collected his wits and remembered where he was.

Well might she dream...he put her down gently. But now she was wide awake, shivering with fear and choked with sobs. He sat with her, trying to soothe her, but it was useless for the moment. Shock and irregular food had upset her system; she struggled to her feet and gave one piercing howl of dismay before disaster overtook her. She stared in horror at her predicament.

'My nighty, my nighty!' she squealed. 'It's sticking to me—take it off!'

He looked in pity at her panic-stricken face. 'It's all right, you couldn't help it,' he said. He stripped off the offending garment and sponged her down. He bundled her up in one of his shirts, rolled her in a blanket and snugged her down between two pillows on the bed-place.

'Have a bit of thumb,' he invited, pushing it towards her mouth. She smiled drowsily under wet lashes and was instantly asleep. He lit a cigarette, and tackled the bedding.

Night after night she awoke in terror, sobbing wildly, incoherently, while he patiently held her and lulled her back to sleep; he lost a lot of sleep himself, but in the process she laid a ghost for him: the time came when a scream in the night was no longer Georgia about to die...it was only Honey, having another bad dream.

At length his plaster was removed. With two good hands, he knew he would soon be called to sea again. The shortage of seamen was so severe that he had been lucky to stay ashore that long. He notified the Company and set about making his arrangements.

He was concerned about Honey and her night terrors, not wanting her to have to sleep alone. He approached Lizzie Bassett.

'Could you have her in your room?'

'Of course I will,' agreed Lizzie cheerfully, and failed to see the pale cold gleam of jealousy that lit My David's eye.

Soon it came, in its little red envelope: the priority telegram calling him to sea. He went to join the new ship believing he had done all for the best. Whatever might happen to him, Honey would be all right. He took a last look around the farm before he went. He might see it again but you could never be sure these days.

Honey cried for three days and nights after his departure. She had stared at him, stricken, when he said that he must go.

'Stay with me! Stay with me!' she pleaded, her heart-broken tears running down inside his collar. Sam held her tenderly, awkwardly, helpless in the face of such distress.

'I have to go. You stay here with Bassie and David and I'll be back one day.'

'Don't go! I don't want you to go...'

'I'll bring you back something pretty from New York—'

'I don't want you to go!'

In vain he tried to explain, to reason with her; her mind was too young to grasp time and distance. He could not reach her, walled off by her anguish. When he promised to return, she asked, 'Will you come back at teatime?'

He smiled faintly, acknowledging defeat. 'Not today. But one day I will.'

She clung to his neck, still hiccuping, while he rocked her and rubbed her back. He gave up trying to explain and hummed to her softly, under his breath:

'Well I'm goin' away for to stay a little while,
But I'm comin' back, yes I'm comin' back
If I go ten thousand mile...'

When she woke up, he was gone. She ran all over the

farm, calling 'Sam—Sam!' but only Bassie came to answer her.

'I want Sam!' she wailed distractedly.

Bassie said brightly, 'He's gone, my lover. Gone on a big ship. Don't you fret, now, you'll have My David for company.'

She was brought back indoors and sat up at the table. It was only laid for three. Honey felt her face pull apart and knew she was going to cry.

'I don't like David. I want Sam!'

'That's naughty!' Bassie spoke sharply, her fat face quivering with indignation. Then she said more kindly, 'Come along now, eat up your tea.'

Honey said between sobs, 'I want my tea with Sam...'

Lizzie Bassett heaved a sigh. She hoped she wasn't going to have trouble with this one now that her dad had gone.

3

Honey waited and waited for Sam to come back.

Every time she thought about it she asked Bassie, 'Is Sam coming home today?'

At first Bassie just said, 'No.' But then she began to sound cross, and Honey thought, She doesn't want him to come. When she woke in the night and was frightened she remembered that, and thought, Supposing Sam comes back and she sends him away again! Bassie said crossly, 'It's no use you screaming for Sam,' and she knew she had been right. Bassie grew angrier every time she asked; it must be that she did not want him back.

The night she worked herself into a state; she cried and screamed and could not stop and for the first time Bassie smacked her. When Bassie was not looking David

smacked her too, only he did it with his fingers doubled up so it hurt much more.

She tried to tell Bassie that David had smacked her but Bassie only said, 'What a wicked thing to say about My David!' and shut her mouth up tight like a buttonhole.

Honey was afraid of David. He was bigger than she was and all the toys were his, even the ones that Sam had given her. He hid them in secret corners while he went to school and if she found one when he was out and he caught her with it she knew what to expect. She knew the toys were his because Bassie never made him give them back.

'Mu-um! It's not fair!' he would pipe as they both reached for the last biscuit.

'Don't be silly, my lover. We don't mind you having it, do we, Honey?' and the prize would find its way on to his plate.

'Mu-um! It's not fair!' And Honey would be taken indoors leaving him in sole possession of the swing.

It wasn't that Bassie was cross or unkind; it was just that you didn't count with her. It was only David who counted. Honey withdrew into herself and waited for Sam. When he came back she would have someone of her own again.

'How many days till Sam comes home?' she asked tearfully, night after sleepless night until Lizzie Bassett grew as short of patience as she was of sleep.

'Mu-um, it's not fair!' nagged David, who resented Honey sleeping in his mother's room, and eventually Lizzie persuaded herself that he was right. It wasn't natural to push out her David in favour of another child. Certainly, she had promised, but then Honey needn't be alone—not if she slept with David in his room. Children were best company for each other; and she could care better for both of them if she got her proper sleep. In fact, the more she thought of it...

'I've got a nice surprise for you, Honey. You're going to sleep in My David's room from now on. Aren't you a lucky girl?'

Honey heard with dismay that she was to be couched in the lion's den. The one time she felt safe from him was at night in Bassie's room.

'I don't like David,' she wailed, 'I want to sleep with you!'

Bassie buttoned her lips up tight and went on making up the bed.

After a few stormy nights there was silence. Pleased, Lizzie told herself that her David had found a way to quieten the child. He had indeed. Lizzie could not hear his methods through the wall...and would not have believed her ears if she had. After a time Honey ceased to ask for Sam, and Lizzie heaved a sigh of relief to think she had forgotten him.

She had not forgotten him. She had given up hope. He had not come back; he was never coming back. He had broken his promise, forgotten her, gone away...she tried to feel angry when she thought of him but there was only a dull sad ache.

In six weeks she had built on him a new and fragile world. Now it had been swept away and she was lost again. Broody and silent, she spent hours at a time gazing out of the window and sucking her thumb. Lizzie put bandages on it, bitter aloes—even sticking plaster; but to no avail. It was to Honey the only thing in life worth doing.

One day a stranger came to the farm.

Bassie said, 'Look who's here!' in the special voice she kept for treats for David.

Honey did not want to look. It was only Sam she had wanted to see, so she kept on staring out of the window and refused to turn round. He strode across the kitchen and she felt herself lifted from behind.

'Go away!' she cried, hiding her face in her hands, in dread of the violent emotions that threatened her. He had promised to come back and he had never come. He had betrayed her—did he expect her still to love him—it wasn't Sam, it wasn't, it wasn't...

Carried out to the caravan, still with tightly shut eyes, she pummelled him with every step of the way.

He did not try to make her talk; he sat her on the bed and began unpacking his case. He held out to her a new pair of scarlet shoes: she would not take them so he laid them on the floor. There followed a doll, a hat and coat and a party dress with a skirt like a powder puff. There was a white fur muff into which she longed to plunge her hands, it had a ribbon for hanging it round your neck...

But these things represented loneliness and abandonment to her; she could not touch them. She sat with

33

averted face while he set them out upon the bed.

He lit a cigarette and set the kettle to boil for coffee. When he glanced over his shoulder she was stroking a tentative finger over the soft white fur. He took a pad of paper from the locker and sat down with it, tore off a sheet and folded it from corner to corner; he folded and turned and folded again until a swan appeared, tiny and delicate. Soon a whole fleet of swans cruised across the table, to be followed by a sealion, a fish—and a bird whose wings moved up and down when its tail was pulled.

Honey by now was spellbound at his elbow. He offered her the flying bird but she would not take it, glowering her face against his sleeve.

He felt in his pocket for the orange he had brought from the mess room table. He held it high, where she could not quite see, and began gouging at the peel with his thumbnail.

Honey strained up on tiptoe, craning her neck to see what he was doing. He watched her amusedly, holding it just out of sight. How dared he laugh at her after what he had done! She stamped a rebellious foot and turned away . . . but she had to look back. What was it he was doing with that orange!

He held it up at last: in the peel he had carved a little scowling face. It had exactly the expression she could feel upon her own. He blew on it, and magically the face was smiling.

'You do it,' he said. He blew on it again and the face scowled back. He was teasing her . . . She wanted to giggle, to yell, to hit him . . . she did none of these things. Instead she stood quite still where she was and slowly, painfully melted into tears.

He pulled her on to his knee and held her warmly in the circle of his arms.

'I don't love you any more,' she sobbed, and the plea for pity was for her plight, not for his.

'Never mind,' he said. 'We'll have to start again.'

Just when she had given in and admitted to herself that it was Sam, she did not know. But from then on everything was different. The sun came out and her heart sang and shouted for joy. She danced about him wildly while he finished unpacking, pulling out this and that in her eagerness.

34

'Can I wear it now?' she asked excitedly of everything she found.

'Sure you can,' affirmed Sam, and dressed her up in the lot.

He released her hair from the straggling plait that Lizzie had made and tied it into a tassel with a bright new ribbon.

'I want this one!' she cried, seizing another one. 'All of them!'

'Yes, ma'am!' said Sam, and tied them all on in a multicoloured bunch. 'Now you're all dressed up for Carnival.' He tossed her up and caught her again. 'Now we'll show 'em!'

They went in to the farmhouse to have tea and she danced beside him, hanging on to his hand: an ocean-going liner with a bobbing dinghy in tow.

She reached for the last piece of cake and David's hand shot out.

'We'll cut it in half,' said Sam before anyone else could speak.

Oh, yes... everything was different now!

At night she slept in the caravan with Sam. When she awoke in the night it was to the glow of the little stove, the scent of tobacco smoke. And even if Sam was asleep he was always there. By day she hung close to him, fearful that he might slip away without warning.

'I won't go without telling you,' he said, 'I told you before, remember?' She did remember, vaguely... but it was all so long ago. He had brought a present for David too, though David did not seem to care for it.

'He's cross because he didn't get his first,' said Honey with some perspicacity.

'Well, isn't that just too bad.' They shared a smile. 'What are you going to call your doll?'

She answered promptly, 'I'm going to call her Sam.'

He managed not to laugh. 'How will you know which is which if we're both Sam?'

'You're not a girl!' A piece of feminine logic which left him with nothing to say.

He had been away for almost a year; winter darkened the afternoons and in the wagon the lamp on its angel bracket was lit early. 'Will we have a Christmas tree?' asked Honey.

'We'll have our Christmas before I go,' he told her, and

35

looked around for a treat to soften the parting.

Circuses had vanished, and the few theatres still open were in the city, the last place he would choose for her to go. So he took both children on the wheezing train to a holiday resort further down the coast in the hope of finding some entertainment there. Travel for pleasure was discouraged; posters on the station at Southcombe wagged admonitory fingers: 'Is Your Journey Really Necessary?' Yes, said Sam to himself, looking at Honey's glowing face. On the train he was further exhorted to avoid spending his money—the Squanderbug was after it, warned the poster on the grimed bulkhead. He wondered what there was to spend it on, he had never seen shops so empty in his life. At every stop he had to hang out of the window to discover where they were, since platform names, like signposts, had been removed in case of invasion, and when at last they alighted from the train and battled their way against the full force of a gale to the Promenade, it was to find that the Pleasure Beach was closed for the duration. The cafés and ice cream parlours that had once flourished were untenanted behind their peeling shutters, the iron pier stood rusting in two sections, its centre demolished by the War Department; apart from a one-mile stretch where a few elderly couples were exercising their dogs the beach was mined for miles along the coast, cut off by barbed wire and warning notices.

On this bleak remnant of muddy sand they ran races to keep warm until the light failed, and then made for the shelter of the town in search of a meal. After a feast of beans on unbuttered toast, washed down with synthetic orange squash, he found a News Theatre showing cartoons and took them in. But he felt that as a celebration the outing had fallen short. On the home-going train he said, 'Sorry there wasn't much open, kids.'

'It was mouldy,' pouted David. 'I want an ice cream.'

'You're horrid!' said Honey. She added as an afterthought, 'What's ice cream?'

The next day it snowed for the first time in years. The village children rushed to get out their improvised toboggans, those who lacked the real thing acquiring teatrays, driftwood, anything which would carry them over the bright surprising drifts. Sam walked up over the hill to watch them. Honey dancing beside him, her nose a small cherry, the white muff bobbing like a rabbit's scut.

'Will you make me a boggan, Sam?'

'Toboggan,' he corrected her, overemphasising the first syllable.

'No, not two boggans—only one boggan. Will you?' She did not want him making one for David. He tossed her up, laughing.

'All right, if that's the way you want it.'

He found some oddments of wood around the farm and started building the toboggan. But the next day he was called away, and had to leave it—and so much else—unfinished.

'I want Girl Sam to stay in the caravan,' Honey announced to his surprise.

'Don't you want her in the house with you? The wagon will be locked, you won't be able to get her out.'

'I know I won't,' said Honey.

They sat her on the table where Honey could see her by climbing on the wagon wheel, and there she sat throughout the next long trip, a gesture of defiance to David, and to Honey the promise of returning spring. But promises were cold comfort...

She watched his retreating figure through a kaleidoscope of tears in a world that had suddenly grown dark.

Bassie said brightly, 'You'll be back in My David's room tonight.'

She had forgotten about that for the moment. The realisation was more than she could take. 'I don't want to, I want Sam!' she sobbed hopelessly.

Lizzie heaved a long, deep sigh. 'Now, don't say you're going to start that all over again!'

And now, in addition to her sense of loss, she had My David's jealousy to contend with.

He stole the precious white fur muff and cut it into shreds with the kitchen scissors.

'There now,' said Lizzie comfortably, 'look what a mess you've made for your poor old mum to clear up.' Her voice sharpened, 'Now Honey, you can just go out of the room until you stop that dreadful noise!'

Pocket money and sweets for them both were given to David to be shared. Honey's share was usually one sweet—the sort that David didn't like—and even for that she had to work. It was worse than useless to take her grievances to Bassie: she was learning what not to say about My David.

37

The knowledge that Girl Sam was locked away in the caravan was a constant thorn in his flesh; in vain he nagged his mother, she did not have the key.

'What's the good of a doll stuck away in there!' He kicked angrily at a hapless blade of grass.

'She's a fairy,' declared Honey, sketching wings in the air with her arms, 'she's keeping it safe for my Sam.'

'He's not your Sam!'

'Well, he's not yours!' Honey's tongue came out in an unfairylike gesture and the discussion evolved into a contest.

When their ingenuity was exhausted David, still sulky, wandered off in the direction of the pond. Honey smiled, knowing herself for once the victor. She clambered up on to the wheel of the wagon and pressed her nose to the glass.

'You like it, don't you, my darling?' she crooned to the plastic face within.

But the moment of triumph past, she came to regret it.

'He's not your Sam,' taunted David repeatedly, delighted to have found a new way to provoke her.

'He is, he *is*!' yelled Honey, beside herself.

'Oh no, he ain't!' David grimaced and danced out of reach. 'If he was you'd have to call him Dad, same as everybody—'

'Shut up, shut up! I hate you!' She hurled herself, fists flailing, to be arrested by Bassie in defence of her cub.

'Now, you behave yourself, my girl! Such nonsense, of course he's your dad—can't you take a joke? I never did know such a child for flying off the handle!'.

She was hauled indoors to bed 'to calm down', leaving David grinning.

Sam was largely unaware of this facet of Honey's life. While he was there her days were too full and too happy to be spoiled by thinking about the times when he was not. And David, uncertain of what she might have told him, gave them both a wide berth.

Sam knew, though, that he occupied a vital place in Honey's life, and realised that a year or more was far too long for her to wait between meetings. Unless he lost a ship from under him, in which case the survivors could generally count on a few days' respite before being reassigned, it would normally be two years before he ac-

crued enough paid leave to take a voyage off; and while men with wives could occasionally bring them aboard when they made home port, for a child of Honey's age it was out of the question.

He left the employ of the Company and joined the shipping pool. It meant sailing on any vessel to which he was sent, on tankers, troopers, banana boats or any other perilous lame duck lagging in the rear of the convoy asking to be picked off; it meant going anywhere, the notorious Malta run or the trip to Archangel under the muzzles of the German shore batteries—he did that twice and scarcely expected to return. But it meant too that at the end of each trip he signed off and went home until he was called again; it might be for a day, a week or even a few hours, but however brief the reunion it was something, and however bad the ship he was not committed to sail in her again.

He looked forward to his visits to the farm, they were a lifeline under his hands through the doubts and dangers of his daily life. And he was growing attached to the little girl for something in herself.

She would sidle up to him and slip a hand into his; not looking at him, not needing to look, confident of her welcome in a way he found touching. If he pressed her fingers the small sleek head would turn—somewhere on a level with his knee—and the grave face smile up at him, a kitten-faced kind of smile with the corners of the mouth tucked upwards, the round eyes trusting, and his heart would warm unpredictably, giving him pain.

Oranges ashore were as rare as platinum and when he came from a ship he always tried to bring her one.

'Cross face or a funny one?' And she would straddle his knee while he conjured it out of the peel.

David was jealous of the oranges. When Sam brought chocolate or other scarce goodies from the ship, they were for everyone: he was sure of a share, even though it was not the lion's. But the oranges were only for Honey, something secret and infuriating between them, like the hated doll that lived in the caravan. In response to his goading, Lizzie dropped a hint to Sam.

'I can only bring one at a time,' he explained, 'they're supposed to be eaten on the ship.'

'Oh.' Lizzie was somewhat dashed, but she caught David's eye and pressed on. 'Only it seems such a pity when she doesn't eat them.'

'She doesn't?' enquired Sam, surprised.

'No, look you here,' and she opened a drawer to show him a collection of every orange he had brought so far in various stages of mould or dehydration, the more aged withered and dry as coconut shells.

'Looks as if she's taken up shrinking heads,' he commented, looking at the dessicated grins. ''Oh, well . . . they're her oranges.' And that was all the progress Lizzie made.

When they were alone, he asked her, 'Don't you like oranges, Honey?'

'Oh yes, I love them!'

'But you don't eat them. Bassie showed them to me in your drawer.'

'I don't want to spoil the faces. When you've eaten them they're gone.'

So that was it. He showed her how to remove the peel carefully in two halves, without breaking into the face; he fitted the two back together, threaded string through the top, and there was a tiny hallowe'en lantern made of orange peel.

One day he asked her, 'Why do you keep your doll in the caravan?'

She was sitting on his knee, laboriously colouring with crayons the pictures in a story book. At his question she stopped, then went on scrubbing as if she had not heard.

'Honey?' he prompted. The crayon in her hand stopped moving; she leaned her head against him and breathed faintly.

'I don't like David . . .' It was as much as she dared to say. It was not enough for Sam, to whom it seemed a strangely inadequate reason for denying herself the solace of a favourite doll.

'Why don't you like him?' he encouraged her gently, holding her in his arm.

Honey fought a battle within herself, her fear of David warring with her need to confide in Sam. And there were so many reasons for not liking him . . . she remembered the muff and her fears died a death in the anger that burned in her.

'He cut up my muff!' she blurted and burst into tears, knowing she would be punished for the telling.

Sam said quietly, 'I'll bring you another one.' But inside himself he was angry. He went in search of David

and when he found him said, still in the same quiet voice, 'I've something to say to you.'

David stood in his shoes and trembled, recognising the menace in the tone. He fixed his eyes on the ground, and felt himself growing smaller inside his clothes. The words, when they came, surprised him.

'If you want girls' toys to play with, I'll bring you a doll next time.'

He glanced up at the unsmiling face and felt the jibe go home. And then a massive hand shot out, lifted him off the ground by a handful of his shirt. He squirmed, whimpering.

'But you touch another thing of Honey's,' thundered Sam, 'and Mum or no Mum I'll beat the shit out of you!' David scrambled up from where he was dropped and scuttled away like a rabbit.

Honey had crept up behind him unobserved; she gasped, entranced by his vulgarity. 'Oh Sam, aren't you rude!' she giggled nervously.

Sam pinched his nose in a gesture that betrayed his confusion. 'You just better forget I said that,' he said

David did not forget the humiliation of being afraid of Sam, and waited to be avenged for the loss of his self-esteem. Honey knew it, and watched in dread for the little red envelope that would take Sam back to sea. To her, a red envelope always spelt disaster.

Sometimes when he was away a pale blue envelope would come, covered in stamps and stickers and heavy black crayon marks. 'A letter from your dad,' Bassie would say, carefully peeling off the stamps for My David. 'When you go to school and learn to read you'll be able to have letters.'

A new world opened suddenly for Honey, a world in which everything in her was concentrated on learning to read. When she started at the village school her progress startled her teacher. When she realised that geography meant Where-Sam-Is, she excelled in that too. They were the only lessons that ever held her attention.

4

The war ground at last to a close. In the country the effects of peace were slow to be felt; food was still tightly rationed and although blackout restrictions ended most people were hard put to it to find material to replace the black curtains at their windows. Clothes were still on coupons, and petrol almost unobtainable. A thin straggle of returning men was demobilised with maddening slowness.

'Will you be coming home for always, Sam?' wrote Honey in her careful hand. 'David's uncle Eddie is coming back and so are the men from the farm. Bassie says the Land Girls will have to go...'

'I am a peacetime sailor,' Sam wrote back, and Honey scarcely sighed. She had known that was too bright a world to hope for, and her heart was learning patience.

At sea, things began to ease up. It was no longer necessary to sail in convoy to secret destinations and careless talk ceased to take its toll of lives. Guns and degaussing gear gradually disappeared and the little ships bustled confidently about their business once again. Now that Sam could tell Honey where he was going she felt less as though the sea had swallowed him. She carefully plotted his course on the yellowing world map on the schoolroom wall and calculated the days to his return; but still the greater part of her life was spent in waiting, her world revolved on an axis she could seldom see. As she grew older she tried consciously to centre it elsewhere; but after weeks of effort she would see his peaked cap bobbing above the hedge and her spirit would go flying out to meet him; he dabbed a clumsy kiss on her forehead and everything else was forgotten.

After the incident of the muff she did not try again to

tell him how things were at the farm. David had taken his revenge for that and she was more often than not at his mercy. When Sam was home she put behind her the times when he was not, and he went on his way unaware that for her the only days when the sun rose were when his ship came in.

For himself, he was neither happy nor unhappy. Sometimes he was bored, occasionally depressed, thinking of ambitions once cherished that he would never now fulfil; but then he was hardly alone in that. Life was all right as long as he kept the door locked firmly on the past.

Nancy he had ruthlessly trampled from his mind. He did not admit to himself that she had left him with a fear of women but the mistrust was there, hidden at the back of his mind where he did not see it; there were women from time to time, but he drew back from every relationship before he could be trapped.

'That's all the woman I've got room for in my life,' he told Arthur Colby, pointing to the barefoot child with sea-water soaking up the edge of her dress. He was as close to the Colbys as he was to anyone. In as far as he had a home, it was the village.

Georgia he dared not remember. Everything about her was tied up with Nancy and her death still scalded him. Such memories as he cherished were of Honey: Honey with lemon meringue pie, asking for 'some of the eider-down'. Honey in the village church-yard among the crumbling gravestones, asking 'Will they put me in one of those when I die?' and a few days later seeing a display in an undertaker's window—'Oh Sam, look at all those things waiting for people!' Honey, dear and uncritical, loving him whatever he was, whatever he failed to be. Life flowed smooth and uneventful; and time gnawed away unnoticed at the short years of his youth.

Whenever he could he took Christmas ashore and they spent it together with the Colbys. When he could not manage that, he took his leave in summer and lazed it away on the beach among the children. He was always in demand; he could identify any kind of shipping from the shore, split an apple neatly in two with his thumbs or prise the top from a pop bottle with his teeth. To the holiday-making small fry these were achievements beyond price, and they attached themselves to him without encouragement. He had only to appear on the cliff to become the centre of a little group: 'Are you going in the

sea, Sam?'...'Sam, will you blow up my beach ball?'...'Sam, will you teach me to swim?'...He would grin and go on walking and they would all follow on. When they came out of the water they sprawled about him on the sand or breathed down his neck while he gouged out little boats from scraps of driftwood or discarded cork floats. On one occasion a grandmother intervened; there was a squeal of protest and Sam looked up to see one of his small admirers arrested by the arm.

'I want to stay with Sam, he's making me a boat—'

'You're coming back with me this minute. Going off like that with strangers, someone might run off with you!' she added pointedly.

Sam opened his mouth to say he had enough kids to go on with, thanks, but the look on her face was enough to close it. He had seen it too many times not to know what it meant. He went on chipping, drawing impassivity down over his face like a blind, and the child was led unwillingly away.

The others exchanged grins at her expense and returned their attention to the growing boat. Only Honey seemed to read his thoughts, and wound a small wet arm about his neck. Young as she was, she always knew; it was as if a mysterious current ran between them. When the boat was finished he handed it to her and said, 'Take it over to her and come straight back.'

She returned with it still in her hand, an angry blinked-away tear on her face. 'They wouldn't let her have it—they're horrid!'

'What did they say to you?'

'It wasn't what they said, it was how they looked.'

'Looks can't hurt you.'

'They can—they hurt you and that's the same as hurting me!'

'Aw, Honey...' He laughed and chucked her under the chin. 'Look at me, I'm not crying.'

She had always been like that. When she was still tiny she had howled when he brought down a hammer on his thumb. Between her bawling and his swearing there had been pandemonium for a while...

She was growing rapidly now, he thought, watching her wading out into the shallows. She was still small but her limbs were neat and strong, the muscular development so well defined that he sometimes wondered if she

were older than he guessed. She was a better swimmer than David despite his four years seniority—a fact that he strongly resented but could not deny. David cast envious eyes at the raft that was moored for the convenience of bathers some half a mile off-shore, and to which Honey was allowed to swim with Sam while he was not. He failed to see the difference between swimming half a mile with the tide alongshore, and swimming half a mile through a strong cross-current out to sea. He felt that Honey was being favoured, and the prohibition rankled.

Sam was sorry for David, understanding him better than he knew. A boy needed a man in his life, a man to call his own, and David had none. Petticoat government might smooth his path but it offered no stimulus; it could not take him over rocky crags or give him a day's fishing in the silent fellowship of men. He bore this in mind and made allowances, knowing how the boy must be galled by the sight of Honey with a sea-going 'father' while he must make do with the company of aunts; he would have made it up to him if he could. But David was unresponsive: if he could not have the whole cake he disdained to accept a slice.

Honey was thinking of David too, as she dredged along the sandy bottom for shrimps; she was wondering idly what way he would find of getting even over the raft. She would find out soon enough... It could not be long now, she thought with a sinking of the heart, it must be nearly time for the little red envelope. The envelopes were not always red now, but they always meant the same thing. Sam seemed to be expecting it, too, he had been hanging around the farm all day; every little while he would be missing from the beach and she would know he had gone to look for the telegram. Honey hated suspense, it would almost be better when he had gone. When all the things had been done for the last time it was dreadful, just waiting. This afternoon, when they swam out to the raft, she had known it was for the last time... for a wild moment she thought of asking him to swim out with her now, this minute, to make sure of going just once more—but she knew he would say no: they were both too tired and you needed to be fresh for that. Besides, the tide was on the turn—only David was daft enough to swim on a turning tide. David... soon, perhaps even tonight, she would have to sleep in his room again, with its mingled smell

of lino polish and David's chamber pot. Old as he was, he still slept with it under his bed. She would have disdained to use such a thing herself, and used to pull the pillow over her head to shut out the sounds of David doing so, but even had she needed to Bassie would have been shocked. Girls could wait longer, Bassie said.

If only Bassie would let her sleep in the caravan...In vain she had pleaded that she was too big to sleep with David now. If she wasn't too old to sleep with Sam, Bassie said, she would come to no harm sharing a nice room with My David. She was silent at that; David was different, he tried to look up her nightdress as she got into bed, but she didn't dare say that to Bassie. But her heart still yearned for the caravan; to her it was not a second hand dwelling discarded by the gipsies but a fairyland, the fulfilment of her dreams, the one place where she rose to her full stature, where she was loved and valued for herself. It had the cosy smallness of a doll's house, and it was home to her as no other place could be. Bassie never understood. No one understood except Sam.

Sometimes when he was reading late at night she would lie awake thinking, listening to the faint flickering of night moths on the windowpanes; sometimes one would come inside and try to destroy itself on the hot glass of the lamp, and then he would catch it in his large gentle hands and put it carefully out of the window. Sam never killed anything unless he had to...

One night when she had been worrying, she had blurted out, 'I wish I'd never asked you, it's all David's fault!' She turned her head to look at him. 'Will they take me away if they find out?'

He came over and sat on the edge of her bunk. 'You mean if they found out I'm not your father?' He spoke quietly, taking her hands that were nervously twisting and untwisting the edge of the sheet.

She nodded, 'I'm afraid they'll take me away.'

'They might...though there's no one to claim you as far as I know. But you don't have to worry, nobody knows but us. Nobody will unless we tell them.'

'But suppose they ask?'

He squeezed her hands reassuringly. 'Nobody's going to ask. Why should they—no one ever has, not even when we first came here. People don't ask those things, it's not polite.'

That was true. Even David had not asked, he had merely taunted her. With her worst fears reduced to a matter of politeness, she felt better. She smiled half-heartedly. 'I can't help worrying...'

'You leave the worrying to me.' He straightened the covers and tucked her in; she watched him with troubled eyes.

'I wish I didn't know,' she said.

'If I'd lied to you you'd have never trusted me again.' She couldn't imagine not trusting him. And yet...

'Play me some music,' she said, and he took down the guitar and played very softly, until she fell asleep

But if someone else should guess, she thought now! If someone looked hard at us both, and started asking questions... suddenly she had to be close to him, to make the most of the time she could be sure of. She threw down the shrimping net and went running over the beach to where she had left him, stretched out on the sand. He got up as she reached him, catching her as she blundered against him, her nose squashed flat against his stomach.

He laughed and released her, then started collecting the towels. 'We'd better go up, now. Getting late and we've had a long day.' He stifled a yawn and looked around. 'Where's David?'

Honey looked. 'I don't know. He was shrimping a minute ago.'

'See if you can find him, tell him we're going up.' Sam lit a cigarette. He had been in and out of the water all day and he was tired and cold. He didn't want to hang about for David, he wanted to relax with hot coffee and a nice warm sweater. But David was with him and he felt responsible.

Suddenly a shout went up. 'Someone's swimming out to the raft!'

The tide was turning, the swimmer must be mad—or else a visitor who did not know the cross currents. He strained his eyes to make out who it was, but could not see past the knot of people at the water's edge yelling good advice. Apart from yelling, nobody seemed to be doing much about it.

'Oh, damn...' He stooped and crushed out his cigarette in the sand before going down to join them.

'It's that boy, David,' somebody told him, but he would

have known by the way he was swimming, three strokes above the water and the fourth under it. The little fool, he thought exasperated, he knows he can't do it— couldn't even if the tide was right! And yet—take off your hat to him, he's got what it takes to try.

He stood irresolute at the water's edge, slowly pulling the towel from his shoulders, reluctant to haul David ignominiously ashore, to humiliate him when he was trying so hard, so dangerously to shine...

Honey read his mind, and clung in terror to his hand. 'Sam, don't go!'

But just then he saw what he expected to see, that the boy was caught in the clawing current and was being drawn alongshore away from the raft, the plaything of the tide that could suck him out to his solitary death.

'Man, he's in trouble!' He shook her off and raced into the water.

He shivered as it swallowed him, chilling his tired limbs to the bone, but he forged on purposefully, anger and anxiety between them boosting his strength. The sea had turned choppy, the wind whipping up white horses on the surface and making it impossible to keep David in sight for more than a moment at a time, bobbing about incessantly as they both were. The boy had given up all attempt at swimming by the time he reached him and was wildly floundering in an effort to keep afloat. Sam shouted advice to him but he was either too deafened or too scared to hear. He made for Sam, his eyes wide with panic, and grabbed at him with the inevitable result that they both went under, thrashing about helplessly in the churning water until Sam realised that they would have to do it the hard way and contrived to knock him out. He turned on his back and pulled the inert body across his chest. He was dead weight but at least he wasn't struggling: the way he had been going he was set to drown them both.

Sam pulled for the raft. It was against the run of the tide but it would be shorter than swimming to the shore, burdened as he was and with only his legs and one arm to force them through the turbulent, dogged water. It was a fight every inch of the way and before long he knew that both their lives were at stake. His eyes throbbed, his lungs were bursting, he was swimming lower and lower in the water—again and again he felt it wash over his face. He swam on because there was nothing else he could

do, while exhaustion dragged like a slave-chain at his legs...

His head struck something: he blinked water from his eyes and peered up at the barrels lashed to the underside of the raft. Unbelievably, there it was, cavorting capriciously on the temperamental sea, towering like a cliff above him, unscalable as a glacier. Desperately he tried to catch the lifeline, treading water and supporting the sagging David on the other arm, dreading that he might let him slip, aware that if he did he would never find him again. He cursed impotently as the raft evaded him, lifting on a roller only to come crashing down into a trough, threatening to brain them both...at last he got a hand on the lifeline and hung gasping for breath, while the raft loomed dark and forbidding above him. For a moment he had to be content with that. He had no strength for more. But he knew he could not support the boy's weight indefinitely. His arm would grow numb and give up its burden to the sea.

If only David were conscious. He tried to rouse him but he had done the job too well. Somehow, he must heave him up on to the raft himself. But it was one thing to support him in the water and another to lift him out of it. His weight increased tenfold—he was a trailing mass of sliding arms and legs, formless—shapeless—lifeless—and utterly indifferent to his peril. At last Sam got a shoulder under the body, waited for a rising swell and heaved. At the third attempt he got the head and shoulders up on to the raft, and then, on the breast of the succeeding wave, the rest of him.

As he hauled up to get aboard himself, the lifeline broke. It was old and rotten and the strain of their combined weights had been too much. It tore loose from under his hand and cast him adrift.

By now he was so spent that it was as tough to get back to the raft alone as it had been burdened with the boy. It was even harder to grab a handhold and he knew that if he did he could only hope to cling for a few minutes before he was washed away again. He had no longer the strength to climb aboard. The sea rocked him, swayed him, tossed him within inches of the raft—and wickedly, tantalisingly swung him away again, a gigantic and malevolent cat at play with a helpless, drowning mouse...

Sam made one last effort, and scarcely knew that it was not enough...

Alone on the distant beach, Honey screamed and her frantic feet beat the sand as the gloating waters closed over his head.

5

Hands grasped him as he surfaced, boiling upwards through the glass-green water, but he was not aware of it. Only that he was cold, cold while the icy worms of nausea squirmed in his stomach and his limbs were a greater weight than he could lift.

Something pressed painfully against his chest, scraping the skin. It was the gunwale of the boat: he collapsed in the bottom, his numb face pressed to the planking. Someone was working on him, torturing his lungs. Without warning, unable to raise his head, he off-loaded a stomachful of seawater. His briny vomit sloshed about between the ribs that whirled in a drunken reel about his head. He groaned and tried to twist away from it.

'A-ar,' came the voice of someone bending over him. 'Tha's better out nor in, I reckon.' Weathered hands came searching under him, gnarled and strong as old willow, probing his queasy stomach. 'You reckon you got any more aboard?'

He managed to shake his head, contrived to prise on to his elbows the inert weight of his body. There was something that had to be done—something forgotten—

'Boy—' he gasped, and the effort of speech choked him. He lay helpless while water trickled from his nose and mouth.

'That's all right, my son, you'm going to be all right.' The old fisherman crouched over him, kneading at his back, kind as a woman in the face of his distress.

'Where's—boy—' he gulped when he could get his breath.

The old man jerked a disparaging thumb towards the bow. 'There,' he growled. 'Right's a bloody trivet. Tan his arse, I would, if he was mine.'

Sam grinned feebly, and after some moments of determined effort managed to drag his reluctant knees up under him and roll back on to his heels, where he squatted, swaying, until his companion tipped him backwards and propped him up against the bulkhead. He stretched his legs as well as he could and after that he was content to lie still, filling his lungs with the good air; it seemed he could not get enough of it. Its keeness rasped his throat and he longed for a cigarette. The old man lit a Woodbine from a tattered packet and stuck it between his lips, but he could not smoke it. He coughed uncontrollably, spattering his hands with little flecks of foam.

It was a pleasure launch that had picked them up; a small hardworking craft that with its crew of two fished for seafood or holidaymakers, according to the season. With the roughening of the weather it had been making for harbour and had come up on them unnoticed, the throb of its engine muffled by the roar of the sea in his ears. Lucky for him, he was thinking, a few more minutes would have seen him out...

David was sitting up in the prow, pale and sullen, nursing a swelling face.

'You all right?' Sam asked him through chattering teeth. He was cold through and through, shivering uncontrollably.

David turned away with a surly mutter, his thin body huddled against wet, comfortless wood.

'Better have this—catch!' Sam threw him the rough thick fisherman's sweater that had been offered to him.

'Thankless young bugger!' The old man was angry, affronted on his behalf. 'Didn't you hear what he said?'

'He's just a kid,' said Sam. He closed his eyes and tried to glean comfort from the warmth of the sun, the gentle rocking progress of the boat. But the warmth penetrated no further than his skin and the light craft pitched and wallowed over the choppy sea. Before they reached the shore his stomach rebelled again.

Honey ran splashing through the surf and clambered aboard, still clutching a sodden, useless towel, to stumble

51

upon his inert body lying athwartships. She fell across it and burst into hysterical tears.

'He's dead—he's dead—' she sobbed, her frantic fists beating on his chest.

That made him cough again. He wrenched his mind back from the inviting darkness to try to tell her David was all right, that he hadn't killed him, only knocked him out, before he saw through salt-bleared eyes that her fear was for himself. He was deeply touched.

'Why, Honey...' He drew her little scared body into the shelter of his arm, and she crouched there, biting her knuckles, her emotions switched so abruptly that she was left bewildered in mid-air.

'I thought...I thought...' she said at last in a very small voice.

He shook her gently, trying to bring a smile. 'I couldn't die that way. My engine runs on seawater.'

She tried, obligingly, to laugh. But her face contorted and the tears began to flow, natural healing, washing away the shock and the confusion. He let her cry for a moment; then, 'Come on, let's go get some coffee.'

He struggled up awkwardly, still comforting the child, and lurched on uncertain legs up the beach. He felt better now that he was on his feet and moving. All he needed was to get warm...

Someone asked him if he was all right. He said lightly, 'Oh sure, I've got my wife here...' and Honey giggled nervously and looked up to see if she was being teased.

He glanced over to where David was the focus of a little buzzing knot. 'Get him better quick,' he called amiably to the clucking Lizzie Bassett, 'because I'm going to warm the seat of his pants for him—but good!' He grinned at the purple-faced boy and made his weary way on up the beach. Honey still clung to his side and he leaned on her more heavily than he knew. She bore up bravely, her angry face pressed to his icy flank. Angry, because everyone was fussing over David while nobody seemed to be bothered about Sam: and her every instinct was telling her that someone should be.

The little group on the beach dispersed; the boat put to sea again and the incident was over. But in Sam were sown the seeds of a desperate illness, a lasting impairment to his health.

And in David the germ of an enmity that was even more deadly.

Time fell to pieces for Honey.

She awoke in darkness from a nightmare and went groping through the unlit wagon for Sam. There was a terrifying noise in the caravan: it had been in her dream and it was still here, filling the darkness like the breathing of some monstrous animal. She was not sure that her nightmare was only a nightmare—not sure that she was really awake...

She called uncertainly, 'Sam?'

He did not answer. The sound seemed to be coming from his bed. As if something dreadful had devoured him, and was crouching there, waiting for her...She shook herself awake. She made herself cover the few steps to his bed.

'Sam,' she whispered uneasily, peering down into his face. He did not respond although his eyes were open a crack. She could see them burning like coals between the lids. When she touched his arm the skin seemed to scorch her fingers. The terrible sound was his breathing. Something was dreadfully wrong...She stood looking down at the stricken figure of all that was good in her world, and felt real fear take the place of fantasy.

'Sam,' she whimpered, but still he did not stir; she shook his shoulder, timidly at first, then in panic as she found she could not rouse him. She stood there shaking and sobbing by turns until it was borne in upon her that she must get help.

She remembered running barefoot to the farmhouse through rain that poured with the tears down her face and being bundled into the warm bed Bassie had just left: but she could not stay there. She had to creep out and listen for what was happening.

She sat shivering in the gloom behind the closed door, her ear pressed to the narrow crack of light, straining to catch and untangle the mysterious sounds below. She heard Bassie go out. Almost immediately she returned, slamming the door, and Honey could hear her talking low and urgently. There was only one voice: Sam was not with her. She must be on the telephone. She heard her say, '—so quick as you possibly can!' and then the tinkle of the phone being hung up, and Bassie went out again, leaving a nerve-wracking silence prowling through the house.

She got up and went to the window, but she couldn't see the caravan from here, only a pool of light on the

grass, shed from one of its windows. Bassie was out there with Sam. That was where she should be...she went back to the door. But she could not open it; Bassie had locked her in.

After an endless time she heard the swish of car tyres and saw shadows blurring the little square of light. Then the front door opened at last and someone was using the telephone. She recognised Dr Colby's voice and her spirits lifted — he would know what to do for Sam, everything would be all right. Then she caught the note of anxiety in his voice. Dr Colby was always right: if he was worried about Sam... Numbed with dread, she knelt on the floorboards, listening to the silence. After an eternity she heard another vehicle arrive, the sounds of muted voices, the closing of doors. She looked out and saw an ambulance, for her for ever after the symbol of grief and isolation, disappearing up the lane.

Although no one came to tell her, she knew that it had taken Sam away, and her soul shrivelled with the conviction that he was never coming back.

Time fell to pieces, and left a terrifying blank. At some point during the days that followed she was taken out to where the Colbys sat waiting in their car.

'Get in, Honey, you're coming with us,' said Mrs Colby, kindly. 'Now, let's have a wee smile, eh?'

Honey smiled dutifully. 'Thank you, Mrs Colby.' But her heart was not obedient. It knew nothing nice could ever happen to her now.

They drove for a long time through the countryside in the brightness of a summer that had lost its warmth. Hedgerows gave way to houses, and finally the car turned in at the gates of a building that towered forbiddingly above a city street. It was hot inside, with a queer sort of smell, clean and yet sickly at the same time. They walked along endless corridors, passing doors through which she glimpsed long rows of people in identical beds. There were signs up everywhere, telling where to go for X-rays, for waiting rooms, for Casualty — what was Casualty? Another sign said Theatre I—

She glanced up at the faces of her companions, but they were silent and preoccupied and did not appear to notice her. She puzzled until she caught sight of a nurse's white cap and blue uniform — of course! This was Dr Colby's hospital, where he worked. They must have

called in here on the way to wherever they were going...

The nurse stopped when she reached them, and said, 'Is this the little girl?'

Honey shrank a little from the hand that reached for hers. Was she to be left here? Someone at school had been taken to see a hospital; his mother had disappeared and they had kept him there and taken his tonsils out...

'Come along,' said Dr Colby, his voice tinged with impatience. Mrs Colby took her hand and they were on the move again, walking down the middle of an endless room between two rows of beds. An elderly man smiled at her, overcoming her with shyness. One of the beds was covered by a shiny white tent. Beside it stood a cylinder with a writhing assortment of pipes. On the other side of the bed was a chair. Dr Colby lifted her on to the chair and she saw that in the top of the tent was a window.

She stood staring down at the man who lay in the bed, thin as a match and fragile under the stiff bedclothes. He opened eyes like holes charred in parchment, and she saw that they were Sam's.

She hung there, helpless in Dr Colby's arm, unable to grasp at once that this was Sam: that he was not yet dead but dying in this distant place, changed out of recognition and unable to speak to her—that this was not after all the ultimate agony, the worst was still to come. Knowing why she had been brought here: they had come to say goodbye.

Suddenly it was all too much for her. She clamped her hands over her mough but she could not keep from crying, a dreadful noise broke from her that would not be stilled. They hustled her away quickly, Mrs Colby and the nurse. They took her into a tiny room and fed her with sweets from a tin. As soon as she was quiet she was escorted to the car and returned in embarrassed silence to Lizzie Bassett.

She was not taken to the hospital again, nor did either of the Colbys come to visit her at the farm. Although the incident was not mentioned she knew she had disgraced herself. She went about silent and shamefaced, unable to voice the despairing question that never left her mind. Only Dr Arthur would know if Sam were still alive; Bassie was too taken up with My David and the harvesting to know anything. So she stayed out of doors from morning to night, walking herself to exhaustion to escape the thoughts within. Even had she not been locked out of the

caravan she could not have borne to go in there. No one seemed to notice where she was; it was as though they had forgotten her, locked in her anguish like a prisoner. Nobody spoke to her of Sam and as time went on she dared not ask. She shrank from hearing the words that he was dead and the mention of his name was enough to send her scurrying from the room.

In the midst of the confusion Lizzie Bassett collapsed and died of a heart attack. For Honey it was as if someone had withdrawn a pin and the whole structure of her life had fallen apart.

Bassie, slapdash and cheerful, partial and impatient but basically kind, had vanished, and in her place a gaunt unsmiling aunt of David's went methodically through her sister's belongings, discarding old worthless treasures and tutting her disapproval. 'That's my Mum's!' protested David unavailingly, and Honey felt for him, imagining those unloving hands rifling the contents of the wagon.

'Not any more, it's not. Gone to a better place, she has,' as the dustbin swallowed a cheap enamelled brooch that Bassie had worn all her life.

'The caravan's mine,' put in Honey fearfully. Sam had always said it was hers. Only he had kept the key—who had it now?

'That's as may be, and no concern of mine. No doubt the Council will move it when the farm's sold. And something must be done about you. You can't stay here.'

David and Honey looked at each other in mutual misery. Then David said, 'Where will I go, Auntie?'

'You'll live with me, over the shop. I hope I know my duty.' She folded her mouth grimly. 'You can go down there now and bring me back a bar of carbolic soap. There's nothing in this house that doesn't need a right good scrub, fair disgusting.'

Honey knew the shop, cold and bare-floored and meanly lit by a single naked electric bulb, forbiddingly stark with its aura of cheap disinfectant. It was just like David's aunt. For the first time in her life she felt sorry for David. It must have been good to be loved by Bassie, and this dreadful lady had no warmth for anyone. When he came back she said diffidently, 'Poor David, it must be awful for you.'

David's self esteem had suffered two blows in a painfully short time and Honey's pity was the last straw. Keeping his reddened eyes averted he said gruffly, 'At

least I got a home, that's more than you can say.'

Honey reminded herself that she should have known, and made no more clumsy overtures. When the time came, he departed unlamented to his fate.

Honey herself was taken to the Colbys at the big grey Stone House. There she was tucked away in a little bedroom that overlooked the garden; she ate her meals, or toyed with them, at the long table in the dining-room where they had shared so many Christmas dinners, only now there was only her, with one or the other, and only occasionally both, of the Colbys, and it was all so different that she wanted to cry. The rest of the time she was looked after by a lady with large black shoes and bony ankles whom Mrs Colby addressed as Ellen. Ellen called her 'Miss Honey' and put her straight hair into curlers that hurt when she lay on them at night; but she was kind and quiet and never scolded, not even when Honey woke her up at night because of her nightmares. Ellen hardly talked at all: she just said, 'There, there, Miss Honey,' and went down and brought warm milk in a glass with a silver handle, and sat beside her bed until she slept.

She lived one day at a time, not looking at tomorrow. Without Sam, no sort of life was imaginable. His loss was a chasm over which no bridge could be thrown; she moved in a limbo where nothing she did was of importance. On the day appointed she allowed herself to be walked to the school by Ellen, and dully sat through lessons with the same blank face that she brought to everything.

The next morning she found a letter propped against her breakfast plate.

6

She stared in joyous unbelief at the familiar upright hand. She looked from one to the other of the Colbys, smiling

indulgently over their breakfast cups. At last she gasped,
'It's from Sam—he's alive!'

Dr Colby rolled his eyes towards heaven and Mrs
Colby laughed and said, 'Well, of course he's alive, do
you not think we'd have told you!' and still she sat drinking in the envelope, until Maggie said, 'Well, are you not
going to open it?'

She came out of her trance and read:

> Honey,
>
> Get the wagon all shined up, I'm on my way. OK
> now but missing you, nobody here knows how to
> pour my coffee. Sorry I couldn't talk when you
> came—what did you think of my tent? It was full
> of oxygen, helps you get well quicker. I felt like an
> orchid under all that cellophane. See you Friday—
>
> > Ever your loving
> > Sam

And today was Thursday!

'I can't go to school,' she cried, 'Sam's coming home,
I've got to get things ready! Oh, please, Mrs Colby—'

'Now, now, now—' began Dr Colby, irritated as always
by her outbursts, but Mrs Colby cut him short.

'Of course you can't, dearie.' She smiled her sweet
smile, and Honey knew it was going to be all right. Next
to Sam, she liked Mrs Colby best of anyone. Especially
now...She jumped up from the table, wanting to go now,
this minute, to get on with her life that had suddenly
started again.

All day she scrubbed and polished in a frenzy of nervous energy. She could barely tolerate that any other
hands but hers should touch the caravan: Sam had asked
her to make it ready and she wanted to do it all. But she
was forced to admit that she could not light the stove and
Mrs Colby insisted on airing the beds herself. Sam had
been very ill, she pointed out, and must be properly taken
care of. As if she didn't know, thought Honey rebel-
liously, forced to stand by while someone else did things
for Sam. She consoled herself by remembering his letter,
every word of which she knew by heart. He missed her,
he had said—he had missed her; he had never said that
before.

When darkness fell she had to be carried off bodily to
bed, and daybreak found her back at the caravan, waiting

forlornly on the steps for someone to arrive with the key. When she had done everything she could find to do, she started again from the beginning and did things twice; it was so much easier than doing nothing. By mid-morning she had achieved a brightness of welcome she could not improve upon; she had cleaned the windows, shopped for stores at Mrs Figg's, laboriously carried water from the house. Her stomach was in knots, her eyes worried the windows, she arranged and rearranged the jam-jar full of field flowers that were all she could provide.

Maggie Colby, who had robbed her garden of a few late roses, tactfully took them home again unseen. She had come to take Honey back with her to lunch, but a glance at the child's tense face made her say instead, 'When Sam comes, tell him you're both invited to supper. You've some milk and biscuits here if you want them, I suppose?'

'Yes, thank you,' said Honey politely, her eyes still on the lane. She remembered, and added, 'Thank you for having me.'

Maggie brought her little case in from the car, set it down, and said, 'He won't be here for quite a while yet, Arthur's only now gone to fetch him. You wouldn't like to come back with me for a little? You're sure?'

Honey said quickly, 'Oh no, thank you—' as if she were threatened with eviction. She blushed, and added, 'I mean—' and stopped in confusion.

'It's all right, dearie, I know what you mean.' Maggie stooped to kiss the burning cheek. Laughing, she stepped down from the caravan. 'I'll away, then, and leave you in peace to await your darling.'

When Maggie had gone, Honey sat on the top step by the open door, her eyes fixed relentlessly on the lane. Little by little her head drooped towards the gingerbread of the canopy, time after time she jerked it upright...A dog pattered up the lane, poked an inquisitive nose round the gate, caught her eye and wagged his tail once before moving off. A fly buzzed in the warm October sun...the fly and the dog went buzzing off together, looking for blackberries...

'Honey?' And there he was, thinner and paler, but still unmistakably Sam.

Her lids flew wide and she launched herself, burying herself in his arms.

'Oh, Sam, you didn't—you didn't...' Even now she could not bring herself to say what he had not done, as if even the mention of it was perilous. But he seemed to understand.

He hugged her and said tenderly, 'No, I didn't.' He brought her inside and sat down with her on his knee, and he moved slowly, as if he were very tired or very old. But she could feel his contentment as he looked about him, and knew he was glad to be home. He sat smiling at her while she tried to collect her wits, and presently he said, 'Guess I could use a cup of your coffee, now,' putting himself in danger of strangulation before she ran to fill the kettle. She had forgotten to buy butter; Sam said, 'Who needs butter?' and spread syrup on the bread and toasted it by the fire. It was delicious, warm and sweet and crisp, consoling to her stomach which had suddenly awoken and was clamouring for food.

She was bursting to tell him all her news. He listened gravely while she poured out the accumulated trivia of weeks, mixing the great and the small, the tragic and the comic, because nothing was too big or too small to tell Sam, he was always interested. The frogs had left the pond and gone hopping about in the long grass, their brown bodies looking like little wet pebbles so that you had to be careful not to tread on them. David had beaten one all to pieces with a stone—she had hit him and kicked him but he wouldn't stop—he had laughed and kept on laughing...Bassie had died in the middle of cooking dinner, the custard she was making had boiled over the stove, it had poured down all over the front like a curtain and smelled terrible...Mrs Colby's cat had five kittens, and one of them was white all over with blue eyes...David had gone to live with Mrs Figg and he said he could eat all the chocolate in the shop...The milkman's horse had taken an apple from her hand...David wanted the white kitten and she was afraid Mrs Colby might let him have it because no one else seemed to want it—oh, Sam, it would be awful, it was such a darling kitten...

Sam smiled and said he would see that David did not get the kitten. He picked up the end of her plait and tickled her face with it. No one else ever did that. She lay along his lap in the firelight and felt happiness seep into her.

After a time they both fell asleep; Sam through ex-

haustion and weakness, Honey simply because she was tired out.

Sam awoke refreshed in the autumnal dusk. He lifted the sleeping child and carefully laid her down upon his berth, taking off the scuffed little shoes and pulling a fold of the covers over her. He stood looking down for a moment at the tranquil face, the window on a devotion he still found astonishing. There were times when he felt impelled to say, 'Don't give me so much that I don't deserve: I can't live up to it...' He never said it because she would not understand. But sometimes when his mind was full of it he would find her looking at him curiously, as if his thoughts were reflected in his face, and would be humbled. This homecoming was not lost on him; he was glad he had insisted on coming straight here from the hospital.

There were times, he thought, when a child was asleep, when you could catch a glimpse of the woman to come: this was one of those times. The features might change and remould, but this expression was already there, a serene sensitivity that would never be lost. Some little boy somewhere was running around with ink-stained fingers and his pockets full of string, not knowing of the firelight glow that would one day fill his life; collecting car numbers, bubble-gum, old nails, dirt behind his ears—maybe even stones for killing frogs—despising all girls; thinking himself sufficient, his life complete—until suddenly one day, wham!

He straightened up and strolled to the door. He stood, leaning his elbows on the hatch, looking out over the countryside. Life must be peaceful here, he reflected, watching the hedgerows turn blue in a dusk that wreathed like bonfire smoke. All evenings were probably like this, cool and quiet and pierced with birdsong, with cattle wading kneedeep in the white mist of the watermeadows...too quiet, maybe. Shipmates ashore said as much. They missed the very things one complained of when at sea. The reek of diesel, the clang of steel plates underfoot, the groan of a fuel pump at night—the rootless existence that weakened every tie...With few exceptions they went back to sea.

With a sigh he turned back to the caravan. It looked smaller than ever by contrast with the spaciousness of the wards. But Honey loved it—its doll's-house proportions were better suited to her size than his!

He shivered. The fire had gone down. He looked into the hod and it was empty. He filled it from the bunker outside and noticed its weight for the first time. His brow streamed with sweat and he had to set it down every few paces. When he finally wrestled it to the stove he had to sit down, half annoyed, half amused, and wait to recover the strength to lift it up.

'Sam…aren't you strong any more?' came a bewildered voice from the berth, and he looked up from mopping his face to meet her worried eyes.

'Still strong enough to beat you up,' he said. 'Here, come give me a hand.'

Reassured, she came to help him and between them they made up the fire, laughing a bit at their struggles and spilling some of the coal on the floor.

When Arthur Colby put his head round the door, Sam was in his shirtsleeves, frying chips; his clothing hung on his bones in an alarming way. Arthur said, 'I thought you were coming to us for supper—I came to pick you up.'

Honey's eyes widened in guilt for her omission, but Sam said quickly, 'Sorry Arthur, I forgot. Have some coffee while you're waiting.' He pushed a cup towards him and grinned. 'I could eat two suppers,' he lied, 'how about you, Honey?'

'Three suppers!' she declared with truth. She felt as if she had never eaten before. Sam piled most of the chips on to her plate, turned off the gas.

Sipping his coffee, Arthur said, 'Well, have you decided about your future?'

Sam hesitated, 'I'll need your help—but I want to talk to Honey about it first.'

Honey stopped eating and gripped the edge of her chair. Her eyes went questing from one face to the other. What was going to happen? She had not thought beyond Sam's safe return, it was too soon to face the thought of his departure…her stomach went back into its familiar knot. She pushed her plate away.

Sam pushed it back. 'Eat up,' he said. He turned to Dr Colby, 'Won't be a minute, Arthur. We'll join you in the car.'

Dr Colby looked at him hard for a moment, then said, 'Hmph,' and went out, leaving them alone.

When he had gone, Honey gazed anxiously at Sam. Waiting for him to tell her, not daring to ask.

He lifted her up and stood her on the chair, her face level with his. 'Don't look so worried. Hey, you're trembling...' He smiled encouragement, gently joggled her. 'Nothing bad's going to happen—I just wanted to tell you myself. I'm not going to sea any more.' He paused and looked at her. Her face was completely blank. He went on, 'How would you like me to stay here and look after you?'

'Oh, Sam,' she whispered, and again 'Oh, Sam!' and her head dived down on to his shoulder and her thin arms gripped his neck. When he looked she was crying, in a strange adult sort of way, not howling in the familiar manner of children but with tight-shut eyes and bitten lips, the tears pouring down her face with not a sound.

He sat down with her, talking to her softly and rubbing her back. At last the words came, 'Don't ever leave me again...promise!'

He promised, lightly, not knowing what it would mean.

7

New tenants were coming into Bassett's Farm.

'You'll have to move the caravan,' said Arthur, 'the new people don't want it there, they've complained to the ground landlord. Luckily he's a friend of mine; well, to cut a long story short—he's let me have the small paddock by the cliff edge. You can keep it there for as long as you want. Not much to speak of but there's a stand pipe and plenty of room for a caravan.'

They strolled down together to look at the site, Honey running excitedly ahead of the two men.

'Oh, Sam, it's lovely—you can see the sea!'

'So you can,' he grinned, remembering what the fishermen said: Foul with the corpses of the lost. He didn't

care, he liked the sea. And it was well enough diluted—
yes, this place would do fine. Just fine. High hedges facing
the road and the farm, and a gate giving on to the lane;
on the third side of the triangle, the cliff and the ocean
beyond. Peace, he thought. And privacy. And space for
a kid to run wild in...He turned to Arthur.

'Thanks,' he said. 'Couldn't be better. Only...' He hesitated.

'Only what?'

'I'd want a business arrangement, pay rent as I did at
the farm.'

'Don't be ridiculous!' Arthur was affronted.

'It's not ridiculous!' Aware that he had snapped, he
forced a laugh. 'You're a great guy, Arthur—a sucker for
the underdog, but—hell, we're friends. Don't make me
into one of your charities.'

'It's not a question of charity, it's a matter of principle.
Knowing my views, that should be obvious to you.'

Too obvious, thought Sam. But if he was stung by this,
his first intimation that Arthur's friendship was based on
patronage, he was not going to show it. He dropped a
companionable hand on the other man's shoulder. 'Come
on, how would you feel in my position?'

'I should have thought it was a little different,' said
Arthur stiffly.

Sam removed the hand. 'Yes...I guess it is.' He looked
with regret to where Honey skipped ecstatically through
the wind-tossed grasses. 'Maybe I'd better look for somewhere else.'

Arthur said quickly, 'No, no—I won't hear of it. Of
course you must pay if your pride's involved, I didn't
realise you'd take it like that. What were they charging
you at the farm?'

'Ten bob a week.'

'Hm-mm. But you had the use of their lavatory and
the water-pump. There's nothing down here; we'll call
it five.'

'Done!' He was delighted.

But having secured the site it proved far from easy to
move the caravan. It was a gipsy showman's wagon,
heavy and high wheel-based, sturdily built of timber, the
sort known to travellers as a 'horse-killer'. Jim Carney,
whose two-pump garage serviced Arthur's car and a spat-
ter of farm machinery, scratched his head.

'Looks to me like it's sound enough. But reckon what

you need for that's a dray horse. Look, see, you got shafts and all, sound's a bell. Bearings is all right. And you're only going down the road.'

'Where can I get one?'

Jim shook his head, drew his breath in through his teeth in a long sibilant negative. You might as well ask for the moon, said his expression, and now it was Sam's turn to do the head-scratching.

As usual it was Arthur who solved the problem. On a visit to an outlying farm he spotted a massive Suffolk Punch, and persuaded the owner to come and do the job.

On the following Sunday the great horse came clopping proudly down the lane to the farm, his bronze coat shining like an autumn leaf and half the village children prancing behind him.

'What's his name?'

'Can I pat him?'

'Can I have a ride?'

'What's his name?'

'His name's Copper. And yes, you can pat him, and no, you can't have a ride. Not yet, anyway. Now stand clear, there's good kids. We've a job to do, Copper and I.'

It took the better part of an hour with a grease-gun and some good sea-going language to free off the arthritic bearings. Copper, urged on by his owner, obligingly threw his weight into the collar: nothing happened.

Sam emerged from under the wagon. 'Looks like a pick and shovel job.' In the years it had stood in the same place, the iron-shod wheels had sunk into the ground and would have to be dug out. Reinforcements were needed; three of the boys went home to fetch their dads, and Sam went up to the Rose to lay in some beer.

'And a Guinness for Copper,' called John, his owner, 'I reckon he'll have earned it by the time he's shifted this!'

Sam grinned, not sure if he was joking, but he brought the Guinness anyway. Copper heard the clink of bottles and his ears swivelled forward, his whiskery muzzle came searching towards his titbit.

'Work first,' said John, 'don't want you drunk in charge of a caravan.'

Copper shook his head to the amusement of the children and John laughed. 'Booze all day if I let him.'

The necessary excavations made, they tried again. By

this time Copper had decided that the operation was just one more vagary of the human race: as the thing was plainly rooted like an oak and not meant to move, all that was required of him was to go through the motions to satisfy the boss. This he did, and returned to cropping the grass. John opened his Guinness and held it before his nose and the three men pushing the wagon from behind abruptly found themselves face downward in the mud as he lurched off in pursuit of his prize.

Out of the farm gate they turned and went creaking and swaying down the steep lane, an extraordinary equipage followed by a crowd of yelling, excited children, with Honey hopping from one foot to the other and Sam holding his breath and crossing his fingers every time he thought of the axles. At last they turned in at the gateway; Copper was unhitched and tossed off his Guinness from a bucket held for him by an entranced Honey. Sam and the others manhandled the wagon into position and sat down to broach the beer.

And that was how Arthur found him, sitting on a shaft in a sweat-soaked shirt, drinking beer in the fresh breeze from the sea. He shook his head.

'And you not long out of hospital,' he said despairingly, 'I give you up.'

Sam grinned, opened another bottle and held it out to him. 'You do that. Here, have a beer.' Honey snuggled up to him and they laughed, conspiratorially, into each other's eyes.

Later, Arthur said to his wife, 'He's too much wrapped up in that child, you know. She's going to break his heart.'

'It's the fate of all parents,' said Maggie, 'and there's nothing you can do about it.' She looked at her husband and suppressed a sigh. If only she could have given him that fate.

In the months that followed Sam learned that there was more to moving house than he had suspected. It was one thing to use the caravan with its primitive arrangements for a few weeks' holiday; quite another to live in it with some kind of permanence. For comfortable living you needed a little more, and there was always Arthur hovering anxiously at his elbow, pointing out such minor details as sanitation or the unsuitability of stand-pipe water for drinking. And that Honey ought to have a room of her own. It was true, he thought, looking at her. She

had long outgrown the chavy bed and graduated to a camp-bed slung athwart the wagon: with their sleeping quarters divided only by the panelling of the bed-place there was nowhere she could dress or undress in private. More than seven years had passed since they came to Bassett's Farm and her limbs were learning a grace that was new to them. A room of her own she should certainly have, and he went out and bought timber.

Arthur rolled his eyes to heaven. 'You can't just build—they'll make you take it down!'

'Why—and who's they?'

'The Council. You have to have planning permission and a licence.'

'How long will that be?'

'As long as it takes. You can't hurry these things. I'll do what I can, of course...'

Sam sat thoughtful, gnawing his lip. 'You mean I can't build anything without a licence? Not even a toolshed? Or a thunderbox?'

'That's different, of course—now, Sam!'

Sam smiled beatifically. There was always a way round.

While Arthur imagined him to be patiently battling with authority, he screened off a corner of the plot behind the wagon and built there a shed of luxurious proportions. When the fast-growing conifers he had planted were tall enough, he divided the shed into a bedroom and a wash-house, lined the walls and concreted the floor. When he had cut a doorway in the bulkhead of the caravan and connected the two with a covered step-way, their makeshift home was complete.

'Looks a bit like a dog house.' He scratched his head. 'What do you reckon—will it do?'

Honey nodded earnestly. But she did not smile. 'Will I have to sleep out there?'

'Well, that's the general idea—'

Her eyes snapped and she burst out passionately, 'You want to get rid of me now!' and rushed out into the rain.

Sam shook his head and fished for a cigarette. He lit up, put on the kettle, and waited quietly for her return. Presently she would be back as always, cold and deflated and in need of comfort. But it was no use going after her...

For Honey it had all been the realisation of an impossible dream, something that could not be expected to

last—and the crash was already overdue. To the bewilderment of the childless Colbys she had reacted not well but badly to the change. For the first time in her life the sun was shining and the unaccustomed touch of it went to her head. She could not, dared not, trust her luck, knowing that at any moment it might be snatched away, and her nervous tension vented itself on Sam. If he corrected her, she flew at him—'I hate you! I hate you!'—fists pounding him, face ablaze, until her fury dissolved in painful sobs, in pleas to him not to leave her as she succumbed to his restraining arm.

When she came back he was sitting with his back to the door. She crept up behind him and leaned damply against him.

'I don't know why I get like this,' she said miserably, huddling into his arm as he drew her forward.

'Maybe I do.' He pushed back a wet straggle of hair, brushed away her tear with his thumb. 'Why don't you just leave the worrying to me?'

Honey sat wrestling with herself, her struggle reflected in her fingers that twisted and untwisted the hem of her dress.

Sam stilled them with a large tranquil hand. 'Can't you...?'

'No, I can't—' She searched his waiting face, the understanding expression that meant he didn't understand.

'If I leave it to you I can't trust you to do it!'

His eyes flew open round as pennies and they stared at each other for a full moment before his mouth twitched and they burst out laughing together. And after that things began to get better. A few days later she came into the caravan to find him sitting, head between knees, earnestly gnawing his fingernails.

'Sam! What's the matter!'

He looked up, his brow furrowed. 'Tomorrow's the end of the month.'

'But—but what about it?'

'Gotta catch up on my worrying—didn't do any this week—' The rest was lost in laughter as she ran to punish him. But in the end the infection spread to her, as it always did. It was impossible to be serious with Sam for long.

It was impossible to upset him either, or so it seemed to Honey. He was always there and always calm, a rock on which her storms could break without damage to any-

one, and slowly her wild seas grew calm, she felt the ground safe and firm beneath her feet. Only occasionally she would run down on to the beach, unable to support the pressure of joy within her, and would run and run for the sheer relief of physical movement, throwing herself down exhausted at the end of it; only to know sudden panic at the distance she had put between them so that she had to go back immediately, breathless as she was, to make sure he was still there.

On the day he started work at his new job her doubts undid her for the last time. He would finish work, he had said, at five thirty. Honey, eager and literal-minded, expected him home by six. By seven thirty she was wandering in the lane, hollow-eyed and taut-faced, too distracted even to stay in the caravan. She recognised his moving shadow from far away and hurried along the dark lane towards him.

'I thought you'd gone,' she accused him, her voice tight with anguish.

Sam, who had missed his train and spent a cheerless hour in the bosom of British Rail, was less than amused.

'Child, child, child...' he began. Then he turned her about with a lopsided hug and walked her along beside him. 'You know I wouldn't go anywhere without telling you, I never did even when you were little—'

'Only once...' Honey hadn't meant to say it; even in her own ears it sounded like a reproach, and she sensed that this was not the moment for it. They both stopped walking. Then to her surprise he smiled.

'But I came back, and that's what you have to remember. Come on now, quit your devilling—' He nudged her shoulder. 'Race you to the gate—'

'Help!' cried Honey. 'I left the kettle on!'

They ran but they were too late. They hooked it off the stove, burned their fingers, dropped it on the floor and the bottom fell out.

'Tell you what,' said Sam. 'Time I took my girl friend out to dinner. Wash your face and we'll go up to the Rose. Besides, we have something to celebrate.'

'Celebrate?' She looked up, diverted from the disaster.

'Sure—new job.' He chuckled, remembering Arthur's gloomy prediction. 'It's not going to be easy, with the war over good jobs don't come ten-apenny...' He hadn't said, 'Especially for you,' but the words had been in the air. Sam had shrugged. His skills had brought him a welcome

before where his appearance might have kept him out. 'Come on, Honey, full ahead or there'll be no food left. And see if you can think of a name for the caravan.'

'A name?' her eyes widened in surprise. 'Why do we need a name?'

'We have to have an address if we want to get any letters. So what shall we call it—Chez Nous? Dunroamin? Or something really original—how about Sea View?'

'I know!' cried Honey, suddenly inspired. 'Let's call it Mango Walk.'

'"Mango Walk",' he repeated doubtfully. 'But that's not a place name, Honey, it's just a song.'

'Oh, but it could be! And it would sound just lovely...'

'M-mm. I don't think... anyway mangoes don't grow in this country. I bet you don't even know what they look like—and neither does anyone else around here.'

'But, darling Sam, it sounds so beautiful! Please...oh, please...'

About to say firmly that it wasn't suitable, he caught the expression on her face.

'All right then. Mango Walk it is.'

She flung ecstatic arms around his neck. 'Oh, I love you and love you...'

What the hell, he was thinking... let them laugh.

They ate their chop, chips and peas in the back room of the Rose, and afterwards christened Mango Walk—'God bless her and all who sail in her!'—with a flagon of cider brought home for the occasion and broken in proper style across her bows. And for three whole years nobody died or had hysterics and nothing more earth-shaking happened than that Honey conceived a whim to be a ballerina and Sam had regretfully to tell her that it was out.

In fact life was flowing smooth and peaceful. And then Nancy turned up.

8

'You've cut yourself!' Honey's jaw dropped. Sam was always so neat with his hands; yet he had cut himself just slicing bread and did not seem to have noticed.

She hurried through to the wash-room to find plasters and when she returned he was still as she had left him, staring like a gundog at something outside while the blood ran down unheeded on to the bread. 'Here, let me...' She was fumbling with a plaster but he shook her off with a 'Ssh!' and his eyes did not leave the window.

With an anxious glance at the taut lines of his face she pushed her way between him and the window, trying to see what it was that had so disturbed him. He took no notice of her. It was as if he had forgotten she was there.

Someone was moving in the lane outside, passing their entrance and then passing it again as though looking for something. The third time the searcher stopped, a hand on the gate, and looked up. Honey had an impression of strong colours, of a mass of vivid hair, a brightly over made-up face—

Sam rasped suddenly, making her jump, 'Go through to the doghouse and shut yourself in! Don't come out till I call you.' Still not looking at her he shoved her roughly towards the door, and she ran, shaken and trying not to cry.

In the dog-house, sitting small and tight on her narrow bed, she hugged Girl Sam for comfort while the voices rose and fell in the caravan. She did not know why she was frightened but she was. Sam was alarmed, and a sense of premonition had come down on everything. Cold and scared, she sat straining her ears, trying to make out the words.

Sam had recovered some of his composure. He noted

with satisfaction that Nancy's beauty no longer affected him. Or perhaps it was no longer potent. He said, 'What brings you here after so long?'

'Do I have to have a reason?' She crossed her legs and he noticed that her knees had gone bony.

He looked at her levelly. 'You need a reason,' he said.

Nancy rearranged her smile. 'That's cosy, I must say. I mean, you don't have to leap up and embrace me but you might manage a smile for a long-lost wife. How about it?'

Sam was not going to be stampeded. He eyed her warily while he lit a cigarette. 'I don't remember it being cosy the last time we met,' he said cautiously. 'You told me to send the money and keep out of sight. Remember?'

A hard gleam showed in the friendly eye and was instantly snuffed out. 'We were young then, Sam, young and hot-tempered. That's no reason we can't let bygones be bygones.' She leaned forward across the table, confidential, smiling. 'We ought to be taking care of each other—after all, we're not getting any younger...'

So that was it. She wanted what she had always wanted—money. He looked her over dispassionately. The bright hair showed signs of re-touching, the once pearly skin was opaque with a chalky whiteness. And the lines of petulance were now clearly etched about the mouth.

He nodded his agreement. 'On the other hand it's nice to grow old in peace.'

Again the gleam, the immediate extinction. Again the refurbished smile. 'I knew you'd understand. You were always generous with money, Sam, I have to give you that. Until we lost touch, of course...'

Sam smiled faintly at the euphemism. 'Only GI Joe looked after you so much better.' He added with mock concern, 'Don't tell me he "lost touch" too!'

'He went back years ago,' she snapped, 'they all did.' She reached over and took his cigarette, drew on it fiercely and then stubbed it out, frowning through the smoke. 'Fact is I'm down on my luck'—her tone was businesslike—'and you're my husband, the one responsible for me.' Remembering her role she dragged out the smile again. 'After all, you owe me something—'

Impatient, he cut in, 'What about your parents? They've looked after you all this time—' Without Georgia she must have been able to go home.

72

'I haven't been with my parents—' As if to cover an indiscretion she said quickly, 'My present—fiancé was living in Scotland and I moved to be near him.'

'Your—fiancé,' he said, unkindly stressing her hesitation. 'I see—' He fished for his cigarettes and lit another one. 'Then I suggest you try him.'

Nancy reached for his second cigarette. He held it out of reach and tossed her the packet. She fumbled with it, took three shots at striking a match, her hands shaking, before she said, 'He's gone to Canada.'

'Quite an exodus,' Sam remarked drily. 'Maybe you should take more care of your friends.'

He saw her bite back a retort, control herself with a conscious effort. She must really be desperate, he thought, and his conscience nudged him. Her next words stifled it.

'Sam, look—' She was trying the old wheedling sweet-talk that had worked in the early days. "You loved me once, there must be something left—for old times' sake? I've got no one to turn to but you, and I—I've got a kiddy, a little boy—'

'And of course he looks just like me!' The cold disgust he had cultivated was slipping, the old hatred beginning to burn, eroding his hard-won calm. He stood up and opened the door. 'If you know whose it is get a paternity order. If not, try National Assistance. But don't turn to me, I've forgotten I ever knew you. You've come to the wrong house.'

'You can't just—' She checked herself and the struggle was apparent, the determination not to quarrel before she had gained her end. 'Sam,' she persisted, 'you've got to help me! A kid has to be looked after, you should know that.'

It was the very last thing she should have said.

He roared in her startled face, 'Like you looked after Georgia! Leaving her alone to die in the Blitz while you went chasing your fancy men—'

'Oh, don't be so melodramatic! Georgia was all right, I saw you both with my own two eyes. She might have been a bit shaken up, but—' She broke off, staring at him curiously. 'She was all right ... wasn't she?'

'If dead's all right! If smashed to a pulp's all right—it should have been you, you heartless bitch! You know what she was doing? Right up to the end? Crying for you, screaming her head off till the last bomb fell because you

73

weren't there. I heard her from way down the street and I couldn't get there in time—I was too late! Woman, I'm telling you if I could have laid hands on you then you wouldn't be standing there!'

Nancy continued to stare, her face whitening. 'I didn't know.' Her voice was diminished to a whisper. 'I—all this time, I thought she was with you.' She wilted abruptly as if her bones had been stolen by the news. Her eyes, still on him, for the first time apprehensive. 'Oh God, I feel awful...'

Sam's outburst had cleared his head. 'I'm not interested in your feelings,' he said coldly. 'I'm not interested in you, or your byblow or your problems. Don't come whining to me again—I don't want to know.' He picked up her handbag and tossed it out on to the grass. 'Now get going, and don't come back.'

She got up slowly, avoiding his eyes, and left the caravan without a word.

When she had gone, Sam sat down, his head in his hands. His knees had turned traitor and he was shaking uncontrollably. He reached for a cigarette and remembered she had taken the packet. There was one half-smoked on a plate and he lit it, but the flavour was soured and tainted by Nancy's mouth. He lurched through to the wash-room to throw up.

Leaning over the basin sloshing cold water he heard a gentle tapping.

'Can I come out now?' Honey's face, wan and anxious, appeared in the crack of her door. He smiled at her over the edge of the towel and she slipped through. 'Are you all right?'

He nodded and put down the towel, saying nothing. He took her by the hand and led her through into the wagon where he sat down, trying to collect his thoughts. Honey sat beside him, an occasional shiver running through her, saying nothing, asking no questions. Her trust was complete. Now in a moment of anger he had betrayed that trust, and he sat with closed eyes, aware of the light pressure of her head against his arm, her cold little hand between his, searching for the words with which to tell her what he had done.

Suddenly he felt her stiffen. 'Sam...'

He looked up to see Nancy framed in the doorway. She was speaking as she came up the steps, 'They said at the farm—' and as she came into sight she stopped

dead. Staring at them both, thinking...it was all too clear what she was thinking. 'Jesus Christ!' she said slowly, her eyes taking in the clasped hands, the shrinking girl. 'Glory be to God, I should have known! Little girls is it, now? No wonder you wanted me out, you filthy old—'

Sam launched himself, blood pounding in his ears, a red glow blurring his sight, the table crashing to the floor in a shower of broken crockery. He was aware of his hands on Nancy's throat, of her moist flesh squeezing between his fingers, of her eyes widening in terror as the fight for breath became urgent, of his deadly intent to see her lifeless, crushed, beaten, pulped, annihilated ...Somewhere in the distance Honey screamed as a hot bright pain seared into his shoulder bringing his mind back into focus. He let go and staggered back, clutching his arm as a warm flood swamped his sleeve. Nancy gulped, choked, tried to spew out more words even before she had caught her breath. They crouched like two animals, glaring at each other in mutual hatred. Neither heard the footfall on the steps outside.

'Oh—excuse me,' said Arthur Colby politely. 'I didn't know you had company.'

Nancy whipped round to face the intruder and something clattered from her hand to the floor. 'What the hell—' She spluttered, coughed, tried again. 'Get out! Can't you see this is—'

'Come in, Arthur,' Sam said quickly. 'Come in and close the door.' He shot a venomous look at Nancy. 'We've said all there is to say. This—woman is leaving.'

She rounded on him, spitting defiance, 'If you think I'm going—'

Arthur took in the scene with a quick glance. 'Perhaps you could come back some other time,' he said blandly. 'My patient seems to have had rather a nasty accident.' He picked up the bread knife from where it had fallen, examined the smear on the blade. 'It...was an accident, I take it?'

Nancy's expression changed. She snatched up her handbag from where she had dropped it and made for the door. On the steps she flung over her shoulder, 'Don't think you've heard the last of me!' and then, mercifully, she was gone. Sam sank down on to a seat and his shoulders began to shake without a sound.

Arthur said quietly, 'Right, let's clear up the mess.' He bent and picked up the broken table. Then he drew out

75

the shivering child from her refuge with one of his rare smiles. 'Come along, Honey, help pick up the pieces. And you'd better get my bag from the car. Sam may need a stitch in that cut.'

Honey wriggled out from the bed-place and stepped over the debris on the floor. She peered anxiously out before venturing outside, looking for the enemy. Then she ran hell for leather down the path, feeling like a soldier under fire, like a heroine risking her life for her beloved: she was doing it for Sam.

David was lingering in the lane outside, casting envious eyes at the once-despised caravan. Three years with his 'Aunt Figg' as he was compelled to call her had nibbled at his pride and he thought with longing of the cosy life within. 'Got company, have you?' he said.

'Yes, we have,' snapped Honey, 'and we don't want you. Push off!'

Smarting from the rebuff, he moved on towards the beach.

Arthur said briskly, 'Come on Sam, brace up, you'll frighten the child. Tears can be more alarming than blood, you know.'

Sam nodded mutely and tried to get a grip on himself. It seemed as if the grief and bitterness of years had risen up to unman him. The sound of Honey's returning feet on the steps came to his aid and with a harsh, painful gulp he dashed the back of his hand across his eyes and got to his feet, taking the bag from her as she came in at the door.

'What would I do without you?' he joked, but she was not deceived and they shared a moment of silence while Arthur busied himself with the contents of his bag. Then—'Ready?'—and he stripped off the torn shirt for his friend's ministrations. The blood was still flowing freely and Honey stood solemnly by with a saucer to receive the swabs.

'Good as new,' said Arthur when it was stitched and dressed, 'but I don't think much of your taste in women.'

'She's not my taste, I never thought I'd see her again. I thought she was dead. At least; I suppose I did.'

'That's what you told me at the time. Honey's mother, is it?'

'Oh, no!' Honey's face was aghast. 'She couldn't take me away, could she?'

'No, no, no,' Sam consoled her. 'she's not your problem, only mine. That's Nancy—that's my wife.'

Only when it was too late did he realise what he had said.

9

'I don't want to go into a Home,' sobbed Honey. 'Please, Mrs Colby, don't let them take me away!'

'Now, now, now, child,' soothed Maggie Colby, 'we don't know yet, it may not come to that.' But she was troubled for the pair of them, so unworldly, so devoted—so vulnerable in their crazy situation. What on earth had possessed Sam to do such a foolhardy thing! Yet it was typical of him to think with his heart instead of with a cool clear head. She had lived long enough to know that people could not be changed; all one could do was offer comfort when the hard knocks came. Now she smiled at Honey, who was trying to staunch her tears. 'If it came to the worst, you could come and live with us. You'd still be near Sam and you could see him whenever you liked—'

Honey shook her head. 'It wouldn't be the same. I want to stay with Sam and look after him when he's old, like he looks after me. You don't understand, Mrs Colby, you just don't understand.' She turned her sodden handkerchief over and over, trying to find a dry corner.

'I do understand, dearie,' Maggie said gently, 'but it's bound to get around the village that he's not your father. And you know, people can be so unkind....'

Honey hiccuped. 'You mean like that...that...' She had no name, no words to describe the hurricane that had laid waste her life.

'Yes,' said Maggie, 'that's just what I mean.'

She was thankful not to have to repeat what Arthur

had been saying the night before. His orderly mind, outraged by the irregularity of the position, had been filled
with anxious forebodings. 'Whisht now,' she had said at
last, 'it's no crime to give a home to a child, he'll have
done it for the best, you know Sam. And you surely must
have had some idea she wasn't his. Why, you only need
to look at them.'

'But he said her mother was Austrian, a refugee.' He
stopped in mid-pace. 'Do you mean to say you knew?'

'No, no, but it was obvious to anyone with eyes to see.
Well, to anyone who cared to stop and think.'

'Then for the love of God why didn't you say something?'

She picked up her knitting. 'Because I didn't think it
was any of our business,' she said firmly. Arthur knew,
when she picked up her knitting, the topic was closed.
But silencing Arthur would not silence the village.

'Now, you want to help Sam, don't you?' It was unfair
to appeal at this moment to the woman struggling so
painfully for birth within the child; but it had to be done.
'The only way you can help him is to do what's asked—
whatever it may be—and not make a fuss and upset him.'
Silence. She prompted, 'You'll not be the one to let him
down, will you?'

Honey drew a long shivering sigh. She shook her head
slowly and said in a small flat voice, 'I'll do anything you
say, Mrs Colby. If you're really sure it's right.'

Maggie said with relief, 'There now, that's better.
When Arthur and Sam have finished their chat we can
tell them what we've decided.' She leaned forward to pat
the disconsolate face. 'And if you're coming to live here
you must stop calling me Mrs Colby, it's Maggie from
now on. Now let's have a wee smile.'

Let's have a wee smile, thought Honey. That was what
people always said when they saw you were wanting to
die. Like that day at the hospital. And now...So it was
'decided'—and already, not waiting to see what might
happen. She had been rushed into agreeing to something
that she had had no chance to think about. But they were
grown-ups and her vote no longer counted. If she argued,
if she angered the Colbys—then it would be the Home,
miles away, she did not even know where—and they
might never let her come back...She wrenched her face
into a smile. 'Yes, Mrs Colby.'

'There, now. And it's Maggie, remember. After all,

you'll soon be grown. Thirteen is it, next birthday?'

Next birthday. They had made plans for it...Her eyes brimmed in spite of herself and she buried her face in her hands. 'I'm sorry, Mrs—Maggie,' she stammered between sobs, 'but I do love Sam and I wanted to be with him always.'

Maggie, her own eyes damp, put her arms about her and held her while she wept.

'As I see it,' Arthur was saying, 'by far the best thing would be a good boarding school. No attention would be called to the situation but at the same time nobody could raise a voice.'

Sam stirred uneasily in the deep leather chair.

'I'm afraid you don't understand, Arthur. I don't make that sort of money, I only wish I could.'

'Mm...perhaps not. But it really would be the answer. What do you earn?'

Reluctantly, Sam told him. 'You see what I mean, I couldn't even scratch up enough for the dancing lessons she wanted.'

'Dancing...' mused Arthur. He sat thoughtful, tapping his front teeth lightly with the end of a pencil. 'Was she keen?'

'Yes, very.' He was a little surprised that Arthur should be interested, aware that in his friend's serious world of devotion to duty such frolicking had no place. 'She was very good about it,' he added. 'Hasn't mentioned it since, though she must have been disappointed.'

'Hmm...' Arthur got up. 'Back in a minute,' he said from the door.

Sam heard him call to Maggie through the door of the other room. 'Maggie, how badly do you want that Chinese carpet?'

Oh, no! he thought. God, he mustn't do that...

'You can stop worrying about fees, now let's go into the practicalities—'

'No!' said Sam firmly. 'Sorry, old friend. I appreciate the thought but I can't let you—'

'You can't stop me,' said Arthur. 'I'm sorry to be the one to say this to you, but perhaps it's better me than somebody else. You have no rights, no responsibilities where Honey's concerned. So don't feel you owe me anything if I choose to do this for her. You're in no position to say no.'

Sam stared at him, stunned. He had always thought of Honey as his: now he felt bereft. Only Nancy was his. And she had promised him no rest. It was only she who had rights—the right to shatter the peace of Mango Walk whenever the mood took her. The thought made him cringe. But at least he could see that Honey was beyond her reach. " Yes,' he said at last. 'Yes, I see...of course. Well, then. I guess that's the best solution.'

He got up heavily from the chair and went in search of Honey to break the news. Suddenly he was feeling very tired.

'Well, Honey,' he said brightly, 'it seems there's a silver lining—you're going to be able to dance after all. Arthur and Maggie are sending you to ballet school.' To avoid her eyes he started hunting for his cigarettes.

Honey looked from one to another in bewilderment. Ballet school—the dream she had cherished until she had seen that it meant leaving home, and had swiftly backpedalled. 'But I thought I was coming here to live with you,' she said timidly.

'And so you shall,' agreed Maggie, 'every school holiday. And we shall all watch your progress and come to see your shows...' Her voice trailed off under Arthur's warning look.

Honey did not see it. She was wrestling with a confusion of feelings, not least of which was a sense of disloyalty at the throb of excitement still evoked by the magic words 'ballet school'.

'I'm much too old,' she said. 'You have to start at seven or eight to do it properly. You won't be able to find a school to take me.' She felt better when she had said that. She had eased the burden of guilt and saved herself from banishment at the same time.

Arthur Colby smiled and folded his hands, fingers interlaced. 'Then we shall just keep trying until we do,' he said, leaving her wordless. It was the first time she had met his tanklike determination head on.

'Do I have to go?' pleaded Honey. Under her earnest supervision Sam had repaired the caravan table and now they sat in the glow of the stove. 'I mean, I can see how it would make things better for you if I went to stay in their house, but—this school idea,' she hesitated, unsure of how to express her misgivings. 'I might not see you

for weeks on end! And if they spend all that money on me it means I can't say no to anything. It's almost as if they were buying me...'

Sam compressed his lips. The same thought was in his own mind; he had hoped it would not cross hers. He said, 'It's a great chance for you. If you pass it up you might regret it.'

If only I had the chance to pass it up, thought Honey. She said, 'Do you want me to do it?'

Sam considered. She was losing so much that she cherished, so much he had wanted to give her that he could not now fulfil. He wanted her to have something...'I want you to,' he said.

She looked at him long and steadily. 'All right.'

'That's my girl!' said Sam. 'Get out there and make me proud of you.'

The beginnings of a smile curved the wan cheek. 'Will you be?'

'You bet! When you get famous I'll be kicking strangers in the street, bragging how you were my girl when you were knee-high to a grasshopper.'

'I'm always your girl, wherever they send me, whatever I have to do—when I'm old enough I'm coming back, I can live where I like when I'm grown-up, isn't that right?'

'That's right.' His glance took in the socks at half-mast, the scuffle of school books spread across the floor. 'But when you're grown you'll want to live somewhere else.' He was not sure why that saddened him but it did.

Honey reached for his hand. 'Not without you...' A new doubt assailed her and she looked at him anxiously. 'You will be here?'

He drew her hand through his arm. 'Where else?' They sat for a long time in silence.

It was the last time they were to talk to each other in peace. Honey was caught up in a whirl of activity, of shopping for new clothes and equipment, two-legged stockings called 'tights', strange garments referred to as 'leotards', shoes enough for a centipede...Maggie was in charge, Arthur was paying, and Sam, who could only watch from the sidelines, was slowly eased to the edge of the picture. Even the move from Caravan to house was achieved without trauma. Maggie saying, 'We've an early start in the morning—your wee room upstairs is all ready for you...' Arthur smiling courteously, 'I hope you will

always regard this as your home ...'and the absences from Mango Walk became one long absence, when Arthur no longer ferried her back asleep in his car only to pick her up before breakfast the next day.

The day of departure came. Sam was invited to see them off at the station: Honey, and Maggie who was to take her to the school. It still felt strange to Sam that it should be someone else who took her.

He arrived at the station to find them already boarding the train, with Honey hanging out of a window, anxiously scanning the platform for a sight of him. She flung her arms around him impulsively, hugging him hard through the carriage window. 'I never thought it would be so far.' Her voice was taut with distress. 'Oh Sam, I'll write every day!'

'You do that,' he soothed, patting her back. 'How far is it, anyway?'

She drew back, eyes brimming. 'Look!' She indicated a smart new leather suitcase on the seat beside her.

The destination label read 'Paris'.

Part Two

❧❧ ❦❦

The Dreadful Light

'Sleep, sleep, beauty bright,
Dreaming in the joys of night...
When thy little heart shall wake,
Then the dreadful light shall break.'
William Blake

I

Sam relaxed in the late spring sunshine on the caravan porch. He took a long swig from his bottle of beer and regarded the airmail envelope with its French stamp. It was a long time since he had heard from Honey, years since he had seen her. She must have grown in that time, he reminded himself, up and away from him, as Arthur wanted her to do.

In the first few weeks her letters had come like a swirl of autumn leaves, lonely, heartsick, blotched with tears yet ending repeatedly with the plea, 'Don't tell Maggie, I don't mean to be ungrateful...' She had not found it easy to make friends; few of the students spoke English and those who did 'don't understand me at all. They're all wrapped up in their dancing and excited about getting away from their parents. And all I want to do is come home, I miss you so terribly...' 'The work is much harder than I thought only the others say it's easy and I get

laughed at. When I ache all over at night I can't get to sleep and then I start thinking and it's awful because there's no one to talk to...'

He answered them patiently, each as it came, though it stretched his wits to know what to say to her. It would not help her to know that he rattled about the empty caravan like one pea in a pod. In the end he confined himself to detailed accounts of the trivia of daily life at Mango Walk, hoping to comfort her with the illusion of being in touch with the home she had lost. He had no way of knowing whether it helped; her letters gave no clue and the promised holidays with the Colbys did not materialise. There was always some insurmountable obstacle to her being brought home: an examination, a show to be rehearsed for, the Christmas in Paris on which Maggie had set her heart—how nice that Honey would be able to join her—the daily regime of practice that must not be broken for more than a few days... when he finally got the message he stopped asking.

By that time Honey herself had ceased to mention the subject. Her letters had dwindled abruptly to mere weather reports with love, to the dates of tests and their results, such impersonal data as might have been found on the school reports he was never shown. Did he guess he was not offered a sight of them? He wondered what they told that Arthur did not want him to see... or maybe it was just one more handy barrier to be raised between them.

They had been breaking it gently over a long time now that she might not return to live in the village: promising students sometimes went on to jobs at the end of training. In a moment of depression he had asked if he was ever likely to see her again. They responded with cries of laughing reassurance—of course, of course, don't be silly, just not at the moment... It was always the same moment.

He had said nothing. Arthur had taken over; the life she had been given was more than anything he could have done for her and he was sensitive to their reminders to let her settle into it undisturbed. But he still sent birthday and Christmas presents with stubborn regularity, although he had no idea of what she would really like. And she wrote polite notes of thanks that told him nothing.

Yet here, out of the blue, was a letter for no obvious reason. A real one after all this time, one with something to say...? He ripped it open.

Dear Sam,

The best laid plans, as they say, often come adrift. Now they tell me that my feet will not do for ballet! This means I shall be returning to England and hope to see you while I am there.

Honey

Sam read it several times before he could believe that was all there was. He turned it over and around looking for a postscript, searched the empty envelope for another page, a few words somewhere that came from the Honey he had known. There was nothing.

Only—'come adrift', his own seaman's phrase that she had caught from him, and still used. He would have to be content with that. He sat thoughtful for a long while. Maybe she was trying to show how grown up she was— not a little girl now to be overruled, not at sixteen? Seventeen? Whatever it was—not in her opinion, anyway. That must be it. He thrust the note into his pocket and finished his beer.

Maggie walked slowly down the lane to Mango Walk. She enjoyed chatting to Sam and her Sunday walks when Arthur was called out on a case often brought her this way, but today she was in no hurry to arrive. The locals were right to hold her husband in such high esteem—she was proud of him, indeed she was, and no one could say she did not support him all the way. Only sometimes, just sometimes, when she thought of Sam in his lonely caravan....

She could hear him whistling as she approached the gate and as he caught sight of her he waved a cheery brush in her direction. Balanced on a ladder, he was painting the outside of the caravan, picking out in gold the intricacies of the carving between the panels.

'My,' she said, 'you've a job there and no mistake. What brought that on?'

Sam stopped whistling. 'About time it was done,' he said, 'only I'm not sure this is the right stuff for it. Been painted before but it looks like gold leaf underneath. Could be some time I'll clean it right down and find out. But this'll have to do for now—don't want Honey to see it looking neglected.'

Maggie caught her breath. 'Well, it looks very nice the way you're doing it.' She said casually, 'You could get

a good price for that now, you know. People are buying them for holidays.'

Sam's brush stopped moving. With Honey about to come home...something in him withdrew, cautiously. 'I live here,' he said, and added provocatively, 'besides, I promised Honey.' Maggie said nothing. Now what's Arthur campaigning for, he thought. Am I supposed to leave the village too? He probed a little further. 'It belongs to the kid; I said I'd look after it for her—that hardly means selling it, does it?' He waited. Maggie, apparently absorbed in the antics of gulls overhead, did not respond. He fired his broadside. 'When's she coming home?'

Maggie looked flustered only for a second. Then she side-stepped neatly with, 'She's not a child, Sam, not now. My, you wouldn't know her...' and then, realising perhaps that it was not the happiest thing to say, glanced at her watch. 'I'm away, now. Arthur'll be wondering where I am. Bye-bye—' She reached the gate and turned back. 'There now, I was quite forgetting what I came for!' She rummaged in her large untidy handbag and came up with an envelope. 'We had some studio portraits done, I thought you might like to have one. You'll see what I mean—quite the young lady...well, well—I really must go...' She stood, holding out the envelope.

He said, 'I'm all over paint. Can you put it inside?'

'Where?'

'Anywhere. In a drawer some place.'

She tucked it into a drawer in the little dresser, with a table cloth stained with coffee and two cork mats. And there it stayed.

Sam sat pensive for a moment, listening to her sensible shoes walking away up the lane. Then he dipped his brush and went on painting.

Maggie's thoughts were uncomfortable as she climbed the dusty hill towards the village. She had not forgotten what she came for: she had lost her nerve. The photograph was an afterthought, a sop to soften the blow. And if that wayward wee girl had written—as well she might—oh dear, oh dear...she really ought to go back now, harden her heart, tell him the truth. The thought was still in her mind when she reached her own front door and let herself in.

By June Mango Walk shone like a fairground with fresh paint and polished brass. The little copper pots winked again from their hooks along the ceiling, the mirrors spar-

kled and the rail of the overmantel smiled a brassy welcome. The curtains melted in the water when he tried to wash them; he went into town and bought material, pink with big red roses, as near as he could match it to the old ones. The woman in the shop raised a derogatory eyebrow at his taste but he knew he was right when he had hung them at the windows, laboriously made with his own hands, stitched with a darning needle and thick white thread for sewing buttons. He had scrubbed the worn lino and polished it. He had even polished his guitar. The caravan was decked like a bride—but where was the groom?

A telephone call to Arthur, reluctantly made and cagily worded, told him nothing. Yes, it was true that Honey might have to give up dancing, but that didn't mean that her education was at an end. Sam, whose formal education had ended the day he was old enough to work, saw this as a pretext. 'I see,' he said, and rang off.

Was Arthur trying to keep her at school for ever, or just until he could think of something else to do with her? What did he and Maggie know about children, anyway? Maggie had been brought up by strangers while her parents were in India and Arthur he could not imagine ever having been a child. Maybe they were about to learn the hard way; Honey as he remembered her would not always remain biddable!

He went back to the caravan and took down the dangling pots that always caught in his hair and put them away in a locker. Then he took his guitar and sat down with it near the cliff edge where he could watch the sea.

The sun dipped, drawing long spiky shadows from the marram grass, making blue drifts among the dunes. Sam got up, stretched, and thought about taking a walk before turning in. It was an evening of rare beauty, too good to be wasted indoors. The tide was low, leaving a broad sweep of wet sand darkly glistening in the afterglow. Away along the beach something moved rhythmically in and out of the water, moving with the pull of the tide. A boat maybe, or paper floating...no, it was a figure, a girl in a fluttering skirt, playing in and out of the water as Honey had played as a child. But it was more than playing. She was swaying like a young tree in a breeze, leaping and lifting, dipping and turning, skimming and swooping like a bird in flight until she came to rest at last upon the sand. Sam watched her intently, motion-

less, as if he were indeed watching a bird and a false move would send it flying away. For a time she sat watching the sea. Then she got to her feet, slowly, as if she were tired, and stood shading her eyes, looking he could have sworn in his direction, looking towards Mango Walk. But the light was fading fast and he could not be sure. She dropped her hand and walked away along the beach; a few moments and the dusk had swallowed her. Sam remained sitting in the fall of dew for a long while after she had gone.

When he returned from work the next day, he phoned Arthur from the call box in the village. It was Maggie who answered and she sounded uneasy. 'Oh—Arthur's not here I'm afraid.'

'It doesn't have to be Arthur.' It was a sign of the times that he was expected to have a reason for ringing them. 'I just want to know if you've any news of Honey.'

A hesitation. 'News—what sort of news?' The evasion was clumsy and obvious.

'News,' he said firmly. 'I thought you might have changed your minds and brought her home.'

'Oh—oh dear—' She was flustered. Poor Maggie, he thought. She said brightly, 'Would you like to ring later? Arthur will be in soon—'

'You tell me,' he said. He sensed Arthur in the background, mouthing and shaking his head. 'Come on, Maggie, what's going on that I'm not supposed to know?' An embarrassed silence. 'Maggie?' he tried coaxing. 'Come on now, I've the funniest feeling Honey's around—I'm very psychic, you know that?—and I want to see her. Not to interfere with anything you and Arthur want to do, just see her, say hello, is that so unreasonable?' Seeing fooling hadn't worked, he added soberly, 'You can't just leave me out you know, because I'm not convenient.'

Maggie lost her head. She said hastily, 'Oh, here's Arthur—he's just come in—Arthur, you're wanted on the phone!'

Arthur's voice said blandly, 'Yes, who is it speaking?' as if he had indeed just come in.

'You know perfectly well who it is, quit sashaying around and tell me what's going on!'

'Perhaps you'd better explain yourself.' The professional voice was impeccable.

Sam took a grip on his patience. 'I want to know,' he said slowly and carefully, 'if Honey's coming home, and

whether she's already here. Now Maggie appears to have had her wits scattered by this simple question; let's see if we can get more sense out of you.'

There was a pause at the other end before Arthur said, 'Sam, I don't think this is something we can discuss over the telephone.'

'Then I'll come up and see you—'

'No!' Then in an altered tone, 'No, I'll come down and see you, it would be better that way.'

'Why can't you tell me over the phone? What is it you're trying not to say?'

Another pause; when Arthur spoke there was tension in his voice. 'Very well, if you must have it. I'll let you know when Honey comes home for good, I promise you'll be the first to know.' That'll be the day, thought Sam. 'But in the meantime while her education continues I see no point in disturbing her with things best forgotten. Frankly, she wouldn't thank you for it. She'll be going straight on to school in Switzerland, it'll all be in French and she'll need all her concentration for her studies. There's nothing to be gained by raking over old ashes, upsetting everyone concerned.' There was a pause at the other end, then he added more kindly, 'You do understand, Sam. It's nothing personal.'

'I understand,' said Sam bleakly, and rang off.

Arthur stood for a moment with the dead receiver in his hand, aware of Maggie's eyes on him, before he too hung up. Damn that girl, he was thinking, why couldn't she have done as she was told! She should have been in Berne by now...

'Yes, what is it?' he said curtly to Ellen, who was standing quietly awaiting their attention. He wondered how long she had been standing there, how much she had heard. You could never tell with Ellen, her face betrayed nothing.

Ellen cleared her throat. 'Miss Honey says she won't come down to dinner.' She turned to Maggie, 'am I to serve without her, madam?'

'Oh—oh dear,' said Maggie helplessly, 'yes—yes, you'd better. Take her up something on a tray.' The last thing she could face at this moment was another set-to with Honey.

Sam walked slowly back to Mango Walk and stood leaning on the gate. Poor old wagon, he thought, all tarted

up like a kid for a party and then—no party. It looked back at him glumly under its gilded gingerbread. 'Never mind,' he told it aloud, 'you needed a coat of paint.' It occurred to him that even now Arthur had not committed himself as to whether or not Honey had returned. And yet he could have sworn—

He went indoors. Where was it Maggie had said? In a drawer somewhere...he found the envelope and in it, in a thick parchment folder, the photograph. He opened it and sank down slowly on to the seat behind him. A strange young woman stared back coldly from the paper, aloof, unfamiliar even without the bizarre costume—totally unapproachable. This was a picture of Arthur Colby's ward: his Honey had sunk without trace.

He put the photograph back in the drawer. He was glad those eyes had not fallen on Mango Walk; it was home only to the barelegged sprite whose hair he had washed, whose socks he had picked up from odd corners, whose tonsils he had worried over; the careless uncritical child who had needed reminding to brush her teeth. Arthur was welcome to his chromium-plated creation, he was right to keep her away. But then Arthur was always right; it was the most trying thing about him.

He locked the door behind him and went out.

The shadows were lengthening across the lane and a little haze of gnats hung above the hedgerows. A fine day tomorrow. A fine day for what? He moved on down the road towards the Gap, where the roadway dipped and poured itself out in a flurry of crumbling cliff on to the dunes. Dew was beginning to fall and the air was warm with the scent of honeysuckle. He reached up and plucked one of the pale trumpets to put between his teeth; its fragrant sweetness caressed his tongue and pervaded his nostrils. It was a trick he had learned from Honey but he could not imagine her doing it now.

His listless feet took him down to the shore. The sand crept into his shoes and he kicked them off, burrowing into its cool softness with his naked toes, scuffing his way to the water's edge like a boy kicking at a pebble. Down there the sand was firm and wet and shone darkly under an opalescent sky. He stood for a long time watching the sea, gilded with a sullen silver that lay upon it like a skin, feeling in his mind its muted rock and sway, its plashy whispering, breathing its green shrimp smell. Then he turned and started walking.

He walked until he had lost track of time and then stripped off and went swimming, cutting through blackberry dark water under a faint phosphorescence on the surface. When he finally plodded up the beach his limbs were heavy and he shivered. Perhaps now he would sleep. As he pushed open the gate a figure rose from the shadows by the caravan.

'Hello, Sam' said Honey. 'May I come in?'

2

Sam peered through the gloom into a face almost level with his own. 'Of course,' he mumbled. He went ahead of her into the wagon and lit the lamp, fumbling with damp salty fingers for the matches, and trying to think of something to say. He did not know what to do with this alien creature who did not even look like Honey. Maybe he should forgive Arthur for trying to spare him this; it was too soon to say 'The Queen is dead—long live the Queen!' Some time, some day, he might have made the effort, but now he was tired and hollow and in no mood for polite entertaining. Now, conscious of the sand between his toes, the trickle of seawater dribbling from his hair, he only wanted to be left alone to sleep. He shook out the shirt he was carrying and started to put it on. The fabric clung damply to his skin, making his movements clumsy. Irritated, he rolled it up and tossed it into a corner. 'I'll make coffee,' he said, and turned away to light the gas.

He found himself staring intently at the gas jets, at the kettle, anything to avoid looking at the stranger who had taken Honey's place. She had followed him in sedately, not arriving with the old familiar thump against his chest. Now she stood watching him gravely as he moved about.

'It takes twenty minutes to boil. Shall I sit down?'

He glanced at her sharply. Was she really waiting for an invitation? Even her voice was different, measured, not springing from the heart as it used to. He cleared a seat for her. 'Imagine you remembering that,' he said drily.

She looked up at him and then quickly away. After a moment she enquired politely, 'Do you still play the guitar?'

He wrestled with a moment's wild impulse to say, 'Yes. Do you still pick your nose?' Instead he said, 'How was Paris?'

It made things worse, as perversely he had known it would. She shrugged, a little French gesture. '*Comme çi, comme ça*, how did you?'

'I never went there.' He added bluntly, 'No oil wharf!' and wished she would go away.

She smiled—a studied smile like everything else—and he noticed that the teeth that had crowded her jaw had straightened. But he no longer knew her well enough to say so. He no longer knew her. He sighed, and fished for his cigarettes.

She held out her hand. 'May I?'

Depressed, he handed her the packet, struck a match. Then he turned away to unpack the new mugs he had bought for her homecoming. He could not bear to see her. He hated the smoking, the varnished nails, the breasts that had sprouted unasked on the tubular body he had known...

'Those are pretty,' she said.

'Woolworth's,' he said shortly. He could not wait for her to go.

In the stillness she said, 'You're angry.'

He did not answer. She stubbed out her cigarette and sat looking down at her hands, nervously pleating and unpleating the hem of her dress. For a moment in the soft glow of the lamp, despite the make-up, she looked vulnerable. Then she stood up. 'It was a mistake—I didn't know it would be like this. Arthur was right, I shouldn't have come. I'll go—'

Crazy that it should jolt him, yet it did. As if it confirmed her contempt. He heard himself snap, 'You only just got here—didn't they teach you manners at that school!'

She sank down again, cheeks burning, and sat staring

fixedly at the door. Sam smoked furiously, the silence stretching between them brittle as ice. Christ, he thought, why did I have to say that…what a mess…

'Why did you come?' Before he could stop them the words were out.

'Because Ellen said—' She turned on him with glittering eyes. 'I wish she'd mind her own business! I wish I'd never come—' and before he could speak she was through the door and blundering down the steps.

Sam went after her. He could hear her sobbing as she ran up the lane. He put on a spurt and caught her up. He caught at her wrist. 'Honey!'

She froze into calm with an effort he could feel. He grasped her shoulders and shook her, trying to prise open the chink in the armour he had briefly seen. 'Please let go,' she said coldly.

He released her and stood back, staring miserably at her locked and barred face. Now he would never know if there was still a real person inside. And the fault was his. She at least had made a gesture, had come to see him. It was he who had torn it up. He said, 'I don't know why I said that. I didn't mean…' What had he meant? For once in his life he was lost for words.

'I know what you meant,' she said, her head held high. 'They told me, Maggie and Arthur, only I didn't want to believe—you know how it is. So when Ellen—' Suddenly her voice cracked. 'I won't bother you again!' and she burst into tears and fled.

Sam stood stunned for a full minute before he could get his feet to move. When he found her she was crying quietly against a tree-trunk, her hands spread like starfish against the bark, her wayward hair escaping from its pins. He leaned beside her and put a hand over hers.

'Go away!'

Go away…I don't love you any more…the same voice. The same problem. Was it worth trying to start again…was it wise even to try? He picked up the hand from where it clung, the fingers very young and fragile against his own.

'I wish I hadn't come,' she said wretchedly, her face still hidden.

'I'm glad you did.'

Slowly she turned her head to look at him, a furtive, mistrustful look across her shoulder, her face familiar

now by the grace of tears; a child's face, lost and unhappy, the endearing roundness still lingering at the angle of the jaw.

He nodded. 'I'm glad,' he repeated.

Honey stopped crying. 'I don't understand.' She sniffed and rubbed her other hand across her eyes. 'Arthur said— and then—just now . . .' She stopped, a bewildered frown between her eyebrows.

Sam made a gesture of impatience. He felt he was accumulating bones to pick with Arthur. 'Look,' he said, 'whatever you may have been told, I haven't changed. Not where you're concerned. I'll come up there tomorrow and sort the whole thing out.'

She gave a loud hiccup and released her hold on the tree. 'Promise?'

'Promise.' He pressed her hand and released it. 'Now dry your eyes and I'll walk you back up to the village.' He found her a handkerchief in the back pocket of his jeans. 'I see you still get hiccups when you cry.'

'I'm sorry,' she said when she had blown her nose, 'I thought I'd grown out of all that.'

Sam smiled for the first time. 'Thank God you haven't,' he said.

The Colbys' spacious garden was rich with roses and the carolling of birds. Honey in summer cotton, hair hanging loose, bare feet thrust into sandals, looked every inch the rebellious schoolgirl. But her voice, steady and assured, was at variance with her appearance.

'I'm not going back,' she said, 'and there's an end to it.'

Arthur opened his mouth, and closed it again at the sight of Ellen who came tinkling and rattling her way towards them across the lawn, bearing a laden tray. She set it down near Maggie, smiled conspiratorially at Sam, and withdrew discreetly, looking more than a little smug.

When she had gone, Arthur said crossly, 'It's not for you to decide.'

'It's my life,' retorted Honey.

'And you don't feel you owe anything to the rest of us?'

'That's not fair! And anyway whatever I owe I owe Sam, not anyone else. The rest is money and can be repaid. I'll get a job, you shall have every penny—'

'Don't be absurd,' said Arthur, nettled. 'That's not what I meant at all.'

Maggie looked flustered. 'But dearie, you must finish your education first, then you'll get a much better job—why, they say an English girl in New York...' Her voice tailed off under Honey's withering gaze.

'I'm not going to New York or anywhere else—I'm staying here. I'll get a job in town and—and go up on the train with Sam.'

Arthur's tone was chilly. 'If indeed you had a job in town, you would go up in the car with me,' he said.

'I'll go with whom I please!'

'Not while you're under my roof!' he barked—and instantly saw his mistake.

Honey paled but she did not flinch. 'Then I won't stay under your roof.' She avoided Sam's eyes as she said, 'If there's really not room for me at Mango Walk I'll find somewhere else.'

Sam blinked. 'What's that supposed to mean?'

Honey's voice shook a little. 'Ask him!' she gestured towards Arthur, who coloured uncomfortably. 'And at the same time ask him why he told me the whole village was gossiping. And why he told me your life had been made so wretched you wouldn't want to see me again! Just ask him—'

'Oh Honey, Honey.' Maggie's voice was full of distress. But Honey was under way and could not stop.

'Go on,' she prompted Sam, 'it explains a lot, doesn't it? Or didn't you ever wonder why I stopped writing to you?' She sat down on the grass, moodily hugging her knees. 'God only knows what he's been saying to you all these years.'

Sam drew a deep breath, and let it out again slowly. 'Well, old friend,' he said to Arthur. 'It looks like you have a little explaining to do.'

Everyone looked at Arthur, Honey with open antagonism, Maggie with a confused expression in which concern and reproach wrestled. Sam's faint smile was enigmatic.

Arthur sighed. For a long minute he sat with pursed lips, studying the tips of his fingers. Then he interlaced them across his chest and looked up to face his accuser.

'Well, well,' he said, 'I am the villain of the piece, aren't I? And all with such good intentions. It seems I

must admit to a few white lies—' he held up his hand to silence Honey—'yes, they were white, whatever you may think. You must realise it was all for your own good. And for Sam's. Now he has been wonderfully good to you, I'm the last to deny that. But the time comes to ease the burden on those we love, to stand back and let them get on with their own lives. You have to understand this was the best, most painless way of achieving that.'

'But it wasn't painless!' cried Honey. 'And suppose he had been my father? Or suppose you hadn't known?'

Arthur frowned. 'That would have been different. But it's beside the point—I did know.'

'But nobody else does. The village doesn't know—not even Ellen. It's no good, Arthur, I know the truth—Sam let it slip last night before he knew what you'd been saying. You had no right to lie to me that way!'

'Honey, that's no way to speak to Arthur!' Maggie was shocked.

'It's beside the point!' Arthur, harassed, was becoming testy. He turned on Sam. 'Make her see sense.'

'You mean, make her see it your way. I don't know that I can.'

'Of course you can, a girl of her age should do as she's told. Tell her she can't live with you, you know very well it's out of the question.'

'Why not?' said Sam with disconcerting directness.

Arthur moved uneasily in his chair. 'Must I spell it out for you? It would be insulting—I mean, I give you credit for more common sense...'

'You mean you don't trust me?'

Maggie winced inwardly. Arthur frowned. He had not meant to say that. Not quite that. He had not even expressed it to himself in those terms. 'Of course not, that's ridiculous. It's just that a young woman can't live alone with—I mean, she's not a child any longer, it wouldn't be right. There are conventions to be observed, you know. And your place, it's not suitable, no locks, no privacy...' He floundered, embarrassed.

'You mean you don't trust me,' said Sam.

Into the silence that fell Honey's voice came softly and without rancour. She smiled at Sam. 'I'll go and get my things,' she said.

3

'You've upset Arthur,' said Honey as they strolled down to Mango Walk.

Sam rubbed a hand over the nape of his neck. 'That sort of double talk isn't like him. I couldn't let it pass. What about you, anyway, all that about owing him money, that wasn't very nice.'

'I know,' said Honey uncomfortably, 'I suppose I'll have to apologise. But it's true, you know, he didn't do it for me. He doesn't care if I dance or drop off the cliff, it's you he worries about.'

'Me? You're crazy, you heard what he said.'

She nodded. 'He thinks more of you than you think. It's your reputation he's guarding, not mine, he doesn't want your halo to slip. Caesar's wife must be above reproach—'

'Caesar's what?'

'Just a silly old joke.' She nudged his shoulder. 'Come on, race you!'

They ran the once habitual race to the gate and arrived laughing, Sam out of breath; for the first time ever, he had not let her win.

'Time to tank up with water, want to come?'

'You're not still going up to the farm for it?'

'Only some. That old standpipe's all right for the heads but I wouldn't trust it for drinking. You can stay here if you want. I'll go on my own.'

'No, I'll come.' How long since she had heard a lavatory referred to as 'the heads' ... she could not remember. So much she had forgotten that she had thought she could never forget. But she was home now, here to stay

97

and with the bad times all behind her. 'Wait for me!' She snatched up a comb and stood tearing at the knots in her hair, listening to the sound of him whistling as he collected the empty carriers. She caught sight of her reflection smiling into space through the ornamentation on the little mirror. 'We've won!' she told it excitedly, and danced down the steps to catch him up. Soon, perhaps tomorrow, she would have to go and see Maggie, take flowers, make her peace with Arthur. But she would not be doing it for them, or even for herself. Her first and deepest loyalty was to Sam; she was not to be bought for a mess of education.

Over supper he asked, 'Did you mind about the dancing?'

Honey gazed into her cup for a long time before answering. 'Yes, I did, I minded terribly—it was all I had.' She looked up and smiled unexpectedly. 'But it's all right now.'

'Want to tell me the details?'

'Not really, it's all a bit technical. Basically I started too late. And I'd never have got out of the back row anyway, I'm not limber enough—that means I couldn't get my leg as high as the others. So it's all a bit of a lost cause, even without the feet.'

'What was wrong with them, anything serious?'

'Oh, no.' She laughed, looked away. 'They just kept pointing towards England.' Before he could ask what she meant she added, 'Sorry I didn't make you proud of me.' Under the teasing manner he caught a note of wistfulness. 'That was the one thought that helped me to go, and I bet you don't even remember.'

He said, 'I do remember, of course I do. I didn't realise you took it so seriously, but if it helped I'm glad, that was the only reason I said it.'

'The only reason?'

'The only reason. Hey, look—you don't have to do anything to make me proud of you, you're a very fine young—young—'

'Well?'

'Well, stand up, turn around and let's have a good look at you!'

She stood up, moved to the only open space in the wagon and did a neat pirouette. 'Well?'

Sam looked at her where she stood poised, hands spread, head tilted, her expression sweetly comic: it was

a nice little face—it might even be beautiful one day. He groped for words. 'You're a menace to shipping,' he grinned.

Honey laughed, threw her arms wide as if to embrace the world. 'Oh, you're wonderful—only you could say that!' Her hand touched the panelling to the bed-place. 'Oh, I must look at the horse on the ceiling. I haven't seen him for so long—you haven't painted him over?' She moved the cups and stowed the sliding table.

'Now, would I do that?' He pushed back the panels for her and removed a pile of music from the bed.

She crawled in to look. 'Yes, there he is, just the same. I used to fall asleep looking at him and listening to your watch...' She broke off, abashed, aware of him for the first time as a man.

'You were very small,' he said. It was as if he had read her thoughts.

She handed him the guitar. 'Will you play me something?'

'What do you want?'

'Anything—whatever. Wait a minute, what's all this?' She rummaged through the stack, pulling out music sheets. 'Schubert, Chopin—I didn't know you liked this sort of music.'

'You were only up to Glenn Miller yourself when you left.'

'But this is all piano music, surely. Isn't it difficult to play it on a guitar?'

'You have to transcribe the Chopin but the Schubert's easy. Most of his music was composed on the guitar—he used to sit up in bed and play it, God knows how, he couldn't have lived in a caravan!' He took the instrument from her, began to coax music from it. 'What do you want to hear?'

Honey sat back and regarded him, head on one side. 'And where did you learn to transcribe? Don't tell me you picked that up in the engine-room of a ship!'

He laughed and bent his head over the strings. 'Well, if it helps you to know, you're not the only one who didn't make it. I once won an entrance to a music college.'

'What happened?'

'Nothing. My brother wanted to be a doctor and there wasn't enough money for both.'

'But that wasn't fair, it should have been shared between you—'

'...and three others? And the two girls as well? No one would have got anywhere. No, my father was right, though of course I couldn't see it his way. I stormed off to London bragging how I'd do it on my own. It looked easy from where I was standing, it always does. But it didn't work out. Even with a scholarship I couldn't make ends meet. I was too proud to go home and admit I'd failed and I couldn't get a job anywhere. Then the war came, they were yelling out for men to crew the ships—you know the rest.'

She said thoughtfully, 'Nothing ever goes right for you, does it? I think that was a shame.'

'Not really. I play for pleasure now, not because I have to.' He hesitated. 'The way you dance.'

She looked at him curiously. 'How do you know that?'

'I saw you the other evening on the shore.'

'Oh—I thought the beach was empty.'

'I watched from the cliff. I thought...'

'Yes?' The query was tense, breathless.

'I thought, She has the music inside her.'

He watched her warily, half expecting her to laugh, this altered Honey that he hardly knew. Instead she said, 'You understand that? We're so alike, you and I. I never realised.'

'Nor me.' He smiled. 'We might go to a concert some time. If you'd like to.' It occurred to him that he might not be her choice of escort. He wished he had thought of that before he said it.

Honey jumped up. 'Where's the paper—haven't we got a local paper? There must be something on somewhere—'

'I'll get one tomorrow.' He noted with pleasure that she had said 'we' and not 'you'. He said, 'The tide's out, why don't we go down there now—I'll play, you can dance, we'll have a perfect audience, just us!'

'Oh, yes!' cried Honey, 'come on!' She seized his hand and drew him after her, still clutching the guitar, feeling alive as he had not felt for years.

Two hours later Arthur Colby, returning from a visit along the coast road, saw on the beach below a tiny figure moving on the amethyst bar of the strand, dipping and gliding like a hovering seabird. He pulled in and rolled down his window. Yes, it was Honey. He knew, because he had made out a second figure in the shadows at the base of the cliff, a man who sat with his arms across his

knees, a guitar untouched beside him: Sam, watching her with rapt attention.

Honey fell asleep to the sound of the guitar that night. She was sitting up on the bed-place, feet dangling, as she had as a child. The sea air, the warmth and the music dragged her eyelids down and, abruptly as a puppy, she was asleep. Sam laid her carefully back on the bed and, not for the first time, drew off her shoes. Then he drew a fold of the covers over her and put out the lamp.

Through in the doghouse on the camp bed that was too short for him, he smoked a final cigarette and lay smiling into the darkness, asking himself what he had done.

But up at the Colbys' Maggie and Arthur lay for a long time talking before they slept.

4

A loud rap on the window jerked Sam awake.

'Hey—it's a fine bright morning, come and swim!'

'I have to go to work.'

'You've got time, it's only five o'clock.'

'Oh, Jesus!'

'I'll see you down there—don't go back to sleep!'

The impish face vanished from the window and feeling like Lazarus he went to find his trunks.

On the beach the sun was brilliant but the breeze reminded them that it was early in the day. They came out of the water and threw themselves down on the sandy towels to get below the wind. Honey lay on her stomach, stealing glances at the strong blunt profile outlined against the vivid sky; she had known it all her life, and yet it seemed to her that she had never seen it before. She listened to the lisping sea and hummed softly under her breath. She was entirely happy.

A pair of early bathers ran past them down to the water's edge in a feather of sand and kicked up spray; they romped and splashed in the shallows, the girl hanging back while the boy tried to pull her in, until she was caught up and carried out through the breakers, squealing, clinging, unable to save herself from being jettisoned with a loud splash. He dived after her and they came up gasping with laughter and the coldness of the sea to swim off side by side.

'Bet they're in love,' said Honey wistfully, 'lucky things.' She laid her smiling cheek down on her arm and looked at Sam. His expression flickered briefly and was bland again. 'What was that for?'

'Nothing,' he said.

'You don't think they're in love?'

'Oh, sure. Covered in authentic dew.'

'Then you don't think they're lucky?' she persisted.

Sam hesitated. 'Let's say, I wouldn't go out of my way to find it. Trouble comes soon enough without looking for it.'

She thought of the young man's laughing face, the girl's arm curved about his neck. 'But they looked so happy,' she said.

He shrugged. 'You know how it is with dew, it dries up and leaves the same old world as yesterday.'

Honey dribbled fine sand through her fingers. 'But surely,' she said thoughtfully, 'it's not like that with people.'

'It's like that,' he said. When she looked at him he was staring straight in front of him, his face a mask.

She did not know how to reach him, the depth of his hurt was outside her experience. But she wanted to. Shyly she laid her cold hand on his arm. 'Sam, you're not old, it's not too late for you. You'll find happiness one day, I know you will.'

Sam stood up, freeing himself from the disturbing touch of the girl who was not quite Honey. 'I don't need that kind of happiness.' In sudden agitation he paced the sand.

Honey watched him, sitting on her heels, her hands lying light upon her thighs. 'I do,' she said at last. 'I believe everyone does, it wouldn't be natural not to.'

Sam noticed her expression and stopped his pacing. He forced himself to relax and said with an attempt at flippancy, 'Well, don't let me put you off, I shouldn't be

spreading gloom and despondency to the young.' He smiled. 'With my record I shouldn't be dishing out advice at all.'

She laughed, a little gurgle of waywardness. 'I don't suppose I'd take it if you did. I believe in taking life as it comes, not running away from things.'

He glanced at her, half amused. 'You've found things to believe in already, have you?'

Her eyes met his with unassuming candour. 'Oh yes, haven't you?'

'Must you really go to work today?' said Honey over breakfast eaten on the sunny porch. 'Haven't you got any holiday left this year?'

'I usually work it,' said Sam. 'I take the money instead.'

'But you should have a holiday!' She was shocked. 'It's not good for you to work right through the year.' She realised that she had forgotten the days of shortage, or maybe she had been too young to notice. Money was no problem with the Colbys and she had never thought to ask herself where it came from. For the first time it occurred to her that her return to Mango Walk would cost Sam money. 'I've got lots of clothes,' she said anxiously, 'and I don't eat very much.'

Sam laughed. 'No need to go mad—just go easy on the brandy and cigars, we'll manage fine. Right?'

'Right,' she said dubiously. 'But Sam'—she turned his watch towards her to check the time—'apart from money, because it's not what matters—' She ran out of words. It was harder to say than she had thought, 'Oh dear, it's so difficult...'

Sam leaned forward, 'Hey, come on, this is me, remember? You used to say you could tell me anything.'

She forced herself to say it. 'It's just—well, I know I landed myself on you yesterday. I mean, you don't have to have me here if you don't want. I wanted to win over Arthur—and to come home of course...' She stopped, seeing a subtle change in his expression. She was making a mess of it as she had known she would. Why hadn't she waited until tonight, worked it out properly, rehearsed what she wanted to say...it was too late now, she was committed.

Sam said, 'If you want to change your mind, no hard feelings.' At the back of his eyes there was an indefinable shadow. Why couldn't she say what she really meant—

but she couldn't. Suddenly it was too important.

'Not me, you. You didn't say you wanted me here, I took it for granted. So if you'd rather be on your own—I mean, you never said you missed me or anything—not in your letters . . .' She could not say any more. She could not even look at him. She waited, tense and uncertain.

She felt his finger under her chin, turning her face towards him, and quickly blinked to clear her vision. He was smiling, the broad brown crumpled smile that had warmed her shattered childhood.

'Don't tell anyone I told you, but it has been getting a little peaceful around here.'

'Oh, Sam!' She hugged herself, the brightness back in her day. Because she felt she should, she added the rider, 'But you must promise to tell me if you want me to go.'

Sam stood up, glanced at his watch. 'I must go. While I'm gone you better decide which promise you want me to keep.'

It was a moment before she remembered. Promise you'll never leave me again . . . it seemed so long ago. 'Both, Sam,' she said soberly. 'I want you to keep them both.'

She followed him to the gate, leaning on the top bar to watch his departure, his step lithe and springy in the morning air. He isn't old, she told herself happily, he isn't old at all.

'Don't forget the paper!' she called after him. He waved from the top of the lane to show he had heard, and then he was gone. After a while she turned back towards the caravan, but it was too fine to go inside. The day stretched before her, blank and empty with nothing to do until his return. She pushed the breakfast things to one side and settled herself on the porch, her knees drawn up and her back propped in the corner. It did not fit her as well as it used to but she closed her eyes against the glare of the sun and drifted into a reverie.

'Anybody home?'

Maggie's voice, accompanied by the click of the gate, awakened her.

'Come in, Maggie,' she yawned, 'I was just daydreaming.'

'Och, and with all the dirty pots laying there. Let's away in and wash them before Sam gets home.'

'But he won't be in for hours yet, there's loads of time.

Oh, do come and sit in the sun, it's so lovely here.'

Maggie bustled past her, picking up the dishes as she went. 'Och, and the bed not made, even! My, my, you'll just need to pull your socks up, Honey my girl.' Still scolding cheerfully, she lit the gas under the kettle. 'Where's the bowl?'

Honey got up with a sigh. 'I don't know, Maggie, I'll have to find out where Sam keeps it, probably in the pan-box under the caravan. We don't have a sink in the wagon, you know.' She came in reluctantly, peering into the dark interior, made her way through and straightened the bed, closing the panels over it. 'Do leave that, Maggie. Did you come to see me or to inspect the caravan?' She said it in irritation at having her sunlit solitude disturbed, and was surprised to see the quick colour rise on Maggie's cheek. 'Come and sit down,' she said, turning off the gas. 'I've made my bed, now can I go out to play?'

Maggie looked startled. 'But surely that's...'

'Sam's bed?' Mischief made her add, 'Yes, but I slept in it last night.' Something in Maggie's expression warned her not to persist with the joke. She stopped laughing and said crossly, 'Sam slept in the doghouse, of course. You were ready to believe bad things of him, I can see you were, he was right when he said you didn't trust him!'

'No—no of course not, you mustn't say things like that. It's just—'an embarrassed fumble after words—'well, that's really what I came to talk to you about. Now, you will be careful, won't you?'

'Careful? What do you mean? Did Arthur send you?'

'No, no.' The words carried no conviction. 'But I can see his point, my dearie. I mean, you will put on some clothes before he comes home, won't you? That thing you're wearing, it's barely decent—'

'It's a bikini, it's the latest thing, all the French girls wear them—'

'Well, you'll not have to wear it where Sam can see you!'

'He's already seen it, we went swimming this morning, I woke him up at five—' Her anger was building against Maggie who had ruined her beautiful day.

'Oh, Honey!' The kindly face was shocked, reproachful. 'I do believe Arthur is right, you are a wayward, naughty wee thing! Do you not know how unfair you are to Sam, putting temptation before him like that?'

'I don't understand you!' she shouted in defiance. She knew very well what was meant. She wanted to push the words back down Maggie's throat, make her cancel them, unsay them, climb down and exchange them for something she could bear...

'I mean—' began Maggie, but Honey could not listen. She turned away, her hands over her ears.

'I don't want to hear,' she cried. When she turned back, Maggie was still there.

' I'll not be going till I've said my piece,' she said with a smile. 'Now, are you ready to listen?'

Honey resigned herself. She was familiar with Maggie's gentle persistence. She nodded, hoping to get it over quickly.

Maggie composed herself. 'Now, don't think I don't know how attached you've been to Sam. Maybe Arthur doesn't but that's just his way, it's hard for him to understand about feelings.' She paused, looking down at her hands, and Honey thought: It must have been hard for you too. 'But the time comes,' Maggie went on, 'to grow up, not just in the body but in the heart. The time to protect the ones we love, to learn to set aside what we want if it saves them sorrow. Do you understand what I'm trying to say?'

Honey swallowed. 'You want me to say I'll go back to school. But I won't and all your preaching's just a waste of time. I can't, Maggie, I just can't.' She could not say any more.

Maggie sighed. 'There, there now, don't upset yourself. If you really can't...' Then she said briskly, 'I'll away now and leave you to your sunbathing. Just mind and get dressed before Sam gets home. You know, my father served in India, and when I was your age he said to me, "Never let a tiger taste your blood, my girl—not even if he does sit purring at your fireside." I've always remembered that,' she forced a laugh, as if she thought that by wrapping her reproof in a joke she could somehow blunt its sting.

Honey said, 'If you think I'm—well, you're wrong, you couldn't be more wrong!' Why must Maggie come airing her opinions, she understood no one and nothing...She said, 'I shan't wear it again.' Stupid woman! she was thinking. As if I'd flirt with Sam...

'There, now!' Maggie's tone showed her relief. 'I knew

you'd be sensible. After all, you're a grown woman now, and it's not as if he were really your father.'

'I know!' burst out Honey, and then stopped her mouth with her knuckles. It would not do to say to Maggie: Why else do you think I came home.

When Maggie had gone she returned to her roost on the porch. But she could not settle, her thoughts were still angry, they boiled up inside her, pushing her eyelids open. At last she got up with a sigh and went in search of a bowl.

She washed up on the porch in the sun and threw away the water in the hedge, remembering the many times she had sat and watched while Sam did the same. 'Are you my slave, Sam?' she had once asked, coming home from school to find him scrubbing the floor. 'You could say that,' he had grinned, sitting back on his heels, 'watch out for the soap.' The memory made her wince. She had been so awful, he so understanding...That he had taken it in his stride somehow made it worse. She had taken so much for granted, made insatiable demands—maybe other children did the same. But then they had the right, she had had none. And now that at last she was old enough to give something back, to reduce the debt that could never be redeemed, here was Arthur interfering, spoiling everything, sending Maggie to lecture her—not content with lying to her, keeping her away. She would never forgive him for stealing those years of her life! And Maggie...

Don't think about Maggie, she told herself in an effort to be calm. Think about Sam. He'll be home at tea-time, with the whole evening ahead. There'll be music and laughing and this morning won't matter any more. She returned to her perch but the sun had gone in. The day had lost its flavour. She dropped her head on her arms and tried to sleep.

When Sam came home he found her huddled by a window, gazing out at a blackening sky.

'I got a paper—hey, what are you doing sitting in the dark?'

'I wasn't sure how to light the lamp,' she lied, her spirits lifting now that he was there.

Sam peeled off the duffel coat he always wore to work.

'Right.' He fished in the pockets for his purchases, 'Matches, light, kettle on—then we can eat.'

'Right!' She got up, shivering in spite of his thick sweater that she had borrowed.

'Hey, what's this?' He had noticed the damp patch on the seat. 'You been sitting in wet things all day? I thought you were a big girl now.'

'So I am.' She made a quick dab at his cheek as she passed on her way to the washroom.

'What was that for?'

'To welcome you home.' She hesitated, added lightly, 'It's more than I got from you.'

It was a moment before he answered, 'I'd better owe you one. After all—'

'I *know*!' she said with controlled exasperation. 'I know you're not my father!' She came back with the damp bikini, not looking at him. 'What shall I do with this?'

'Hang it out on the cratch, the rain will wash the salt out.'

She could feel him watching her as she clambered across the bed to the open window and leaned out to hang it on the rack. She did not trust herself to look at him. She felt wounded, pushed away. She had not fought her way back to him to be put in her place like a child. She sat on her heels with her back to him, staring out into the dripping hedge. 'What makes you think I'd let you, anyway.'

She heard him set something down on the stove and walk towards her. But she could not look round.

'Somebody's upset you. Has Arthur been down?'

She shook her head, 'Just Maggie—' She stopped, the tears not far away.

He hitched himself on to the edge of the bed, 'And what's she been saying—or can I guess? She caught you in that fancy swimsuit, right?'

Honey sniffed, and tried to laugh. Trust Sam to reduce a mountain back down to its molehill. 'She thinks I'm flirting with you.'

'And are you?'

'No, certainly not!'

'Oh...now I'm disappointed, man—you know, treats like that don't come my way too often.' He was smiling, teasing her, trying to see her face. 'Come on now, don't

take it to heart, you know Maggie—old-fashioned as the hills. And if you can't flirt a little with me, who can you practise on? Mmm?' She nodded but the tears still threatened. She could not bear that he should think she would use him for practice. He reached across, nudging her ribs with his hard knuckles. 'Hey, come on, flirt with me! Come out fighting and break clean—'

'Stop it!' She tried to fend off the knuckles, laughing after all. 'Look, stop it! Maggie says you're a tiger and not to be trusted. Are you?'

'A tiger, eh?' He leaned back, his hands behind his head, and his whole frame shook as he chuckled. 'Well, I guess we all like to think we're tigers so at my age maybe I should take it as a compliment! But don't worry about Arthur and Maggie. It's our life, right? Yours and mine. We'll live it our way. Now let's eat—'

'Sam—just one thing...'

'What now? I'm starving—'

'It's important. I want you to promise.'

'More promises?'

'Only this one. One day Arthur's going to tell you to send me away. Don't do it, promise me you won't let him talk you round!'

Sam stopped laughing. 'I'm not that easily persuaded.'

'I think you are. You defer to him too much, and you shouldn't. If you don't make a stand he'll end up dictating both our lives.'

A corner of his mouth twitched. 'So that's it, you think he might stop you getting what you want.'

'Yes,' She dragged her eyes back to the hedge, to the dripping bikini on the rack outside the window. 'Yes, I really think he might.'

For a moment they were both silent. Then Sam said, 'I told you, I'm not that easily persuaded. But if it should ever come to that—I say if—it won't be because he's Arthur, but because he's right.'

Honey shivered. The indignation that had warmed her earlier had melted and run down into a small damp chill. She put on a bright face and said, 'Yes...well. Let's have something to eat.'

They dined on buttered rolls and cheese and ham, with apples for dessert, washed down with a flagon of cider that Sam had been hoarding in the cool of the pan-box, and while they ate they searched the paper for a

concert. But there was nothing within striking distance; they decided instead to spend Saturday afternoon browsing through record shops.

'I brought a portable record-player back from France—quite small and it works on batteries—I could fetch it from Maggie's...' She tailed off.

'Let's get one of our own,' said Sam. 'We'll choose one Saturday.'

With a fire lit in the little stove they sat in its golden glow, drinking the notes of the guitar like drops of wine. Sam sang his half-forgotten songs and Honey hummed softly the bits she remembered, while the rain whispered on the roof and the wind sang boisterous descants in the trees outside. And the music stole away hours as it always does, and it was late, very late and still they went on singing, not wanting the time to end. And the sky was beginning to lighten over the sea when Sam said, 'God! I shan't wake up,' and lurched off drowsily to his short camp-bed, and Honey crawled under the covers in the bed-place thinking, tomorrow I'll throw the bikini away.

She didn't want Sam to think she was flirting with him. Nothing could have been further from the truth.

5

The concert was a doomed project. The town's one concert hall had been gutted in the war and not replaced.

'Well,' said Sam, 'maybe we could go up to London. There's the new Festival Hall on the South Bank, I bet you haven't seen that.'

'No, I haven't. Oh, they say it's wonderful!'

'We'll find out what's coming on. It'll have to be a Saturday...'

A week later Honey announced that she had received an answer. It was perhaps unfortunate that Maggie Colby was present.

'Let's all go together!' she cried enthusiastically. 'I play the piano, you know, and I'm very fond of music. Arthur can get a locum and take us in the car, much nicer than a stuffy old train—won't that be nice, Honey, just like old times?'

To Honey, inescapably reminded of a miserable Christmas spent in Paris, it sounded altogether too much like old times. She faltered, 'Yes...I suppose so...' then she saw Sam's eye upon her and added, 'Actually it's Ram Gopal's Indian Ballet, I don't know that you'd care for that.'

'Well, well,' said Maggie cheerfully, 'it doesn't have to be that, I'm sure there's a nice musical on somewhere, we can go to that. It'll do Arthur good to get away for a break, he hasn't had one since I don't know when. Och, it's a lovely idea, I'm so glad you thought of it!' And she hastened away to spread the glad tidings to Arthur.

'Oh, dear,' said Honey, when she had gone.

'Oh, dear,' echoed Sam, looking quizzical. 'Come on, it's not the end of the world.'

'No, but—' She thought of the long hours squashed in the back seat of the car with plump Maggie, the inevitable changes of plan. 'They won't want what we'd want, you know. We'll all finish up at a Whitehall farce, I know Maggie's taste in outings, I suffered them for years...' She broke off, aware that she sounded—as she was—ungrateful. She couldn't expect Sam to understand that. 'It just...won't be the same if they come.'

Sam looked puzzled. 'Can't quite see why they want to come with us,' he said.

'Can't you?' Honey's laugh had an edge to it. To make sure it's a 'family outing', she thought. Three adults and a child: Come out, you're surrounded...outnumbered three to one. 'Oh, let's call it off! We can always say we can't afford it.'

He shrugged. 'If you like. I thought you wanted to go.'

'I did.' She added with a confidence she did not feel, 'But there's always another time.'

Arthur brightened visibly at the news. 'Well, that's a relief. I must tell you, Sam, that the idea of you two going off alone overnight was quite unsuitable. Bad enough you being together in the caravan—'

'We're not together in the caravan.'

'No, thank God! Maggie told me. Just the same—'

'You really don't trust me, do you?' He rose to his feet,

his anger beginning to smoulder. 'What kind of a randy old goat do you take me for—leching after my own kid. I still got my own teeth, is that it? You're afraid I might gnaw through the panelling—'

'She is not your own child,' said Arthur, very slowly and distinctly, 'and please sit down again. It's not like you to fly off the handle over nothing.'

Sam sat down. 'I know, Arthur. But maybe it's not such a good idea to keep reminding me. You say it enough times I might come to agree with you.'

'What's that supposed to mean?' Arthur's eyes were on him, cool but suspicious.

Sam shook his head. 'Oh, all this fuss about nothing.' Why the hell had he said that, aggravating the bee in Arthur's bonnet? He said, 'Look, mine or not, how could anything happen with all those years between us? Use your head.'

Arthur looked superior. 'Age, my dear Sam, is a state of mind, not an accumulation of years.' He sat back, fingers interlaced, savouring the point he had made.

Sam let him enjoy it for a moment. Then he said, 'If you believe that, it's not my age you're concerned about, old friend.'

Arthur was annoyed and changed the subject. Sam walked slowly home, a nebulous depression settling over him. It was so good to have Honey home, to find her unchanged underneath the surface varnish—and yet Arthur's attitude, her reaction to it, bid fair to spoil their friendship. Try as he would, it was beginning to involve him too. Maybe time would sort it out...He quickened his step, pushing it to the back of his mind. But still it was there on the horizon of his thought: a cloud, no bigger than a man's hand.

He arrived home to find Maggie enthusing to Honey, who listened with dutiful interest. '—and then if Arthur's called out it won't need to break up the party!'

'Hello,' he said, 'what's hatching?'

'You're to come up on Sunday, we're going to have a concert of our own! I'll play the piano and you can bring your guitar. It'll be just as good as going to London.'

'Fine,' cut in Sam. 'What time do you want us?'

Honey looked appalled. He ignored her. Maggie said, 'There now! I told you Sam would be pleased, did I not?' and beamed all over her innocent face. 'Come to lunch,' she insisted, 'you can't possibly eat properly down here—

I don't know why I didn't think of it before, you must have lunch with us on Sundays—now, no arguments! We'll be expecting you.' And waving gaily, she was gone.

'How could you!' Honey reproached him, seeing with despair the end of Sundays as they knew them. Fine Sundays spent gardening, or in and out of the water; wet ones in music and firelight, staving off hunger with fruit and ship's cocoa 'thick enough to hold the spoon up'—while rain drummed companionably on the roof.

'I know, I'm sorry. But we can't say no.'

'Why not?'

'Because—look, I just had a bust-up with Arthur. If we don't go he'll think it's more serious than it is. You can kick me if you like.'

'With Arthur? What about?'

'Well—no, never mind.' He had recognised the impossibility of repeating the exchange.

Honey coloured. 'I suppose it was private. I shouldn't have asked.'

'Not really, just silly. I should have kept my big mouth shut, but—well, I get sick of variations on the same old theme.'

She smiled. 'I suppose he was on about us not being related. I might have guessed.' She added lightly, 'As if it mattered, anyway.'

There was a silence. 'It does, you know. You're a hostage. I have to give you back.'

Honey sat very still. She said in a small voice, 'Suppose I didn't want to go?'

Sam seemed not to hear. 'Coffee time,' he announced briskly, and went to fill the kettle.

On Sunday, shaved, combed, scrubbed and laden with guitar music and a kingsize box of chocolates as peace offering, they presented themselves at the Stone House in time for lunch.

The Colbys were hearty eaters, the meal they offered as solid as a brass band concert. It opened with a heavy leek and potato soup and plodded doggedly through steak and kidney pudding with three vegetables—'A root and a leaf, my girl, are absolute essentials'—to wedges of apple pie three inches thick and swaddled in double cream.

Arthur ate his meal with the speed of a greyhound, a habit bred of years as a slave to the telephone. Maggie's disappeared almost as quickly, despite her constant flow of chatter, her pressing on everyone of extra helpings.

Honey, used to the austere regime of the ballet school, earned a rebuke for picking at her food.

'But I'm so full!' she protested, surreptitiously unfastening the button at her waist. 'Honestly, I feel six months pregnant.'

'No need to be vulgar,' said Arthur curtly, and Maggie's mouth formed itself into a little shocked 'O'.

What was vulgar about being pregnant? 'Sorry,' she sighed, stood up—and her skirt fell off.

For a moment she stood red-faced, confused, aware only of Maggie and Arthur rigid in their chairs. Then, unable to look at Sam, she snatched up the skirt and clutching it around her fled through the open French window into the garden. She did not stop until she reached the shelter of the willow tree, where she crouched on the nobbly ground among its roots, nursing her humiliation and wondering how she could ever go back indoors.

She always seemed to disgrace herself in this house. She had never forgotten the day of Maggie's cat. She had found it swollen and crying in a cupboard and rushed with it in distress to Maggie who was entertaining guests. The cat had looked around at the circle of faces and miaowed unnervingly before she produced three boys and a girl on the drawing-room carpet. Tiny and isolated in the centre of the vast acreage of Wilton, frightened by the strange turn of events, the scolding of Maggie and Ellen, the nervous titters among the guests, Honey had burst into tears. Only Sam had said nothing. She had slunk down behind his chair and crouched there in the darkness, clinging to his consoling hand with her eyes shut tight against the laughter. She could still remember the dusty smell of the chair, the carpet that prickled her bare knees. She had covered his hand with kisses, there in the shadow behind the chair; it was the first time she had known how much she loved him.

She sighed. It was easy to express love when you were four years old.

It was Maggie who came to find her. She had no idea of how long she had been sitting there, only that when she emerged her knees were stiffening and a little pattern of twigs was impressed into her insteps. She smoothed the offending skirt and said, 'I'm sorry. Perhaps I'd better go home.'

'No, no, no,' protested Maggie, 'come in and have tea, you can't go before the concert. They're deep in talk now, nothing will be said. Just come in quietly with me and behave as if nothing had happened.'

Honey shook her head. 'I don't know—it would be just like Arthur to think I did it on purpose.'

'Och, what an idea! Though I must say I had a shock when I saw what you had on underneath. Where in the world did you get such things?'

'In Paris, of course.' She caught Maggie's expression and added crossly, 'It was you who sent me there!'

'Maybe so, maybe so. Still, I'd have thought your own good sense would tell you.'

'Tell me what?'

'Why, that nice young girls don't go about in black lace underwear, things like that are sold for women of a—a certain sort. Why, you can see right through—and not so much as a petticoat!'

'How was I to know? I bought them because they were pretty!' And grown-up. And feminine... Was it only bad women who enjoyed feeling feminine? Did everybody know these things but her... did Sam know? She felt her face beginning to burn again. She hung back miserably as they approached the house. 'I can't go in.'

'Whisht, now! It's not the end of the world,' Maggie laughed unexpectedly, as if—too late—she had realised the distress she was causing. 'After all, I'm sure Arthur has seen such wonders before, and Sam—' she hesitated; Honey held her breath—'Sam is—a nice man. I'm sure he will pretend not to have noticed. Now put it behind you and come away in to your tea. Remember, you have to face them sometime.'

Arthur was formally polite, avoiding her eyes. She could not bring herself to look at Sam. She passed plates and cups for Maggie, thinking of the day in London that would never happen now. She could feel disapproval chilling the air in the room like frost.

Tea was consumed in a silence broken only by polite comments on the cake. Maggie said, 'Honey, would you ring for Ellen, please, we need a little more milk.'

'I'll go!' she cried, and made for the door before she could be stopped. She got as far as the kitchen, where Ellen's homely shape was bent over the sink. 'Oh, Ellen!' and she burst into tears.

'There, there, Miss Honey,' said Ellen, 'there, there,' just as she had done long ago, asking no questions, patting her with damp hands smelling of kitchen soap. As the sobs abated Ellen sat her down on a wooden chair, found her a clean handkerchief from somewhere and heated milk on the top of the Aga stove. She offered it in the familiar glass with the silver handle, on its tray with two aspirins. 'Drink it up, Miss Honey, it'll stop the hiccups.'

'Dear Ellen...' She sat looking down at the knobbly black shoes that were discreetly slit across the swollen toe joints and felt a sudden rush of warmth towards their owner. 'Do you still have b-bunions?'

'Yes, Miss Honey.' Ellen looked pleased. 'Fancy you remembering that.'

'I do hope they don't hurt you,' she said. Someone as kind as Ellen should not have to suffer pain.

Ellen smiled. 'Only a twinge or two when the weather's on the turn,' she said comfortably, 'mustn't complain.' She took the empty glass. 'Now you go and bathe your face and I'll tell them you're lying down with a headache. Then you can go back when you're ready.'

Honey went slowly up the stairs to the bathroom. When she had washed her face in cold water she walked along the landing to the room that had been hers. It was as she had left it, pristinely white and juvenile, from the chaste single bed to the teddy bear she had left behind in her flight to Mango Walk. He had been given to her by a fellow-student at the ballet school—'You must have a mascot, everybody does'—and had accompanied her through shows and examinations like a watchful aunt. Now he sat forlorn and sagging on the dressing-table, wearing a resigned expression and a round straw hat that had once belonged to Girl Sam.

She picked him up and sat down with him on her knee. What was it Maggie had said? Something about growing up, not just in your body but in your heart...

She sat for a long time with the toy between her hands, gazing through the window towards the distant elms, where rooks, about to settle for the night, were weaving and skeining like a swarm of bees. At last she put it back on the dressing-table and went out, closing the door behind her.

She was composed as she descended the stairs. She had reached a decision in the little white room. The days were past for Maggie to scold her, for Arthur to humiliate

116

her, for her to go running to Ellen for consolation like a child. To be accepted as a woman, she must take her place as a woman. The time had come to put away childish things.

From the drawing-room the sound of the piano came faintly. Maggie was playing a selection of Gilbert and Sullivan airs which was part of her repertoire. Honey had heard it before. She knew just where Maggie would strike a wrong note, just where she would lose the tempo. It did not matter to Maggie as long as she reached the end without stopping. She smiled; she was willing to bet that Sam knew too.

At the drawing-room door she hesitated. For all her new resolve she was reluctant to make an entrance; it would be easier to go out through the kitchen and try to enter unnoticed by the French doors from the garden, to enjoy a moment's obscurity before she had to answer for her absence.

Ellen looked up as she passed through the kitchen. 'A breath of air,' she explained, and then she was out in the summer dusk among the cabbages, making her way round the side of the house to the terrace where the long glazed doors stood open.

Standing in shadow, she could see into the room where Maggie had brought her recital to a close with a reverberating discord, hastily corrected, and now sat smiling modestly at the keys while the polite applause petered out.

'Now, Sam, it's time we heard from you. What about one of those nice songs of yours?' To Maggie, anything played on a guitar was a song; 'proper' music was played on a piano.

'A song,' affirmed Sam, amusedly. He began drawing chords from the guitar, checking the tuning, striking harmonics to go chiming through the air like bells. 'Honey not down yet?' He looked up and caught sight of her. She shrank back. 'Well, anyway, this is for her. The song's one I picked up in America, I don't think you'll have heard it.' Without betraying her presence, he began to sing:

> 'Go 'way from my window
> Go 'way from my door,
> Go 'way 'way 'way from my bedside
> And trouble me no more...'

117

She looked up, startled. What was he saying? His face told her nothing; he went on singing in his soft warm voice:

> 'I'll give you back your letters
> I'll give you back your ring,
> But I'll remember you, my love,
> As long as songbirds sing...'

He would never say that to her. It was Nancy he had loved, Nancy who had worn his ring...and this sad song was out of character for him; could it really be that he missed that awful woman—that behind the hatred and the bitterness, the inability to speak of her, in some dark hidden corner of himself he still loved her and wanted her back? She hung back forlornly among the pale stars of the tobacco plants, young and gauche and inadequate in the face of her old rival.

> 'Go on your way without me
> Go on your way at rest
> But always know that you're the one
> I really did love best...
> I really did love best.'

Sam had finished singing. Instead of laying down the guitar he went on playing, changing the rhythm, improvising on the melody. Honey caught her breath—it was music she had never heard before, and more than dexterity of hand went into it—it was as if she herself had been translated into music, as if it held out arms to her into which she fell and was warmed, consoled, understood...Suddenly she knew why he had said 'This is for Honey.' It was not for the song but for this, this music he had made—and made for her! Understanding flooded her with happiness. She felt her face warm into a smile, there in the shadows, listening with closed eyes in a world that held only the two of them.

The last notes dropped into the stillness like pebbles into a pool. Everyone was silent, alone with his thoughts. Honey looked at Sam. He was not, as usual, intent on his left hand, but was watching her with an expression that

118

told her he knew of the ordeal this day had been for her; that he knew, and was sorry, and this music was his kiss to make it better. This is still our day, he was saying: this is for you . . . Her eyes misted suddenly. Dear Sam, if only someone could have made him truly happy. If only she could . . .

She must have moved forward into the light, for Maggie looked up and said, 'Ah, Honey! I see your headache's better.'

Taken by surprise, she said, 'My—oh . . . yes, thank you.'

There were two new faces in the room, introductions to be made, and the spell was broken. One of the newcomers, a man with high colour and a bristling white moustache, said, 'Well now, and where have you been hiding? Come and sit by me, m'dear.' He moved fractionally along the sofa to make room for her. 'I understand you've just come back from Paris?'

It was clear what his notion of Paris was and it was something she would have preferred to forget. But she did not want to add rudeness to a fellow guest to her list of offences so she crossed the carpet reluctantly, her arms folded across her clinging sweater, and knelt on the rug beside him. From the look his wife was giving him, she thought uneasily, it was a toss-up which of them she was more likely to offend.

He patted the cushion beside him. 'No, no, come up here. Not becoming for a gel to sit on the floor, dash it. Not becoming at all.' He had narrowed still further the gap between him and the end of the sofa and was sitting with his arm along the back. ''Come along,' he coaxed, 'plenty of room for a small one.'

'But I like the floor, really—'

'Do as you're told, dash it!' He was still smiling but his grip on her arm was relentless, pulling her towards him.

'Honey, we'll have to be going,' said Sam. 'Did you bring a coat?'

'Oh, yes—' I'll go and get it!' She jumped up thankfully and make her escape.

'Och, Sam—' Maggie, unaware of what had been going on, woke up to the fact that they were leaving. 'Must you go so early, it's only half past nine, will you not play us one more tune?'

119

'Sorry, Maggie, another time. I have to get up in the morning. Thanks anyway. Where's Honey, is she ready?'

He need not have asked. Cardigan in hand, she was already at the door. 'Goodnight, Maggie, thank you for everything. Say goodnight to Ellen for me.' She waved her goodbyes from the porch.

'Goodnight Maggie, Arthur. Goodnight,' Sam nodded towards White Moustache, who ignored him, and his lady, who bestowed a tepid smile. As they crunched down the gravelled drive Honey heard a voice: 'See here, Colby. Damn it all! D'you let that fella call you by your Christian name? Not quite the thing, you know...' She glanced up at Sam. He was wearing his impassive face and she knew that he had heard. She said, 'Thanks for rescuing me.'

He smiled in the darkness, saying nothing. They walked home in silence through the lanes, a space between them, not even touching arms. It was as though no words were needed. At their gate she said on impulse, 'Let's go and look at the sea.'

He followed her down. Standing on the sand beside him she released her hair from its slide and let the night wind lift it.

She heard him say, 'You want to dance?

She shook her head.

She did not want to dance. She did not want anything remotely likely. What she wanted could never happen while he still thought of her as a child. She was eighteen, and a woman. Girls married at her age... 'How old are you, Sam?'

'Why?' The question was shot at her so abruptly that she jumped. He laughed, shaking his head. 'Never mind. Want to swim?'

She started to say No, then caught her breath and nodded.

'Better go and change,' he said, and turned to go.

Honey stood still. 'No,' she said, 'we don't need to. It's dark. No one will see.' She waited, holding her breath. It was a challenge, a dare so audacious it frightened even her.

For a moment he hesitated. A moment in which her head swam as his eyes bored into hers. Then he said, 'It's late. We'll swim in the morning,' and strode off up the

beach so fast she had to run to catch up with him.

Oh God, she thought, panting after him, I should have known this wasn't my day. 'Sam!' she cried, 'Sam— please wait...' At the base of the cliff he stopped, and stood waiting. She plodded through marram, the soft sand dragging at her feet, in dread that he would move on again before she caught him up. And then she thought, What am I going to say? Pretend it was a joke? He won't believe me...

'I'm sorry,' she said lamely, 'I didn't know you'd be shy, people are different in France.'

'You mean, you—'

'No! No, not me, I mean...'

'Then why now?'

'I...I don't know...it was stupid, really...' She looked helplessly at the sea, the dark horizon, but they offered no solution.

Sam's expression softened. 'I bet I know what it was, you were trying to shock me. Just to see if you could. Isn't that it?'

'Yes,' she pounced gratefully, 'yes, that was it.' She laughed, a touch of hysteria in the sound. 'And I did, too! You should have seen your face...' She turned away, unable to look at him and lie. She was a coward, too. Playing along with him, helping him putty up the crack in her image, to keep it the way he wanted. Because it was better after all to be loved as a child than rejected as a woman. Better at any price...

Walking beside him, small and subdued, she knew she would never try to force the pace again. If a child was what he wanted, was all he could accept, a child she must remain.

When they reached the caravan he was smiling, his confidence restored; they were able to chat without restraint. And though most of her was thankful, a part of her was growing sadder as the minutes ticked by.

He looked at his watch. 'Goodnight, don't forget the lamp.'

'Goodnight, love...' she whispered as he vanished through the door. He did not hear. She heard him running the water in the washroom and then the door to the dog-house closed.

Alone in the darkness of the bed-place her eyes

brimmed suddenly, drowning her in tears. Oh, tiger, she was thinking: dear and distant tiger...taste my blood.

6

After that disastrous Sunday, Honey held her breath. But Saturday came and no mention was made of going to the Colbys; on Sunday she rose and dressed, praying that Sam had forgotten. She spent the day on thorns, not sure which she dreaded more, a day spent there or his possible reproach if she failed to remind him. But it passed into evening, nothing was said, and at last she relaxed again.

Life flowed on as if nothing had happened. Sam was beginning to write music of his own; evening after evening the caravan was filled with it, while the moths danced in the lamplight and Honey listened enthralled. Arthur was preoccupied with a patient who was not responding to treatment. Maggie went about her work with habitual cheerfulness as summer drew to a close; but her days were shadowed, her nights frayed, by the conviction that down at Mango Walk Sam and Honey were once more inseparable, were sending tendrils into one another's being that would soon be impossible to tear free...She did not admit even to herself what she feared most. Such a disaster did not bear thinking about.

Perhaps they could be saved, she told herself, as long as they did not realise—if some way could be found to part them before they woke up to what was happening. Yes—that was the thing. It could still be all right, as long as they did not know.

Sam knew. He had known since the day he had tripped and measured his length down the caravan steps. Honey

had been there in an instant, her arms about him, her eyes dark with concern, and for a dizzying moment he had pressed his face into her shoulder. They hung close in joy and terror while the universe reeled about them, not speaking, hardly daring to breathe. When he had sat up at last, rubbing his shins and trying to laugh, her hands still loved him and he could not crush the tenderness from his voice. Afterwards, for a long time, he could still feel the print of her fingers in his hair.

Sam knew. He did not know when the change had come about but he knew that it had, and that for him it was irreversible. A little bit of a girl had filled his life with a warmth he had never expected—that same scrap of humanity he had once hated for not being Georgia. He knew too, and was shamed by the knowledge, that if he could change her for Georgia now, if by some miracle by giving up Honey he could bring Georgia back, restore her life, he could not do it.

How had it happened? How could it have happened, had they not been safely insulated by barriers of bed-wetting, threadworms, tussles over homework? If she had stayed through the stormy teens, if they had had the usual battles of will, the childish defiance and the heavy father bit—would it have helped? Perhaps. But Arthur in his wisdom had seen fit to remove those years from their calendar. It was ironic, he thought.

But apportioning blame did not help. Even all else being equal the whole miserable thing was a non-starter. In the mornings when he shaved he avoided his reflection, unwilling to see the grey at his temples, the lines accumulating about his eyes. At forty-three he was still in good shape, hard work and swimming had seen to that. But Honey was eighteen; he could not stay young while she caught up with him. Five years, ten if he was lucky...And the things that women cherished, marriage, a decent home—these were not in his gift. He could not be the one to cheat her of those things. It was for his generation to protect hers, not to plunder it. There were names for men like him, brutal but accurate. 'Little girls is it now, you filthy old—' Was that what he wanted for her?

He fell into the habit of going into brooding silences, from which he would awake to find her watching him, gentle, speculative; and then just her eyes would smile,

because no more was needed between them. Only once she asked him, 'What were you thinking about?' And he came back from a distant memory and said, 'About not having string in my pockets,' and left her wondering.

More and more he hid behind his guitar, because it saved him from talking, and he no longer knew how to talk. What he wanted to say was unthinkable, what he had to say, unbearable. He retreated further and further from the moment: 'You remember I promised to tell you if I wanted you to go...' He could not do it.

He could not do it and he dared not let her stay. He went down and down in a descending spiral of despair. He knew it must devolve on him to do what had to be done; but his predicament was too fresh, too painful for the taking of decisions. Perhaps when it had healed a little...decisions of that sort had a way of making themselves. Already he found himself watching her as if under sentence of death. Already, he snapped at her for no good reason. He tried to control his nervewracked temper, tried to keep his mind on other things. At work he drove himself frenetically, which earned him the resentment of his mates but did nothing to release his tensions. All the time the thought of her tugged at the corners of his mind; he could not wait to get home and yet on the steps he would hesitate. He would stall, search for keys to unlock an unlocked door—and then it would open from within, framing a face that lit at the sight of him, and his laboriously built defences would crumble into dust. By bedtime his pride was vanquished, his courage battered to a pulp, and he would pace the doghouse chain smoking until, exhausted, he could throw himself down, to doze uneasily until morning offered escape. Aware of Honey's hurt and bewilderment he found himself for the first time unable to help her. He could hardly bear to look at her. The jaws of the situation tightened, notching him up by slow degrees towards breaking point.

Honey, aware of the change in him, drew back. What had she done? Teasing her memory for an offence and finding none, she looked elsewhere for a reason. She could date the change to the day, almost to the moment...had she thrown herself at him? Did he feel that she had? But she had only held him, had offered no more, not even a whisper that might have bruised the magic. She had waited, tremulous, for the tightening, the deepening of the bond between them. Instead he had retreated

from her by the hour. Their easy camaraderie was gone, in its place the polite consideration due between host and guest. It was as if he had cut all ties at a stroke and she was frightened and cast adrift by the betrayal.

Was there someone else, someone already in his life that he had not told her about? Her stomach turned over at the thought. She wished there were someone she could talk to. But there was only Maggie.

She would watch him evening after evening as he sat withdrawn and silent behind his guitar, learning the lines of his cheekbone and jaw until she could have drawn them from memory. If he were any man but Sam she might have found a way through the wall he had built, for the legacy of childhood had left her even now a little in awe of him. But if he were any man but Sam she would not have loved him.

'Maggie, can you spare a minute, I want to talk to you?'

Maggie followed her husband into the library and closed the door. An uneasy sensation disturbed her. Arthur was wearing his 'into battle' face.

'I've been thinking,' he said, 'about Sam and that girl down there.'

'Yes?' Her tone was carefully non-committal. 'What about them?'

Arthur interlaced his fingers. 'I think I've come up with the answer.'

'The answer?' repeated Maggie. 'The answer to what?'

'The answer to what! Really, you can be very slow at times. To the problem, of course, the problem of getting her out of the way and started on something worthwhile. Just shows how little thought you've been giving it.'

'Och, Arthur—'

'Don't interrupt, Maggie, you break my train of thought. What was I saying—ah, yes. I don't know why it hasn't occurred to me before; she must go into nursing, of course.'

'But why *nursing*?' To Maggie it seemed the last thing to suggest itself.

'I should have thought it was obvious. She's been down there sponging off Sam for quite long enough. She can learn a useful job, justify her existence. Repay her debt to the medical profession.'

'And?'

'And nothing. That's it.'

'You mean, that's all there is to it? She can do all this from home?' Instinct told her he had obscured his real reason. He was going to have to come out with it if he wanted her co-operation.

He said testily, 'Of course not. You know as well as I do the best teaching hospitals are in London.'

Maggie was silent. So Arthur was going to try again. Was there never to be any peace?

'Well?' he prompted at last, his patience fraying. Her shilly-shallying, as he called it, was trying to him who always knew the answers. 'What's the matter, don't you agree it's a good idea?'

'I suppose so, but...'

'But what?'

Maggie hesitated. 'I sometimes wonder if we've the right to interfere.'

'Right!' exploded Arthur. 'This isn't a question of rights, it's common sense. It's obvious she can't stay there indefinitely—what better than a good job in a hospital?'

'Aye, aye,' said Maggie with a sigh, 'what better...' What better, indeed, she asked herself. They had known all those years ago that Honey would have to leave Sam when she grew up. To that end they had pinched and saved to keep her at boarding school. But she had been a child then, and Sam a much younger man. No one had envisaged her return—unless it was Sam—or that the operation would have to be repeated. It would not be so easy now, the trauma more severe. To have a hand in it would make her feel like a murderer. 'They've none but each other in the world,' she protested weakly.

'High time they had!' said Arthur, his tone so emphatic that for a moment she wondered...but no, he would notice nothing less tangible than black lace underwear. He was concerned with the proprieties; the true perils of the situation escaped him. She said reluctantly, 'Aye, well...perhaps. But is it for us to meddle? I mean, Sam's a grown man—even Honey's no longer a child.'

Arthur leaned forward, his worn face lined with concern. 'Sam's good nature will be his undoing, you know that as well as I. That damned girl will be the ruin of him if we don't do something to help. Don't say you're going back on me, Maggie—not now!'

Maggie sighed. She was not happy about it, not happy at all. But looking at her husband's face she said, 'No— no, of course not. I'll not go back on you. I'll do what I

can.' She managed a smile. 'Just because I have my doubts doesn't mean I'd let you down.'

She said no more, reminding herself sharply that Arthur, as always, was likely to be right. Had she not prayed for something like this to present itself? Honey was a silly young thing who, left to her own devices, could make a fool of Sam and maybe break his heart into the bargain. Her own was too young and too supple to break, Maggie was confident of that. Yes, Arthur was right, and she must keep that thought uppermost. His plan was sensible, and right—and inevitable...but why must sensible people inflict such pain, why must quixotic people like Sam bring down such sorrows on themselves? She sighed deeply once again.

Arthur had already applied himself to his pile of NHS forms. He said crossly, 'Maggie—for heaven's sake! You're blowing all the papers off my desk.'

There was silence in the caravan, broken only by the hiss of the oil lamp, the ticking of the cheap alarm clock. Sam sat with bowed head, elbows on knees, his face unreadable.

Arthur said at last, 'She'll be back soon, the patient only lives just past the farm. I'll be able to give her the forms.'

Why not, thought Sam: let him do the dirty work, endure the stricken look...

'No,' he said hastily, 'I'd rather tell her myself.' He reached for his cigarettes. 'Alone, if you don't mind.'

'Just as you like.' Arthur's tone was huffy. 'Those things will be the death of you.'

Sam tossed the packet aside with a gesture of weariness and irritation.

Arthur smiled sardonically. 'You can give them up, just like that?'

'You can give up anything you haven't got.'

'I'm glad to hear it. I shall want your assurance where Honey's concerned. No letters, nothing to encourage her to come back. Maggie and I will keep an eye on her, see she's all right.'

It was Sam's turn to smile, his eye dark and dangerous. 'Yassa, Mr Boss Man!' he drawled. 'Anything you say...'

Arthur said sharply, 'I don't like your tone.'

Sam stopped smiling. 'And I don't like the things I hear you thinking. More still I don't like some of the

things you say. You don't have to think for me, Arthur, you don't own me, you're not responsible, I'm old enough to think for myself—and believe it or not I know right from wrong! You tell me Sam do this or Sam don't do that, and because you're my friend I let you—but it's not your God-given right! So help me one day you could push me one little inch too far.' He reached for the tossed aside cigarettes and lit one with a shaking hand. 'You asked me once what I meant by saying don't remind me I'm not her father—well I'm telling you now, I never thought of her any other way until you started harping on it. I'd have killed the man who looked at her the way you had me looking! And I'll give you something else to think about, and for free, and that's if any bad thing should come to Honey through me, don't tell yourself you had no part in it. God help you, don't ever deceive yourself that far!'

A sound on the steps outside plunged them both into a tightlipped silence.

Honey came in, her shoulders golden in the lampglow, lighting the room with her presence. She smiled at him, at Arthur. 'The old lady was sleeping, I left the tablets with her son.' Then she set about making coffee, looking down into the kettle as she filled it so that he saw again the silken droop of fine straight lashes, the delicate veining on the lids. He dragged his eyes away. The occasions on which he dared not look grew more, not fewer, as time went on. He found himself wishing the summer weather gone, to be spared the hunger touched off by her innocent sun-worship. He wanted her swaddled in overcoats, her femininity muffled, her unconscious challenge muted— how could he say so? But God! When she came and stood near him . . .

'Don't think I'll wait for coffee,' Arthur said heavily, collecting himself with a visible effort. He stood up. 'We're still friends, Sam? No hard feelings?'

Sam shook his head, thinking: For how long? Only while I walk your way. 'Goodnight . . .' He closed his eyes, alone with his wretchedness. He heard Colby go out, closing the door, his steps on the path, the click of the gate. They echoed through the shadowed cell in which he had locked himself, where once again, as in a bad dream, he sat searching for the words to break bad news to her. And as before, the fault was his. Why couldn't he have cared for her sanely, safely as a father should! This

was what came of trying to play God. Now for the second time she would be cut from her roots, because he in his madness could not be trusted with the thing he cherished most.

He started as her hand touched his arm.

'Are you all right?'

She was crouched beside him, barefooted on the linoleum, her toenails little pink shells still set with a few pale grains of sand. How long would he remember all the colours of her hair, the warm mushroom shadow behind the ears, the veiling of silver at the temples where the sun had caught it...or the shape of the little scar beneath her chin, the relic of a fall when she was three? No one else would ever know her that well; even she had forgotten.

He dredged up a smile. 'I'm all right.' It had to be said. And now. If he didn't do it now he would never be able to. He put a hand over hers. 'Honey, I've been thinking—'

She was looking up into his face. Alerted, questing for a source of danger she had already sensed.

He returned her gaze. He had to have strength for both of them. He must somehow find that strength. He heard his own voice saying, 'How would you like to go to London...and be a nurse?'

He was reminded of a man he had once seen at the moment of stopping a bullet. The eyes blank and incredulous, the face slowly draining of expression. For a moment he thought she was going to faint. Then she snatched her hand away and went scuttling away into the bed-place, shutting the panels behind her. She had vanished without a sound. She remained there in absolute silence, a terrified animal hiding in its burrow.

Sam did not move for a long time. Then he extinguished the lamp, turned off the gas and went slowly to bed.

7

At daybreak Sam dragged his bones through to the caravan in search of coffee. He tapped lightly on the bulkhead and waited. There was no response, so very quietly he went in, lit the gas under the kettle and sat down. He had no more cigarettes. He had finished the packet last night in the first hour of sleeplessness; and he was desperate for a smoke. He thought briefly of walking up to the shop before he remembered he was an hour and a half too early. All he could do was try not to think about it—so much for giving it up, he reflected, words, empty words...

When the kettle boiled at last he got out the tin of Nescafé and two mugs automatically, then wondered if he should put one away again. Honey was still in the bed-place with the panels closed over her. Maybe it was unfair to wake her if she slept—or would it be worse to go out without a word? Increasingly, he found even the most trivial decisions were beyond him. Still undecided, he made two coffees and started to drink one. Then talking the other he went and stood close to the panelling, trying to discern whether the shadow he could see through it still lay in the aftitude of sleep. He could not. He whispered, 'Honey?'

'Yes?'

She had not moved. The answer was immediate, and he knew that she had not slept.

'You want coffee?' God, he thought, you banished someone from your life, and the next thing you said was 'Do you want coffee?'

'No.' Her shadow turned away from him, the face towards the window.

He stood there with the cup in his hand, at a loss.

After a while he went to the table and sat down. He drank both mugs of coffee and made more, his brain labouring like over-revved machinery. He did not know what he had expected from Honey. Tears, arguments—a tantrum perhaps. But not silence. It was the last thing he expected and he did not know how to deal with it. There were things he must talk over with her, details to be discussed—but what could he say to her? It was clear that she was in a state of shock. How could he callously force on her the practicalities of her departure. Yet if he did not, Arthur would. Someone was going to drag her through it and he would be the gentler of the two.

Before he left for work he wrote a note and left it propped against the coffee tin.

> Honey—we have to talk about this. Let me know when you are ready.
> Sam

He stood frowning at it for a moment. Then he turned off the gas under the kettle, picked up his duffel coat and closed the door softly on his way out. At the gate he paused, waiting or hoping for some sound to call him back. Maybe she would break down now that she thought him out of earshot, weep or show some other sign of life—shout, swear, smash the windows—

The silence was absolute. At length he made himself move on, but his legs were reluctant to carry him to work. Nothing had disturbed him like the stillness that now fell on Mango Walk.

He spent the day only half aware of what was going on around him. He spoke to Birdy and called him Mick. To Mick and called him John. And when someone spoke to him he failed to answer. He came back to a chorus of catcalls, an inventory of female attributes and an exchange across his head that was only half in fun: 'Found her down the supermarket—' 'Got her packet of OMO, had she—' 'Yeah, cheaper than down the High Street!'

'OMO?' he echoed stupidly, his attention caught for the moment.

'Yeah, OMO—Old Man Out,' volunteered Birdy. 'Here, better not be mine or I'll have your guts for garters!'

'Yeah—you seen Birdy's missus? Right bit of crackling, she is—'

'Who you calling crackling—watch it!'

They were off again, and he was left in peace. If you could call it peace. He could think of nothing but what he had left at home. At lunchtime he could not eat. He downed two pints of lager which gave him the illusion of calm and would have lost him the tip of a finger in the compressor had not Birdy snatched his hand away in time. 'Dozy bugger!' Then he stopped and stared, his colourful stream of words dried up; he said, 'Here—you really got problems?' and then, 'Look, it's only larking about, like. No hard feelings, eh?' Sam shook his head, No hard feelings, he thought, that was what Arthur had said. People tried to needle you, tried to take a rise. Then when they thought they'd managed it they lost their nerve and said No hard feelings, and that was supposed to make it all right. You weren't allowed to get angry once they'd said that. Like kids playing tag; they yelled 'feign-its' when the pace got too hot and they were safe. If only he could find a magic word to say and be safe.

As the day wore on he began to dread going home. Once on the bus, he could not get there quickly enough. Every time they stopped to pick up a passenger or to set down a shopper laden with bags, children, push-chair, he wanted to jump off himself and run the rest of the way. Only common sense kept him on the bus which for all its exasperations did travel, albeit fractionally, faster than he could. But at the stop before the farm he got off and cut across the fields on foot.

Cattle were grazing in the lower meadow; they raised their heads to watch him as he sprinted alongside the hedge. Were they bullocks or cows—was there a bull among them? He did not know. He kept his head down and went on running through the drenched grass in the falling dew of evening. He flung himself over the last stile and stopped dead. The caravan looked uninhabited. Not even the faint glow of firelight tinged the windows. No sound came to meet him as he approached and he felt his stomach tighten with apprehension.

Perhaps she had gone out, he told himself, gone up to the Stone House to raise hell. But he knew it was unlikely; she had been in no state to tackle Arthur when he had left this morning. The door was unlocked, as he had left it. He shouldered it open and went in. Maybe, after a sleepless night, she had dozed off in a corner—

Something inside him took a downward plunge as he

132

saw two mugs and the coffee tin, the square paper showing up palely in the gloom. Everything was as he had left it. The panels to the bed-place still closed.

'Honey?'

No answer. He went over and peered through the glass, trying to make out her shape through the gathering dusk. Then a sound from within, a sort of gasping snore, jangled him into action. 'Honey!' He flung open the panel with a crash and as he did so something fell to the floor. He retrieved it, a small empty bottle—aspirins! God, how many? He didn't know. The bottle had held fifty but some were gone. What to do—Jesus, what to do! Get Arthur—no, she could be dead by then—no phone, no nothing in this godforsaken place—Jesus wept! He jerked her upright and as he did so she vomited weakly, an evil-smelling posset that was powdery between his fingers. Thank God she had brought some of it up! She was still unconscious and he held her forward, in dread that she would choke. If she dies, he thought viciously, I go up there and kill that man. With my bare hands I kill him, so help me God. He heaved her up, head downward over his shoulder, and carried her through to the washroom. He ran cold water into the basin and tried to revive her with it, sloshing great handfuls into her face, pouring it on the nape of her neck, sluicing it over her skin that was clammy and sweating. All the time he talked to her, shaking her, shouting her name, 'Come on now, wake up! Honey, you hear me? Wake up! Honey, come on...' Still she did not respond. He heard himself sobbing, 'Honey, come back, come back! Please, Honey, please...' Sitting on the bathroom stool clutching her inert body, rocking her helplessly to and fro, to and fro...

After an eternity she began to moan. Frozen into silence, he watched as her eyelids opened a crack, were instantly squeezed shut again as if the light were painful. Then she began to tremble, normally at first and then rising in malarial shudders to a terrifying shaking that he could feel through his own body, a violent uncontrollable tremor that threatened to tear her apart. 'It's all right,' he whispered, pulling her head down onto his shoulder. 'Don't, my baby, it's all right!' But still she shook, it seemed as if she could not stop. He lifted her on to his bed and rolled her in the blankets, rubbing her hands and feet that were like ice. It came home to him for the first time that she was naked. He drew back, abashed, but only

133

for a moment. The next he was lighting the gas under the kettle, filling a hot-water bottle, rolling it in an old sweater to guard her from burning. He roused her, 'Take this, it'll warm you,' and put it into her hands. He dared not touch her, now that he had thought of it. She accepted the bottle, her movements slow and unthinking, her teeth still chattering. He lit a candle, peered into her face. It was deathly, the lips grey. He got up from his knees, 'Won't be long.'

Her eyes opened in alarm, the pupils dilated, and her head made a negative movement—'No . . . Arthur . . .'—her cold fingers clawing at his. He crushed them reassuringly, his hand a nutcracker. 'Just brandy—I'll be back.' He went through to the wagon, lit the lamp, began searching shelves and gutting cupboards. He went back to her. 'I got to go out. Don't move, don't do anything, try to stay awake—*Honey, for Chrissake*!' Her lids were already drawing together, drowning her eyes. He seized her shoulders and shook her roughly. He looked about for some way of propping her upright. There was nothing, the camp-bed was useless, offering no support. He bundled her up again, manoeuvred her up the steps and, awkwardly, treading on trailing blankets, back into the bed-place. He stripped off the sour sheets and propped her between pillows in the angle of the bulkhead, wound up in the blanket like a newborn baby in its shawl. She stared at him bemused, ready to slide into sleep again; but the trembling was diminishing. Thank God! he thought, oh, thank Christ! He was uncertain if he should leave her, unsure if he should be keeping her awake or letting her rest. But brandy was a stimulant, it would warm her—he would run both ways—he squashed her face between his hands and kissed her fiercely, clumsily, without hunger, feeling nothing but relief. 'Don't go to sleep!' And he fled towards the Rose. He burst into the 'Public' and thumped on the bar for attention.

'I've told you not to do that,' said George. 'You wait your turn like the rest,' and he turned away ostentatiously to serve another customer.

Sam opened his mouth to say, 'It's an emergency!' and realised he must not. 'Sorry,' he mumbled, and stood aside trying to catch his breath.

George, savouring the situation, went round everyone present, whether or not they had been served, enquiring their pleasure. Sam waited, fuming. He had been in this

position before and knew there was nothing he could do to hurry it. When George was quite ready he came back to him, his large red hands spread along the bar. 'Now, my son,' he said with the air of having just administered a lesson in behaviour, 'and what can we do for you?'

Sam crushed an urge to snap that he was not his son and push his front teeth up his nose for emphasis. Instead he said, 'Brandy—a half-bottle.' With an effort he added, 'Please.'

'Well now, that's more like it,' said George expansively, 'I like to hear please and thank you, it makes life pleasant. Only I don't sell half-bottles, you want the off-licence up the road.'

'But they're not open!'

'Out of luck then, aren't we?' George smiled with unmistakable satisfaction, picked up a glass, held it to the light and began to polish it. 'Only full bottles here,' and he turned away.

Sam rummaged in his back pocket, counted out the price of a bottle on to the counter. 'Full bottle, then.' He was ignored. He repeated the request a little louder. George half turned towards him, cocked an eyebrow. 'Didn't quite hear you?' Lesson time again, thought Sam, his pocketed hands clenching into fists. 'I said, a full bottle—please.' He levelled his eyes at the display behind the bar, not trusting himself to look directly at George. Beyond him in the 'Saloon' he glimpsed a flushed face, a bristling white moustache. And instinctively stepped back out of sight.

'Three Star or Five?' The glass that had been polished impeccably was again held to the light, found unsatisfactory, breathed upon and addressed with leisurely determination.

'Three will do.'

'Ah—well now, that's a pity. I only keep five.'

'All right, I'll take five,' Sam said quickly before he had the chance to turn away again. 'How much?'

It was a mistake. George said promptly, 'Five seventeen six.' As Sam's jaw dropped he added, 'Bar price!' clinching his victory. Sam did not have that much and they were both aware of it. Unhappily he searched his pockets, knowing that the price was fictitious and knowing that he could do nothing about it. He spread his remaining cash on the counter and it came to four pounds and some loose coppers. Even at that he would walk to

the station for the rest of the week, but the brandy was vital. He said wearily, 'That's all there is, take it or leave it—'

George ignored him to beam at someone behind him. At the same moment a hand swept the money back towards him across the bar.

'Have one with me,' said the White Moustache cordially. 'What's his tipple?' he enquired of George, 'whatever it is, make it a double.'

'Brandy, would you believe,' sniffed George, eyeing Sam with distaste. 'Like giving a donkey strawberries! But that's up to you, Colonel.'

Sam was startled. He had no wish to drink with anyone at the moment, least of all with the Colonel. But to refuse might cause unpleasantness and waste more precious time. He nodded 'Thanks' to the Colonel and said 'Rum and coke' to George, who ignored him. As he usually did. He tossed off the brandy that appeared before him, wishing he could take it back to Honey instead of drinking it himself, frustrated and at a disadvantage. He disliked hospitality he could not return, it made him uneasy, made him wonder what was behind it. And almost immediately he knew what it was.

At a sign from the White Moustache the glasses were instantly recharged. 'And how's that little filly of yours, eh? Must say I wouldn't have believed you were from the same stable, dark horse, you, what?' He drew up a bar stool, edged confidentially close.

Sam thought he saw a potential ally—and any was better than none. 'Not well at all,' he said, 'been sick all day, something she ate. I came to get her some brandy but they're charging fancy prices around here.' He indicated the coins spread on the counter. 'Seems that's not enough.' He raised his glass and hoped for the ploy to work.

'Bloody ridiculous!' rumbled the Colonel. 'George! Bottle of five star and look sharp about it!' As George nodded deferentially he sorted out two of Sam's pound notes to push towards him. 'Plenty there—and don't forget the change.' He turned back to Sam, 'Have to watch these chaps, y'know, get above themselves if you let 'em...yes, well.' He stopped, cleared his throat noisily, as if he had caught himself up in an indiscretion. 'Now, about this little gel of yours...very promising, very promising indeed. Quite the little flyer, in fact, quality there—

oh yes, no mistaking it! Pass her off anywhere with those eyes, that bearing.' He leaned towards Sam who stood stiffly, palm extended to accept his change, and laid one finger against the side of his nose. 'Keep you in your old age, if you use your head.' He sat back, nodded in satisfaction at his own observation. Then leaned forward again, 'Mother a stunner, eh? How'd you manage it, fellah like you, eh? "When lovely woman stoops to folly"—what? You lucky dog!' The loaded smile, the wink . . . He's been drinking, Sam warned himself. Take the brandy and get out . . . but George had disappeared.

'She's ill, right now,' he glanced meaningly at his watch, 'I have to get back to her—'

'She won't die for ten minutes, damn it!' The tone was testy. 'Stop fussin' like an old woman. I want to talk business. Fact is,' he leaned forward through a haze of cigar smoke, 'fact is, I've taken quite a fancy to that little gel of yours, quite a fancy. And I could use an able-bodied fellah like you up at the house—bit of gardening, handyman—drive a car, can you? Well, you know the drill, you and the little gel could move out of that junk-heap of yours and into the Lodge. All cosy and discreet, no wagging tongues—can't have the wife upset, y'know, not the thing, not the thing at all.'

'I don't understand you,' Sam said stonily. He wished to Christ he didn't. He wished he had never enlisted the man's help. He wished—he could hear George moving with deliberate slowness in the cellars below. Somehow he had to get out of here before he lost his temper. Conversation in the bar had stopped and the barmaid was standing at a distance looking uncomfortable. Sam managed to catch her eye. 'Could you ask him to hurry?' But she shrugged apologetically; she couldn't leave the till. He looked again at his watch. Twenty minutes . . .

'What the devil are you fidgeting for, sit down when I'm talking to you! And stop pretending you don't understand me, dammit, it's plain enough.' He leaned forward, lowered his voice but not far enough—'A taste of the old Dolce Vita, do her the world of good! Like mother like daughter, what? See you didn't lose by it, of course, can't have any outraged fathers tearin' up the show . . .'

Christ, thought Sam, was that brandy never coming! He set his jaw, staring savagely past the Colonel, noting with contempt the faded watery eyes, the fiery nose, the

whiskers waxed into twin phallic symbols above the discoloured teeth, the sagging body...tossing scraps to his slavering rage to keep it quiet. Another brandy stood on the counter and he gulped it down, praying for calm: Jesus God—get me out of here before I lose control!

The Colonel babbled on unaware of the brewing storm. 'Fact is, wife not up to it these days, health, y'know. Finds it all a bit of a strain, poor dear—discretion's the thing, discretion...a nice cosy billet in the Lodge, eh? Just the ticket—and I can be generous, oh yes!' He paused to peer up into the granite face of the man who stood over him, gritty-eyed and swaying slightly from the effects of raw alcohol on an empty stomach. 'Well,' he prompted thickly, 'what do you say?'

George reappeared with the brandy. Sam reached across and snatched it from his hand, flung his fistful of coins down on the bar towards the Colonel.

'Not for sale!' he rasped, and slammed his way out through the doors into the understanding darkness. He heard the Colonel's voice protesting drunkenly, 'Damn lucky to be asked—fellah like that, damn' lucky!' and other voices in varying degrees of embarrassment or amusement trying to hush him. He paused only to pound into the bark of a tree the blow he could not land on his tormentor. And then, nursing his wounded knuckles, he began to run.

He ran and kept on running, heart bursting, fists flailing, feet pounding the road in an agony of frustrated fury, covering ground faster than he knew in his desperation to get back to Honey, to put distance between himself and the man his every nerve longed to murder, to let down with physical effort the pressure that was building up in him. Halfway home he was jerked back to reality by the scream of brakes, the jangle of a motor horn, and flung himself to the safety of the verge. Must have been weaving all over the road, he thought. Flourishing the brandy bottle too. Lucky they hadn't picked him up—or knocked him down. God, it had been close! Now it was his turn to shake; he tried to open the bottle but his hand was too unsteady and he plunged on again, spurred by anxiety no less than by the need for refuge. It seemed years before he reached the gate and fell against it with a thump, hanging on for support, sobbing for breath. He couldn't go in to Honey like this, he must pull himself

together. Still shaking he sniffed hard, spat in the dust, scrubbed his wet face with his sleeve. Yet still the shame and the rage broke through, rose up and flooded from his eyes. Stop it, stop it, he told himself: but he could not.

He remembered the brandy. Still his hands would not serve him and he cracked off the neck on the gate-post, pouring it into his open mouth, sucking it down, slopping some of it over his shirt. He choked a bit and coughed, then he began to feel better; he stood against the gate drawing in the cool air and felt curiously light. Must be the effect of so much running—he had done no running for years. Calmer now, soon be able to go in. Cigarette...why hadn't he thought of that before? He searched his pockets slowly with fumbling fingers, found one a bit crushed, the packet flattened where he had sat on it, and tried to light it with a match torn from a book. He took three shots at it and decided it must be more bent than it looked—no way could he get the flame to meet the tobacco. He gave it up. Another swig of brandy would do just as well. He raised the bottle and then remembered he must save some for Honey. It was all right, there was nearly half left. But he'd better keep it for her. He started searching for the cork—or was it a cap? He couldn't remember. Whichever it was it was missing, he must have dropped it in the grass. He tried groping around for it, holding on to the gate with the other hand, but he couldn't manage that and the brandy bottle, keeping it upright. And his knees were giving out. It was all that running...and no sleep last night. It made you forget things. Like something funny that had happened to the gate, it was on the wrong way around with the hinge where the latch ought to be. Someone must have turned it round to keep him out, someone wanted to keep him away from Honey, Arthur—or that other one. He chuckled. Poor old fool, he'd never hold up anyway...He went hand over hand to the other end of the gate and found the latch. He must go in, go in and see Honey, see she was all right. He took a firm grip on the bottle. Driving his legs like pistons he staggered towards the light. The first step was all right but he missed the second and fell, barking his shins. He sat there for a moment, vaguely waiting for her to come and take him in her arms.

A scared voice from within called faintly, 'Who's there?'

'It's me.' He hauled himself to his feet. Coffee, he thought dimly, black coffee when you feel like this... he pushed open the door and stood swaying.

She had crawled to the front edge of the bed-place to look out, the lamplight dusting gold over her skin. She was lovely, he thought; yes, beautiful—his Honey! Her wan face cheered at the sight of him. 'I stayed awake,' she said, her voice still weak. 'I'm so tired...' The rest was lost in a yawn that showed her teeth, her little pink tongue. She pushed back her hair, her eyes still trying to close, looking unbearably young and undefended. Girl, girl, I love you...

'Darling...' he mumbled. Smiling fatuously, he lurched towards her.

8

Sam stumbled to his feet and groped his way through darkness to the washroom. A dull pain thudded at the base of his skull and his stomach bobbed like a cork on a sea of nausea. Relieving his bladder, he felt the sweat break out under his hair. He retched painfully, bringing up nothing, hanging on to the lavatory for support, overwhelmed by the reek of mingled brandy and Elsanol—never again! How had it happened? He could not remember. He had had a bad day at work, had been worried... was that it?

He seized the wash-basin as it floated past and doused his head in the water. Slowly he shuffled as far as the door to the doghouse. There he stopped, stupefied. There was his bed—but where were the blankets, the pillow? The thing was stripped down to its frame, its bleak canvas. He stood holding his temples, leaning against the door-post, trying to work it out. Had he not just got out

of bed? Then there must have been covers—must have been. And they were not there.

He made his way over and, leaning down, felt along the floor. Nothing. As his hand fell on the bed he noticed that it was cold. He had not slept here. Alarm stabbed the fog in his brain like a searchlight, suddenly it was vital to know where he *had* slept. Out of the confusion he unravelled a recollection: Honey had been ill. Had he sat up with her... would he find his bedding on one of the seats...

He negotiated the stairway with difficulty, and peered through into the caravan.

'Sam?'

He turned to see Honey looking out from the bed-place. The panels were wide open. In the moonlight shafting through the windows he saw one breast clearly outlined as she leaned towards him. He stared, unbelieving. She was naked, covered only by a fold of something entangling her knees. It looked like—no! But it was. The blanket from his bed.

'Sam,' she whispered, 'darling... are you all right?'

'Darling'—Jesus Christ, what had he done? He turned and reeled away towards the doghouse, threw himself down on the unforgiving canvas, down, down into the black pit of despair.

In the morning Honey, dishevelled but fully dressed, emerged from the bed-place more silently than usual.

Sam, already on his second pint of black coffee, flinched at the sound of the panels opening, dreading what her first words might confirm. He would know as soon as he saw her eyes. If he had—if the unthinkable had happened, there would be fear there, disgust and loathing. She would shrink away from him and he would know. He sat staring into his cup. Waiting for sentence to be passed. But she said nothing on her way to the washroom, only giving him a curious glance as she went by.

He sighed and pressed the heels of his hands against his eyes. His mind though wretched was clearing now. He remembered the nature of her illness, the reason for his errand to the pub, his encounter with the White Moustache. Even had a vague recollection of coming back. But the rest—the vital time—was still a blank. He sat very still and tried to lay hands on last night.

She came back, pale-lipped, her hair damply combed, made coffee and sat down with it, her thin hands huddled round the mug for warmth. Looking at him furtively from time to time, leaving it to him to speak first. But he did not know how to.

After a while she got up, and came back with a fizzing glass which she held out to him from an uncertain distance, as if half afraid to approach him. 'For your headache.'

He took it from her. 'I was so drunk last night.' Making excuses, he thought. Despising himself...

'Is it a very bad hangover?' Her voice was filled with the concern he did not deserve.

'I'll live,' he said, and drank the seltzer to silence it. The bubbles in the glass were going off like hand grenades.

'I didn't do it to frighten you,' she said, 'I wouldn't do that.'

'You scared me witless—God, how could you do a thing like that!'

'Don't—don't...' She had turned away, her head between her arms as though she were trying to protect her ears. 'You don't understand.'

If only I didn't, he thought. If only I didn't have to go through with this farce. He said, 'You don't want to go to London, is that it?'

Her voice was choked. 'I thought you knew.'

'Not even...after last night?' He held his breath.

She raised her head at that. 'Oh, for God's sake—do you think I've never seen anyone drunk before!'

So that was all! Relief flooded through him like adrenalin, giving him strength for what he must do. He could not wait to get her away, put her safely out of reach, put an end to the daily torment of wanting her. He said with brutal cheerfulness, 'Right, so somewhere else. But you have to go some place, being difficult only makes it tough all round.'

He could feel her pain from where he sat. She knelt very still on the lino, shrunk into herself, her neck slight as a flower stem under the pale tassel of hair. The sight of her knifed him. But if he weakened she would be drinking sorrow all the days of her life. He reminded himself of something Maggie once said: Young girls fall in and out of love like ducklings in the water...Yes, time

would take away the hurt; life would move on and take her with it. He wished to God she would say something. He pushed himself to go on, 'That's settled, then. London, unless you can think of something better. Just as long as it's soon. But a hospital's as good as anywhere. You'll be safe there.' Safe. Safe from me. And from the White Moustache.

'But why?' The words seemed wrung from her.

'Because I say so!' he snapped. A typical parental brush-off, he thought; just the sort he had always despised.

To his dismay she shook her head. 'It's not enough to say that.' She raised her wounded eyes. 'You have to give me a reason, I want the truth.'

He moved his head restlessly and its throbbing punished him. The truth. And if I told you the truth—all of it, all the sad and sordid details, the headaches, the wet dreams, what happens when your breasts move under your dress—what I'm driven to—what do you know of the cruder facts of love? I'm too old, too earthy, too experienced for you. And I don't want to be remembered with my naked lust grinning in a corner... He closed his eyes. 'Look—' They flew open again in alarm as he heard her move.

She was on her feet, her arms outstretched towards him. If she touched him! In a panic, he thrust her violently away and winced as her face struck the sharp corner of the dresser. A little cry was jerked from her and she crouched where she had fallen, a hand pressed to the weal already whitening on her brow.

Distraught, he covered his own face with his hands. 'Oh God,' he mumbled miserably. 'Oh God, I'm sorry. Arthur's right, you're not safe with me any more.'

After a time without dimensions he heard her say softly, 'Don't be upset, it doesn't matter. None of it matters, don't you see? I love you.'

He stared at her, dumbstruck, rocked by the enormity of what she had said. It was as if the earth had been jolted out of orbit. For a moment of unreality in which he suffered the crazy illusion that she was the adult, he the child, their eyes held. Then his were wrenched away.

'Of course you do, Honey.' He spoke with the effort of a lifetime; slowly, carefully choosing his words. 'And I love you. Just like always. Just like any real father and

daughter . . . just exactly like that.' He fumbled for a cigarette and turned away to light it, unable to look at what he had done.

As if from a great distance he heard her say, 'Yes . . . yes. Of course.' She was on her feet now, standing by the window, staring out through heavy drops of water that burst against the glass. He saw her nod, shake her head, press her hands together. Confused, trying to recover herself . . . A flurry of rain hit the caravan. A gull flapped his loud galoshes across the roof. Sam sat still, aching with the weight of unspoken words.

She said in a lifeless voice, 'How long?'

'I hadn't worked it out. I suppose till you're—till Georgia would have been eighteen. They won't take you before that.'

'I see . . .' She turned her blank gaze towards him. 'If they did I suppose you'd want me to go now?'

He did not answer, thinking of the bleak weeks ahead. They were going to be the most punishing of his life.

'Would you?' she persisted. As if even now she searched for a crumb of hope.

Sam pulled himself together. 'Yes, I would.' He stood up abruptly and crashed his head into the underside of the ceiling locker. 'Ah—shit!' he roared and bent double, cradling a firework display in his arms.

And Honey, unable to go to him, turned and ran out into the rain.

9

October brought a shortening of the light, coaxing mist from the sea to shroud Mango Walk, where two people locked in their separate griefs lived not together but under one roof.

Summer died softly that year, dirged by the low in-

sistent voices of foghorns, calling and answering. Like us, thought Honey, calling and answering, never allowed to meet. Even now, she could not accept the facts as Sam would have her see them; could not believe that he wanted her gone, that perhaps he was really locked for life to the dreadful Nancy, too crippled or too bruised to love again. She dwelt endlessly, fruitlessly, on the early weeks of happiness, so sure that he had shared it, convinced that there must be something—a word, a touch—that could unlock him, release him, bring him back to her—if only she could find it. Her heart like a ferret ran searching, searching for a way leading through to him.

Each day she spent hours in composing appeals to him. Each evening, hearing his step outside, her mouth would dry, the words evaporate from her mind. The meal would be eaten in silence and he would disappear into the doghouse, only to emerge for a silent breakfast before going to work. The time of ordeal dwindled. Alone in the caravan she worried the windows, or sat immobile for long hours at a time, not knowing how to get through the days. Yet each nightfall brought a sinking of the heart: one less between her and the horizon beyond which her thoughts could not be forced. She made no plans. She was not living, but merely enduring time.

The last day came, inexorable as death. She woke in an agony of tension. Today was her last, her very last chance. It was Saturday, he could not escape to work—and still she did not know what to say to him, how to win him round. The first thing was to prevent his going out, she told herself, dressing in a ferment, rehearsing what to say: Let's work in the garden today, I'll give you a hand before I go away...She could not contemplate going, had not even packed. But there was only today in which to turn the tide.

At seven o'clock she laid the table for breakfast and sat waiting. Eight o'clock. Half past eight. Nine o'clock. Had he gone out before she was awake? Swimming—he might have gone swimming...for two hours? At nine-twenty-five she heard a footfall on the step and her heart gave a lurch.

'Is anybody home?'

Maggie! Dear God, of all times, it was Maggie. She looked at her blankly, unable to find words.

'I've come to take you shopping,' said the visitor brightly. 'Arthur has promised me a new winter coat so

I thought you'd like to come and help me choose one. There'll likely be some wee thing you'll be wanting yourself, something to take with you—'

'I—no, I can't, I haven't packed.'

'Och, you should have done all that long ago. Well, never mind, you'll have time this evening. Away with you and get changed, or we'll miss the bus.'

'But...Sam...' she protested weakly.

'Sam's away up with Arthur, did you not see him go?'

So that was it. Defeated, she changed her gardening clothes for a dress and duster coat, drank a glass of water, and followed her captor. Hour after hour she trailed behind her through the dusty streets, the overheated dress shops of the city—the Southcombe shops were useless, Maggie insisted—trying to appear normal, to feign interest in her kindly but uncompelling chatter; trying to eat the luncheon pressed upon her, while the knowledge dragged at her that Sam must have returned by now, that the hours were slipping by and she could not be there, this last vital day with him filched from her like the years of her exile in France. Weary and dispirited she took her leave of Maggie and turned towards home at last, empty-handed in the sunless afternoon. On the green by the bus stop some children were singing:

'Who shall we send to fetch her away,
Fetch her away, fetch her away...'

Maggie smiling, trying to cheer her: 'We'll be there in the morning, don't be late now! You'll be able to go to that Festival Hall of yours, now won't that be nice?' She hurried on, trying not to hear them, but the voices followed her chanting down the hill:

'Who shall we send to fetch her away
On a cold and frosty morning?'

Sam was there. He was squatting on his haunches, dividing polyanthus roots, the splittings spread on the grass beside him. He glanced up briefly at the click of the gate. In silence she came and stood behind him, all the words she had so carefully marshalled slipping away from her. In that moment it came to her that she had lost; whether she was beaten or had given in hardly mattered, she had no more hope. For what use were words against

146

feelings? She had to concede at last that he did not want to know.

'Too many yellow ones,' he said in a flat voice. 'Be a jungle by the spring.'

She did not answer, inescapably reminded that she would not be there. She stood looking down at him, trying to fix his image in her mind. She already had so many memories to cherish, funny or poignant; yet with time they would dry and blow away like leaves, she knew it from her own sad experience. She watched numbly as he cleared up, collecting the trowel and the knife, heeling the unwanted plants back into the soil. He would never just leave anything to die. When he had finished he remained staring before him, as if he had lost interest in what he was doing.

At last she said, 'I'll make tea.' Because it was all she could trust herself to say. A tear escaped her to splash on his neck and she reached down hurriedly to brush it away.

Without looking up he said, 'Go put the kettle on while I wash.' He stood up and gave her a little push towards the caravan. Then he disappeared into the wash-house.

She climbed the steps and lit the gas under the kettle. She cut bread and buttered it, mechanically set the table with no thought for what she was doing. The Last Supper. She wondered if that was blasphemy. She sat back with closed eyes and waited for the kettle to boil. It always took so long. But she would not have to wait for it again. She would never do any of this again. This was the day she hadn't believed in, the day she couldn't face. The day of the little red envelope—only this time the summons was for her.

Hearing Sam come in she opened her eyes. He was drying his hands on a towel which he rolled up and tossed back through the doorway. She noticed that he was freshly shaven and when he pulled a clean shirt from the locker she felt a throb of fear.

'You're going out?'

'If you'd rather—'

'No!'

The silence snapped shut again like the jaws of a trap. They eyed each other unhappily, unable to spring it. Then Honey found something to pass for a smile.

'Come and have tea,' she said. Pax: no more wounds, no struggling. I know when I'm beaten...

147

The kettle boiled, its thin reedy whistle cutting across her thoughts. She brought it in from the porch, moving about mindlessly, making tea that nobody wanted. But she did not know what else to do. She warmed the teapot, filled it from the kettle; sat down again to wait for it to brew. On her plate a small square box had appeared.

'They said you'd need a watch.' He reached across the table, nudged it towards her. 'Not pretty, but it's the right kind—the sort nurses wear.'

She looked at it, a round-faced Ingersoll on a businesslike fob. Her going-away present. The final seal on her departure. While she had paced the caravan he had been pacing the streets, finding her a gift from his meagre savings. He was saying something.

'I had them write on it for you. See, on the back.'

Would it say 'with love'? Or their two names—a token to carry with her through the empty world...She turned it over. Engraved on the cheap white metal was her name: Honey McLeod. And the date, 18th October 1956. Her birthday—Georgia's birthday, given to her with so much else. In all her life she had not given him a birthday present; and now it was too late...

Letters and figures swam together as her eyes filled. She swallowed, managed a little nod, unable to speak; wanting to say thank you, to say something, anything. She poured milk into the cups, lifted the teapot that seemed suddenly too heavy for her, and stared uncomprehendingly at the colourless stream of liquid trickling from its spout. His hands took it gently from hers and set it down.

'You forgot the tea,' he said.

Suddenly it was all too much for her. Failure to make a pot of tea and failure to achieve her heart's desire became one; her head went down on her hands and she burst into tears among the teacups, wept hopelessly, the tears running down between her fingers.

Sam was devastated. In the past weeks, seeing her silent, quenched, her eyes burning holes in her face, he had told himself that he wished she would break down and cry—if only to God she would, he thought, then they might both feel better. Her unnatural calm had unnerved him, kept him on thorns for what she might do. And yet now that she had found the release of tears he could not endure it.

He left his seat to go and crouch beside her but he did

148

not know how to console her, how to reach her, what to say. He was not even sure who it was that sat there weeping, the child who was lost or the woman who was promised...but not to him. He tried to enfold her but she sat rigid, unyielding. He leaned his head against her shoulder. 'It'll pass, Honey. It all passes, in time.'

Honey shook her head, unable to answer. It would not pass. Everything else but not love. She had read that somewhere. She tried to stifle the sobs that tore loose, slow, painful, one after another and would not be stopped.

'Let it all come out,' said Sam, rocking her gently until she gave way and wept despairingly, holding him close with tear-wet hands.

'Why couldn't you have loved me?' she sobbed. 'I so wanted to make you happy.' And she was dragged down under a fresh surge of grief.

'I do, you know I do.' He blundered painfully into his own brick wall, as lost and confused as she. 'But I have to love you enough, that's what you don't understand.'

'Like a daughter. That's what you said.'

Her desolation pierced him leaving him weak. He had no more use for lies, no more strength. 'I know...I know, I had to say something.' He felt another great sob building up in her. 'Don't cry any more, my baby. Please don't...'

'I hate you to call me that.'

He smiled, his face hidden. 'That's because you don't understand.'

He felt her draw back to look at him, trying to see his face. Suddenly vulnerable, he kept it turned away. He could have got it all wrong...she might laugh. Or be kind. Or lie—he didn't know which to dread most. But he had already said too much to turn back.

'Sam...' The crying had stopped abruptly.

He felt himself lowering his head as though the blow she could deal him were physical. 'Did you think I was too old to be in love with you?'

It seemed as if time itself had jarred to a halt. And then he felt her begin to tremble. He sat back, fished in the pocket of his jeans. 'Honey, don't...'

She was not listening. 'You should have told me, you didn't have to lie.' She dashed at the tears on her face, took the proffered handkerchief. 'Darling Sam'—she laughed unsteadily—'you can be such an idiot!'

He had to look her in the eyes. But he could not make

himself smile. 'Honey...dear Honey, don't get excited. It doesn't make any difference how I feel.'

She looked at him as if she had not understood. 'But it does...of course it does.'

'No.' He took her bewildered face between his hands. He could feel her waiting, tensed for the fall of the axe. He brought it down quickly. 'Honey—I'm putting you on that train tomorrow if it's the last thing I do.'

For a moment she stared. 'You can't mean it.' Then she shook her head. 'Yes, you do mean it.' Her mouth began to quiver. 'But why, *why*?'

'Oh, girl...' He sighed despairingly. 'Because and because and because. Because whatever sort of life you have out there will be better for you than staying here with me.'

'You really believe that?' she said in a crushed voice. 'Is that what you meant about loving me enough?'

He nodded, staring past her into the dusk. 'Don't think this is easy for me, it hurts like hell. But I have to do what's right, what's best for you. That means giving you a chance of happiness the only way I can.'

'But Sam, you've got it all wrong—'

'No, I've got it right. I know it's right, I've been thinking it through for weeks. We can't make a good life together like other people. All we can do for each other is for you to go free and for me to let you.' He took her cold hands in his. 'So when I take you out, turn you round three times and point you to the future, you're going to start walking. Oh yes, you must! If you don't, I'll have gone through this for nothing. Don't do that to me.'

She turned away from him, her face against the window, crying into the curtain. 'You shouldn't have told me if you wanted me to go.'

'No, I shouldn't.' The sight of her so utterly destroyed reproached him. 'Sometimes when you try your best is just when you snarl things up.'

She nodded, blindly. 'I know...I've made you unhappy. And I wanted it to be so different.' She mopped at her swelling eyelids with the sodden handkerchief.

'It hasn't all been bad.' He reached up, kissed her drowned cheek; she looked pathetically young, almost comic, racked by hiccups with the tears running off her chin. 'Come on, don't look so tragic.'

Her head came blindly against him and he held her

in silence, crouched on the floor beside her, unmoving although his feet were going numb; savouring the stillness, the rare sweetness of having her in his arms. At last she stirred.

'It was all right, wasn't it, some of the time? Maybe right at the beginning.'

'I wouldn't have missed it.' He stood up, flexing his knees. 'Trouble was we both tried too hard. Ended up wanting something that could never be.'

'But it could have been, if only you could see it!' Her eyes pleaded with him through the gloom. 'We could have made it work, I know we could. Oh Sam, it's not too late—I'd do all the hard part, you'd only have to sit back and be loved.'

'I know...' He drew her to her feet and into his arms where she clung, swallowing tears. 'I know you would.' He pressed his face against her hair that fell heavy as cornsilk over his hands, assailed by a moment of weakness unequalled since the day of his fall. 'But you don't know, you just don't know how it can be. I saw what it did to Nancy...'

'Sh-sh,' she whispered. 'I'll go, don't say any more...please, don't say any more...'

He groped in the darkness of his misery for something to lessen hers.

'There'll be someone for you some day, you'll see. Someone who can really look after you. You'll be happy and forget all this.'

Her head moved in a gesture of negation. 'It won't be you.'

'No! Not me, nor anyone like me—someone quite different who can keep you safe!' He grasped her shoulders, shook her. 'Listen, I'm not giving you up so you can rush into some other crazy thing!'·

'Oh, Sam—' She raised her head and caught him off guard, her arm came up and drew him down, her wet cheek drove against his. 'I'm going because it's what you want, because I'd do anything for you. But it's not being safe that matters, not to me.' She sighed. 'You've known me so long, and you still don't understand...'

They threw out the unwanted food—'a feast for the birds!'—and sat handfast on the windowseat, watching their lost garden, their life together, slipping away into

the dusk. Shadows gathered behind them in the caravan, their last day drew to a close. Unseen in the hedge a blackbird piped a single phrase and was silent.

'He's singing her to sleep,' said Honey. She looked down at their clasped hands. 'Funny, the things that keep you awake when you're little; I used to be frightened of dying. Then I'd think: Sam will be there, I can hold his hand. And it would be all right.'

He smiled.

'I'd be long-gone before you anyway.'

'Oh, no!'

'You must have known that?'

She shook her head. 'I have to know you're somewhere in the world!'

Her eyes appealed to him, as if he were all-powerful and could change the logical processes of time. Suddenly he was weary. He wanted the night to pass, the ordeal to come and be over, to have it all behind him and be at peace. Maybe people awaiting execution felt this way, wanting to have it all done with and be dead.

'Sleep now,' he said, 'tomorrow's going to be tough.' He gathered her up and carried her over to the bed-place, drew off her shoes.

She pulled on his hand, 'Don't go.' He hesitated. 'No—I mean, just stay with me.' She reached up, kissed him gently. 'It's sad that we can't make love, because it would be beautiful. But you wouldn't forgive yourself. I know that now ...'

He said, 'I want you to go away whole. Nothing between us dragging you back.'

'I know ... but don't go, don't leave me, not when we've only a few hours left ...'

He kicked off his shoes and climbed up beside her, and they lay in each other's arms, dozing and whispering, until the sky grew light.

10

At daybreak Sam got up and lit the fire, and when it was burning she followed him. They sat before it side by side, saying nothing, because there were no more words for what they felt, no more time, no anything. They hung close to each other as the hands on the clock moved round, eating away the hours. She sat on the washroom steps and watched while he shaved. He stood beside her while she packed the last of her possessions; then he corded her suitcase and stood it outside on the porch. Silence tightened its grip.

They drank black coffee, scalding hot and sweet, dividing the last of the brandy between the steaming mugs. Honey drank it without enjoyment but it helped her to stop shivering.

They put on their coats and stood looking helplessly at each other. Then Sam held out his arms and she came into them; they stood for a long time without speaking, she with her eyes closed, conscious only of the steady rocking beat of his heart, the warmth of his arms, the movement of his breath against her hair.

'How long?'

'Just a few minutes.'

'Kiss me goodbye...'

She turned up her face, their lips met, but it was a sad ghost of a kiss, the fire and the magic eluded them. 'It's no good,' she said, 'we've lost each other already.'

'There's still a little while,' he said. They clung like drowning swimmers, desperately. She said, 'I thought you kissed me once. But I can't even remember it. I wish I could.'

Sam groaned inwardly. It was nothing to what he could not remember. 'Honey,' he said hesitantly, 'that night, when I was drunk...'

She raised her head, said softly, 'When you passed out, you mean?' She met his eyes but he could not read her expression. 'Don't look so worried. It was me, it was what I wanted.'

'What—you wanted?'

She lowered her eyes. 'To sleep with you, just once. I knew I'd never have another chance. Then you woke up and ran away.'

'But—' He stopped, seeing her again leaning forward in the moonlight, her breasts illumined, the nipple tautly outlined by the light...Sam—darling, are you all right...he caught his breath.

'I know...' she sighed, her mouth against his as the remembered moment glowed in both their minds. And now it was different, their heads pressed foward, their arms tightened ecstatically as the world and its hurts receded. Honey felt her blood sing white-hot through her veins; felt as though she were naked, her clothing a caress upon her skin; felt Sam's sudden response as his mind read hers, his fingers learned the contours of her body through the fabric that covered it...Oh God, why did we waste last night...

Outside in the lane, in another world, the car drew up without their knowing. They heard neither the slam of its door nor the impatient beeping of its horn, cocooned as they were, fused in a sweet sensuality they had only begun to taste. They finally drew apart to become aware of insistent knocking on their door.

'Coming!' called Sam without taking his eyes off Honey. She swayed as he released her, dizzy and trembling. 'Such a baby,' he whispered as he steadied her. He bent and brushed his mouth very lightly over hers. 'Go bathe your face before Maggie sees you. She'll think you've had a fate worse than death,' and she nodded, with the ghost of a smile, and went.

'Sorry,' he said as he opened the door, 'we weren't quite ready.' He turned away and lit a cigarette to avoid their eyes.

'Oh, my dear, I know—' Maggie came breezily in. 'There's always something at the last minute!'

Oh, yes, thought Sam, drawing hard on his cigarette, there was always something...He picked up the case from the porch and stowed it in the boot of Arthur's car, and when he came back Maggie was still chattering, fill-

ing the dreadful silence with her voice that went babbling on like water over pebbles. 'Honey,' he called, 'Arthur's waiting,' and she came through from the washroom, her face freshly bathed, her eyes stillborn. She followed Maggie out, not looking back as he locked the door behind her, but their hands caught as she passed and they went out to the car together, their fingers tightly locked under the concealing folds of her coat.

At the station it was much worse.

Honey stood on the platform looking down at the rails, aware that Sam was with her yet not with her, talking of nothing to Maggie, his face a mask. He neither spoke to her nor looked her way. She was reminded of long-ago visits from his ship, when he had chatted with Arthur while she waited unnoticed, forgotten, until at last she could bear it no more and wrenched his face towards her, crying, 'I'm here...' It was like that now. She was cut off from him as if by an ocean.

The station began to fill. People with the expressionless faces of travellers stood about in groups waiting for the train, for the journey, to be able to get on with their lives. She fixed her eyes on the track, her stomach contracted into a tight knot of misery. A piece of dirty paper was blowing along between the lines, where someone had dropped a lemonade bottle. It lay there now, grey and opaque with grime, and the shabby white paper caught on it and stayed feebly flapping, a forlorn little flag of defeat.

A ripple of movement ran along the platform as the lines vibrated to the thunder of approaching wheels. Her mouth dried as she moved forward with the others towards the oncoming train...

Sam was never sure about what happened as the train drew level. Only that his hands flew out involuntarily and snatched her to safety as she lurched towards the edge. Whether she fell or fainted from lack of sleep he could not tell, the deafening roar of the steam engine drowned his question, her answer was muffled, her face buried against his coat. One or two people who had seen gathered around them as the train drew to a halt. 'She overbalanced. It's all right, she's travelling with her aunt,' and they went hurrying off to find their seats.

Maggie fussed, 'What happened, I didn't see?'

'She nearly fell under the train. Don't worry her.' To

155

Honey he said, 'Time to get aboard,' and she turned her ashen face away and walked beside him in search of a place.

He found an empty compartment and installed them in it. Others came after them and claimed seats; they parked luggage in the racks and disappeared to take leave of their friends. Maggie went off to buy something or other, because there were a few minutes to wait and she was by nature incapable of waiting, and they were alone. As alone as one can be in a public place.

Sam stood with one foot on the platform and one in the carriage, effectively blocking the door. 'You won't forget your promise?' She looked away, and in a lowered voice he added anxiously, 'No more aspirins—'

'Don't!' After a pause, 'I'm wearing the watch.' She turned back her coat to show him.

He leaned forward to finger it. 'I wish it was nicer.'

'I don't. I shall wear it always.'

'It might not always go.'

She said, 'I shall keep it always,' and caught at his hand, unable to say more.

He glanced around nervously. 'Someone might see.' He pressed her fingers and drew away. 'When Maggie comes back I shall go. You won't mind if I don't watch your train go out?'

She said, 'No...no, all right,' because you couldn't throw your arms around him and beg him not to go, not on a busy railway station with everyone looking on.

He straightened up. 'I'd better go and hurry her up.'

He slammed the door between them like a guillotine, she was shut away from him, could see only his head and shoulders framed in the window, remote as a photograph. She caught at his sleeve—'Sam!'

He leaned back in through the window, wearing his distant going-away face. For a moment her courage failed her. It was so selfish, what she wanted to say. She ought to be brave, set him free as he had her. But she could not. He waited, while she wrestled with herself; then with a smile that was a mere warming of the eyes he reached for her hand, 'What is it?'

'Don't forget me.' It was all she could say.

'No chance.' His thumb caressed her wrist. 'I know you by heart.' With a quick look behind him, he leaned forward, kissed her cheek, and was gone.

Maggie was still dithering at the bookstall. He picked

up the first magazine that came to hand and thrust it at her. 'Maggie, I've got to go, will you go to Honey now?'

She protested mildly because she didn't understand. There was plenty of time.

'Please, Maggie, do this for me. Go all the way with her, right to the door, don't leave her alone, don't let her hang about on the station the other end—' He broke off. She was looking at him curiously.

He said, 'Get her off the platform quickly,' and left her to think what she would. He fished in his pocket, paid for the magazine. 'Oh—and give her this for me, she's never got one.'

Maggie moved off looking slightly bewildered, a copy of *Playboy* and a square of folded linen in her kid-gloved hand. Beyond her he could see Honey's face, a white blur at the carriage window. He wrenched a smile out of the nothingness inside him and waved an arm to her. Then as the slamming of the doors reverberated along the length of the train, he turned and escaped from the station in a few rapid strides.

Where he went, what he did for the rest of that day, he could not afterwards recall. He arrived at Mango Walk in the evening and stood leaning on the gate, stunned and exhausted as if he had been in a fight. His eyes burned in their sockets, the lids as he closed them were raw from lack of sleep.

A patch of something pale showed up on the grass and with an effort he made out the remains of the bread they had thrown out: a feast for the birds, she said. Watching from the window, her hand warm in his. Now she was in some distant building whose shape he did not know, among strangers he could not visualise. Remembering, perhaps...

He pushed open the gate and walked slowly up the path. The polyanthus roots now wilted where he had left them. Water, came their withered pleading: water, or slow death... You can do without anything—he envied the smug Sam who had once said that. But then, he had only been speaking of cigarettes. On the porch he paused, fumbling for keys with fingers stupid from fatigue, and noticed five bottles of milk standing under the caravan. What in the world had they done with so much milk, he asked himself, stooping to right one which had fallen on its side, and saw Honey, dear and unpractical, wasting

157

as much as they used because she always let it boil over...Tomorrow he would leave a note for the roundsman. Tomorrow...He pushed open the door and was greeted by the odours of stale coffee, brandy, tobacco smoke. The fire had died in the stove, a whisper of ash in a narrow iron coffin. The cups and the bottle still stood on the table; hers would have the imprint of her lip still at the rim. He looked at the debris, the overflowing ashtray, the breadcrumbs and dead matches littering the floor. Tomorrow he would clean up. Tomorrow, tomorrow, tomorrow...

He moved wearily to the bed-place, shrugging off his coat and letting it fall. He sat for a moment looking at nothing, unable even to think. Then he laid his face on the pillow that still smelled faintly of her skin and sank at last into analgesic sleep.

He awoke a few hours later, just before dawn. He struck a match and looked at his watch: it was hardly worthwhile to undress and go to bed. He kicked off his shoes and loosened his belt, then settled back to sleep again, driving a hand up under the pillow out of habit. His fingers encounted a handkerchief screwed into a ball, still damp with tears: he pushed it aside with the thoughts it evoked, and met with the crumpled edges of the leaves of a book.

He drew it out and struck another match. A tattered blue exercise book of the sort she had once used for homework. Something of Honey's...and then he remembered. 'You mustn't ever read it,' she had said, blushing scarlet: 'even if I forget to hide it away. It's a diary. Diaries are sacred, so you mustn't look...'

The book fell open and his own name caught his eye: 'My darling Sam...' He pulled it towards him and read on: 'My darling Sam, who has been as good as—' the last three words were crossed out and replaced with '—better than a father to me all these years, has today discovered that he loves me. His confusion is so touching...'

He lit the lamp and sat up. It was a patchwork of disjointed jottings going back to the year of her banishment, of diary entries, dates of shows, the beginnings of school essays: 'The human spirit, deprived of love, grows grudgingly like a plant without the sun, waiting for the first sharp wind of adversity to cut it down.' Or perhaps she had copied that from somewhere. And there were pages of letters to himself, the sad and loving letters

pleading with him to bring her home, the letters he had expected and which had so abruptly stopped. She had written them instead in a book from the school stores, and only posted to him the polite and cheerful notes she imagined he had wanted to receive.

Through its pages stalked a bent figure with a silver knobbed cane, wearing black with a grey lace shawl to cover her thinning hair: 'We call her Madame Corbeau because she looks like a jackdaw, but not to her face—nobody would dare...' Honey seemed to have lived in dread of this woman, a famous dancer crippled by arthritis whose frustrations were vented on the hapless ankles of her students, her vicious cane falling on Honey's more than most. Something else she had not told him in her letters home. An entry near the end of her spell in France read: 'Sent for to Madame Corbeau. Will never forget what she said. "You are wasting your time and ours; to become a dancer one must be an artist—you are a pussycat, go home and curl up with the man you love." Oh, the scorn in her voice, in her eyes! But if only I could.'

The final entry she must have made last night, at some moment while he was asleep: 'If only you could see, I would rather be wretched with you than safe and comfortable with someone else. But even now I can't make you understand, you're determined to make martyrs of us both.' The page was blotched like the early letters from France, the paper crumpled as if she had pushed it away in despair.

He turned back and read from the beginning and when he had finished he knew the extent of his loss. He was still sitting there with the book in his hands when the sparrows and chaffinches awoke in the hedge, and a half-hearted sunrise tinged the breasts of gulls wheeling hungrily over the strand.

She would not forget easily, as he had persuaded himself. Forget she must; for his own harsh reasons he knew it to be so. But he watered the wilting polyanthus on his way to work.

Ellen was at the bus stop, going to town for her day off. She looked at him tentatively before saying, 'Good morning, Mister Sam.'

'Morning, Ellen.'

'Miss Honey went off then, yesterday?'

'Yes.' Was it really only yesterday? Would his life be made of days as long as this one?

Ellen looked up the road for the bus, saw it was not yet coming. 'Expect you'll be missing her for a while,' she said kindly, 'till you get used to it.'

'Yes,' he repeated, his eyes on the distant trees. So many of them grew and flourished between him and his love.

Ellen fell silent. As the bus rounded the corner she rearranged her belongings and moved a little nearer to the stop. 'Ah, well, Mister Sam, we never know. Perhaps it's all for the best. You being,' she added diffidently, 'a gentleman of colour, as you might say.'

Sam stood still where she had left him, watching the bus drive away that should have carried him to the station. He had lived so quietly all these years, kept himself to himself, been careful to offend nobody. Yet now, when the chips were down, in came the knife...

At last he began to walk in the direction of the town. *Gentleman of colour, gentleman of colour* drummed his tramping feet along the road. It was the first time anyone in the village had said it to his face.

PART THREE

❖❖❖❖

The Foggy Dew

The only, thing I did that was wrong
Was to keep her from the foggy, foggy dew.

I

'What's the matter with Sam these days?' Maggie Colby asked her husband. 'He looks about ten years older.'

It was true. The lively sense of fun which had characterised him seemed to have died, leaving him stolid and grey-faced. 'Smoking too much,' suggested Arthur, but he knew it was not the whole answer. He suspected that in some mysterious way Sam had set himself to grow old, as if he felt life had let him down and had turned his back on it. One sensed that something vital had gone from his life taking the best of him with it. Not that girl, thought Arthur, not still that damned girl! It had been such a struggle to bolt that stable door, he could not entertain the thought that the horse was gone. Yet he could see no explanation for the change in Sam. Not that they saw much of him these days: since the disaster of Christmas when dragged to their house he had sat like a log throughout the festivities and finally retired with a skinful, he had kept out of their way. Of course that could have been due to the Colonel's presence on that

occasion, since for no good reason that Arthur knew of there was clear hostility between them. He compressed his lips. If the colour of Sam's skin was the problem the old warhorse could damned well take his prejudice elsewhere!

The next time he saw Sam on the road he hailed him as usual and pulled in a little ahead. As he drew level he opened the passenger door. 'Hop in. Only two more calls and I'm free, then we can go home. Maggie's been wondering where you'd buried yourself.' It was not perhaps the best chosen phrase. As the other man hesitated, too obviously casting about for an excuse, he added with a touch of impatience, 'Come on, no alibis, there's no one waiting for you.' He shot a searching glance at Sam, who said 'No' very quietly and got in and closed the door.

Colby put the car up through the gears. 'I was watching you coming along the road. You were walking with the cares of the world on your shoulders, head down, chin on your knees, what's the trouble?'

'No trouble,' said Sam. And added with chilling politeness, 'Thank you.'

'You haven't been teasing the natives?' No answering spark of amusement. 'Bad news from home, perhaps?'

'Home?' A faint frown of perplexity. 'Oh...no.'

'From Honey, then?' Again the watchful glance. Again the unreadable profile, the bald flat 'No'.

Arthur tried again, 'Don't burn much midnight oil these days, do you? I passed by the other evening about nine, you were all in darkness. But maybe you were out.'

'Not so young any more,' said Sam, 'I go to bed.'

Arthur made a last determined effort. 'Look here, Sam, this is not like you. You don't even work in your garden, it's knee-high with weeds. It's not normal for a chap like you to shut himself away and not see anyone. You don't go out, you never meet a pal. Good God, man, isn't it lonely?'

Sam said simply, 'I prefer it that way.'

They were passing the lane to Mango Walk. Arthur stopped the car. 'If that's how you feel there's very little point in your coming any further—'

'None whatever,' agreed Sam, and got out and shut the door. 'Goodnight, Arthur,' he said equably, looking in through the window, 'thanks for the lift. And give my regards to Maggie.' And he moved off with his long-legged stride down the lane.

Oh, Hell, thought Arthur, foolishly sitting there, Hell, Hell, Hell...He was left with nothing to do but drive away. Which he did, profoundly troubled on his friend's behalf.

Sam let himself in and sat staring moodily out of the window. The fire was out, the inside of the wagon chilly and uninviting. He was sorry to have dealt roughly with Arthur. He was a friend, after all—perhaps the only one. It was only his taste for vivisection that was the trouble, he had felt he could not do with it tonight.

He had been right about the garden, though, it was a mess. Better turn it back to grass, leave only the shrubs. In the failing light he could just make out the shape of the winter cherry Honey had given him, so young it had just two branches, one nearly vertical, the other at right angles to its trunk. 'Like a dancer with her arms in Second Position' she had laughed, slipping gracefully into the pose to show him. She had walked with it the two miles from the nursery to surprise him, arriving pink-faced and breathless, her sandals dusty and clothes shedding peat. 'It'll bloom for you every Christmas.' She had shyly turned towards him the card that read 'To Sam with love'. He still had that card. Not Arthur nor anyone else could take it from him.

He ought to move away, he told himself with a sigh. The gipsies burned a woman's wagon when she died and he began to see that they were right. It was too close, too intimate, like her clothes; to live in it was unbearable—to abandon it to strangers unthinkable. They burned it, and that was that. But while Honey was alive, he could not destroy it. And anyway, he had nowhere else to go.

So there was nothing to be done after all. He knew that. He knew it every time he came home tired and cold and missing her more than usual. He always decided to move away—and always stayed where he was. Maybe some day he would live it down, would see the wind stir the marram across the dunes without a dancing shadow running before it; time would write his own name on Mango Walk, if he could wait until he was old enough——and tired enough—God send that day...

Time passed while he sat inert upon the window seat, gazing from darkness into darkness. He was cold. He must pull himself together and light a fire...in a minute. He huddled into his damp duffel coat and thrust his hands deep into his pockets, finding emptiness where this

morning her letter had been. It had lain there for almost a week. A small thing she had warmed and touched, curled scroll-shaped by the heat of his own hand. He always kept them a little while before he sent them back.

He turned his thoughts to the coffee he would presently make, savouring its fragrance, the glow of comfort it would bring to his empty body. As he mentally found the matches and lit the gas, his eyelids drooped... he awoke with a jerk as his head fell forward. He propped it against the window frame and drifted off again, his thoughts weaving in and out, over and under as if they were plaiting hair... the way she plaited her hair before swimming, threading the ends back into it like the tail of a horse on Mayday... sitting in her dressing-gown under the lamplight, rosy and moist from the sea with the aromatic steam from the coffee rising up between them. 'Why didn't you read my letter? I told you I was coming...' He, reaching across the table, clumsily—'Ah, Honey'—and she, smiling, 'I'll be here any minute— what's that knocking? Go and let me in...' Then retreating, her smile fading as the room grew darker; his hands finding nothing, eyes seared by lightning as thunder crashed and rumbled overhead... thinking, She's run into the rain again, run away to cry... 'Honey—come back...' and her answer not reaching him, distant and desolate as the cry of a gull on the wind—fear seizing him, nameless and dreadful—'Come back—come back!'... His own voice woke him. The thunder resolved itself into the banging of the knocker. He was alone in a darkness filled with the clamour on the door.

He gained his feet still drunk with sleep, staggered to the door and flung it wide. He stood reeling, wild-eyed, slashed to the bone by an icy wind, trapped and dazzled by the lights of a turning car. He put up his hands to shield his eyes.

'Why, Sam, my dear, whatever is the matter?'

With a plunge of disappointment he saw that it was only Maggie.

She had come, she said, with a message. Honey was worried about him... or maybe it was her... or was it Arthur? He was dazed and unable to take in what she said. He stared at her stupidly and moved aside to let her in, trying to bring his senses into focus. He fumbled vaguely with matches with his stiff cold hands. Maggie sniffed surreptitiously as she passed and it came to him

that she thought he had been drinking. He grinned sheepishly. 'I was just asleep,' he assured her.

'Just so, just so,' she said, anxious to cover her mistake, 'but it's nice to see that smile again—I began to think yon lassie had taken it with her.'

He squirmed at her want of tact and wished her dead. But he had to forgive her. With Maggie there was no dissembling, she said whatever came into her mind, and no barriers to friendship sprang up as a result; if she was tactless it was because she was not censorious; her own blameless life she felt to be a matter more of good luck than special virtue, and if others fell from grace, so might she, given similar trials. Her affection for backsliders continued undiminished and her idols never fell because she made none.

'I miss her, naturally,' he admitted. She patted him vaguely and proceeded to light the lamp. She pulled off his damp coat and told him briskly to get the fire going while she prepared a meal.

'You've not much in the house,' she accused him, raking through cupboards in search of food.

'I mostly eat out,' he evaded, bending to the stove and attacking it with vigour.

'And what have you had today?'

'Oh...something. I forget.'

She clicked her tongue disbelievingly and he grinned. 'Give me up, Maggie.'

She clicked again, exasperated. 'I do believe you're living on nothing but endless cups of coffee!'

'I'm addicted,' he teased her, 'if I don't get my fix I go into withdrawal symptoms.'

As always, she took him seriously. 'Och, Sam, you must eat proper food—what on earth are you trying to do?'

'Nothing,' he said mildly, and went out to get firewood, leaving her to shake her head over him. He heard her retort, 'Just so, you're plain not trying!' and when he came back she had found eggs and was making an omelette. Butter sizzled in the pan on one gas-ring while the kettle sang on the other, and soon the crackle of the kindling fire added its small bright voice. Rain was still falling in sheets outside, driven in rivers across the caravan windows by the gale that was getting up, drumming on the roof while the bulkheads creaked in protest as the buffeting gathered strength. But the weather no longer

165

seeped in to dampen his spirits as it had before. Perhaps it was Maggie who was keeping it at bay. It used to be always like this: the warmth, the comfort—and something else, the thing which translates a mere commodity into terms of personal experience. Reason reminded him that he could do all these things for himself; could cook, make coffee, light a fire...but it was not the same. Even Maggie's presence evoked only an echo of how it had been. Perhaps without Honey it would never be the same; dread stirred in him as he glimpsed a loneliness that stretched through unseen years to the ends of life. He squatted staring into the fire, bleakly aware that it did not burn for him: it merely burned.

Something of what he was feeling communicated itself to Maggie standing behind him at the omelette pan. She looked down at the powerful curve of his back, the dejected droop of head and wrists, and thought inconsequentially, Poor tiger...

She laid a hand on his shoulder. 'Sam, my dear, is it always this bad with you?'

Sam clasped his hands together and looked down at them for a moment before he spoke. 'No, not always. I had another letter from Honey.'

'Oh, not bad news, I hope?' she said quickly, her cosy face anxious.

Sam looked up in concern. 'I wouldn't know, I didn't think of that. I sent it back like always.'

'Like always?' repeated Maggie faintly. 'You mean you don't read them—not ever?'

'Not ever. Like Arthur said, it's better for her that way. And he's keeping an eye on her, he promised.' Doubt drew his eyebrows together. 'He is, isn't he?'

'Of course, of course.' Maggie's tone lacked conviction. 'She's just fine and doing well with her studies, don't fret yourself—'

'Then why did you ask me if I'd had bad news?'

'It was the way you were looking, nothing more—now, come away to your food while it's hot. Once an omelette goes cold you can sole your boots with it.'

He insisted that she share the omelette, and afterwards they chatted over the cigarettes she had found concealed behind the coffee tin. She had also found a near-empty rum bottle.

'You've not a full one hidden away?' She sounded quite serious.

Shamed by his Christmas performance, he said stiffly, 'I don't drink alone. Coffee's my vice, like I told you.'

Maggie said soothingly, 'There now, don't take it to heart, it's only your health I'm concerned with.' When he did not respond she added, 'Now, you know we'd think no less of you if you did.'

'Arthur would. I have to be perfect for him—not just all right, perfect. Honey tried to tell me that and I wouldn't believe her. I had to learn the hard way.'

They found little more to say. A constraint had fallen on their conversation. Sam watched her furtively through the haze of tobacco smoke and wondered how much she really knew. She would have had to be blind that day at the station not to have guessed the way things stood. Looking back he saw that it must have been written on them both like a neon sign...Honey with her taut white face, her eyes full of pain...and the thing that had nearly happened on the platform, the thing so awful that whenever he remembered it the train loomed nearer and larger than before. Always the thought of it set him nervously pacing...maybe he should have told Maggie, told someone...

He saw her regarding him speculatively and realised that he had stubbed out the cigarette he had just lit. Not only stubbed it but broken, split, reduced it to fragments. It lay in the ashtray like a tiny haystack ripped to bits by a storm. He said a shade too quickly, 'Smoking too much, I can do without that one,' and Maggie smiled in answer and began to collect up the plates.

He took them from her hands—'I'll do them later'—and set the kettle on the stove, and Maggie began her elaborate ritual of leaving. It never varied and was seemingly indispensable: nose to be powdered, hair to be arranged, hat set on at precisely the proper angle. And all, thought Sam with amusement, for a walk through the darkened village in a downpour. Maggie was very feminine. And nice. But he did not want to tell her about the train, or any of it. Not Maggie or anyone else. His personal feeling for Honey was his own. He did not want to share it.

'Can you lend me a torch, Sam?'

'Torch, nothing, I'm coming with you.'

Characteristically, she began to fuss: his coat was not dry, there was no need...He banked the fire and picked up his coat and she was right, it was not dry. He put it

on without comment and waited while she searched for her gloves. When at last she was ready she stood waiting, like a Pope, he thought, about to give audience. Some devilment prompted him to say 'Got everything?' to see the small panic produced in her by doubt. As they were going through the door she turned to him an anxious face, 'Have you got your door key?' He jingled the bunch in his pocket and teased her, 'What do you think I do when you're not here?'

'I know very well what you do when I'm not here!' retorted Maggie.

They trudged in silence up through the lanes, the cold rain stinging their faces, their ankles assailed by puddles. At her gate he halted, remembering that Arthur was within. 'I'll get back now, Maggie, before I get any wetter.' He smiled disarmingly under his battered old cap.

Maggie stood looking up at him in the reflected light from the house and thought she saw something of what Honey had seen. She felt a deep surge of affection for him, of compassion for his lonely existence, and impulsively reached up to kiss his cheek. But at the last moment she drew back, abashed. He was too young, too male, his eyes too darkly eloquent for the peace of even her matronly breast. Suddenly shy and awkward as a schoolgirl, she drew back. Then, in dread of hurting his feelings, she made a clumsy dab at his face with her gloved hand and turned away quickly. 'Aye, aye, well off you go then before you catch pneumonia. I think Honey would never forgive me if I let you do that.'

He did not answer. When she looked back from the porch he was still standing there, watching her with a face that said nothing.

'Away with you, now,' she said gently with a little shooing gesture, and he raised a hand and turned away, swallowed at once by the whispering rain-wet darkness.

Maggie saw him go with a heavy heart. She was angry with herself, knowing that she had increased his burden of rejection when she had most wanted to lighten it. She had tried and made a mess of it, which was worse than not having tried. Had she lived these fifty years and not learned how to help another human being without she must blush and turn coy because he was a man? Had she not brought herself yet to feel the way she looked: stout and middle-aged and maternal—it came to her with a shock that Sam was only a few years younger than herself.

Somehow he lacked the serenity one hoped to achieve with middle age. It was as if he were still lost at the beginnings of life, still troubled as the young are troubled, still searching for the answer to his need...but perhaps he had found an answer, and had to accept that it was not for him? A bitter lesson at any age: cruel at forty-three. And Honey. She remembered her last words before she left her at the hospital: 'Look after Sam for me, don't let him be lonely—' She had turned her face away as the smile fell apart. Poor Honey...poor wee thing.

It was of Sam she was thinking as she fitted her key into the lock. How ironic to be condemned to loneliness—not because you were lacking in charm, but because you were too attractive!

Sam plodded back between the dark hedgerows, his sodden coat a cold plaster across his shoulders. He could feel the water beginning to ooze from it and run down the channel between his shoulder blades. He watched the trickle of water falling past his face from the peak of his cap, and felt the flesh around his mouth settle back into its habitual mask of silence.

It had been good to see Maggie. She had been friendly and kind; she had almost kissed him good night—why not quite? His mind veered away from the old chewed-over question—not Maggie, so sane and sensible and kind? Yes, kind...and that was it. She had put too much weight on that kindness and it had cracked and let her fall. At the moment of contact she had quailed, and had to look away...

He reached home at last and put his clothes to steam before the fire, and then stood for a long time with his hands plunged up to the wrists in the bowl of hot water he had prepared for the dishes, listening to the crackle of the fire and the faint ticking of collapsing suds. He thought of Honey's letter, and the odd look that had flitted across Maggie's face when he had told her about sending it back unread: maybe if she wrote again he ought to open it, just in case. But there was another reason that held him back. It was more than pride that prevented his asking Arthur for news. He did not want to be told when Honey found her new man. He could accept it because he wanted her happiness...but only if he did not have to watch.

He raised a hand flecked with irridescent bubbles and examined his finger pads, ridged and runnelled like the

bed of the sea. How long did it take for immersion to do that, half an hour, an hour? Maybe longer. He had stood there all that time letting the water grow cold. Now he would have to wait for the kettle again...

Not that it mattered. So much of what he did was just killing time.

'I'll want to see you again in about a week.' Arthur filled in his findings on the record card. The patient nodded, buttoning his shirt.

They both looked up at the sound of a commotion in the hall outside.

'But you can't, you can't go in! He's got a patient—'

'I don't care if he's got fifty patients—'

'Excuse me,' said Arthur, recognising the voice. He came out from behind his desk and reached the door just as it burst open.

'What the Hell's this mean—"Gone Away", it says—she's not at the hospital. Where is she, Arthur? What have you done with her?' Sam waved the envelope clutched in his hand under Arthur's nose. Arthur bundled him out of the surgery and closed the door behind them. 'For God's sake keep your voice down, I tell you she's all right.'

'So why don't they know where she is? Why has it come back?'

'I suppose because she didn't leave an address—'

'But you know where she is. Come on, where is she? I have a right to know!' Arthur did not answer. Sam went on. 'Come on, you have to understand—I'm not going up there, I just want to know where she is.'

Arthur lowered his voice. 'I thought you weren't going to write,' he said accusingly. 'Look, I have a patient waiting in there, you'd better see Maggie about this. Maggie!' he called through the living-room door. Maggie emerged looking flustered. 'Sam wants to know where Honey is, give him her address, will you?'

Maggie looked bewildered. 'Her address? Why, is she not at the hospital?'

'Well, you should know, you've been keeping in touch with her.' Arthur turned to go. Then turned back again. 'Haven't you?'

'Well, I—' She turned pink. 'I wrote once—twice I believe—but she didn't answer.' She turned helplessly to Sam. 'I thought you were...' she offered weakly.

Sam looked from one to the other, his eyes cold as jet. 'You mean nobody has?' he said evenly. 'And now nobody knows where she is?' He unleashed his voice suddenly like a blast of gunfire, 'Sweet Jesus, you're supposed to be looking after her!' He lunged towards the door.

Maggie caught at his sleeve. 'Where are you going?'

'I'm going to find her, that's what! And if I don't, so help me I'm coming back here—' he thrust an aggressive finger towards Arthur—'and I'll be looking for him!'

Back in the caravan he moved fast. He stuffed a clean shirt and underpants, two pairs of socks, razor and toothbrush into a duffel-bag and pushed his Post Office Savings book down the side. He raked out the fire, made fast the windows and went through the cupboards, throwing away perishable food. He had no idea how long he might be away. He was going to find Honey and it would take as long as it took.

He locked the door, stowed the buckets and padlocked the pan-box. Then he set off into the night. There was no one waiting at the bus stop so he set out to walk the seven miles to Southcombe, where with luck he could catch a train to London. But even had he known that a bus was due he could not have brought himself to stand and wait. The scourge of anxiety drove him forward, his legs eating up the miles, Honey's letter in his pocket now curled into a tight tube by the heat of his clenching hand.

It had wandered around the various blocks in which the hospital was housed for three weeks before it was returned to him. What he had not told Arthur was that it was marked not only 'Gone Away, No Address' but also, and in older ink, 'Try Maternity'.

2

'Tip-tap...tip-tap...' whispered the blind-cord against the carriage window. 'Fiddley-dee, fiddley-da, fiddley-

dee, fiddley-da,' muttered the joints in the track as the rails kissed the wheels and streamed away lost in the endless night behind them.

Sam stirred restlessly as his head dropped with a jerk. Sleep on the train, he had told himself; wake up fresh for the search ahead. But he could not. Although tired from the long tramp, only his body relaxed. His mind, still savage, ran in endless circles, dipping him into brief confusions of dreams only to rouse up and run on again in pursuit of unanswerable questions. He sighed, his forehead against the clouded glass, and his breath disturbed particles of soot on the window-frame and set them dancing.

He had the compartment to himself. He got up and paced the short space trying to ease the panic knot in his stomach. He slid open the door and walked up and down the corridor, conscious of the angry looks of other passengers who were trying to sleep. He retreated again into his own small area of hell and closed the door.

When the train pulled into Paddington in the damp chill of early morning, he opened startled eyes on the face of a small man with the bright eyes of a terrier under a peaked railway cap, who was roughly shaking his shoulder.

'All change here!' he was barking. 'Come on, son, you got to get off!'

Sam staggered to his feet, groped for his duffel-bag. The bright eyes turned shrewd. 'That all you've got? Want your winter woolies here, you know, this isn't Darkest Africa.'

Sam stumbled out on to the platform and stood rubbing bleary eyes. 'Yeah,' he said through a yawn, 'it's all I've got.' He fumbled through his pockets and produced his ticket, swaying a little from fatigue.

'Barrier,' said the other with a jerk of his thumb. 'Single, eh? Got somewhere to stay?'

Sam shook his head. The thought had not crossed his mind.

'Blimey—another one! All the bloody same, come here with nowhere to go, nothing in your pockets. No—'as Sam noticed a seat and moved towards it—'you keep going, you can't sleep on the station!'

'I didn't come here to sleep!' said Sam, irritated. 'Haven't just stepped off the boat, either. I've come to—I'm on business.'

172

The man caught the hesitation and laughed derisively. 'Here, Stan!' he called along the platform. 'Got one here, says he's on business—haven't heard that one before!' As he shouldered his duffel-bag and moved off Sam heard a shout follow him, 'Try the Sally Army, they'll take anybody.'

Beyond the barrier a woman in stiletto heels and a cartwheel hat stood besieged by suitcases and a pair of excited toy poodles on a twin-leash, alternately shouting 'Down!' to the poodles and 'Porter!' to the unresponsive air. Instinctively, Sam picked up the cases. 'Where you want to go?' he asked her.

'Taxi,' she said shortly, and tugging at the entangling leads she hurried after him into the street. On the pavement's edge he hailed a passing cab and was mildly surprised to see it promptly respond, then he realised that she was also hailing it. He saw her into it complete with bouncing poodles, handed in her luggage and turned to go.

'Just a minute!' She was leaning, hand extended, through the window; offering to shake hands? There was no smile, only an expression of faint impatience. She pushed the hand towards him; slowly he raised his...

'You really should wear uniform,' she said disapprovingly. And then the taxi had driven away and he was left on the pavement, staring at the sixpence in his palm.

For a moment he frowned, still confused and dull with sleep. Then a watery sunbeam found its way between the tall buildings to brighten the coin in his hand. He laughed, tossed it up and caught it, and dropped it into his pocket. Perhaps it was a sign of good luck.

He checked again the address of the hospital and moved off into the frowsy bustle of London's waking and scratching. A homing cat, moth-eaten and soot-grimed, streaked purposefully across the pavement, tail down, feet twinkling, to disappear through a grating into some underworld of its own. Pigeons pecked and bobbed about the broken shoes of an old woman who with grimy hands was feeding them crumbs from a tattered paper bag. They erupted before his feet as he approached, spraying upwards through the morning haze like the bow-wave of a ship. Overhead, starlings squabbled and chattered, shrieking shrill as costermongers against the growing grind of the traffic.

From an imposing hotel on his right came a rich scent

of coffee, and he was tempted—he could look for a coffee bar, even a roadside stall . . . but he did not know this part of London. He walked on, down to a T-junction with a broad street of unopened shops and littered pavements. 'Praed Street' read the sign, but it meant little to him. He stood for a moment undecided. Then he saw the underground symbol and headed for it.

In the train tunnelling energetically under London's streets he felt a growing confidence. He was heading towards the hospital, on the last lap of his quest. Someone there would know what had happened to Honey, would at least be able to tell him where she had gone. He was going to find her, nothing would deflect him from that; what happened then was in the lap of the gods, but one thing was certain, he was through with listening to Arthur. He had tried it his way and the result had been this mess. Owing Arthur so much, he had felt obligated, compelled to respect his wishes, accept his advice. But in trying to save Honey he had cast her adrift—and now . . . he hardly dared to think. He could not be sure that his way would be any better; unable to marry her he had so little to offer. But he could find her, scratch up some sort of a home—and he could *care*. Which was what Arthur couldn't. Or didn't . . . but maybe that was unfair. Keeping a watch on the Underground map on the opposite bulkhead for the station at which he must change trains, his attention was caught by an advertisement: 'How you feel tomorrow depends on what you do tonight!' But it was only trying to sell him Beecham's Pills.

He moved on to the back of a newspaper read by the passenger opposite. He managed to catch a line or two between movements of the train. 'AMERICA OFFERS PILOTS IF EGYPT WILL OPEN SUEZ!' He suppressed a smile; they wouldn't know if they were up the Suez Canal or on the Goodwins. The next one sobered him: 'RACIAL TENSION MOUNTS IN NOTTING HILL.' With Honey alone in London . . . The rasp was at his nerves again, and by the time he reached his destination his cheerfulness had evaporated.

He took the stairs two at a time and asked directions at the ticket barrier.

'Over there, man,' the collector waved an arm between customers, 'can't you read?'

Sam looked. On the pavement outside a street market was setting up, fruit stalls, racks of clothing, cheap jew-

ellery and hopping fur toys on leads appearing from no-where, each taking its appointed place. Directly in front of him two women were expertly rigging a canopy over a stall, and behind them, on the far side of a road already teeming with every kind of vehicle, he saw the hospital.

It was vast. It towered, blackened and forbidding, rank upon rank of identical windows rising floor after floor, occupying a whole block, approached by a flight of steps and a porticoed entrance in which a woman with a chair and a basket was preparing to sell flowers.

Sam's heart sank. He had not envisaged anything on quite this scale. He had been imagining something like the cottage hospital near home, or even the City Infirmary where he had recovered from his ducking. A place where the lodge porter knew all the staff, their life histories and their family connections. This was something different altogether, and he realised now that he should have been prepared for it, should have known that in such a place one might come and go and not even be remembered. Well, it was too late now. He might as well push on.

On a nearby stall a record-player brayed above the roar of the traffic:

'Che sera, sera! Whatever will be, will be...
The future's not ours to see...Che sera, sera...'

He took a deep breath and forged through the rush hour crowd to escape from the station. He looked both ways before crossing the road. No point in throwing his life away at this juncture, it would be a waste of effort. Maybe the effort was wasted anyway—maybe she had already been discharged, had gone and taken the baby with her. Maybe this whole thing was a wild goose chase on his part. But he had to know. He could not just sit and worry.

He hurried up the steps and in through the swinging doors—and stopped. He was in an entrance hall of intim-idating proportions, a place of entrances and exits, of seats and signs—but none of them said 'Maternity'. He looked around for a porter's desk but he could not see one. The place seemed thronged with people coming and going on secret missions of the utmost urgency, who passed and repassed him as if he were not there. He stood like a fool, not knowing what to do now that he was here.

Two nurses, one sandy-haired and one dark, walked

by him, cloaked and chattering on on their way to the street. He stepped forward, 'Can you tell me—'

They paused in their flight. 'No visiting yet, dear, not till much later. Come back this afternoon.'

'No,' he said, 'you don't understand, I want to find Maternity.' They exchanged smiles that said, 'Another anxious father.' 'When did she come in, during the night?'

'I don't know, not exactly. I've come a long way.' It didn't sound convincing. They couldn't have thought so either for the sandy-haired one said, 'But you are the father?'

'I'm—related,' he said.

'But not the father? You see, only fathers can visit. It's the rule.'

'But I could find out about her,' he persisted, 'if she's here. That's right, isn't it?'

The girl looked doubtful. 'Are you sure you're a relative? You don't seem to know much about her.'

'Yes, I'm sure,' he said hastily. 'Just tell me where to find Maternity, I'll manage.'

The other girl stepped forward. 'Look, I'll show you, you never find it on your own, it's in another building,' and taking his arm she steered him towards the doors. Outside in the street she giggled richly. 'What happen, man, you nine month late with the wedding?' Her voice was as Jamaican as rum.

Sam found himself smiling. 'Something like that,' he admitted. 'What do I have to say to make them talk?'

'You just make like you related some way. She your woman?'

Instead of answering, he said, 'It's been a long time. I only just heard.'

Another peal of laughter. 'Oh, score! Better not say you she husband—she maybe catch another one by now.'

Sam stopped walking.

'Hey, man—you all right?' His companion turned to look back. 'You not looking so good, like you been up all night. Why you don't come in here, have some coffee, think the whole thing out 'fore you go busting in there?'

She drew him towards the doorway of a sleazy little café and he followed unresisting to sink down at an oil-cloth covered table ringmarked by hot cups. She quickly joined him with two cups of coffee and a boxed fruit pie. Sam dropped his head on his hands. 'I never thought of that,' he mumbled, 'Jesus, I never thought of that.'

She sat down opposite and pushed a cup towards him. 'Here, drink it hot, warm your belly. Look, me only joking—she like you, she don't marry someone else. You her man, she wait for you—I would.' Her broad brown face was troubled, he felt sorry for her as she went on. 'My Mama always tell I should mind me own business. Look, you don't want me go chop out me tongue, you better start smiling quick!'

He wanted to tell her not to feel bad, that she didn't have to mind her own business, that he was glad of her concern...he felt an overwhelming urge to talk to her, to confide in someone, to listen to advice, be it good or bad. But he had kept his own counsel so long he no longer knew how. He said with difficulty, 'It's all right, I should have thought of it myself. It's good you said it—really.' He took a long swig of the scalding, tasteless liquid. 'But it's like you say, I can't just go busting in there.' He found his cigarettes, lit one, pushed the packet towards her. 'And I've got to know. I've just got to know.' His knuckles drove hard into the palm of the other hand. 'I can't go away not knowing.'

The cigarettes were pushed back towards him with a fat brown hand. 'Look—I'm off duty, I go in there and find out for you. They maybe tell me what they don't tell you.'

Sam looked up, startled. Warmth from strangers, once so familiar, now took him by surprise, so long had he lived without it. She went on, 'Tell me her name and I'll ask. Then you wait here till me come back.'

'McLeod,' he said, 'the name's McLeod, same as mine.' He spelt it out for her and added, 'She's young, about nineteen.'

She looked at him a little oddly then. But she said, 'Don't go away,' and smiled, and went.

Two nerve-racked cigarettes later, she was back. 'Sorry.' She sat down at the table. 'Nobody that name in the last six months. Only a nurse, but she left a month ago. Anyway she not one of us.'

Sam stared...a nurse! But of course—a nurse! 'Try Maternity.' Yes—but not to have a baby, just to work there! He jumped up eagerly. 'That's it, that's her!'

'Hey, what you saying, man, you playing games with me? You saying—'

'I know what I said, I'm crazy, I was wrong! Look, did she leave an address?'

'I don't ask.' The warmth had gone out like a light. 'Like I telling you, she not one of us. So I not asking. And you don't go bustin' in there, not if you got any sense—people thinking you halfways decent, let them think it!'

With an angry rustle of starch she marched out, slamming the door behind her.

Sam stayed where she had left him, his head spinning in the wild conflict of relief that his worst fears were groundless and a new misgiving: that Honey had vanished into the wilderness of London, and now no one could trace her, no matter what. Should he push on, go to the Maternity Unit himself, ask for her forwarding address, insist? Even supposing she had left one—and she might well have left without, she had made no friends at the ballet school, maybe she had made none here either—if he did, would they give it to him? He knew they would not. They would no more accept than the nurse had that he had any right to demand it. He lit his last cigarette and drew deeply on it, trying to clear his mind.

A movement behind the counter caught his attention. A round man in a greasy apron, entrenched behind a stack of wilting crisps and an orange-cooler with three distinct tide-marks, was wiping down the counter with a grubby tea-towel. He eyed Sam with disfavour. 'You having anything else?'

Sam sighed, recognising the signs. 'Ten Gold Leaf,' he said, and got up, shouldering his bag.

'One and fivepence halfpenny. Haven't you got anything smaller?' He looked sourly at the proffered ten shilling note. While Sam scoured his pockets to produce a shilling and a sixpence, he added, 'All right for some, nothing to do in the middle of the morning but sit about spending the dole on cigarettes. It's us poor buggers has to work to keep you lot!' He slapped down the halfpenny change with a belligerent glare.

Sam regarded him evenly. Then with deliberation he took a box of matches from the rack by the till and pushed it towards him with the ten shilling note. 'Sorry,' he said pleasantly, 'it's all I've got.'

Outside in the street, his moment of satisfaction behind him, his spirits drooped again. Further along the road on the opposite side he could see the Maternity Block. To his eyes it had 'Dead End' written all over it. Yet, he could not bring himself to give up, having come so far. He walked slowly towards it, peering at its win-

dows as if he hoped to find an answer there. But he did not. He walked on and past it, and then turned and walked back again, gnawing his lip and trying to think what to do. And again...he took out her letter and read it again, the brief note that had so disturbed him. 'I can't take any more, please forgive me. Honey.'

He failed to notice how long he had been walking up and down until a rough hand grasped his coat collar.

'Right, son—no arguments! Just get in the car.'

3

Jane Fisher pushed back her plate. 'What did you say?'

The others exchanged glances across the canteen table. Nurse Fisher, busybodying as usual.

Jill said, 'There was a man picked up outside the Maternity Block this morning.' And got up to go.

'No—hang on a minute.' Jane smiled blandly, aware that Jill did not welcome her interruption but undaunted by her chilling look. It took a great deal more than that to daunt Jane.

The daughter of a country parson, she had grown up in large untidy vicarages half-furnished and smelling of cabbage, her life regulated by matins and evensong in the confident expectation that she would grow up to be a missionary. She had suffered her family's exhortations with equanimity and when the time came to enter the theological college had said No: she was going to be a nurse, which she felt to be more useful. She had watched her father grow old and disheartened, his valour worn thin by people who, in his own words, 'bowed to Heaven on Sunday and danced with the Devil through the week'. Jane had smiled at his turn of phrase but she knew what he meant: she too had no time for churchgoers who trampled their neighbours when it suited them. Besides

which, Jane had fallen for a Malayan student, a Buddhist, and was not convinced that she ought to ask him to exchange his religion for hers. Shocked by this double rebellion her parents had taken up a panic stand: they had refused to consider the match and forbidden her to see him. Jane, unruffled, had bidden them a smiling goodbye on her eighteenth birthday and signed on as a probationer. In her third year, still working with an earnest dedication, she had found herself sharing a room in the Nurses' Home with a strange unhappy girl whose withdrawn expression had disturbed her; a girl who cried quietly at night when she thought no one heard, yet who fended off sympathetic probing with forced smiles and assurances that she was all right, really...Jane had not believed a word, and when she had suddenly disappeared a month ago was deeply concerned. Now she said, pleasantly but firmly, 'I thought you mentioned Nurse McLeod?'

With exaggerated patience Jill sat down again. 'A man came to Maternity this morning asking about a patient called McLeod, said he was a relative. At least he didn't, Topsy did. She said he was coloured and afraid to ask himself. Anyway, she went back and told him there was no one there by that name and next we heard he'd been picked up by the police.'

'Why, what was he doing?'

'How should I know? He'd been pacing up and down outside for God knows how long, I suppose someone got nervous and rang them—after all, the Pharmacy's in the same block. Anyway, they came and took him away. Satisfied?'

Jane coloured. But she was not to be put off. 'Not really. I don't see how you can be sure it was the same man.'

'Topsy should know, she was talking to him. If you're so interested why don't you go and ask her?'

Jane hesitated, looking down the crowded canteen to where one dark face stood out among the others. 'That's not really her name, is it?'

Jill shrugged. 'How should I know?' she said again. 'I mind my own business. Not like some I could mention...'

Topsy was as usual sitting alone; she did not look up as Jane drew up a chair.

'Sorry to disturb your lunch, but I heard there was

someone looking for Nurse McLeod. They said you spoke to him?'

The other girl looked defensive. 'Didn't say no Nurse McLeod. Said *his* name McLeod, he looking for a patient. Maybe not the same gal.'

'Oh,' Jane sank down, disappointed. 'Are you sure about that?'

'Sure I'm sure. What he want with no fancy white nurse, brown-skin man like him?'

Jane sighed. 'I see. Well, it must have been somebody else. Only she was a friend of mine, so I hoped... Sorry I bothered you.' She had risen and was moving away when she heard, 'Wait—'

Topsy said reluctantly, 'Look, he say... it could be her. But that's all I telling you—don't want me mix up in any bad thing. I got me own problems, y'know?'

'Of course, thanks anyway. And I won't remember who told me.'

She glanced at her watch. Half past one. At two she was down at the Police Station.

A man was standing on the steps outside, dabbing blood from a broken lip. A dark man, West Indian perhaps. He looked weary and bewildered, searching his pockets as if for cigarettes. After a moment he gave up, glanced at her as though he might speak and apparently had second thoughts. He turned to move off.

Jane hesitated. Suppose he were the wrong man...? Onward, Christian soldiers! Heart pounding, she marched up to him. 'Is your name McLeod? I'm a friend of Honey's.'

'So you don't know either,' he said, as they strolled towards the hospital, 'I was hoping—'

Jane shook her head. 'I thought you might have some idea where she'd go, that's why I came after you.'

'You mean, she didn't leave any address, not even a message.'

'Not a word. I was her room-mate and I didn't even know she was leaving. I suppose Matron knew, must have or there would have been an enquiry. But she didn't tell anyone else, not even me.'

'She didn't leave a note anywhere, in her things maybe?'

'She took everything with her. Just a few sheets of paper torn up in the waste basket. I was worried about her so I picked them out, but I couldn't make any sort of sense out of what I found.'

He drew on his cigarette. 'You say you were worried about her. Why was that?'

'She was so terribly depressed,' said Jane. 'I felt she might do—anything.'

'Did she tell you what about?'

'Well, she didn't like the work. Let's face it, she was never going to be much good. She wasn't cut out for nursing. But it was more than that. There was something in her life, something she wouldn't talk about. And whatever it was was getting worse, not better. I wanted to help her but she was so secretive. You can't help those who won't be helped.'

'No,' the man sighed, his expression withdrawn and unhappy.

'Look,' said Jane anxiously, 'there must be some way of finding her and I really think someone should. No one else is going to bother, isn't there something we can do?'

'Did you save the bits of paper?'

'Yes, but—'

'There just might be something I could pick up that you couldn't. I've known her a long time, since she was a child.'

'Oh—' She stopped, confused by something half-remembered. 'Then I suppose you know her guardian?'

He smiled unexpectedly. 'How did you know I was at the Police Station?'

'I heard at the hospital you'd been picked up, so I just took a chance on your still being there—as it was I nearly missed you.'

'I thought I was there for keeps—they frisked me for drugs, knives, you name it. If it wasn't for my doctor at home I'd still be there on a "sus" charge, they just wouldn't believe a word I said. They even checked his number with Enquiries before they rang him in case I'd invented him—but he must have made the right noises because in the end they boxed my ears and turned me loose.'

'So I see,' said Jane drily. 'Just the same, you'd better get an address in London before they pick you up again. It's different after dark, the law's on their side. Look, meet me here—no, wait, not on the pavement—in that Es-

presso bar, see it? I'll be off duty at seven and I'll bring the papers with me. Maybe we can work something out together. Now I must go.'

He said, 'Thanks for your help, Nurse...'

'Fisher. Jane Fisher. You can call me Jane. Now go and have a meal and get yourself a place to sleep. Try the—'

'I know, the Salvation Army!'

'Right. And I'll see you here at seven.'

She went back to the hospital encouraged by the progress she had made. It was not until long afterwards that she saw how deftly she had been side-tracked.

For the rest of that day Jane found her mind continually sliding away to the problem of her vanished roommate. For some reason she could not define she was uneasy about the man who had come looking for her. Not that she was prejudiced. No one could accuse her of that, but—he was somehow...unlikely. Yes, that was it. If anyone came looking for Honey she would have expected it to be a relation, a woman; or maybe even the guardian she had spoken of so briefly. And this man could hardly be that. Although she knew so little about Honey that almost anything was possible; it struck her that although she had replied frankly to all his questions he had answered none of hers; was she really helping Honey by helping him? By what right did he come looking for her anyway, a man claiming the same surname—which might or might not be his—of whom she knew nothing, who offered no proof of identity, a Negro—but no, that smelled of prejudice, and she pushed the thought away.

She put the scraps of paper into an envelope and made her way to the promised meeting place. But she determined to know more about him before she laid them on the table.

She arrived a few minutes early and secured a corner table and almost at once she saw his face at the door, smiling a greeting across the heads of the crowd.

He made his way over to her, balancing two steaming cups and snaking between the couples, 'Excuse me...excuse me...'

'Getting a bit sunburned around here, aren't we?' a voice said pointedly, 'getting like bloody Nairobi.'

'Got your tot of rum in it, Sambo?' enquired another. His girl friend nudged him and said fiercely 'Shut up!' and he contented himself with chanting mockingly under his breath:

'Take her to Jamaica where de rum come from,
　　　De rum come from, de rum come from...'

Jane felt her neck flush uncomfortably. 'Really! Sometimes my countrymen—'

'It's all right, I'm used to it, I've been here more than
twenty years.' He spoke quickly, soothingly, as if he
wanted to hush her. 'Sugar?' and he pushed it towards
her.

'I'll never get used to it, I don't think people should.
Neither did Honey.'

The black eyes came to attention at the name. 'What
did she say about it?'

'It was funny,' said Jane, 'it was the only time I ever
saw her animated, really alive. She really flew at this
person who said something nasty about a patient who
was—well—like you...'

'You're allowed to say it.' A corner of his mouth
twitched.

'You have to admit it's embarrassing, one is never sure
how people want to be referred to—for instance, you.
Would you rather be called coloured, or Negro, or black?'

'I'd rather be called Sam,' he said, and took a swig of
his coffee. 'Anyway, what was it Honey said?'

'I can't remember all of it, it was quite a diatribe, but
the gist was that people like—like him were the salt of
the earth, the best, the kindest—'

'She must think they're all like me,' he said with a
lightness transparently false. 'Did you bring the papers?'

'Yes, I've got them with me. But I think you should
tell me a little more about yourself before I show them
to you. To start with, who are you?'

'A friend. Like you.'

'Not a relative?'

The hesitation was barely perceptible. 'Not a relative.'

'Yet your name...'

'Sam McLeod,' he affirmed, his eyes watchful.

'I don't recall that she mentioned you,' she said doubtfully, 'for all I know you could be a debt-collector.'

'She didn't talk about me?'

'She hardly talked at all. All I knew was she was
adopted and she couldn't go home, because—' She pulled
herself up short. It was happening again, here she was
obediently giving information without getting anything
back! 'Look here,' she said firmly, 'don't think I'm un-

184

helpful but I want to be sure I'm doing the right thing. Before I give you these papers you'll have to show me one good reason why I should.'

'Can you find her without me?'

Again he had countered with a question but this time she was ready for him. 'But why you? I'm sorry, but you're going to have to tell me why you're here.'

For a moment their eyes locked. Then he said, 'Let's have another coffee. Smoke?'

She sat in angry silence, smoking the proffered cigarette and smarting with defeat. He was not going to tell her. She would have to co-operate blind or else give up.

He came back with two more coffees and sat down; took up the plastic spoon and skimmed some of the froth from his cup. 'Reminds me of something the high tide left behind.' Then, as if he sensed her antipathy, 'Look, I want to tell you something.'

'When I was a boy in Jamaica I had a pet mongoose. Her mother had been killed, she was too young to feed herself—anyhow, I managed to rear her. She'd ride in my pocket, eat out of my hand, I was real proud—but it was wrong.'

'How could it be wrong?' Jane was perplexed, caught up for the moment by the diversion. 'Surely...'

'It was wrong. She'd learned to trust, you see, to trust me and anyone who looked like me. It's dangerous to do that to a wild animal. One day she went missing. Gone to find a mate, my father said, and I tried to believe him. But a few days later I found her beaten to death. The boy who did it thought she was wild, she rushed up to him and he thought she was after his parakeet—so he killed her. It wasn't his fault. But it cut me up because I knew I was to blame.'

'You? But I don't see...'

'Me. Because I'd taken away her natural fear and left her vulnerable.'

After a silence, Jane said, 'I don't quite see what this has to do with Honey.'

'Don't you?' He leaned back, breathed blue smoke down his nostrils. 'I just don't want another mongoose on my conscience.'

Jane said slowly, 'You're not...' She had been about to say, 'You're not her guardian?' But of course that was impossible, such an adoption would never have been sanctioned. She lowered her eyes. 'You're not to blame,'

she said instead, 'the best of intentions backfire sometimes. You can't go through life regretting them, feeling
guilty. It's silly. You can only do what feels right at the
time, and hope.' She pulled out an envelope. 'See what
you can make of this.'

They pieced the fragments of paper together on the
table, trying them this way and that like a jigsaw puzzle.

'Are you sure you've got all of it?' he said.

'All I could see. It seems to be bits of several things,
not even in the same handwriting.'

'Mm-mm. Some of it's hers. Letters and answers,
maybe. But who from?' He mused, lips compressed. 'She
didn't mention looking for a new job?'

'No—but there was an evening paper in the basket
folded at the "want" ads., with some phone numbers
underlined. I rang one or two but they weren't very helpful, said they were looking for dancers, not nurses. They'd
never heard of her. Perhaps it wasn't connected after all,
it could have been someone else's paper thrown away in
our basket.'

'Dancers...you say you rang them, what were they
like, what sort of places?'

Jane searched her memory. 'Night clubs, as far as I
remember. One or two sounded pretty dubious, I thought.
You know, the sort you find tucked away round the back
streets of Soho. No addresses, just phone numbers.'

'What were the voices like?'

It was an odd question and she hesitated.

'Come on, come on,' he said impatiently, 'you can tell
from voices, what were they?'

Embarrassed, she said bluntly, 'They were like yours.'

He said wearily, 'Oh Jesus,' and passed a hand over
his face. 'Did you keep the paper?'

Jane shook her head. 'It didn't seem relevant. And
anyway, whoever it was had cut out part of one column—
presumably to act on so the rest would be useless anyway.
You don't really think it was her?'

'I wish I didn't,' he said with feeling. 'Now do you
see what I meant about the mongoose? I'm the only black
man she's ever seen, I've been like one of the family since
she was a baby. She's liable to walk into anything—imagining that all black people are kind and friendly and
harmless!'

'And they're not?' Jane was a little shocked. She felt

186

he should speak well of what she thought of as his people, at least to her. Especially to her.

'What do you think?' He spread the pieces again. 'There could be something here, look for figures. She could have jotted a phone number, something like that.' They shuffled and reshuffled, finding figures in three different hands. 'Must be dates on the letters,' said Jane. 'Can you tell which are in her writing?'

He sorted out a sequence of eight figures. 'But that's too many for a phone number,' said Jane. She found another three figures, a four, then a five and seven close together. 'But look—there's a dot after the four, right on the edge, where the paper's torn. That could be a date.'

'April '57,' he confirmed, 'that means we can eliminate two more. Or one. When exactly did she leave?'

'Mid-April—and that was odd because she should have finished out the month.'

'So she must have had a job to go to. We're getting warm. Right, can you remember the exact date?'

'Not without a calendar.' She glanced about her and saw one advertising Pepsi Cola hanging behind the counter. Luckily the previous month's page had not been torn off. She strained her eyes, 'Yes. It must have been...the fourteenth, I remember we had—'

'Right, so we look for ten, eleven, twelve or thirteen that look as if they belong together. If we don't find them we're back to square one.'

They found them, and assembled the date 12.4.57. They were left with four figures which could have belonged in any order and the letters Y, M and A.

'Is there a C anywhere...YMCA?'

'Hardly! It spells Amy—or May. Somebody's name? Or a date in May? No, the other dates are written in numerals—'

'Got it!' cried Jane, 'it's a Mayfair number, that's the exchange, MAY!'

'Come on,' he said, 'here's where we go and find a phone.'

She smiled up at him, the last of her mistrust evaporating. Rain was beginning to fall and they crowded together into a booth. 'Right, Mayfair.' He was busy with pencil and paper noting the various combinations of digits. Jane nodded, standing primly to attention. For some reason she was finding his closeness disturbing; she told

187

herself sternly not to be an idiot. 'I've got more coppers if you need them,' she said.

'Thanks.' He pushed two pennies into the slot, dialled MAY and the first group of figures on his list. 'Hello...' He pressed the A button. 'That's who? You're Carlo's Steak House? You don't have dancers, do you...no, I didn't think—OK, OK, I'm sorry.' He made a comic flinch as the instrument crackled indignantly. 'I don't try her again, that's for sure!' He crossed the number off the list and tried the next. He listened with a growing frown. 'Some old lady, she sounds scared to death.'

'Ring off before she calls the police,' Jane laughed. 'You know, you're not safe to be out alone!'

He tried the next combination. 'Rumba Jamaica,' a rich dark voice reached Jane across the wires. He clapped a hand over the mouthpiece again. 'This is it!' he told her excitedly, his face dark and intense. 'Hello! Hello, you Rumba Jamaica, right?...you give me the address, man, I got to meet me friend there...no, she just give me the name and the number no street...Well, how I find you, take a bus or what?...You don't tell me, why not?...What the difference what she name, no skin off your nose...Look man, you a club, right? You don't tell me I have to ask the police, you want that?' He made a little grimace at Jane, scribbled something on the envelope. 'Right, that's better,' he finished in his normal voice, and rang off. 'She's there, I know it!'

'But how do you know?' said Jane doubtfully. 'It's only a hunch, isn't it?'

'I know,' he said soberly. 'Where can I find a taxi around here?'

'You? But I'm coming with you—'

'No,' he said firmly, 'thanks for the offer, but no. It's not the sort of place for you, my bones are telling me. Better I go on my own from here on.'

Crestfallen, she said a little crossly, 'Then I won't know if you found her.' She felt used, discarded. It wasn't fair...

'You'll know. I'll leave a message at the hospital. It's Nurse...?'

'Fisher,' she told him for the second time. He hadn't even remembered her name. Outside on the pavement she pulled herself together and offered her hand, 'Well, good luck. Tell her to write to me.'

'Thank you, Honey's friend. You've helped more than

you know.' He turned up his coat collar against the drizzle. 'I won't forget.'

She stood stubbornly holding out her hand until he took it in a firm warm grasp.

'Last woman I went to shake hands with tipped me sixpence,' he said, and laughed. She liked the laugh, she decided. It lit the sombre face and ploughed a furrow that might once have been a dimple down one weather-beaten cheek.

'You see?' she said. 'I said you weren't safe to be out on your own.' She smiled her goodbye and watched him disappear into the dazzle and darkness of London. Then she turned, and walked slowly and thoughtfully back towards the hospital.

4

Sam shouldered his duffel-bag and stood looking disconsolately down the length of yet another street. Another stretch of pavement gleaming blackly wet between dustbins stood out for early morning clearance, another decision facing him, another choice to be made between yet more seedy clubs to be tried.

He had been wrong about the Rumba Jamaica. Although his instincts had drawn him there a brief exchange with the management had dashed his hopes. He had stood blinking in the painted jungle of the foyer, squinting through phoney moonlight at fluorescent palm trees, straining his ears to catch a familiar voice above the heavy beat thrumming through the walls and floor.

'Membership card? You got to have membership card to get in.'

The two who closed in on him could have passed for Ashanti warriors without the bulging dinner jackets, the elaborate frilled shirts.

He stood his ground. 'I want to see the manager.'

The younger of the two said, 'Expecting you, is he?' and it was clear that he had been no nearer to Africa than Cardiff Docks.

'No,' said Sam, 'but I won't keep him long. I just want to see him for a minute.'

The taller man leaned back against the desk and slowly wound a handkerchief around his knuckles, a faint smile playing about his lips. 'Well, just mebbe he don't want to see you,' he said in a deep bass. And straightened up.

'Hold on a minute, Lenny. What's the trouble?' A small man, Armenian—or perhaps Greek—had appeared from nowhere. 'What does this man want? Members only, you know the rule—'

Sam put in quickly, 'I'm looking for a girl, Honey McLeod, is she dancing here?'

'This is a private club, we don't give information about members. I must ask you to leave.'

'No, no, no, I mean working here, does she work here?' He was pushing his luck. The man from Cardiff was also pulling a handkerchief from his pocket.

The Armenian shook his head emphatically. 'Just the girls with the band, Terri and Rita. Now if you don't mind—' He nodded to the bouncers who moved forward smartly.

'It's all right, I'm going,' he assured them, but they followed him out to make sure. Outside, their roles were discarded like paper hats. 'What happen, your girl run out on you?'

'Sort of. Look, I've got to find her, she came here looking for a job. Where else could she try?'

'Depends what sort of girl she is.'

That was not so easy. 'She's English—white. But she'd go for...well, this sort of place.'

They exchanged knowing smiles, then turned back to him. 'London's full of clubs, you could try any of them. But don't waste your shoe-leather, man—ten a penny, that kind of gal!'

He had turned on an angry heel and left them grinning.

All that had been nearly a week ago. Now he had lost count of the clubs he had tried and he was running out of money. This morning he had checked out of the hostel in search of something even cheaper. He had not found it. In the windows of boarding houses everywhere the 'No Coloureds' signs stood like grey-faced sentries. Be-

hind the few unguarded windows, behind doors painted in defiant shades of purple, pink, orange, incoming West Indians were taking turns to sleep, sometimes as many as eight or nine to a room. He sighed. Tonight, if he was still in London, it would be a bench on the Embankment or the dusty paper-blown grass of Hyde Park. If he was not picked up. If he was he could look forward to a night in the cells. The price of his rail ticket home he was determined not to use until his mission was accomplished.

He looked again at the choice of doors before him. He had exhausted first the clubs with an obviously Caribbean flavour. Then those with pretensions to smartness, with foyers and lighted signs. Now he was down to the sort whose furtive activities were housed in basements, warehouses, the back of cheap restaurants. Three of the buildings in this street looked likely. None of them had a sign or any form of advertisement, but in each the street door stood open a crack, enough to allow a narrow seam of coloured light to escape. He tried the first. The door gave on to a hallway painted black, walls, ceiling, floor—all black, unrelieved by colour and lit with a faint mauvish glow from concealed strip lighting somewhere. He hesitated, in an apparent dead end. Then in the gloom he made out a heavy curtain partly askew, revealing the head of a staircase leading down from the far end. He started down the stairs, at the bottom of which he could see a crudely painted magnolia blossom filling half the wall and surmounted by a meshed grille. Before he was halfway down a panel slid open behind the grille.

'Membership?' The usual demand, the usual muffled beat, the odours of cheap perfume, sweat, deodorant, tobacco...and one less usual, cannabis.

'No,' he began wearily, almost hoping she was not here, 'I'm looking for—' He stopped. The eyes behind the grille were familiar, and this time they were hostile.

'Stravos—Tony!' barked the Armenian, and 'Right, guv!' came the response. A door to his left burst open and Sam did not wait to be introduced. He heard two pairs of feet thudding behind him—up the stairs—through the door—running—doubling and dodging through the down-at-heel streets in a desperate bid to throw them off. These were not the black bouncers from the Rumba Jamaica and he knew what to expect if they caught him in some unlit alleyway.

Pelting between the dark buildings he asked himself what the Armenian had against him—what it was about him that had thrown him into a panic. Why should seeing the same face twice have alarmed him into launching an attack? Unless he had more to hide than a few clients smoking reefers...something, perhaps, that Honey was caught up in. Suddenly he was sure beyond doubt that she was back at the Rumba Jamaica, somewhere unobvious, discreetly tucked away...and that the club was as unsavoury as this one, one of a chain trafficking in God knew what.

With relief he saw ahead of him the lights of Piccadilly, heard the running feet behind him slow to a reluctant halt. They would not risk beating him up in full view of the public. Just as well, he reflected, hampered as he was by the duffel-bag he could not have evaded them for long. He dodged between cursing taxi-drivers across to the central refuge and sat on the steps of the Shaftesbury Memorial to get his breath. He pulled out his well-thumbed copy of London A-Z and checked his route. He had wasted enough time on a wild-goose chase. It was time to go back. But this time there would be no knocking on the front door. This time he must be a little more devious.

He sat frowning into space. Until he noticed a street barrow drawn up on the opposite curb, the light bouncing and sparkling on mounds of fruit arranged on its gaudy artificial grass. He got to his feet, smacked an exultant fist into his palm, and plunged again into the screeching traffic.

'Aaoow—sod it!' Rita's howl of anguish rang around the cupboard between office and lavatories euphemistically referred to as the dressing-room.

'What the—' echoed Terri, reaching for a tissue with which to remove a large gobbet of cleansing cream from the gold tassel dangling from her left nipple. 'Hey, look at this—' She scrabbled in the mess on the makeshift dressing-table to hold up a king size cream jar. 'It's a frigging orange! Where's it come from?'

Wherever it had come from there was no doubt about where it had arrived. It had wedged itself neatly into the cream jar like a ball-and-socket joint, dispersing the contents in even quantities about the room. Mixed with the cream was a quantity of broken glass.

'It's come through the window,' wailed Rita. 'Oh, Christ, just look at my feathers!'

'Stuff your feathers, I've cut myself!' snapped Terri, trying to staunch a trickle of blood that dripped from the spoiled tassel and ran to join a third, not much larger, which constituted the remainder of her costume.

'Oh, go see the Dummy and get a plaster, you'll be all right.' Rita mopped cream from her bedraggled ostrich plumes. 'Mr Monty'll go mad when he sees this!'

'Oh, very nice, I'm sure—revolving tits trimmed with sticking plaster. I'll have to cut my act!' Terri snatched the box of Kleenex and clutching it to her near-naked bosom stormed out as another missile came in through the window. She collided with the Dummy on the other side. She too was clutching an orange, her face white and her eyes strangely bright.

'Where are these coming from?' demanded the Dummy. It was the first time Terri had heard her say anything. That was why they had nick-named her the Dummy, she was like some deaf-and-dumb thing moving about. Taken aback, Terri stared at her.

'Where, tell me!' repeated the other girl, her expression intimidating. 'These oranges—with faces on them—where did they come from?'

Terri gaped, her head of steam lost for the moment. 'From outside I guess, some nut—Hey, where are you going? Come back, I want First Aid—' But the Dummy was gone. Her dead face had suddenly come alive in the most astonishing way and without another word she was gone. Terri stood for a moment staring after her before it was borne in on her that she was not coming back. 'Up yours!' She stuck her hands akimbo with a gesture that set her luscious body quivering and went back into the dressing-room. As she did so she heard the Dummy's flat-heeled shoes clattering away down the fire escape.

Honey reached the ground in a jumble of drinks crates and empty cartons and stood looking eagerly up and down the empty street. In the half light nothing stirred but a sheet of paper blown by the wind. Her heart dropped painfully. It was not possible. Then she remembered that the dressing-room faced on to another street, and she was running as though there were no tomorrow, no yesterday but only now, the beginning of her life. The short road seemed endless, the ground seemed to hit up-

193

wards at her flying feet—and yet at last she gained the corner, at last threw herself round it, skinning her hands on the bricks and scarcely feeling it and there, unbelievably, was Sam.

He was standing under a street lamp on the further side of the road, head thrown back, arm raised, taking aim with another orange. She saw his fingers curled about the golden ball above the dark column of his wrist, saw his brows drawn together in fierce concentration, the light catching his teeth as he gnawed his underlip, his body drawn taut as a steel spring. And knew that for the rest of her life she would see him as at this instant, this image caught in the net of her thought for ever.

And now he had seen her, was turning towards her, something new and wonderful happening to his face as he ran to meet her. The orange dropped from his grasp and rolled into the gutter where hers went to join it; they lay there side by side among the rubbish, their weird faces upturned like the masks of tragedy and comedy on a playbill.

'Oh Honey...Oh, thank God...'

And Honey was come at last to her longed-for harbour, her world grown small and safe in the warm darkness behind her closed eyelids, her consciousness bounded on the one side by the homely roughness of his duffel coat, on the other by the remembered texture of his shaven cheek, held closed in a wordless happiness.

For a long time they stood without moving or speaking. Then her small world expanded a little; she remembered that she had hands, and moved one of them to encircle his neck. His arms about her tightened, their mouths sought one another's faces and they kissed, very softly and gently at first and then with a slowly kindling warmth as the fires that had burned for so long in secret flared up to consume them both. Afterwards they were silent, because there was nothing that needed to be said, and so much to be felt, seen, thought, remembered...their eyes after long starvation could not look enough, and Honey with her fingertips began to trace the contours of his face, learning the shape of it as if she were blind, while he watched her, a little of his underlip caught between his teeth. She whispered, 'You'll bite that one day...'

He stood her away from him. 'Let me look at you.

194

You're thin, they've starved you. Or haven't you been eating?'

She shook her head, smiling, radiant. 'Doesn't matter now. You can feed me up.'

'I couldn't find you!' It sounded like an accusation, his anxiety stark on his face.

'I tried to tell you. I wrote three times but the letters kept coming back, if you'd read them you'd have known—'

'I only read the last one. I thought—well, never mind.'

They smiled into each other's eyes.

'Oh, I can't believe it's really you, you're here, it's all over. You just don't know what it's been like—'

'I can guess. This is no place for you—they push drugs in these places, didn't you know?'

She shook her head. 'It's heroin, too! Not just purple hearts or the stuff in cigarettes. They wanted me to try but I was too scared—'

'Hell, what were you doing here, why did you leave the hospital?'

'Don't be angry—I couldn't bear it at the hospital, people dying, losing each other, and I thought it would be dancing, they said I could be a hostess. Only I didn't realise what they meant and I upset a customer. I slapped his face and they were furious with me...'

Sam hugged her off her feet, ducked his face against her hair, not sure if it was laughing or crying he had to hide. 'Oh Honey, Honey...what am I going to do with you!'

'Take me home.'

He sobered. 'You know what will happen if I do.'

'I want it to happen. It's how it should be with you and me. How it was meant to be.'

She was trying to look at him but he would not meet her eyes. 'I thought I'd never find you,' he said again. 'You know? I've been in London a week, I was running out of places to look. I was about to try Battersea Dogs' Home.'

'Dogs' Home?'

'Where else would I look for a lost mongoose?' Seeing her bewilderment he added, 'Just a joke. I had a pet once and I lost her. I'll tell you about it sometime.'

And Honey knowing him so well sensed that there was more to it than a joke and stopped smiling. 'You shouldn't have let her get lost, Sam. She loved you, you

should have kept her safe—' The miseries of past months rose up and choked her, she hid her brimming eyes against his coat.

He held her in a crushing grip and did not answer. He's afraid, she thought: even now, he's afraid. She said cruelly, 'You're a coward, Sam. You're a lovely, wonderful person, the only one in the world for me, but you're a coward. You lack faith in yourself. You even lack faith in me. You think I'm crazy to want the good things you're frightened of. But I'm going to show you you're wrong, we're going to be happy whether you approve or not.' She swallowed her tears and raised her head, watching his expression change through hurt surprise to a confusion of panic and pleasure; she stood a little apart from him, pulling gently on his hands. 'I'm coming home with you. You know I am. You can talk to your conscience on the train.' Seeing his lips begin to twitch she smiled encouragement. 'Come on,' she coaxed, 'before we get arrested for breaking windows.'

'Child, child...' He knew he should take her back to the hospital, insist...but...He looked at her, this new Honey, as if he had never seen her before, struggling with a towering elation that filled him despite his every effort to resist it.

'Come on,' she said, smiling and pulling, until at length he laughed and wagged his head, and came along.

They moved off slowly, hand in hand, their eyes on each other, and gradually their pace gained speed until, laughing and running, they went flying down the street like children. They reached the Underground out of breath and hurled themselves upon it, infecting the ticket-seller with their happiness to leave his brown face grinning after them, raced each other down the escalators to the platform and leaped between closing doors on to a waiting train.

It had been so easy, thought Honey, after all. And wondered why she hadn't done it before.

5

At the beginning of every love affair however sad or silly, however outrageous or ill-advised, there is a moment of pure joy. And this was theirs.

They arrived at Paddington with half an hour to kill before the next train they could catch at ten minutes to ten. They went to the refreshment bar and filled in the time drinking coffee. It was terrible coffee—brewed, Sam said, from the cloth they had wiped the pot with—and they enjoyed it immensely between laughter and tears, having become a little light-headed with the suddenness of it all. They sat close together on the hardwood seat, hands clasped tightly in the shadows under a table wet with spilt tea and scarred with stubbed-out cigarettes, and saw the ordinary faces of ordinary people shining with a radiance not of this world. Not needing to talk or look at each other because although there was so much to be asked and answered there was all the time in the world, and words were altogether inadequate.

Honey relaxed in the warmth of the coat he had taken off for her to wear. 'This takes me back,' he had said, fastening the toggles, turning back the too-long sleeves, and they smiled, remembering. He tweaked the cotton skirt with its grease stains.

'What have you been doing in this?'

'Kitchen work.' To his startled look she explained, 'One and six an hour and an evening meal. And they let me sleep on a couch.'

'You're well out of there,' he said fervently, and she smiled, her mind flying ahead to better things. She had stood a little apart to watch him as he bought the tickets, savouring the sight of him, feeling a warm glow of pride that she knew to be absurd: he was no better and no worse than any other man. But he was Sam.

On the train at last they sat facing each other, conversing only with their eyes, making gentle fun of their fellow passengers who were trying not to stare. Not surprisingly, thought Honey, she must look decidedly odd in the dowdy probationer's dress she had worn for washing dishes, black cotton stockings and borrowed duffel coat hanging to her knees—what a way to dress for your wedding! The thought made her laugh. But she shook her head at Sam's enquiring glance; she might tell him one day. But this was not the moment.

As the train rocked swiftly through the night she tried hard to keep him in view, but the movement lulled her eyelids, dragging them down in spite of her. She thrust a foot between his on the carriage floor and imprisoned one of his ankles. It was the next best thing to holding hands. If only they had the carriage to themselves . . . but when the last of their companions alighted at Bath, they were both soundly asleep.

They reached Southcombe in the small hours and stood peering drowsily through the soft West Country darkness in a fine drizzle of rain. There would be no buses until the morning; the only way to get to the village was to walk. Honey was still tired and her knees began to ache after a mile or two, only Sam's arm supporting her kept her going. But as they turned at last into the familiar lane her weariness left her.

'I can smell the sea—oh, and I can hear it—listen!' She stood with head lifted, feeling the breeze on her face, and suddenly was as fresh and as buoyant as when she rose that morning. More buoyant, since the morning had held no knowledge of the day's harvest. Looking back to it was like looking back ten years, and her face made a smile of its own accord. 'Come on!' she cried to Sam, and began to run down the lane towards Mango Walk, in through the gate, thrashing wetly through the tangle of weeds and overgrown roses and up the steps. She waited breathless while Sam unlocked the door, but when he held it open for her she shook her head.

'You have to carry me over.'

'I do?'

She nodded, hardly dared to breathe. 'It's the custom.'

For a moment there was no response. She thought, Oh, God, I've blown it to pieces . . .

Then with no change of expression he raised a finger—'Wait!'—and disappeared inside. She heard him rum-

maging and he emerged again carrying a broom. He took her hand and solemnly led her down the steps again to the dewy grass where he laid the broom down between them and the wagon. Still holding her hand he said, 'When I nod, we jump together.' When they had landed he took her wondering face between his hands and kissed her very gently.

'It was good enough for my grandparents. I guess it will have to do for us.' And then with one of his unpredictable bursts of high spirits he picked her up, swung her around on a gale of laughter and bounded up the steps with her into the caravan.

'Now I really know I'm home,' said Honey, 'the smell of coffee and the crackle of the fire...'

They stood in the firelight, their hands round the steaming cups. She had showered in cold water and stood barefooted on the lino, wrapped only in a towel. But Sam was still fully dressed. He was not laughing now; he was watching her quietly over the rim of his cup, his black eyes catching fire from the red of his shirt. That was something she had almost forgotten, his taste for vivid colours, something that singled him out among men who felt daring if they rose to a blue or a purple...how could she forget, that or anything about him!

They finished their coffee and it was hard to know what to say. And it had to be the right thing. Intuitively she knew that the moment was poised on a knife-edge, a false move now could cost her everything. Knew too that despite all the words they could exchange he was still committed to his role of protector. And unless she could change that commitment to one more powerful she was doomed to a loss she could not survive. She could hear the pounding of her heart above the whisper of the flames, above the ticking of the clock, above every sound in the room. She peeped at Sam and the dark fire scorched her, she had to look away. The tension became unbearable. She moved nervously, clumsily reached to put down her empty cup and the towel fell away. Automatically she caught it, then wished she had not, then stood still, uncertain whether to hold it or let it fall, filled with longing yet not knowing how to bring him close to her. The mechanics of seduction were beyond her; and she could not stand there clutching the towel for ever.

'Must clean my teeth,' she blurted, and fled to the

wash-room. There she stood by the basin, her flaming face buried in the towel, and sobbed just once. She knew she must go back, that the moment once lost would never come again. But she could not, she could only wait alone on the naked concrete, helpless as a rabbit in a snare...

Sam moved soundlessly behind her and he too was trembling, she could feel it through his hand on her arm. But his voice was steady as he took the towel from her. 'What are you fussing about? Come here to me.'

Blindly she turned to him and the love that was between them took over, spinning its fine strong webs about them; it was as if the twin halves of one being had locked together for all time. Honey held fast to the love that she knew; his shirt was unbuttoned, she shrugged him free of it and wound her arms about him, nuzzling her breasts against his skin.

Sam wanted to tell her that he hadn't meant this to happen, to beg her not to hate him for it some bitter day to come...but the softness of her thighs caressed his hands, he could think of nothing as his reason drowned in the fragrance of her hair. 'Honey...' he murmured helplessly, his face against her neck.

'I know...I know,' she whispered, her thirsting body driving against his, her young hands fluttering like wild birds over his back. She felt herself lifted off her feet. There was the softness of pillows under her head, the mattress giving under the weight of Sam beside her, his body sliding naked over hers, tender yet relentless, taking possession...his mouth tasting faintly of coffee and of cigarettes...infinitely satisfying as she settled into his arms.

In the chilly hour before dawn Sam got up to attend to the fire. It was almost out but he raked it without too much noise, threw wood on the embers and produced a blaze. He found his cigarettes and lit one. The smoke curled deliciously around his tongue and he sat smoking contentedly on the floor, the warmth of the flames licking his belly, the flavour of tobacco and the heady wine of happiness mingling in his brain.

He looked over to where Honey lay asleep. Her figure was lost in shadows, only one hand was picked out by the light where it lay palm upwards, the fingers softly curled, thrown up on the pillow beside her. As he watched they uncurled a little as if reaching out to some-

thing and with a stab of pleasure he knew they were reaching out to him. She was his after all and in spite of everything. So be it. He drew on his cigarette, remembering the evening. 'You can talk to your conscience on the train,' she had said. He smiled. 'So where were you when I needed you?' he asked it now: but his conscience said nothing. It too was asleep, soft and cosy as a kitten. 'Look what you let me do,' he accused it, and 'Mm-mm, yes...' It stretched luxuriously and turned over in its sleep.

'Mm-mm...yes,' he echoed in his thoughts. He went over to the bed-place and stood looking down at her, a shadowy creature, a sleeping woman bearing only a distant relation to the child that he had known.

'Worse than death, Honey?' he had asked her half laughing, half breathless, wondering if he had taken her too roughly, and 'Better than life, my love—my love— my love...' Her mouth had pressed fervently against his naked shoulder.

'Honey...' he whispered, almost to himself. He sat on the edge of the bed beside her and stroked the long smooth hair that lay haphazard across her arm. Even in this dim light his hand chimed darkly against the whiteness of her skin. It made them look as though they didn't belong together; did it really matter so much? Maybe not now—the sleeping kitten stirred and spread its claws— tomorrow is also a day...

He wanted her to wake and drive the thought that menaced his happiness. He cupped his hand tenderly over the roundness of her head, tasting with his thumb the silk of her eyebrow. She turned and pillowed her face against his hand, her fingers lightly curved about his wrist. 'Are you really there?' Smiling, her eyes still closed.

'Look and see.'

She did so, her eyes sliding away from his body before they were raised to his face. But they were Honey's eyes, blind and uncritical. Not Nancy's to cut him to the bone. Weren't they...?

'Come sit by the fire,' he said.

She sat up and he caught her briefly in his arms, softly kissing her drowsy cheek before bringing her over to the rug before the fire. She sat with arms folded across her and her knees drawn up; her face was hidden from him

but he could tell by the curve of her cheek that she was smiling. He touched his lips to her neck. 'Poor little Eve,' and felt her body quiver as she laughed.

She relaxed against him and they sat flank to flank, refreshed and undemanding in the calm sweet intimacy after love, her arm lying pale along his thigh. And the painful thought came sidling back to gnaw at the edges of his mind.

'Honey—' He stopped. He had not worked out the rest of his speech.

'Yes?' she prompted after a moment.

'Nothing,' he mumbled, and tried to put it out of his mind. But he couldn't; the contrast had never seemed as sharp to him as now.

Presently Honey drew away. 'Let me look at you.'

He sat motionless, in dread of her assessment, the night's euphoria banished at a touch. 'Well?' he laughed nervously, 'do I look like some sort of a freak to you?'

Honey stared. 'A freak...' She shook her head wonderingly. 'But—but you're beautiful...surely someone must have told you that before?'

'Yes, I've been told!' He spoke harshly, raked by an agony from the past.

There was a silence. 'What is it...Nancy?' Her voice was timid in the shadows.

Sam could not answer. He sat with face averted, held dumb in the grip of bitter memory.

'My beautiful brown boy,' she had whispered, and then 'Such a pity you're black, such a pity...' She had enjoyed him and been ashamed of her enjoyment. 'Ah-h nigger, nigger, nigger...' she had murmured through clenched teeth as the tension of delight grew unbearable between them, using the insulting word as if it were a term of love. And then afterwards she turned away from him in distaste, disgusted with herself and with him. 'Why did you have to be black?' She had pounded frustrated fists into the pillow. 'Why did you?'

'I didn't choose it.' He had seen tears shining on the pearly cheeks and reached out for her, wanting to comfort her.

'Don't—I can't bear you afterwards!' She had pulled away sharply and got out of bed, to hunch moodily in the shabby armchair with a coat to hide her nakedness from his eyes.

That was in the early days when they were still rela-

tively happy; even then she would not walk down the street with him in daylight. He remembered the first time—how she had wept afterwards, reproaching him. 'Now I'll have to marry you, no one else would have me after this...'

He had held her tenderly, his hot face in her hair. 'Don't cry. I love you, I'll take care of you...' He should have seen the way the wind blew then. But he had been too blind, too dazzled to see anything beyond that she was going to be his wife.

He had been drunk when Georgia was born. When Nancy discovered she was pregnant it was the beginning of the end, for it curdled the last dregs of her affection. She fed her resentment by refusing to go into hospital for the birth—she'd be ashamed to let the nurses see what she'd been going with!—and while the long slow trying first labour was in progress had lain moaning, her tongue loosened by analgesia, screaming abuse with each contraction that had shocked even the hardened ears of the midwife and driven him at last from the flat. The midwife had caught at his arm, 'You're not going out!'

'She doesn't want me here.' And he had stumbled blindly down the stairs to tramp the streets to exhaustion in an attempt to escape his thoughts; finally, desperate, to drown them in the merciful glow of rum.

When the pubs turned out there was nowhere else to go and he had come back and sat, disconsolate, on the stairs. The midwife nearly fell over him as she came down them in the dark. She stared with disapproval mingled with compassion, and said at last, 'Don't waken her. You've got a little girl.'

He had forgotten to think of that. He raced up the three flights and let himself in soundlessly. The flat was filled with the unfamiliar odour of disinfectant and the faint sweet sickly smell of anaesthetic. In the cot he had built there was a new roundness; carefully, tremulously he lifted it out. It was warm and lay against him with a feminine softness, a sweetness he had thought gone from his life. He carried it over to the window and peered into the tiny face with its tight-shut eyes, a face that would wear a welcome for him in his loveless home. Nancy's venom might work in her, but she was blood of his blood and would one day turn to him. He had a stake in humanity at last.

Afterwards Nancy had said to her friends, 'Where do

you think he was while the baby was coming? Out soaking up the rum while I was lying in labour! I woke up and found him crying drunk with the baby in his arms...'

He could not deny it, half-truth though it was. And then Georgia had been killed, and only Nancy was spared.

It was all over years ago; he had thought the old ghosts laid; but now the London experience had skinned him sensitive in areas long forgotten; the chance word 'beautiful' had done the rest. Now he crouched wretchedly on the lino a million miles from the white girl at his side, isolated in the black hole of the past.

He stared at the fire and said, 'If that's all there is, you'd better go. Go now before I forget to be nice and try nailing your shoes to the floor.' Then because her silence unnerved him, because he was in terror that she might, he made it worse. 'Go on—what are you waiting for?' he rasped, and turned his cold glare towards her.

She was sitting a little away from him, fiddling with the ends of her hair. She raised brimming eyes and her voice was barely audible.

'For you to come back to me...'

A moment, and he was in her arms, the old griefs slowly receding in a silence more healing than words. As time clicked back into place, he reached for her hand. 'I'm sorry...tell me what you're thinking.'

'That I could kill the woman who made you look at me like that.'

He said with difficulty, 'I don't mean to punish you for her.'

'I know,' she said, holding him, 'but you will, and I'll forgive you...only you mustn't hide from me, lock me out—that's what hurts, you not trusting me.'

He sighed. 'I am what I am, Honey. There's no way I can change if the going gets rough. So I have to be sure you want me as I am, that you're not making excuses for me, wishing I was white...'

'Nancy!' And her hand in his tightened, as if she feared the mere name might put him to flight.

He drew back his head to look at her, searching her eyes. 'Don't ever hurt me that way, Honey. Tell me you hate me but don't ever call me names!'

She drew him back to her and suddenly he was sobbing soundlessly, painfully, a hand across his mouth. She held him serenely, undismayed by the dreadful spectacle of a man in tears. How could anyone do this to him, she

was thinking, how could any woman! Strangers might kick each other in passing and not know, but for Nancy there was no excuse—she must have known what she did. He had really loved her, she thought, her heart turning sick.

He was quiet now, scrubbing self-consciously at his face. 'Sorry, girl,' he whispered hoarsely, 'I guess that had to come out.'

'It's all right.' She ran her fingers through the soft wool of his hair. 'You know it's all right.'

He heaved a deep sigh and lay down with his face against her thigh, shamefaced, embarrassed; trying to laugh it off. She could feel his wet lashes, his hand brushing tears from her knee.

'I didn't mean to weep all over you.'

'I'm happy,' she said, swallowing. 'Don't you know that's what I'm for? I'll make it all up to you, Sam, I swear I will, everything—'

'You don't have to do that. Just be there, it's enough.' He turned on his back to look at her. He ran a light finger down the side of her neck, over the tip of her breast and down her side. 'You're beautiful,' he said, 'you really are.'

Honey smiled. 'You're not allowed to say I'm beautiful. If you do I shall retaliate by calling you names. Such as darling...sweet...my love...'

Sam made a rapid recovery. 'Sounds like a great idea. Come back to bed.'

Honey was awake first in the morning. Hospital habit still roused her early and a feeling of joyous anticipation like the early hours of Christmas gathered along her spine and made sleep impossible.

For a while she lay still, trying to make out the painted horse on the shadowy ceiling above her. When the tightness in her stomach became insupportable, she raised herself on an elbow and lay looking down at Sam, slowly taking shape beside her in the growing light. She could just discern the sphere of his head against the pillow, the powerful sweep of shoulder flowing away into the darkness.

Outside, the dawn was filled with the sounds of awakening. Rain had fallen during the night and drops were still lisping wetly down from leaf to leaf. Deep in the dripping hedge a bird piped abruptly, its small voice

crashing into the silence like a trumpet call. Another answered, and soon the listening valley was filled with their carolling.

The twilight turned rosy, gliding the raindrops along the guttering into a string of opals. They slid slowly past the window in an endless bright succession as the water drained from the roof, merging and blending at the lower end into a roseate ball of fire. The incandescence increased and expanded with each contributing drip, it hovered and danced as its shape distorted and finally shattered in a minute display of fireworks. Then the process began all over again.

The light turned to gold. The birds, their first frenzy spent, called and chirruped to one another in conversational tones as they ranged the spongy meadows in search of prey. Wafting from outside came the curious sweetness of azalea blossom, and in its wake the distant tang of the sea. The light breeze caught the curtain and it billowed out, flooding the room with a luminous glow, lifting it and them from the common ground to swim in oceans of amber.

A tickle of cold air spread across her skin. She reached up to close the window, twitching aside the curtain which moved with a harsh metallic rasp of rings along the wire.

Beside her, still asleep, Sam started violently; she felt his whole body leap in alarm at the unexpected sound. 'My darling...my darling,' she whispered, and bent and moved her lips along the margin of his hair.

He turned on to his back, an arm flung carelessly across his body. Even in sleep, she thought, he moved with a grace possessed by few. But perhaps she would never be able to tell him so: anything that marked him out from other men was likely to be taboo. As she watched, the radiance from the window bathed him, highlighting the cap of his knee, the ball of his shoulder, his face a charcoal drawing with the features boldly splashed across it. She remembered once a gipsy coming to the farm in one of his long absences; looking at her palm she had said mysteriously, 'For you my dear, the face of love is a dark one,' and Bassie had sent her away saying she was bad to frighten children. But Bassie had not understood; only she had understood, and had gone away hugging her secret to herself...

She grew restless, alone with her thoughts. She wanted

Sam to wake up and talk to her. She ran a tantalising finger across his skin and his hand moved automatically to defend himself. But the corners of his mouth began to smile as he caught her wrist. She bent above him, watching the wide mouth with its everted lips that gave his face its bland expression, its slightly upward tilt that reminded her of a child's upturned to be kissed. She laughed. Then caught her breath, remembering the powerful sensations it had evoked in her last night.

A heat haze rose in the valley, sparkling in the morning air. Sam awoke to the warmth of the sun on his eyelids, the silken tremor of her breasts against his arm, and turned towards her with a sigh of happiness.

6

Sam stood in the manager's office before the glass-topped desk. There was a chair on his side of the desk, but in the nine years he had worked for the firm he had not once been invited to sit in it. His appearances in this office had been fortunately few, restricted as they were to reprimands. Now, he suppressed his anxiety and waited.

A clock ticked. A butterfly, trapped in the double glazing, beat unavailing wings against the glass. The man behind the desk continued his leisurely perusal of his mail. Only when he had quite finished did he look up.

'Well, Sam,' he said pleasantly, 'come to collect your cards?'

'No, sir. I came to ask where I should be working. There's someone else at my position and the Foreman referred me to you.'

The name on the door was G. B. HAYTON but Sam knew it was not for him to use. Nine years had taught him where the frontiers lay.

Hayton smiled. 'But you've left us, haven't you? Not been in since—when was it? Ah, yes, the Wednesday before last.'

Sam knew then that he was wasting his time. But he would go down fighting. 'I had two weeks' holiday due, sir. And I'm back before it's up.'

'Holiday dates must be agreed with the Supervisor before the start of the season.' Hayton's smile deepened. He enjoyed his job, especially at moments like this. His favourite occupation was the manipulation of underlings; Sam knew his taste, and for himself would not have pandered to it. But he owed it to Honey to try.

'I'm sorry, sir. It was an emergency. My daughter...'—how he hated to say that now!—'she was missing...'

Hayton laughed. 'Randy lot, you spades! Piccaninny in the offing, eh? Another little mouth to feed? Too bad, you should have thought of it before. Too late to come whining to me now. What do you suppose would happen if I went off without a word to anyone?'

Sam clenched his teeth on his self-control. 'I hope we'd keep the wheels turning, sir.'

Hayton settled back in his chair, his expression one of the deepest satisfaction. 'Ex-actly,' he drawled, 'we must keep the wheels turning. Which means filling vacanies as soon as they arise.' He switched off his smile and set about rearranging the papers on his desk. 'You know the rules. Pick up your cards on the way out.'

Sam wasted no more breath. He strode out, slamming the door, and had the small satisfaction of hearing the glass fall tinkling behind him. Someone shouted after him but he did not turn back.

At the Wages Desk an envelope awaited him. Inside it were his National Insurance Card and Tax Form P45.

'No pay?' he asked. 'There should be two weeks' holiday pay.'

The wages clerk, pale-lipped and bespectacled, said promptly, 'Instant dismissal. You don't get holiday pay. Only if you give in your notice.'

'Instant what? But he said—'

'It's not my fault,' she said nervously, 'I only do up the envelopes. It's not me you want to shout at—George!' She leaned out through the window. 'Run and fetch the Supervisor, I've got a man here making trouble!'

'Forget it,' said Sam, and made for the workshop. Angry or not, he was not leaving his tools behind.

His toolbox had been moved from its usual place and when he found it in the shadows under the back of the bench it felt suspiciously light. He opened it. Of some fifty pounds' worth of tools he had built up over the years, only two spanners and an electrical screwdriver remained.

'Has anyone—' he began. No one looked up. 'Mick ...Birdy?'

Work in the shop continued as if he were not there. He picked up the box and left. As he crossed the yard he heard the laughter break out. It followed him all the way to the station.

He had walked there automatically, but now he stopped to think. Was he going to tell Honey he was out of work? He left the toolbox at the left-luggage department and went out to buy a paper.

By lunchtime he had answered every relevant advertiser in the Situations Vacant column. As he trudged disconsolately back to the station to collect his almost empty box he reminded himself that he had known it would not be easy. Apart from anything else he had no tools of his own any more. And he was over forty. And he was black. Even when he had telephoned one firm and got as far as an interview, the vacancy had been conveniently filled by the time he arrived. He tried to recall how he had got the job with Hayton nine years ago; but of course—it had been Arthur's doing. He remembered the looks of surprise and resentment when they had first seen him; clearly Arthur had not warned them and they had felt tricked. Arthur had some sort of pull with the firm, and for whatever reason they had kept him on. Until now.

He snatched a coffee at the refreshment bar and boarded the train. The afternoon was still ahead of him. Maybe Southcombe would provide the answer, holiday resorts in summer were usually ready to take on staff and there must be something in the way of maintenance. He got off the train and made straight for the Employment Exchange.

Half an hour and an unhelpful questionnaire later, he emerged. Looking up, he saw Arthur approaching with a questioning expression on his face. He held up a hand to silence him. 'I found her. She's home. And I don't want to hear another word!'

Arthur stopped, mouth still open as if about to speak.

Then he threw back his head and laughed, and clapped him on the shoulder.

'Come and have a drink,' he said.

'What excuse did he give?' asked Arthur over beer and sandwiches. 'He must have offered some sort of reason for laying you off.'

'He said I went off and didn't tell him. I guess I should have rung in,' he added reluctantly.

'He's lying,' said Arthur, 'he knew very well where you were. I rang and told him what had happened when I got that call from the Police. Didn't mention them, of course.'

'You did?' Sam looked at him, startled. Such a possibility had not crossed his mind.

Arthur nodded. 'Can't be too careful with a type like Hayton. I guessed he might try something like this. Do you want to make a change or were you satisfied there?'

Sam hesitated. Satisfaction hardly came into it—it was a job, and that was all that could be said for it. Probably any other would be much the same. 'Beggars can't be choosers,' he said. And grinned, lest Arthur should take it for self-pity.

'I'll have a word,' said Arthur. 'He's not going to climb down and give you back your old job, obviously. But there might be something else in the firm. It's worth a try,' he smiled bleakly, 'especially when I point out the...misunderstanding. Meantime I suggest you tell Honey you're on a few days' holiday. Whatever you do won't start before Monday so if you find something better you can let me know.'

Sam did not know how to answer and he was glad when the calling of 'Time!' created a diversion. The thought of going back to Hayton to eat humble pie made his gorge rise. But he could not say that to the man who for a second time was putting himself out to help him. He mumbled his thanks and followed him out to the car. 'No thanks,' he replied to the offer of a lift. 'I've a few things to do, I'll catch the bus later on.'

To his surprise, Arthur said, 'Why don't you both come to lunch on Sunday? It's been far too long...'

'You sure you mean that? You know—she's not my daughter now.'

'Of course I mean it,' said Arthur, instantly his old testy self, 'what sort of a friend do you take me for?'

He was hurt, thought Sam with amazement, sensing for the first time the depth of feeling under the crusty surface. 'The best,' he said.

Arthur revved the engine and wound up the window. Then he wound it down again and leaned out, a rare twinkle in his solemn eye. 'Tell her to put a safety-pin in that skirt,' he said as he moved off.

Sam stood smiling on the pavement, watching him drive away. There were more important things after all than the loss of a job.

He did not find another job that day, but he did not tell Honey what had happened. She accepted that he had taken the week off to be with her and they spent the days before the weekend in idyllic solitude, a time of music and sea-spray, of lamplight and love words, and whisper of late spring rain upon their roof.

All too soon it was Sunday. They looked at each other a little wistfully, closing their door behind them, knowing that the special time was past and could never be equalled, that it could never come again. Saying nothing, they kissed, and set off hand in hand towards the Stone House. As they came in sight of the village they loosed hands and walked sedately side by side.

'Well, Sam, back to work tomorrow, I suppose?' said Arthur cheerily, and Sam knew that he had somehow managed it, that he still had a job to go to after all. Maggie glanced coyly at Honey from time to time and it was obvious that she was aware of how things stood. After lunch she contrived to get her alone, and delivered a little homily on the value of discretion.

'If people here knew, your lives wouldn't be worth living,' she warned. 'You have to remember they still think Sam's your father. And that's by far the best way— let them think it and then nothing can be said. Just always behave as if he were, then no mischief can be made.'

'What—always?' Honey said naughtily, and Maggie coloured pink.

'You know quite well what I mean,' she said primly. 'You know, Arthur's right, you are a brazen wee thing.'

It was Honey's turn to colour. 'Arthur,' she said crisply, 'can keep his opinions to himself.' It angered her that even now Arthur could dim the brightness of her day. 'I'm sorry, Maggie, we just don't get on. I'm not sure why he dislikes me, but he does.'

'Whisht now, don't be silly, it's not Arthur's way to

211

dislike people. I don't know how you can say that after all he's done for you.'

Honey turned away, abashed and unable to speak her thoughts. When she looked back, Maggie had gone and Arthur was standing in the doorway.

'Did I hear my name mentioned?'

'No... yes.' She hesitated. 'Do you dislike me, Arthur? I've always felt you did.'

He frowned. 'Certainly not. I don't dislike anyone, a doctor learns not to. But since you ask my opinion, I think you're a selfish, headstrong girl: you don't care about Sam or anything else as long as you get your own way.'

'It's not true, I do care! I care more than you do, more than you can understand—you don't see him as a person, only as a sort of figurehead for his race. You want to put him on a pedestal and admire him, but I want to make him happy! I want to give him the good things in life, all the happiness he's missed—'

'You'll give him nothing but trouble.' He said heavily, 'The day will come when he'll be ashamed of you.'

Honey did not tell Sam what had passed; and when Arthur reappeared he behaved as though nothing had happened. The rest of the day drifted pleasantly by, and by the time they went home she had pushed it to the back of her mind. There were so much better things to dwell on than the gloomy pronouncements of old men.

Next morning, Sam was back at work. Hayton had been persuaded to climb down far enough to offer him a maintenance job in the boiler house. It was dirty and hot and he missed his old companions, but it was work. He had a regular wage and he had lost only two weeks' pay. He was not complaining.

Honey greeted him excitedly one day with the news that she was going to give dancing lessons to the village children in the church hall. She would teach them on one afternoon a week, for which she would receive the fee of five shillings each for half an hour. Maggie had agreed to play the arthritic piano provided, and insisted it would be unseemly for her to accept payment for this service. Some weeks as much as thirty-five shillings found its way into their modest coffer, and Honey enjoyed the lessons quite as much as the little girls who, solid as young farm animals and less imaginative, sol-

emnly gyrated on the instructions of 'thit furrin miss' from the caravan.

Life flowed calmly, sweetly, like a deep smooth river. Their days passed in happy anticipation of evening; each morning held a little parting, a little loss of life, until they could push the hours behind them and be together again.

'I'm so happy,' wrote Honey belatedly to Jane. 'I wish you could see me—you wouldn't believe it's me!'

7

Sam stretched out on his stomach on the warm sharp sand and tried to convince himself that he was reading. The print danced and dazzled and turned green before his eyes, but he kept them riveted there away from Honey and her friends where they played in sunlit water near the raft.

They had come over from the holiday camp at Southcombe, these young people she had known in London, and carried her along with them on a wave of happy greeting, so that before he knew it he was stranded with his book. He might have gone with them, of course: Honey would be distressed when she realised what had happened. But he did not want to isolate her by claiming her as his, and he knew that he would inevitably do just that: it would not kill him to play odd man out for a while. But it was better to do it at a distance.

He turned his back on the sea, knowing that somewhere behind him her white cap bobbed in and out among the others, and turned his attention to the little straggle of holidaymakers coming slowly down the cliff path.

He lay on his elbows, watching them pick their way

in bathing gear between stones and the rubbish they themselves left as hazards for unwary feet. He looked at the men in particular; old flabby men whose jaded genitals flapped against their thighs, pale stripling boys with acne, their youthful impudence apparent through their trunks. Their skins ranged from pallid pink to scarlet, according to the degree of rashness in the wearer. Any one of them, he thought broodingly, a fitter mate for Honey than himself, any one of them with a prior right to her. All other considerations were waived as long as the skin tones matched. Anger and frustration welled up in him, making him bow his head on his forearms. The sand, disturbed by his breathing, prickled his nostrils. He sat up.

He wanted Honey back with him, needing the solace of her company, the confidence that warmed him in her presence and deserted him the moment she was gone. He sat hugging his knees, his eyes drawn helplessly to the youthful bathers, who had swum inshore and were romping in the shallows with a beach-ball. He could discern the familiar shape of Honey, splashing and leaping among the others, heard their cries and laughter echoing under the topless sky, his own sense of exclusion heightened by the contrast. He was not envious of their pleasure; he did not begrudge it but he longed to share in it, wretchedly aware that if he tried the whole thing would fall to pieces. He felt alone and forsaken on the sunlit beach, and the knowledge that tonight she would lie in his arms was distant consolation. Probably her most lighthearted moments would always be spent with others, and he told himself sharply that he would have to get used to it.

He stared out to sea, trying to divert himself by identifying the faraway shipping as he had done so often for Honey and David in the past. His eye fell on the deserted raft. He had not swum out there since the day he went in after David and couldn't get aboard. That had been a bad moment. A moment that had cropped up in his dreams for years afterwards. Even now if he closed his eyes he could see its green-black wetness looming above him, sucking, churning, slapping at the water, towering unscalable as the walls of Jericho. It wasn't unscalable, of course...He glanced back at Honey. She was looking his way. He waved a hand to her, took off his watch and ran down into the water. There was plenty of time before

the tide turned, and this time the sea was his friend: cold, buoyant, exhilarating, it stimulated his body and effectively numbed his thoughts. And it was not such a bad thing to remount a horse which had thrown you. He drew deep breaths and struck out for the raft.

Honey, watching his powerful crawl cut through the water, grabbed excitedly the wet shoulder of the girl nearest her. 'There goes a real swimmer, look!'

She watched with intent face for a moment and then dived after him. By ones and twos they followed her.

Sam was enjoying himself. He had reached the raft and mounted it as easily as a seal, a single thrust of his legs landing him up alongside his vaulting hands. He sat on the edge, threw back his head and laughed for sheer exaltation. Then he whipped back into the water, playing in and out of the rollers like a dolphin.

He surfaced and saw Honey forging slowly towards him, swimming with her eyes shut as she always did, only looking around briefly from time to time to get her bearings and then battling blindly on again. Swimming was serious work to Honey. He filled his lungs and submerged, swimming under green water that sang and drummed in his ears until he saw her legs trailing in the water above him. Then he shot upwards to break surface directly beneath her, spilling her out of the water in a flurry of water and thrashed up foam.

Laughing, she beat at his dripping head. 'I might have known, I couldn't see you anywhere!'

Sam shook water from his ears like a dog and dived away, preparing to do it again. He circled a little and then launched himself at the hovering feet. Up she went, floundering and gasping, taken by surprise.

But this time it wasn't Honey. It was some other girl in a similar bathing suit, looking around her in annoyance for the cause of this piece of horseplay.

'Oh, it's you!'

With a shock he recognised the girl from the hospital. The girl whose help he had enlisted by a mild deception, and whom he had neglected to thank or keep informed. And now he had crowned it, properly and for all time...

'Excuse me,' he mumbled, treading water and dripping confusion, 'I thought—'

'It's all right, I suppose you thought I was Honey.' She eyed him speculatively. 'So you're the villain after all...'

'That's right. I'm the one in the black hat.'

To his relief she laughed, and they turned and swam side by side towards the raft. Honey was already there, hanging on to the lifeline. He hoisted her up beside him and said, 'You see what happened?'

'Let that be a lesson to you! I hope you were duly embarrassed.'

'Oh, I was,' he assured her warmly, wondering whether to offer his arm to the girl still in the water. But she reached up for his hand and allowed him to help her aboard, and smiled, and sat beside him near to Honey.

'I remember your face,' she said, 'but I didn't catch the first name?'

'This is Sam,' said Honey, and her eyes raised to his shouted out the rest from the housetops. He sent her a secret smile and turned back to the other girl.

'I have to admit...'

'Jane,' she said, 'Jane Fisher. You were pretty worried, I'd hardly expect you to remember.' She looked about her and said, 'This is a lovely place, I must come here again some time.'

Honey turned to her delightedly, 'Come up to the wagon when the others go back to Southcombe, you must see Mango Walk!'

'Shall I?' she looked uncertainly from one to the other.

'Of course,' said Sam, wondering how much she knew, how far she sympathised, how close Honey was to exposing herself to a wounding censure. But if he dragged his feet she might be hurt in a different way. He said, 'Have supper with us,' and left them to make their plans, chattering happily as if he were not there.

He stretched out on the brine-pickled boards and sunned himself. Snatches of their conversation drifted across to him, tossed this way or that by the breeze, bounced off the glittering water to his lazy ears.

'...went back to Malaya.'

'Oh, Jane, I'm so sorry.'

'It's probably all for the best. We could never have married, the way Mummy and Daddy felt about him. They'd have made his life a misery.'

'But don't you miss him terribly?'

'Mm...in a way, I suppose. We weren't together very much.'

'Practical Jane! How I envy you.' He could hear the smile in Honey's voice.

The wind veered, wafting their talk away from him, then fading it in again.

'...the world's not made for dreamers.'

'No...I know.'

He wanted to reach out, touch her hand. He opened his eyes and yes, she was looking at him. He said, 'The world's not made for anybody. We just have to rub along in it best way we can.'

'Quite the philosopher,' said Jane, half serious and half amused.

'If you look like me you have a choice. Either a philosopher or a sourpuss. I got no room for crabby people.'

'But you don't mind being a Negro, do you? Why should you, after all?'

What would you know about it? thought Sam. But he liked her for the intention.

'No, I don't mind. I don't even mind people who do mind as long as they keep their dislikes to themselves. I tell myself it doesn't matter what you look like, it's what you are inside that counts.'

'Of course it is,' said Honey, 'it's the person, not the packaging!' She laid her curving cheek down on his shoulder and delightful though it was it made him nervous. Always he felt the knives at his back.

'People can see us,' he muttered.

'Who cares what they think.'

'You'll care soon enough if they ever find out,' he said soberly. He sat up, bringing her with him. 'Come on, let's swim.'

Jane's face was a blank. It's given her a jolt, he thought, seeing Honey's face on my bare shoulder.

Honey was explaining, 'People here don't realise— Sam doesn't want them to. But it's not easy pretending he's my father, knowing we're—'

'Sh-sh!' Sam could not help himself. There were times when her extraordinary candour rattled him and he had to bite his tongue. He did not want to nag like a fearful old woman. But he hardly knew this girl Jane.

Honey read him, as she so often did. 'I know Jane better than you do.'

Jane smiled, 'don't worry about me, Sam. My Johnny was Chinese, that's why my parents objected so strongly— incidentally, so did his.'

'Did they?' Honey looked surprised.

'Most likely,' said Sam. 'My parents were upset when I married Nancy.'

'You're married?' queried Jane, and for the first time her eyes turned cool.

Sam hesitated. 'Yes,' he said stiffly. 'I am. We're out of touch now. But divorce is against her religion.'

'Against her religion!' Honey repeated with disgust. 'It didn't stop her marrying a non-Catholic, did it? It never stops her doing what she wants to do. I haven't forgotten the day she came to Mango Walk—'

'Honey, please.' He didn't want it all dragged out again, and before a stranger. 'Let it go, she's not here to defend herself.'

'You're still in love with her!' Her voice, her expression were an accusation.

'No...no, you know that's not true,' he said gently, enfolding her cold hands. Honey blinked water from her eyes,

'Then why won't you tell me what she did to Georgia?'

Sam shook his head in a helpless gesture. With Honey's own memory of that night hidden somewhere like a cobra in a basket, waiting to strike? 'It tears me up to remember it, that's why. It's all over, past and forgotten, let's leave it that way.' He squeezed her hands and released them. 'I'll go ahead and warm up the wagon. Jane, you try and talk some sense into her.'

Jane smiled faintly in response. He slipped into the water and struck out for the beach.

When he was out of hearing, Jane said, 'What was it with his wife—did you ever see her?'

'Only once. I'll never forget it, it was horrible. There was blood everywhere—I thought they were going to kill each other. I was terrified—shocked, I hadn't realised he could be violent, he's such a gentle man. I was sent away because of that and didn't see him for years. I'll never forgive her, never—'

'Oh, but you must!' Jane's response was automatic, her Christian saints invoked.

'I can't. I hate her! She ruined Sam's life and even now he's not free of her. You can see that.'

Jane smiled reassuringly. 'But he's all right now. You can see that, too.'

Honey pounced eagerly. 'He is, isn't he? I'm so glad you said that—' She broke off, suddenly self-conscious. 'You think I'm an idiot, don't you?'

Jane laughed. 'No, I don't think you're an idiot; I think he's a very lucky man.'

'Well...at least I'm more his sort of person than she was. Less flashy—God, if you could have seen her!'

'Mm-mm. Seems to be the fate of young West Indians over here. Daddy had a dockland parish once, he saw a lot of it. Sorry if I looked po-faced when he said he was married. Perhaps I'd better not come to the caravan after all.'

'Oh no, do come,' said Honey anxiously, 'if you don't he might think...'

'It's because of his colour?' finished Jane. 'Yes, I'd better come.' She glanced towards the beach and pointed. 'There, now—look at that.'

Sam had reached the shore and waded up out of the shallows, a small bronze statuette from this distance as the light gleamed on the water running off his pelt. He made his way to their heap of towels and began searching in Honey's bag for his watch. The three people nearest sat up and took notice. They looked uneasily at the crouching figure, then anxiously about for the owner of the bag. What they were thinking was all too obvious.

'It's just because it's Sam! If anyone else did that they'd naturally assume he had the right to.'

'It was the same for Johnny,' said Jane sadly. 'No one ever trusts what they don't understand.'

Sam had become aware of the scrutiny and was sitting back on his heels with an enquiring turn of the head. Nobody moved. Nobody spoke to him. The watchers on the raft, straining their eyes against the sun, saw the white glint of his teeth as he said something, saw him spread his hands...

No one answered him. They looked to each other for approval and in tacit agreement turned their backs. Plainly a Negro, like a dog, should know his place: it was like his impertinence to question their authority. He picked up his towel with an angry twitch and strode off up the beach.

Honey took to the water with a sigh.

The girls strolled leisurely up the lane that smelled of hot dust and honeysuckle.

'This is it,' said Honey, her hand on the gate.

Jane took a deep breath of the scented air. 'It's charming,' she said. Honey, proud and happy in the fulfilment

of her life, nodded in agreement. In the past weeks they had scoured the drab coats of paint laid on by successive owners of the caravan from its coachwork to find the original deep sky-blue still good under its layer of varnish, and discovered that, as Sam had suspected, the carving was covered in gold leaf. It sparkled now in the sun, its vine tendrils and clusters of grapes revealed in their exquisite craftsmanship. The garden, rescued from dereliction, was beginning to recover, and the senses were seduced by the scents of rose and bergamot, lavender and the sharp strawberry smell of philadelphus snowy on the bough, the ear wooed subtly by the rustle of leaves in the wind that came in softly off the sea.

'I love it,' Honey said simply, 'it's part of us.'

She took Jane inside and led her around pointing out to her this or that which Sam had planted, or grown 'from a tiny little cutting no bigger than this', showed her the watched-pot cherry tree that had waited until her back was turned to flower, the hedge where the blackbirds nested, the raspberry canes and the strawberry bed, and with pride, the back of the wagon where Sam had built on—'He was a ship's carpenter, there's nothing he can't do'—and Jane looked and listened, thinking, She's so much in love. It will be hard for her when the bad times come...

As they reached the steps they could hear him singing softly under his breath. A rich, savoury odour greeted them.

'Sam must be cooking,' Honey said. 'He always sings when he's busy.' She opened the door and announced, 'I've brought Jane with me.'

'Uh-huh.' Sam looked up from where he was slicing peppers, his fingers dark against the scarlet and the green. 'You like peppers, Jane?'

'I don't know, I've never tried them.'

'Now's the time to find out.' He indicated the three places he had laid. 'You girls better change, show Jane the doghouse, Honey.'

'Through here, Jane. You'll find everything...dear, did you find your watch?'

'I left it where it was, it seemed simpler.'

'I should have been with you, I saw it all and couldn't do a thing!'

'Ah, baby,' he smiled in his enchanting way and chucked her under the chin, 'I'm not crying.'

She wound her arms about him and laid her head on his shoulder, savouring with her cheek the crisp sweet-smelling freshness of his shirt. He held her lightly in one arm and dealt with bacon, tomatoes and mushrooms with the other.

'It was my fault,' she said, and felt his lips against her hair.

'Forget it, Honey. You can't protect me and anyhow it doesn't matter. I'm used to it.'

'You shouldn't be used to it, you shouldn't have to be!'

'Still hankering to change the world? Suppose you make a start with those wet clothes. Jane will be thinking we're up to mischief in here.'

Honey raised her head and smiled. 'She can't help being a bit pious, she's a parson's daughter. I suppose it's bred in the bone.'

Sam said in a whisper, 'Kiss me.'

She offered her lips obediently and felt his mouth sweep softly downwards, capturing hers, blending his darkness with her light, his strength with her tenderness, his maturity, her youth, in a movement of fusion beyond all argument...how could anyone think they did not belong together?

They stood with Jane at the bus stop in the summer dusk; a lime tree in somebody's garden flavouring the air they breathed. The silence was warm and still, reflecting back each small sound they made.

Jane glanced at her watch. 'I suppose the bus hasn't gone? There doesn't seem to be anyone waiting.'

'I'll ask in the pub,' said Sam. 'I want some cigarettes.'

When he had gone Honey asked Jane, 'Do you like him?' needing the seal of words on her impression.

'He's nice, you hang on to him as long as you can. He deserves something better than that woman.'

'As long as I can?' echoed Honey faintly. Her hands and feet felt cold.

'I mean, don't give him up until you have to.'

'Jane...I couldn't give him up.'

'Oh, not yet, of course, but sooner or later...when the time comes. After all, this isn't a very permanent arrangement, is it?'

'Of course it's permanent—what did you think?'

'You mean, you think you can go on like this for the

rest of your lives, hoodwinking people, in dread of being found out—Oh, Honey, you can't!'

'Oh, yes, we can, we can!' Honey was distraught. 'We have to, Jane, it's all we've got, all we can hope for, ever, it's got to be for always! Oh, I didn't know you were thinking like this.'

'Well, never mind, ducky, don't upset yourself. After all, it's only one man's opinion—who knows, perhaps you'll make a go of it—ah, here comes the bus.'

The bus loomed up and she boarded, waving and smiling, her brisk and confident self, unaware of the maelstrom she had raised and left behind her. 'Bye-bye, dear,' she called cheerfully, 'say goodbye to Sam for me, thanks for a lovely evening. Oh, and'—she winked confidentially—'long may it last!'

'Long may it last...' whispered Honey as the bus drew away and left her solitary. When Sam came back she held his hand as tightly as a frightened child. 'Let's go home.'

Indoors, he took her in his arms. 'You're trembling...'

She thought of the kiss they had shared. 'Sam, take me to bed.' Only there would she feel secure, inseparable...

A long time later he asked her softly, 'Honey, what frightened you?'

She opened her eyes on the face that hung between her and the world, filling her vision and wholly possessing her mind.

'Nothing,' she sighed, at peace once more. 'I was jumping at a shadow, that's all.'

It was the single shadow that runs before the storm.

The trouble with Living in Sin, as Sam remarked, was that you had to get up so early in the morning; which was certainly true if you lived in a caravan. In the summer of nineteen fifty-seven tradesmen called for orders and delivered to the door. In country districts they delivered early, and if their knock was not answered promptly were inclined to thrust their goods in through the nearest open window, regardless of what might be underneath. Sam in his single days had risen to find a loaf of bread and some fish dropped neatly through a window into the coal bucket; locking up had resulted in the meat being parked unwrapped on the ground, hygienically covered with the dustbin lid. 'You didn't want a dog to pinch it, did you?'

had been the indignant excuse, and he had admitted defeat. But now there were stronger reasons for rising early.

Smiling wryly at each other as the mornings turned colder and the temptation to lie in grew strong, they hauled themselves from warm bed to chilly lino and dressed before it was light.

It was probably bound to happen in the end: the inevitable dark morning when the alarm did not sound, or having sounded failed for whatever reason to rouse them. It made no difference in the long run, the damage was done just the same.

Sam was awakened by the tramp of feet. He started up, seized the clock and was horrified to see the time. About to wake Honey, he realised that the footsteps were just outside. Someone with something to deliver. Someone looking for a window. And this—over the bed—the only one unfastened. In panic he threw the sheet over her sleeping head, ruckled the eiderdown to disguise her shape and leaned across to forestall the intruder.

It was Harry the postman. His uniform cap appeared between the little curtains, incongruous and unwelcome on this hallowed ground.

'Parcel, for McLeod. Sign, please.' He handed in the parcel the stub of pencil, the yellow slip.

Sam leaned on his elbow to sign the receipt, praying that Honey would not wake and stir.

'Going to be late, aren't you?' Harry began amiably, and then the expression on his gnarled pink face changed abruptly. His faded eyes flashed, he crimsoned to the roots of his sparse grey hair. Seizing the receipt he ducked back from the window and stumped away in a silence more furious than words. Ears still burning, gait stiff with embarrassment, he blundered out through the gate and slammed it behind him.

Mystified, Sam watched him go. Then he glanced down, and saw what Harry had seen. A long strand of hair, unmistakably Honey's, lying straight and smooth as a river across the snowy plain of the pillow.

She awoke to find him still sitting motionless, the parcel in his hands. She started up, took in at a glance the parcel, the open window, the time on the clock. She raised her eyes to his and watched him wordlessly, waiting for his comment, until she realised that in the same way he was watching her. Waiting for her to give the cue

223

to laugh, to cry, to brush it aside or be crushed by it. She reached up to encircle him with her arms and a little smile came unbidden to her lips.

'Never mind, darling,' she whispered, 'breakfast in bed tomorrow.'

Old Harry's embarrassment had somewhat abated by opening time that evening. In fact with suitable embellishments the incident made quite a good story over a pint in the Rose.

Within a week all the village knew that that darky down the caravan was taking advantage of his daughter.

8

Their first communiqué from the enemy was a letter to Honey from the Parish Council, regretting that the church hall was no longer available to her for dancing lessons. No reason was given; she was left to draw her own conclusions.

It made little difference to her budget because her class of nine had dwindled abruptly to one little girl, but it left her with the problem of explaining it to Sam. After some thought she decided that if she found another job immediately there was a chance of his believing that she had made the change from choice. Damn them, damn them all—why could they not mind their own business! What was it to them how she spent her leisure hours, did they really think their kids would be contaminated? Angry and heartsore, she set out to search for work.

Maybe her attitude did not help her; perhaps those she approached really did look on her with a jaundiced eye. Whatever the cause, she ended up in Maggie Colby's sewing room, swallowing indignation with her tea.

Maggie listened patiently to the disheartening recital

and at last said quietly, 'You're beginning to taste what Sam's been up against all his life. I suppose you realise that?'

'Yes, I know. I used to think I understood it but I didn't, I know that now. Although they thought I was his daughter there was a degree of dispensation—"Look alike, think alike," isn't that what they say?—I could "pass". I suppose they said "Poor little thing, it's not her fault," and I never got the full brunt.'

Maggie shook her head, 'You still don't get the full brunt. They're punishing you because you've flouted convention and if you cared to go back to the fold you could live it down in time. But for Sam...' She left the rest unsaid.

Honey squared her shoulders and her eyes were calm. 'Well, I'm not sorry this has happened. At last, I'm standing beside him instead of on the outside looking in. But, Maggie—he fought so hard to keep me from it, I don't want him to know I'm there until he has to. So if you do hear of a job, you will let me know?'

'Of course I'll help you, dearie, you only have to ask. You know how fond we are of you both.'

'Not Arthur, I think,' said Honey dubiously, 'not of me.'

Maggie laughed unconvincingly, 'It's just that you don't understand him. Now, away home with you and don't worry too much. This is a small wee place and folks haven't enough to think about. It'll likely be a nine days wonder and then they'll let you alone and cast stones at somebody else.'

'Let's hope so,' said Honey, and smiled. 'Thanks, Maggie, you've made me feel better.'

Even with Maggie knocking on the door, it was not easy to find work in the village.

The vicar's wife wanted assistance with her children, but when the name McLeod was mentioned, reflected that she couldn't really afford to pay anyone. The Colonel's wife was in need of a companion, but she was quite sure that the girl would be 'unsuitable'. As a last resort she tried to persuade Arthur that he needed a secretary. He replied bluntly that he did not, and if he did he would want someone competent.

'Don't be hard on her, Arthur. After all, it's for Sam's sake as much as hers.'

Arthur appeared unmoved. 'Sam's not a child. He knew what he was taking on.' He looked at her over the top of his newspaper and added, 'Cowan the dentist is opening a part-time surgery in Southcombe. He'll be wanting a receptionist, I imagine.' He glanced at his watch and bolted before she could answer.

When Maggie went to seek out Mr Cowan, she met a shining Honey on his doorstep.

'Oh, Maggie, I've got it, I've got it!' she cried. 'Isn't it wonderful, I can't believe it! Sam will never guess.'

'Well, I'm delighted for you, dearie—but how did you hear of it, was it advertised?'

'No,' said Honey, 'I had a letter offering me an interview.' She looked mystified. 'Do dentists usually do that? He knew I had nursing experience so I suppose...' Her frown deepened. 'You don't think there's something funny about it, do you? I mean, how did he get my address?'

'I shouldn't think so for a moment,' said Maggie. 'You take your luck where you find it and don't worry about where it came from.'

She was smiling as she boarded the bus for home.

When Honey told Sam he looked at her oddly. 'You're really pleased about it?'

'Yes, I am,' she assured him eagerly. 'Why, aren't you?'

A quizzical half-smile pulled at the corners of his mouth. 'That's fine,' he said, and returned to his guitar.

Honey found overnight differences in the attitudes of those about her. In the village shops or at the bus stop, people who had greeted her all her life with 'Hello, Honey' now ignored her, or if compelled to speak did so in the monosyllables they reserved for strangers. No one smiled at her now as she passed, and she learned to walk with unseeing eyes. 'Such a drawing aside of skirts,' she remarked to Maggie, 'it must be audible for miles.' But her laughter had a sharpened edge to it that was new to her.

The volume of their mail increased abruptly and was almost exclusively addressed to Sam. These days it was deposited just inside their gate, weighted with a stone to prevent its blowing away. The affronted postman avoided all contact with them now; if a parcel had to be signed for he hammered on the door until someone came. But he never again put anything through a window.

'What is all this?' asked Honey, handing the inflated

mail to Sam. 'It looks like circulars.'

'Just rubbish.' He thrust it bodily into the stove.

'Don't you want to see what's in it?'

'I know what's in it. Come and get your breakfast.'

She had not yet started work at the surgery and when he had gone she was left to tidy up. The fire was out and as she raked it through out tumbled the cascade of unburnt circulars. She picked one up, franked for postage by a business house but innocent of advertising on the envelope. It was also unsealed. She pulled out the contents and read:

'Dear Sir,
    In view of your recent marriage may we suggest...'

It came from a firm of 'Surgical Appliance Manufacturers' and it was easy to see what they were suggesting. She opened another, and then more. All were similar in content, some discreetly medical, others saucy and in dubious taste. One began by quoting: 'Pity the man who goes to bed to save candlelight and begets twins.' There were so many of them, she thought, more arrived every day. But why? Suddenly she saw the reason for the influx. It was somebody's idea of a joke, somebody with nothing better to do than spend time and postage tipping off all these firms. She knelt among the ash and the envelopes, angry and ashamed to have her secret life, her intimate personal hours with Sam pawed over by such grubby hands. Such matters had to be thought of, provided for; there had been talk in the hospital of an oral contraceptive which would end the necessity for mechanical means; squatting on the cold concrete of the wash-house, fumbling with a diaphragm selected by guesswork from the chemists in Southcombe such a method was a consummation devoutly to be wished. But that would mean going on her knees to Arthur, and if she sometimes thought wistfully of a loving untouched by such premeditation it was only momentary. She was happy to be making love at all.

Yes, such matters had to be thought of. But not like this—

'I didn't mean you to see those,' said Sam's voice behind her and she jumped.

She said, 'Have you seen this one?' as if it were some

kind of funny story, because she did not want him to know how she really felt. And it was all right, he was not angry or embarrassed, and they laughed. But after a moment the laughter died, the funniness would not do any more. He knelt and put an arm around her, screwed up the impertinent literature with his free hand and set a match to it.

'Sorry,' he said.

'Doesn't matter. Anyway, it's not your fault.'

'No, but'—he tried to bring the laughter back—'it's not nice for little girls.'

She said, 'I'm not a little girl any more.'

'You're not?'

She shook her head. 'I'm the woman you didn't want to know. Remember?' She smiled. 'Now run, or you'll be late for work.'

He rose to his feet, picked up the jacket he had come back for.

'You're a very nice woman,' he said, 'I must have been crazy.'

The bombardment of paper had barely ceased when she came home from the new job to find that a fresh ingenuity had occurred to their persecutors. All over the blue panels of the wagon, in every available space, someone had been at work with chalk.

Honey stood for a moment, feeling slightly sick, before she realised that Sam would be arriving close on her heels. She seized the first thing that came to hand and scrubbed at the obscene graffiti until every last mark was erased. She went inside shaking with anger and drank several cups of coffee. Let it be someone else's turn soon, she thought: please let them leave us alone...

It was only the beginning. Every day on her return from work she found the same phenomenon. She took to hurrying home in a frenzy of anxiety to be able to clean it off before Sam saw it; one day, inevitably, she was too late.

She saw him turning in at the distant gate as she ran down the lane and called to him to wait, but to her dismay he dived in through the gate without pausing. When she caught him up he was stooping to throw something underneath the caravan. He turned swiftly at her approach and straightened up, brushing his hands together.

She halted. There was nothing to be seen on the car-

avan. No insulting slogans, no crude illustrations. Nothing but a telltale streak of chalk. And Sam, furtively dusting his hands. Watching her with precisely the tentative regard with which she was watching him.

They stared at each other in disbelief and then, helplessly, because she was tired and overwrought, she began to giggle. Sam reached out for her and they embraced, the ugliness all swept away on a gust of saving laughter.

'You know what?' he said, wiping his eyes. 'I think we're both nice people!'

Honey smiled up at him, happy, not minding any more. 'Maybe we're a little too nice,' she said thoughtfully. 'Do you realise, every time we're driven to deceiving each other like this we're letting those wretched people come between us?'

'Don't you believe it,' said Sam.

Not all the skirmishing ended so happily. One day after school a group of children came racing helter-skelter down the lane on one of the inscrutable errands of children, and one of them fell just outside the gate.

A scream brought Honey running out. She picked up the little figure prone in the road and cradled it on her knee as Sam would have done. It was one of her former pupils, her face grazed, her knees bloody, her hands hugged fearfully against her. Honey mopped at the tears with a fold of her skirt, hardly noticing the other children huddled in a hostile group at a distance.

'Poor Jenny,' she soothed, 'never mind, let's go in the caravan and find some chocolate.'

Fear flickered inexplicably across the innocent eyes. 'I don't want to,' Jenny said bewilderingly, her look full of mistrust.

Honey stood up with her. 'Come on, you're a brave girl. We'll put something nice on your knee, stop it hurting—'

'No, no!' The child's voice rose to a squeal. 'I don't want to. There's a nasty man in there!' And she struggled down and hobbled away still sobbing, trying to cover her hurt knees with her dress. The ranks of the children closed silently around her and her sister with a sidelong glance put a protective arm about her.

Even the children, thought Honey. The little group moved off down the dusty road, leaving her alone with her pain.

Once they ceased rushing to remove the graffiti the spice apparently went out of renewing them and the nuisance fizzled out. The name board on the gate was torn down one night and replaced by one roughly daubed with the legend UNCLE SAMS CABIN. But after what had been, that was a pleasantry.

More disturbing were the letters that Honey began to receive. Ill-spelt and ungrammatical, the first one read:

YOU BRAZEN SLUT HOW CAN YOU ACT SO SHAMELESS WHEN THERES A DECENT WHITE CHAP WOLD OF MARRYD YOU BUT HE WONT BE SEE DEAD WITH YOU NOW I SHOLDT WONDER

SIGNED A WELL WISHER

She sighed, and consigned it to the fire. Perhaps she should take it to the police, but what was the point? Even if they discovered who was responsible—an arrest, a conviction, and hate would have something to feed on; one martyr might find a hundred partisans. No, best to say nothing. But she sighed again, because it was one more thing she could not share with Sam.

Honey still bought groceries and oddments at Mrs Figg's. It was the main shop of the village and was open on Sunday mornings, and although she found with exasperating frequency that what she asked for was 'out of stock' when she could see it plainly standing on the shelf, she stubbornly refused to be elbowed out. She was learning toughness from Sam, although hers was of a defiant nature and lacked his long-term quality of quiet stocism.

Early one Sunday, she went to buy marmalade. David Bassett was serving in the shop, with old Mrs Figg, frail nowadays, just visible in a wheelchair at the back of the shop.

'Morning, Honey,' said David.

'Morning, David,' she looked up and smiled, pleasantly surprised to be greeted by her name, 'I hope your aunt's not ill?'

'No, she's all right.' He reached down the marmalade from behind him. 'I'm just giving her a bit of a break, like. It's a lot of work for one old girl, what with the Post Office and all.' He rested his arms along the counter and

230

his expression changed subtly. 'And what about you, you all right, are you?'

'Yes, I'm all right,' she said guardedly, beginning to mistrust his manner. She put the coins on the counter and heard the shop bell tinkle as more people came in behind her. David did not move. He said, loudly and with a deepening smile, 'Not wearing you out, is he, that nigger of yours? What's it like sleeping with him, enjoying it are you?'

Honey's face burned and her fingers closed round the marmalade jar, but somehow she controlled the impulse to smash it in his face. She waited for the wave to recede and leave her in command. Then she said, 'Very much, thank you,' and had the satisfaction of seeing him flinch, 'it's a lot better than sleeping with you. And,' she added spitefully, 'he doesn't keep a chamber-pot under the bed!' She picked up the jar and walked with measured steps towards the door.

An outraged babble broke out behind her as with shaking hands she fumbled for the latch. 'Well, I never!' and 'Oh, there's brass for you!' Her eyes misted with anger, she could not see what she was doing, she wrestled impotently, hampered by the marmalade.

'Open the door for her, David, I'm sure we don't wish to keep her!' Mrs Figg's querulous voice joined the others.

'Let her fancy man come and open it for her, I ain't waiting on the likes of her!'

Honey rounded on him, her self-control in ribbons. 'Don't bother, I'm very particular who waits on me!'

'Pity you're not so fussy in bed,' snarled David, 'any old rubbish seems to do for you.'

'I *am* fussy, I *am*!' She was sobbing now with rage and humiliation. 'He's the best in the world, you ought to know that, David, you of all people! You should be on his side helping him, not jumping on the wagon with the others—as for you, all of you, you ought to be ashamed!'

Mrs Figg bridled like a pouter pigeon. 'Open the door, David, get her out, I won't have the hussy in my shop!'

Somebody jostled her and she pulled away. 'I'm going, I'm going!' She wrenched the door open at last and turned on David. 'He should have let you drown,' she cried passionately, 'I wish he had, I do, I do—'

A hand fell on her shoulder from behind and she whirled to look.

'Oh, Sam!'

'You all finished here?' he said, unsmiling. She nodded, unable to speak. He took the jar from her hand and led her from the place. The others in the shop might not have been present.

They walked home in silence. Honey held her breath to keep from sobbing, flicking away from time to time the tears that streamed down her face despite her high-held head. Slowly it was borne in on her that he was angry; she could feel it in the pressure of his fingers grasping her arm. 'Sam—'

'Don't do that, Honey.' His voice was cold, the voice he sometimes used to Arthur. But he had never used it to her. 'Don't ever do that again. Don't make a scene.'

'They hate you because of me.'

'So who cares, a couple of old women with tits like vinegar corks.'

'But I have to defend you—you know I do!'

'They know it too, you're just playing into their hands.' But looking at her he felt his anger melting. She was so young, so vulnerable, while he had years of hard experience to stiffen his spine. 'Don't try to fight them, Honey. They'll crucify you, and I shall have to watch.'

'But we mustn't give in! Some day it'll be different for us, I know it will!'

Sam sighed. 'Another time, another planet...here and now is where we live. Don't go crusading, Honey. Crusaders get killed.'

'But if nobody stands up and fights it'll never be any better!' When he did not answer she added resignedly, 'What is it you want me to do?'

'Let it slide over you—do like Brer Rabbit, remember the old story?'

'You tell me,' she said, nostalgic for her childhood.

Sam smiled. 'He jest la-ay low, and he don't say nothing,' he quoted, his voice making music of it.

They went indoors and Honey looked at the breakfast table. 'All this fuss because of marmalade and now we don't want it.'

'Who says we don't want it? I'm still hungry.' He sat her firmly down and lit the gas under the kettle. She shook her head. 'Just coffee,' she said as he brought the pot to the table.

'Not just coffee,' said Sam. 'Look, Honey, if you're

going to lose your appetite over things like this you'll pretty soon starve to death.'

A large tear ran off her chin and splashed on to the empty plate. He leaned across and cupped her chin in his warm brown hand, his dark face illumined by his lovely smile.

'Look at me,' he said, 'I'm not crying.' He drew her around the table on to his knee. Their arms enfolded one another, a curious contentment stole over them and presently, a warmth and a sweetness entirely natural.

But for the first time their loving was spiced with sorrow and the salt of tears.

9

About once a week the anonymous letters came. The second was addressed to Sam and said, 'GET OUT YOU BLACK BASTERD OR WELL RUN YOU OUT SO HELP ME.'

'Lose five marks for spelling,' said Sam, tossing it into the fire.

More often they were addressed to Honey and were variants on the first. All were destined for the fire but if they were together they read them first. It was easier to take them lightly when Sam was there because he could always find something to laugh at. But if Honey was alone when one arrived she burnt it unseen and went out for a walk.

Added to this were petty annoyances such as the pouring away of their morning milk so that all they found were the empty bottles. This happened with such irritating frequency that Sam in an unguarded moment asked the milkman to put the bottles in through a window. He was rewarded with 'Are you kidding?' and a look that set his teeth on edge. There were days when they came home

to find the contents of their dustbin strewn about the garden, the plants and shrubs decorated with inverted empty cans. The first time they laughed. But on the fourth occasion Honey leaned on the gate and said, 'Oh, no, not again, aren't they sick of it yet?' Neither was it amusing to arrive home in the frosty dusk and find that the coal bunker had been rifled, the coal laid down the path in a weird black glistening causeway from the gate to the wagon steps. It was impossible to clear it without treading in it, and it was late that night when they sank down at last to the comfort of fire and coffee, too exhausted to eat. Honey dropped her head on her arms and said wearily, 'Aren't they ever going to leave us alone?'

Sam reached out a hand to console her. 'I don't know, Honey.' He was tired too.

It was like that in the beginning. Always the persecutions were small, nothing that could not be explained away as a mischievous prank of 'they children'. But when Sam attempted to scotch the nuisance by putting a padlock on the coal bunker it was immediately evident that other elements were involved. No child could have unbolted the concrete slabs of the bunker and left it disarmingly still standing, its padlock still in place, ready to disintegrate at a touch and spew its contents everywhere. Sam sighed. At best this was the work of the village lads, aligned, since the fracas in the shop, on the side of virtue and David Bassett. But he was careful not to say so to Honey.

Honey had reached the same conclusion on her own. She had learned too late the wisdom of a still tongue, remembering the David of her childhood who would wait for ever if need be to avenge a slight. A David not far removed from the one of today who palely loitered alone every night in the Rose. 'Poor young chap,' muttered the villagers, 'and him giving up a job in town to come and look after his auntie's shop. Nice welcome for him, I must say! Never looked at another girl, he hasn't—close he might be, awk'ard he may be, honest and clean-living he allus was—not like some you could mention!' and, 'Disgusting, sleeping with his daughter! Still, what can you expect? What's bred in the bone will out in the flesh, you can't expect no other...' Anger against the disgraced McLeods was discreetly fanned, never allowed to die down.

A stone was flung at Honey which cut her face and after that Sam would not allow her to come through the village alone. On the days when she worked, she would wait at the surgery after Cowan had left, and catch Sam's bus as it came from the railway station. Thus it was that on one Wednesday evening, when the village shop was closed, all three protagonists found themselves on the bus together—or almost together.

An ice-cold sleety rain drove in eddies around the group at the stop, gilded sharply by the approaching headlights. Those waiting huddled morosely in their inadequate coats, shifting their chilled feet between puddles in a fruitless attempt to keep warm as the bus drew up alongside. Tempers were short and the bus already full. Sam gave up his seat to Honey and moved out on to the platform, just as several would-be passengers including David Bassett crowded on to it.

It was obvious that some would have to dismount. But no one was willing to wait another hour in the wind and the rain; they herded stubbornly in the confined space while the conductress fought her way down the crowded aisle to turn them off. Shouting shrilly and brandishing her ticket-holder, she descended on them; as she emerged, David slipped behind her unnoticed into the body of the bus.

'All off the bus, *if* you please!' She emphasised the command by shoving at the two nearest to her, one of whom happened to be Sam. He shook off her hand and stayed where he was.

'I was here already.'

'You can't travel on the platform. You'll have to get off.'

'But I was inside. Look, I have a ticket.'

The clippie, annoyed to find herself in the wrong, took refuge in bluster. 'I'm in charge of this bus and I say you can't ride on the platform. This bus doesn't move till you get off. All the lot of you!' She rounded on the others.

Sam hesitated, his good sense telling him to get off, his imagination warning him of the hazard to Honey, left to walk from the stop at the other end alone. There were too many crowded between them for him to catch her eye. And there was David, safely ensconced within the bus. He thought quickly.

'David,' he said urgently, catching at his sleeve, 'I'll

235

have to get off; look after Honey, will you?' It was an old trick, putting the known thief in charge of the safe. Was it going to work?

David twitched his arm away, his nostrils working like those of a mouse. 'Do it yourself,' he snapped all too audibly, 'think I want your leavings?'

In Sam without warning the long thread of his patience snapped. His left hand whipped out and grasped the boy's clothing and his right landed with a satisfying crack under the jaw. David went hurtling backwards, the standing passengers going down behind him like cards along a conjuror's arm. Instantly half a dozen pairs of hands seized Sam and flung him into the road.

The panicked conductress struck out blindly with her ticket-holder and frantically rang the bell. The driver, startled, let in his clutch with a jerk and the bus lurched away just as Sam struggled to his feet, the passengers on the platform clinging on for dear life. Which, when he thought about it later, he realised was probably lucky for him.

Honey, when the argument started, was trying not to lose her sense of humour with the girl sitting next to her.

Her name was Cissie Idle. Her mother Bessie, herself not undistinguished in her way, had been heard to say that she was glad to see one of her daughters with the sense to earn her living on her back. Now Cissie was intrigued by the thought of sex with a strong dark tang to it. Unabashed, she was grilling Honey for the details.

'Come on, tell us,' she nudged her confidentially, 'what's it like—you know? With him, like? I've heard tell it's their noses, is that right?'

'Noses?' repeated Honey, mystified. As long as the questions were confined to noses, she could keep her temper.

'Yeah,' returned Cissie, 'noses. You know, all them twirly nostrils.'

As she spoke the rumpus started. Honey jumped up and Cissie was forgotten as she was knocked aside by the cascade of falling bodies. She had just regained her feet when the bus started violently and threw her down again, but divining that something was amiss with Sam she rang the bell and ploughed her way to the exit, where David among the crowd of sympathisers sat fondling his bloodied chin.

'Hit him, he did.' Someone obviously did not recognise her. 'That black fellow—hit him flying.'

'I hope it hurts,' said Honey as she got off the bus.

The distance travelled by a bus in a matter of seconds is always a surprise. Walking back, Honey began to think she must have missed Sam in the darkness. Perhaps he was lying in a ditch, perhaps—

But then, there he was swinging along the road towards her. In the reflected light from a window she saw him smile and break into a trot.

'Are you all right?' she called anxiously, noting the handkerchief held to his face.

'Sure I'm all right. I'm fine. Never felt so good. When we get home I'll write a symphony—no, two symphonies. And a string quartet before breakfast!'

'Lovely,' said Honey, 'wonderful—just as soon as we've swept up the coal.'

'How do you know it won't be dustbins?'

'Coal,' she said with certainty, 'we haven't had coal for a fortnight.' His arm around her shoulders swung her along with him.

He grinned a little sheepishly. 'OK, now say I told you so.'

Honey laughed happily. 'I'm saving that till I feel mean.'

Still walking they drew closer together, in a silence filled with their measured tread. Then he said, 'You haven't asked me yet why I hit him.'

'Do you want to tell me?'

'Not much.'

'That's why I'm not asking.' Their faces turned to each other in the darkness, and they smiled. 'Stop a minute. I want to kiss you...'

Kissing out of doors under the dark wild sky was strangely exciting, the cold rain and the night air, the warmth of his mouth in contrast.

'We're getting wet,' he murmured at length.

'I know,' she whispered, and drew him down again. At last he freed himself with a little shiver. 'Let's get home quickly,' and they strode out briskly through the puddles, filled with a little glow of cheerfulness.

'Cold?'

'Not now.'

Presently Sam began to sing under his breath and she joined her voice to his:

'I know an old lady who swallowed a fly.
I don't know why she swallowed the fly—
Perhaps she'll die...'

They laughed as they sang, pursuing the strange old
lady through her edible menagerie, and when they had
disposed of her they went on through every song they
could remember, their voices light above their tramping
feet as they put the miles behind them. Out of the town
and through the village they sang, indifferent to the slamming window, the extinguished light, flinging their small
defiance to the winds. Their singing rose up through the
night sky like a curl of smoke from the courage within
them.

Much later as they lay between the sympathetic sheets,
Honey lay looking up into Sam's dark face, the familiar
roofing of the bed-place behind it. She drew a light finger
along his eyebrow and down his nose. 'All them twirly
nostrils,' she said amusedly. Then, as he flinched,
'What's the matter?'

'Nothing—I slipped getting off the bus. What's that
about twirly nostrils?'

'Cissie Idle,' she said, expecting him to laugh, 'she
thinks you're very attractive, with twirly nostrils.'

To her surprise he frowned. 'When were you talking
to her?'

'On the bus. Why not? She wanted to talk to me, not
many people do.' She could have bitten her tongue out
having said that. But she could not take it back. 'I think
she's a bit lonely. Glad of someone to speak to.' Aware
that she had made it worse, she fell silent.

Sam said, 'But you're not like her. You know that,
Honey.'

'I'd rather be like her than like some people,' she said
fervently. 'Heaven defend me from the righteous!'

Sam sighed in the darkness. 'I guess for a man in a
glass house I'm throwing too many stones.'

'You never throw stones,' she told him, and they settled down to sleep. She lay contentedly with the dear
weight of his head on her shoulder, appreciating the softness of his hair against her cheek, and lay for a long time
savouring the quietness, the peace of the early hours
when alone of all the village only they were awake, the
hostile thoughts of the others stilled by sleep.

Only the sick or the dying lay wakeful at this hour. And if their watch was shared by some woman in childbirth she was preoccupied by the stress of labour, her thoughts turned in upon herself and in no way concerned with them. Births, marriages and deaths, she thought, they all take place at night. The real business of living goes on while the world is asleep.

Sam stirred in her arms with a drowsy inarticulate murmur. She held him close and kissed his closed eyelids, counting herself deeply blessed in the love of such a man. She found herself thinking of Cissie Idle, of her shoddy unrewarding existence, shared only with her blowsy mother and her casual indifferent men. 'Poor Cissie,' she said softly to herself, 'what a lonely life...'

But Sam heard her words and sleep fled from him, banished by the conviction that because of him, Honey was learning what it meant to be Cissie Idle.

They still went doggedly to lunch at the Stone House on Sundays; but it was not the pleasure that it might have been.

It was impossible to relax in the face of Ellen's loyal assertion that the scandal in the village was 'Just a mess of wicked lies!' and of Arthur's well-meant preoccupation with the very problems they longed to lay aside; and Maggie was becoming so coy with embarrassment that she did everything short of patting them on the head. Yet go they did. It was partly a clinging to what remained of normality in their life, partly because it was the one outing from which they could be sure of returning to find Mango Walk as they had left it. 'Thou shalt not revile the sinful on the Sabbath' seemed to be the eleventh commandment in the village: or perhaps they were accorded diplomatic immunity while eating the Colbys' salt. Dr Arthur was a figure of some importance in the district. Being the only doctor for miles, he had to be.

'I see young Bassett's lost a front tooth,' he remarked on the Sunday after the bus incident.

Sam thoughtfully tested his own teeth with his thumb. 'Little Black Sambo still got his,' he said.

Arthur looked worried. 'You must watch your step, you know, Sam. I can well believe the little perisher asked for it but you have to remember you're a foreigner to these people and they're very narrow—'

239

'For God's sake,' protested Sam, 'how long does it take to get naturalised around here? I've lived here on and off nearly twenty years.'

'You have to be born here,' said Arthur flatly, 'and your parents and grandparents too. Even I have a taint in their eyes because I went outside the country to get my degree. They'd probably rather I'd stayed here and dosed them with horse pills made of kitchen soap.'

Sam brooded, gnawing his lip. 'Sometimes I wish I'd never seen this place,' he said.

An unmarried couple which was also of mixed race was something entirely new in the experience of the village. The question of incest was one that was argued hotly from both sides; for every individual who believed it, there was at least one other who held that they were not related and never had been—well, you only had to look, how could they be?—and that That Man had carried off a little innocent white girl and waited for her to grow up. There was a nice how-d'ye-do! And it was hard to say which view provoked the greater indignation. Disgusting, it was, and a blot on the whole community.

Naturally, when a visitor from outside the area came to the village, he had to be impressed with the extent of its disapproval, lest he go away with the wrong impression: it was not to be thought further afield that such goings-on were blinked at hereabouts. Such was life in remote places; and such was the state of affairs when the young Brodniks had their cousin Norman to stay.

The only child of a mother whose health had been sickly since his birth, the Brodniks' cottage was his only refuge when adversity pinned her on her back.

Mary Brodnik had married a Pole. Leastways, she said he was a Pole, though you never could tell with a name like that, not really; he could've been one of them Bolshies or anything. During the war, that was. Soon as it was over he'd scampered off home, whatever he was, leaving Mary with a parcel of debts and a couple of brats thrown in. Some said he'd been married already and had gone back to his wife; others that he had been shot as a Red—or by the Reds—or something. Whichever the reason, Mary was stranded, left to work off her debts on Public Assistance and bring up her foreign-looking brood as best she could.

The truth was that Mary had loved Jan Brodnik deeply.

His 'desertion' to the sanatorium where he died had stilled the springs of joy in her, she went about her dim world slavishly, doing only what she must, speaking to no one, hearing, seeing and caring for nothing, not even for the boys. Her marriage to Jan had made all of them outcasts. She knew this, and cared not at all.

But the young Brodniks knew it and cared a great deal. Because of their mother's silence they knew their father only through village gossip and were filled with a cankering resentment that embraced all foreigners. They longed to be accepted by the society which shunned them, to be members of the gang of youths loafing between chapel and church on Sunday evenings. They hated being referred to off-handedly as 'they Brodniks' and brushed aside as though they did not count.

Perversely, this gave them no sympathy with the despised McLeods. Rather, they saw them as a stepping-stone to security for themselves. To come out strongly on the side of the village must, they felt, strengthen their own pretensions as locals, and their support, if unwanted, was at least unqualified.

It was on Saturday, in the late afternoon, that Honey came slowly up the lane towards the bus stop on her own. She was hanging back for Sam, but the Brodniks and their cousin did not know that. Neither did the groups of stragglers walking down from the bus, children and teenagers coming home from their Saturday outing in the town. What they saw was That Girl, alone for once and unguarded, a heaven-sent opportunity for bravado in the Brodniks, a chance to shine in the eyes of their disparagers.

The elder boy, Peter, whistled as she passed, with an obscene gesture that sent the others into paroxysms of delight.

Honey looked away, her face burning scarlet. The boys looked for, and found, a grudging admiration from their fellows: two or three detached themselves, crossing the road to join them.

Honey, aware of a closing of the ranks, tried not to notice the fact that they were now between her and Sam. She hoped he would hurry. There was a quality of menace in their taunting that frightened her.

The boys nudged one another and fell in behind her. They sniggered and scuffled and tweaked at her clothing. Unnerved, she quickened her step.

One of the boys shouted above the catcalls, 'Here—
does the blacking rub off?' and fresh glee broke out among
them.

She said nothing, quickened her pace again, prayed
for Sam to appear...she did not dare to look back.

'Hey! Does it rub off, I said?' the taunt was repeated.
They wanted her to answer. She was being poor sport for
them. But she must not play into their hands. They began
to jostle her, closing in on her, big boys, some almost
fully grown.

'Does the colour rub off, does the colour rub off...'
they chanted, pushing her, shoving her with their shoulders so that she rebounded helplessly from one to another
of them, unable to walk a straight line. She dropped the
scarf she was carrying and, trying to retrieve it, found her
fingers deliberately trodden on. She stifled her cry of pain
and stumbled on, not daring to lift her eyes from the grey
cold road. Fallen leaves from the hedge whirled past her
vision, red, gold, brown, as she struggled with her fear,
while the young Brodniks capered wildly, intoxicated
with success.

'Does the colour rub off, does the colour rub off...'

There seemed to be more of them now, pushing, el-
bowing, trying to trip her. She could feel their steaming
breath on her neck. Oh, God, where was Sam? Had he
been waylaid too? She longed to run, but instinct warned
her it was madness...a sob escaped her. Instantly, they
jostled her harder, bruising her, kicking her ankles,
stamping on her toes.

'Come on, boys, let's have a look!'

The raucous shout, the rough hands on her clothing,
lifting her skirt. The smell of unbrushed teeth and ado-
lescent sweat, the scrape of hobnailed boots upon the
road—the violence of childhood bedded in the strength
of the adult male—and common sense deserted her.

'No—oh, no—please, let me go,' she pleaded, and at
last, 'Sam! Sam, help me!' was torn from her as, lashing
out blindly, she felt herself forced backwards into the
hedge. They fell upon her like animals, just as Sam
rounded the corner into view.

At the sound of his answering bellow the boys froze
where they stood. But it was only for an instant. Then
his head went down, his eyes flashed murder, and he
charged them, terrible in his rage.

They broke and fled, shrieking in terror, in delight,

242

like the children they were, running wildly, blinded by excitement, into the road at the lane's end.

'Honey, are you all right?'

'Yes—God, what was that!'

An agonised scream of brakes, a sickening smack as the wing of the car hit something soft. Then a dreadful, a horrifying silence, broken only by the slamming of the driver's door. As Sam, running ahead, emerged from the lane someone began to scream, shattering the air that had crystallised to the brittleness of glass. But the screams were not coming from the boy who had been hit.

He was lying quite still, his face grey as the road.

'It's Norm,' somebody said in a shocked whisper, 'young Norm, that's staying with they Brodniks.'

They stared at him. It was hard to see where he was hurt until the eye followed the tyre marks in the blood-brown dust and found the dim shape of the severed foot, still lying in the dirt under the car. The girl who had been screaming went quiet, and had to be led away to vomit.

When Honey stumbled up still shaking, on legs that had dissolved below the knee, Sam and Arthur Colby, whose car it mercifully was, were kneeling in the road-way, facing each other across the inert body of the boy; Arthur dealing swiftly, efficiently with the practicalities, Sam stricken with anguish by the thing he had brought about.

'Oh, God...' he muttered brokenly, 'oh, God...'

'Shut up,' snapped Arthur under his breath, then as Sam continued 'Oh, God...oh, God...for Chrissake, Arthur, give me something to do...' he lifted his head and barked full into Sam's unguarded face, 'You've bloody well done enough!'

It seemed to them both on looking back that they had never seen trouble before that hour.

Honey stood looking down at Sam. His eyes were closed, his face impassive. But she had seen the fleeting expressions that had winged across it—the shock, the incredulity, the guilt. The unbelievable pain.

'It wasn't his fault,' she hissed furiously. 'You know that. How could you say that to him!'

Arthur did not answer her. His hands moved smoothly, continuously, as if she had not spoken. Without looking up he thrust his bag towards her. 'Dressings,' he demanded tersely. 'And a hypodermic. Are your hands clean?'

243

'Not clinically,' she snapped, 'neither are yours if you've been driving.' It was a childish retaliation but it eased her tension and stilled his acid tongue. She knelt in the grit of the road and opened the bag, found dressings and handed them to him where he sat grim-faced, his practised thumbs boring into the pressure points.

'Arthur, you haven't answered me.' Her voice shook a little with the effort of control. 'It wasn't Sam's fault. You know it wasn't.'

Arthur said nothing, but Sam raised his eyes, his head moved almost imperceptibly and she saw that he did not want her to say any more, did not want his grief made public. Wanted only to be alone with it, alone and quiet, until he had got its size.

She charged the hypodermic, expelling the air as her hands remembered how, and handed it to Arthur. Someone said, 'Ambulance is on the way, I phoned from the shop.'

Honey stood up, looking at the group in the road, trying to feel pity for the crippled boy. But she could not, he was not real to her, her concern for him lost in her agony for Sam. She saw only him, his stricken eyes, his helpless hands, his bowed shoulders, the gaunt trees clawing the sky behind him.

The picture seared itself into her, never to be escaped. For her afterwards, that moment and that place went hand in hand.

All through the rest of that day she was thinking, Sam will need me tonight; when all this is over and we are alone he will turn to me and I shall comfort him. All through the nerve-racking hours, at the hospital, at the police station, she clung to the thought, answering questions with only part of her attention, her mind turning towards him, watching him with compassion and with love, waiting for the time when they would all go away and she could cradle his aching head between her breasts. She always knew when his head was aching: there was a certain pucker between his eyebrows. No one else knew that about Sam, not even Arthur, and the knowledge made her feel special in a warming sort of way.

But when night came and she went to him, he held her briefly and in silence, as though she were dead, as though she were a stranger. Then he turned away from her and fell at once into a heavy sleep.

She lay awake for a long time, willing herself not to cry and wake him, feeling alone as she had never felt before. For the first time, the gap between their ages made her afraid, because in his deep trouble she could not reach him, because his need was to be solitary, even from her. Something she had said in that poignant summer before they parted came drifting through her thought: 'I've made you unhappy, and I wanted it to be so different...' She hid her face because the sight of his averted shoulder made her desolate, and when later he turned in his sleep and his arms came searching for her she huddled into them gratefully, consoled by his warmth. But the wayward tears ran down between his skin and hers before she slept.

A hush fell on the village. Several weeks passed. Weeks during which the village nudged and muttered to itself, 'Why didn't you say?' and answered resentfully, 'Well, why didn't you?' unable to countenance the truth that Sam was innocent. Feeling against him ran higher than ever, yet the fact could not be blinked that he had not touched the boy, had not even been within reach of him at the crucial moment. He had stayed behind with Honey when the boys took flight, and only raced ahead of her when he heard the sounds of disaster. Too many had witnessed the facts for anyone to risk a lie to the authorities; yet they felt him to be morally responsible, a sentiment they did not credit him with sharing, and burned with righteous anger because of their blind conviction that justice was being cheated.

They wanted him arrested, convicted, punished, scourged—anything. They wanted their just revenge. Their hatred spilled sidelong from their eyes as he passed. An unnerving hush settled on any group at his approach.

Only the eyes followed him, trained like gunsights on his back.

10

'I don't like this silence,' said Honey. 'You don't know what's in their minds.'

'I do,' said Sam, thinking grimly, Someone's going to town to buy a rope. Could it really come to that? He could not imagine this pastel landscape marred by the dangling corpse of the lynched...he shivered, remembering the long ago days of the Blitz: you always thought it would not happen to you.

Honey gave up her job, knowing that he lived in constant fear of her being waylaid. But she missed the companionship, and her sense of foreboding was heightened by the long hours she spent alone. Would it always be like this, would they never be able to jog along in peace as others did? Might not things be easier for them in some other place...She put it to Sam.

'Everyone knows us here, in another place it might be different.'

'Where would we live?'

She thought for a moment, 'I suppose we could take the caravan. A horse could move it. One did before, when we moved down from the farm.' But even as she spoke she knew it was a fantasy.

Sam shook his head. 'We shall have music wherever we go. There isn't any place in the world there wouldn't be someone who feels like this. We have to sit tight and stay where we are, refuse to be driven out. If we lose here, believe me we can't win anywhere. And that's for certain sure.'

Honey sighed. 'All those drab, ordinary people living happy, peaceful lives. Why can't we?'

Sam laughed. 'We could, if we'd give in and separate. We could be peaceful. If that's what we wanted...'

'We wouldn't be happy,' said Honey with certainty, 'anyway I wouldn't be.'

'No, we wouldn't be happy. But we can't be both, not as long as you're you and I'm me.' He smiled through his cigarette smoke, drew her head against his shoulder.

'Sam, what will happen to us?' she said, and her voice was troubled.

'Let's not think about it,' he said.

'No—do you ever wonder what we'll be like? When we're old, I mean.' She sat up, and her eyes meeting his held faint surprise. 'Somehow I can't imagine us old together, can you?'

Something chill stirred in his stomach. Something unexplained.

'Don't,' he said sharply, his mind reeling back from the edge of an abyss.

Winter settled on the village. Birdsong dwindled to an uncertain trickle, overlaid by the plaintive cries of gulls as they veered inland, driven before the wind. The sea roared and howled along the shore; when the wind dropped a thick white mist crawled hungrily up the dunes in the grey-blue afternoon. The rooks in the vicarage elms went early to bed, rising up from their buildings in the leafless trees against a pearl-grey sky, raking the air with harsh cawings in their mysterious ritual of settling for the night.

Sam arrived home in the evenings, chilled by his walk down from the bus, bringing with him into a wagon aglow with firelight the bite of frost, the flavour of bonfire smoke. Honey would rub her face against his, and even his lips were cold.

The morning, when he was newly departed and she had many hours to kill before his return, she packed tight with activity to keep nagging fears at bay. She could rarely settle sufficiently to eat, and afternoon found her on thorns, watching and waiting in the gathering dusk. As darkness fell she drew the curtains hurriedly before she lit the lamp, hating to feel the uncurtained windows like eyes behind her back. From that time on, the hissing of the lamp, the white face of the clock, were the bounds of her narrow world, hemming her in with unadmitted fear.

At the sound of his tread outside it would expand and shatter, the walls of the wagon that had been her cell

would be vibrant with warmth and light, her anxiety melting like mist in the sun with the knowledge that he was safely home and life could start again.

Winter deepened. In Mrs Figg's shop window red and green crepe paper blossomed among the packets of soap, and a tiny spruce died in a blaze of glory, festooned with tinsel and silver baubles, scenting the shop with Christmas. The light from the shop window glowed out across the evening frosty grass, or reflected from puddles under an icy drizzle of rain. Choir practice was stepped up; choristers with numb toes and fingers warbled dutifully in the echoing church, their carolling blessing the frigid air that turned their breath to vapour as they sang. The season of goodwill spread a fire-blanket over the village. Norm was still in hospital, out of sight and temporarily out of mind. The outcasts of Mango Walk drew a breath, and wondered if they were to be granted an amnesty.

On the Friday before Christmas Sam came home late with the first flakes of snow caught like stardust in his woolly hair.

'I met Arthur on the way home. They want us to go there Christmas Day.'

Honey brushed snow from his coat and tried not to show her disappointment. She had looked forward to two days alone with him. 'What did you tell him?'

'I said I'd ask you. What do you want to do?'

As long as they were together, it was not so important where. 'I'll do whatever you like.'

Sam looked at her and slowly shook his head. 'Girl, I do wish you wouldn't say that.'

'Why ever not?'

He hesitated. 'Makes me feel I overlaid you, failed you somewhere along the line. You grew up facing the wrong way around, looking back towards me instead of out towards the world.'

Honey turned from the pot she was stirring on the stove to look up into his face. 'Not that old worry again. What's brought this on?'

'Nothing...everything. I don't know. All this trouble I'm dragging you through maybe. It makes me feel bad. And every time you say you'll leave a decision to me I feel guilty.'

'Oh, Sam...' sighed Honey. She put down the wooden spoon and drew him down beside her on to a seat. 'Look, love...every woman starts out as a child, and someone

has to bring her up. In my case it just happened to be you, but why does it matter to you so terribly, why must you blame yourself for everything I do?'

'Because you never blame me for anything, and you should! You should realise I'm human, liable to make mistakes, to mislead you, to go wrong myself. Not god-head, not infallible, not a pattern for you to follow without thought. I'm afraid for you, Honey, afraid that one day I'll make a bad decision and you'll accept it and come to grief. Look—' he waved an arm in the general direction of the sea—'if I said, "Come jump off the cliff with me," you'd come, wouldn't you?' Honey was silent. 'Wouldn't you?' he insisted.

Honey lowered her eyes. She knew that if Sam were to leap off the cliff she would want to go with him, unable to face a world that he had left. But she was sure it was not because he had robbed her of her will.

'Yes, I suppose I would,' she said sadly. Because a lie could not pass between them and there was no help for him in the truth.

He broke away from her and stood up, pacing restlessly in the restricted space. After a while, Honey said, 'Sometimes I almost wish I had grown up in that orphanage.' He stopped to look at her. 'Yes, I do.' Her voice was gentle, serious. 'I'd have found you somehow, and loved you as I had to. And you wouldn't be tearing yourself apart like this.'

Sam said nothing, merely held her in that curiously intense gaze. He looked older, she thought, there were shadows and hollows in his face she had not seen before.

She said, 'Can't you see, you're tearing me as well?' Her eyes filled in spite of herself. 'Why must you do it, why?'

'I don't know...I don't know.' He came back to sit beside her, took her hands. But he did not meet her eyes. 'I'm sorry. But you put an intolerable weight on me, making me always the one to take the lead—knowing if I go astray you'll follow me. It's better, safer to walk side by side.'

She broke away and stood up, her back to him. 'You want me to love you less. Is that what you're saying? It is, isn't it?' She felt hurt, angry; this was the nearest they had had to a row.

After a moment he said reluctantly, 'Yes. Perhaps it is.'

She whirled to look at him, to see his face, whether he really meant it. But she had no time in which to read his expression. They both leaped violently in alarm and automatically clutched one another, as a rock came crashing through the window in a shower of glass.

11

They stood tense, waiting. Their eyes locked together. Nothing happened.

There was only silence, filled with the sighing of the wind through grass, the rattle of bare azalea branches outside, the myriad faint sounds of which silence is composed. Nothing else.

They waited and listened for so long that when Sam moved carefully to extinguish the lamp the sound of his rubber-soled shoes on the lino screamed in their ears like the tearing of calico. Honey let go the breath she had been holding with a gasp that startled them both.

Sam signed to her not to move. He edged towards the broken pane, lifting a corner of the curtain with one finger as he did so. Instantly a second stone followed the first, smashing the mirror over the stove and falling in a rain of daggerlike splinters to the floor. Sam drew back his head and felt the breeze of it whistle past his face. But he had seen enough.

Keeping his head low he slipped back to where Honey now crouched, bare feet drawn up, on the edge of the seat. He drew her feet towards him, fumbling on the floor with his other hand, smiling up into her frightened face in the darkness, trying to reassure her while he found her shoes. 'Nearly lost the twirly nostrils,' he whispered, but she did not smile. He pushed on her shoes, tapping them first in case of glass splinters, then felt for her hands.

They were cold and trembling. He drew her to her feet.

'Don't make a sound,' his mouth said against her ear, 'we're going through to the washroom.'

She glanced at him in surprise but moved obediently. He kept his body between hers and the menacing grey square of the window and after an eternity they reached the doorway on the opposite bulkhead.

'Thank God I made this,' whispered Sam. He went down first and lifted her after him, afraid she might stumble and make a tell-tale sound. As they reached the washroom a low catcall reached his ears. He moved swiftly to the outer door, drawing her with him, and bent to the lower bolt, leaning his shoulder to the door in order to slide the bolt back silently.

Honey stood shivering beside him, conscious of the smell of soap, the coldness of the draught from the broken window, her stomach contracted into an icy knot of fear.

'Who is it out there?' she whispered through chattering teeth. 'What do they want?'

He was easing the key in the lock now, using both hands to forestall the tell-tale snap of the tumbler. 'Come close and listen carefully. It's just some of the lads, boozed up and out to make a scene. I want you to slip out this way, cut up across the farm and go straight to the Colbys. I'll come for you as soon as I've got rid of them.'

'But it's after ten o'clock—'

'Turning-out time, they'll understand. Tell Arthur what's happened, he'll know what to do. Knock them up if you have to. And don't let anyone here see you go.'

'Sa-ambo-o-o!'

They were getting restive. Another rock came through the window to land with a dull clunk on the linoleum behind them. He realised he must get her away before they guessed there was no one in the wagon. Maybe a movement there would hold them off, deceive them for long enough...his hand closed over a cake of soap and he pitched it up through the doorway into the caravan.

He turned back to Honey, urgently grasped her shoulders. 'Now, this way is open. Wait till you hear me open the front door, slip out and run like Hell. I'll make enough noise to cover any sound you make.'

'But I don't want to leave you!' She was trying to cling to him, pleading, a very small girl again. But he had peeled off his sweater and was pulling it over her head.

'Come on, Sambo, come and get your medicine!' An older voice. Another stone followed it.

'Honey! Hon-o-oney...Honey Tart? Come and hold his hand?' That brought a cackle of laughter and he prayed she hadn't heard it. 'Come out, come out wherever you are...'

Honey was beginning to shake in the alarming way he remembered. He forced some sort of a grimace to pass as a smile. 'Don't worry, everything's going to be all right, just do like I say.'

She clutched at him. 'Sam...'

He said wryly, 'Look, this is one decision you have to leave to me.' He kissed her quickly, bruisingly, thrust her towards the door. 'Please go for me, Honey. Don't you understand? I'm sending you for help.'

Her hand grasped the doorknob as he melted up the steps, and they both listened. Then she heard him rattle the locks on the main door, she had turned the handle and was out, out in the night air, squeezing through the gap in the hedge, out and running across the frosty fields of the farm.

Sam heard the wash-house door open and close again softly, and knew that she was gone. He let go his breath with a faint sibilance, made a big thing of opening the main door and stepped out on to the porch. They fell back slightly as he emerged and he realised they had expected to have to break in. He had surprise on his side. But it offered him a breathing space he could well have done without, it was noise he needed, and plenty of it, noise to cover the sound of running feet when they gained the metalled road above the farm.

'Well?' he said loudly. 'Come to see Honey, have you? Or will I do just as well?' He came slowly down the steps on to solid ground, waiting.

'You'll do to go on with, you murdering bastard!'

'Murder—' He was taken aback momentarily.

'Murder!' came the chorus of voices. They charged him like a herd of bulls.

'That's for Norm—'

'That's for his mum—'

'That's for me—'

'And me—'

'And me—'

He gasped as somebody's skull crashed into his midriff

and fell heavily against the steps with the rest on top of him. At first he tried to defend himself but they were too many and too strong, against their weight and fury he had no chance. His ears rang with the thunder of blows and at length he covered up and took what was coming to him.

Honey ran as she had never run in her life, all her young sinews stretched to the limit. Her heart pounded in her throat, she felt herself slowing almost to a walk only to be driven on again by the terror of Sam's predicament, until she reached a state wherein it was easier to run than to walk. The road between High Bassetts and the village stretched before and behind her, interminable, featureless on this moonless night of black inhospitable air stung through with the fine-cut cruel barbs of snow, of hard ground, pitiless under her flailing feet.

Her lower legs felt lost to her so that in some fantastic way she seemed to be running on her knees. The dark shapes of cottages loomed against the sky huddled like animals—suppose she tried a nearer door than Arthur's to get help? But their windows were dark, they were all in bed, damn them, damn them! Peacefully sleeping, while Sam...No, worse—they might be awaiting the return of one of the attackers from Mango Walk! She forged on, a prickle of fresh fear running along her spine, sobbing for breath on the last lap, the uphill climb to the Stone House out of the village. She passed the policeman's house and thought briefly of calling him out—but Sam had said the Colbys: she put her trust in him as in the Lord.

She became aware that she was no longer running in a straight line but veering helplessly from one side to the other of the road. Aware too that there was nothing she could do to stop herself, only pray that she would not blunder into a ditch and fail to get out of it.

When at last she reached the Colbys' gate she could not take it in. She stared, feeling she should be going on running, since running had become her way of life. Yet there it was, the calm familiar place, the stone gateposts, the brass plate gleaming dimly in the light from an upstairs window, totally out of place in this nightmare world. She tried to turn in at the driveway and her legs

did not respond. She went sprawling face downward in the gravel and for a moment she could not get up, the ground seemed to be pushing her over backwards, rejecting her, pushing her off into space to swirl and reel away with the climbing snowflakes and be lost in the black night sky.

She fought to drag her drowning mind back to reality. There was something she had to do...something for Sam. Arthur! She had to get Arthur...She pushed with her depleted strength against the ground and felt the reassuring pull of gravity before she fell back again exhausted. But something had gone wrong, something she could not bring back into focus...Someone was crying. She recognised dimly her own voice, moaning, gasping for breath.

With an agonising effort she levered herself up from the ground and half crawled, half staggered the remaining yards to the house, fixing her gaze on the lighted window that blacked out with every choking beat of her heart as though the shutter of a camera had clicked across her eyes.

She reached the heavy studded door and hung there, beating on it feebly with her fists, and it seemed to her that the sound she made was inaudible. She must have sunk to her knees, for as it opened she pitched inside.

Ellen stood staring wide-eyed at the strange apparition: the dishevelled girl, hair streaming wildly down over a man's sweater many sizes too big for her, face and hands cut and bleeding, who lay at her feet helplessly howling like a distracted animal.

For Honey had remembered what it was that had gone wrong. She had come in through gates which already stood wide open. And that could only mean one thing.

Arthur Colby was away on a case.

Honey's memories of that night were restricted to vivid snatches like the pictures in a kaleidoscope: Maggie, sponging her face with cold water, the smell of antiseptic, the urgency of voices on the telephone, the police car that appeared from nowhere, the reassuring detachment of its occupants. But most sharply etched of all were the flying figures caught in the headlights of the car, their fantastic shadows skirling upwards against the high

hedge as they scattered like starlings from the huddled thing in the ditch that must be Sam.

There was the doctor whose startled eyes met hers for an instant before he recovered his professional composure and handed her a torch to hold. She recalled that he asked if she were going to faint, and that she replied too quickly, being unsure herself. That between them they unrolled him and drew down his knees, bringing a sound from his throat like the last spent whimper of a child, more eloquent than any cry of pain.

'Sam...it's all right, it's me...'

'He's quite unconscious,' said the doctor gently, 'help me turn him over, he could choke on all this blood.'

They turned him on to his stomach and she winced as the careful fingers probed the lacerated mouth to give him air. He did not respond again, not even when he was lifted on to the stretcher and swallowed up in the ambulance, a stranger suddenly with a swaddled face, a shape that could have been anyone.

She stood in the road feeling lost, abandoned, watching the ambulance doors closing between them; it was frightening to find him unaware of her, as if she had come racing back to find him gone. She pressed her hand hard against her mouth, was glad of the friendly hand of the policeman tapping her shoulder.

'You can come in the car with us, miss.'

And there were questions...questions...the police, the hospital, she could not remember who or where. But always the same questions.

'And you're his wife?'

'No.'

'Next of kin, though?'

'No.'

'But you are a relative—we might need a signature, you see?'

'I'm no relation.'

And the expected appraising stare, the veiled curiosity, the tedious argument because they were both McLeod.

But dominating all, overlaying her vision at intervals like subliminal advertising, the whirling shadows thrown up by the car's swinging headlights as the tortures broke and fled in all directions. Like the hideous spectres of a nightmare they pervaded her thoughts until even they

were beaten into submission by the sting of a hypodermic, scarcely felt in her exhaustion, which released her into a merciful nothingness.

As light seeped through her eyelids she knew only that she did not want to wake. She covered her face and her arms groped unavailingly for Sam. Then she remembered.

'I must go,' she mumbled, struggling up through the darkness to meet the full weight of disaster like a blow. She swung her feet off the bed and sat swaying, her eyes still closed. She heard a door open, a voice saying, 'Oh, now, now, now!' Hands pushed her back, inexorably, to the pillows.

'I must go, you don't understand,' she protested feebly to the nurse who bent over her, 'I must get back to him.'

'Now, who is it you must get back to, eh?' She was being tucked in, soothed, humoured like a child. But this was not the time, and she fought against it.

'He came in last night, my—' She never knew how to refer to Sam to strangers; she tried again, 'He's terribly hurt, I must see him. Please help me, please...' She began to cry weakly.

The nurse said consolingly, 'Well now, if he's here he won't run away. But I can't let you up until Sister's seen you, so you just stay there like a good girl for five minutes. You tell me his name and I'll see what I can find out for you, all right?'

Honey, her head still swimming, nodded helplessly. When the nurse returned, a lot more than five minutes later, she greeted her with, 'Is he all right? Did you tell him I was here—is he worrying?'

The nurse laughed. 'He's not worrying about you or anything else, he's not even round yet.'

'Not round yet?' Honey stared at her in alarm. 'How bad is he—how long has he been unconscious?'

'About nine hours—but that's not unusual with concussion,' she added soothingly. 'He'll be all right, dear, just cuts and a couple of fractures, nothing that won't mend. He's down in Men's Orthopaedic, I expect you'll be able to see him for a minute when the Police have finished.'

'Police?'

'They want to see him when he comes to. It's quite

usual with hit-and-run accidents.'

Hit-and-run, thought Honey, I wonder who told them that. Maggie, perhaps...yes, a hit-and-run lorry with Jim Crow written all over it. And nothing accidental about it.

When Sister had seen her she got up and washed her face, borrowed a comb from the nurse, and went down to Men's Orthopaedic. Hospital training reminded her to see the Ward Sister's permission and she knocked timidly on her office door.

'Could I possibly see a patient who was admitted last night? I know it's out of hours but I promise I won't disturb him.

'Only for a moment, then. What's his name?'

'McLeod,' she said. And waited.

Sister looked down her list. 'Ah, yes—' She looked up, confused. 'I don't think this can be the right one. Are you sure he's in this ward?'

'Yes, Sister,' said Honey patiently.

'But this one's—' The older woman checked herself, smiled and said, 'Well, go and have a look. If you don't find him we'll try another ward.'

'Thank you,' she said. She crept to the bed she had already marked, the one nearest the table with the screens still about it.

She knew him only by the brown hand lying outside on the covers. His face was swathed in bandages leaving only one eye visible, and that so bruised and swollen that the lashes stood out stiffly, painfully between the tight-shut lids.

'Sam...'

There was no response. She stood looking down at his shattered strength and knew that it had been ground into the dust because of her. Slowly into her stomach like cold water seeped the dread that she might never again see a Sam she recognised.

Leaving the ward she came face to face with Arthur Colby.

'Sorry I couldn't get here before,' he said stiffly. 'How is he?'

Numbly she recited the list of injuries, the fractures of ribs and arm, the eye that was endangered, the cheekbone laid bare by somebody's steel-shod boot.

'Quite a party,' he said, his eyes cold as glass.

Honey felt crushed by the weight of the disaster she had brought about. Unable to bear it alone she burst out, 'Oh, Arthur, it's all my fault!'

There was a moment's silence. Then, 'Yes,' he said quietly, 'I'm afraid it is.'

Honey waited about the hospital hour after hour, waiting for Sam's return to consciousness. Hospitals in her life were a recurring nightmare: the first one—this one—which had swallowed him long ago, the one in London to which she had been banished, and now this one again. As the familiar smells and sounds engulfed her they all seemed to merge into one; she wandered listlessly along corridors until briskly requested to wait in the proper place. Alone and forgotten in a waiting room, she sat on the edge of her chair with clenched hands and closed eyes, half expecting to open them and see herself again in uniform, to find that her life with Sam was a dream and she was still and for always an inefficient cog in a vastly efficient machine.

The spell was broken at last by a young probationer, who thrust her head round the door and announced briefly, 'Visiting time! You can come in now,' and disappeared before she could be asked a question.

Honey got to her feet with mixed feelings of relief and apprehension now that the moment was here. But as she moved towards the place where she would find him she was aware of a lightening, a lifting, of something like the old upsurge of joy she had always felt.

At the entrance to the ward she was met by the Sister, who took her by the shoulders and said, 'Just a minute, dear,' before turning her towards the office and drawing her inside.

'I'm sorry, Sister, was I running?' She was breathless, eager to be gone.

The Sister looked into the tense, shining face and was strangely moved.

'No, it isn't that.' She paused, fumbling for words. 'My dear, I'm sorry. I hardly know how to tell you this, but—he doesn't want to see you.'

12

The following day Maggie took Ellen and the gardener Vines with her and went down to Mango Walk to survey the damage. Vines was surly and reluctant at first, unwilling to 'get mixed up in anything', until Maggie reminded him pleasantly that he was employed by Dr Arthur and not by the village, when his resistance capsized to be replaced by an obstinate silence.

Sick at heart, Honey went with them, feeling that life as she had known it had come to an end.

Apart from a few broken windows and some trampled shrubs there was little to show for the night's carnage, and after a cursory glance inside Ellen was sent home, still sniffling into her handkerchief.

'This has upset her,' said Maggie, 'she thinks the world of Sam.'

'Yes,' Honey's voice was shrunk with misery. 'Poor Ellen.'

'Well, now,' said Maggie cheerfully, 'if you've the keys, we'll go in and clear up a bit. Vines, you make a start on the windows.' Maggie was a firm believer in having plenty to do in times of stress; nothing was worse in her opinion than brooding.

Honey produced Sam's keys, which she had brought with his clothes from the hospital. The muddied trousers, the blood-encrusted shirt, the shoes still moulded to the shape of his feet, one sock with a hole in the toe. The intimate personal oddments so familiar yesterday ... She fitted the key into the lock and opened the door of a world in which she no longer belonged, his home in which suddenly she was unwanted, an intruder. Perhaps she should pack up her belongings, spare him the painful business of telling her to go. Surely he had suffered

259

enough on her account. But then he might think she had left out of cowardice. And could she bring herself to do it—she did not know. She could not think, could only wait numbly for the next blow to fall.

Maggie put a broom in her hand and told her to sweep up the glass. The same broom they had jumped over the night they came back from London—

'Don't stand there dreaming,' admonished Maggie, and she began to sweep.

Suddenly under her feet, there was Sam's watch. She could see him, always careful of his watch, his one possession of any value, taking it off before any wet or dirty job. Taking it off, dropping it safely through the letterbox from outside. Knowing what to expect. She picked it up, gently rocked it to set it going, handed it to Maggie who put it into her handbag.

'I'm surprised they didn't break in,' said Maggie, 'the wagon's hardly touched.'

'They didn't have time,' said Honey. 'When we arrived they hadn't finished with Sam.'

'Aye, but how did they get at him without breaking down the door?'

'They didn't need to,' with sad pride, 'he went out to meet them. Just opened the door and stepped out.'

Maggie stared, incredulous of the foolhardiness of Sam. 'But surely he must have known?'

'Oh, yes. He knew. But he wanted me to get away first.' She turned away, scalded. Remembering how she had called him a coward.

Honey could not bring herself to tell Maggie what had happened at the hospital. Time enough when Sam was discharged, when she could think more calmly; and she had to learn to stop running to other people with her troubles, had to bear her own sorrows without leaning on someone else. So each day at visiting time she went to the hospital.

She enquired after his progress and went away again. She left no messages and found none awaiting her. She came away quickly, before she could be asked if she wanted to see him, and spent the remaining time pacing the deserted part or hidden, if it was wet, in a corner of an Espresso bar, seeking the solace of hot coffee as he had taught her to do. She sat with the cup before her, staring out through the rain-barred window at the grey

bulk of the hospital, trying to pick out among the confusion of lighted squares the one behind which he lay. Oh, Sam...I didn't think it could end like this... didn't think there could be an end between you and me.

The sad sleet drove its veils between them, and presently she went out alone through the shining tear-drenched streets to catch her bus.

While Honey drifted in outer darkness, Arthur Colby was watching her. From time to time she would feel his eyes upon her, shrewd and dispassionate. He knows, she thought numbly: he knows and he's not sorry. He always did think I was a bad idea, I should have grown up in an institution if it had been left to him. Now at last events have proved him right and he can't help feeling good.

She wondered why he had not told Maggie. Was he intent on sparing her nothing, compelling her to confess herself...not yet, not yet. She could not endure pity yet. She could not even hide in the caravan: the windows were not yet glazed and Maggie would not hear of her return. So she kept up the pretence, since there was nothing else to be done.

She washed Sam's shirt, watching the dissolving blood colour the water like coils of ruddy smoke between her fingers. And his underwear, still with a few fine black hairs clinging to it. She polished his shoes and sent his trousers to be dry cleaned. But his sweater she did not send, because at night when she could not sleep she would get up and pull it around her, trying to conjure him up out of the darkness; knowing that soon she must give up even that.

She mended the torn places in the shirt, and the long slit made by surgical scissors before they were able to remove it. She stitched and patched with infinite care, creating a small work of art, reflecting that she had never done such a thing for him before. His neat seaman's habits persisted and he had carried out his own repairs. He had been so easy to live with, gentle and undemanding; knowing how her impatient spirit rebelled against the tedium of mending, he had never asked her to do it. She did it now without being asked, putting ungrudged hours into a garment he might never wear again, the last and only offering love could make.

'Sam's coming home!' Maggie sounded as excited as a child. 'Arthur said I wasn't to tell you, but—why, my

dearie—you've gone as white as a ghost!'

Honey gripped the table edge as her knees melted under her. 'It's all right, Maggie—I'll be all right in a minute...' she managed to say. And then Maggie was steering her to a chair, holding down her head in a way that made her feel sick. She sat staring at the revolving carpet while her head swam and Maggie's voice went on...and on...

'Now I've gone and spoiled the surprise!' she was saying. 'Though it seems to me that it's just as well if this is the way it takes you—you'll not need to go fainting all over the place when he gets here. Ellen, get Miss Honey a glass of water, please.'

Honey sat up slowly. 'What time will he be here?'

'Arthur's gone to fetch him now, he just came to collect his clothes. Mind—he'll not be fit for much, Arthur says. But it seems he wouldn't stay there any longer.'

Honey's mind spun helplessly. Since he did not want to see her, why was he coming? Didn't he realise she was here—had Arthur not told him, or was he so eager to have done with her that the telling could not wait? That was not the Sam who all her life had spared her everything, who had always stood between her and harsh facts. But she was no longer sure of anything.

'Did he say why?'

Maggie looked at her curiously. 'What for would he need to say why? He'll be wanting to be back with you, no doubt. You've not forgotten tonight is Hogmanay?'

Hogmanay...was it possible? That Christmas had passed her by and she had not noticed? Maggie was still chattering.

'Did he not tell you when you saw him yesterday?'

She made an effort. 'No—no, he didn't say a word.' That was true enough, she thought sadly.

'Ah well, then, that's it, he was going to surprise you and I've spoiled it all. Don't let on that I told you and disappoint him, there's a good girl. Now away with you and lie down for a bit; I'll call you when they arrive.'

'Yes...all right,' she said weakly.

Maggie helped her up. 'Aye, do that. See if you can get a little colour back forbye.'

Honey was grateful to get to her room but she did not lie down. Instead she sat glued to the window from which she would see the approaching car. Asking herself if she could possibly have misunderstood about Sam. Learning that hope can be a sharper agony than despair.

'Honey!' Arthur's voice boomed up the staircase. 'Someone to see you.'

'Coming—' she made herself reply. Then she sank down shivering on the edge of the bed, unable to force herself further. She could hear the murmur of their voices down below. Sam's rich with music, Arthur's flat and toneless, Maggie's like the chirrup of chaffinches. Yet she could catch no words to help her dilemma. Doors opened and closed again. Then footsteps approached the stairs and paused.

'Honey!' Maggie was calling. 'Did you not hear? Sam's here.'

She called back hastily, 'All right...coming...' and stood up. Sam himself had not called her. Sweating with nerves, she moved to the dressing-table and peered into the once familiar mirror. Her own face stared back at her, gaunt and unprepossessing. She scraped at her hair with a comb. Applied lipstick then wiped it off, mindlessly picked up things and put them down again. What use were any of them at a time like this. If only she could close her eyes, feel his hands on her shoulders: 'What are you fussing about? Come here to me...' Her lips curved softly at the memory—

'Honey!' Arthur was growing angry, muttering under his breath, 'What the devil is she doing up there?'

She turned and threw herself at the door, in the way she had to, the only way she could make herself. On the stairs she met Arthur on his way up to fetch her. He glared at her and for the first time in her life she was unaffected. His opinion of her had only been of value in so far as it could influence Sam's; now there was no more damage he could do.

She said in a low voice, 'Does Sam want to see me?'

'What do you imagine we've been calling you for? He's in the library, he asked to see you alone.'

Her heart took an icy plunge. But she said calmly, 'Thank you,' her eyes on the closed door across the hall. In spite of herself she hesitated.

'Well, go on,' prompted Arthur. 'What's the matter, nervous?'

His lack of compassion stung her to an unexpected self-possession. 'Yes, I am.' She looked him defiantly full in the face. 'How I'm going in there to face him, what to say to him, I don't know. But if he can open a door and step through it, so can I.'

Arthur Colby watched her go in silence, his shrewd gaze tempered with a new respect.

Sam was standing with his back to her, lighting a cigarette with a hand that was not quite steady. He did not hear her come in and for a second that stretched out to the ends of time she stood, indecisive, just inside the door. Then she closed it behind her, and he turned.

'Honey...' His battered face lit with pleasure and he tossed the cigarette into the fire. 'Happy New Year!'

She was hardly aware of crossing the room, only of having arrived, of trying to enfold a body unfamiliar with the rigid shape of plaster, of pressing her cheek to his as she had always done. 'Oh, Sam...'

He held her in his one good arm, brushed his broken lips against her temple. 'I said I'd come here for you, sorry it took so long. We missed Christmas.' His fingers moved softly in the nape of her neck. 'Get tired of waiting?'

She was unable to speak for the constriction in her throat. Aching with love for him, she could only shake her head.

He whispered in her ear, 'Don't cry on the plaster, you'll make a pudding down my neck.'

Honey pulled herself together, sniffed hard, began searching for a handkerchief.

'In my pocket,' he said.

She found it and scrubbed her face roughly, clenching her teeth to keep from sobbing. He was peering at her through one blackened eye. The other was still covered by a bandage. 'Hold your breath and count to ten. Look at me, I'm not crying...'

Somehow she managed it. She stuffed the handkerchief resolutely back into his pocket, produced a smile and pulled him towards a chair. 'Come and sit down, I'll light you a cigarette. Did Arthur say you could?'

'Who worries about Arthur?' he said. He eased his bones carefully into the deep leather chair and took the cigarette she lit for him. It was moist and tasted of her lipstick. He drew her on to the arm of the chair and settled his head comfortably against her. He pulled deeply on the cigarette and felt his taut nerves beginning to relax. But then it was no longer enough. He threw the stub into the grate and dug his face into her ribs.

'I missed you. I never knew a week could take so long.'

'Why wouldn't you see me?'

It was said, she could not take back the words. They had shattered her peace like a bomb. He hesitated, and in the silence she almost cried, 'Don't tell me!' but she bit it back.

At last he said, 'I didn't want you to see me.'

She traced with a fingertip the stitched gashes in his scalp, where the shaved hair was beginning to grow again.

'I've seen worse things. Don't forget I've been a nurse.'

'Yes, but...I wanted my face back, such as it is. I'm not so young and pretty I can afford to lose ground.'

'You don't have to be young and pretty for me! You didn't trust me, that's what you're really saying.'

He said, 'I'm sorry...' and hid his face against her.

'You don't know what it did to me to be told you wouldn't see me. I thought...' Her voice tailed off. He raised his head to look at her, trying to focus with one bloodshot eye.

'What did you think?'

It was Honey's turn to look away. 'You took so much punishment because of me. I hadn't dreamed you'd be the one to suffer...'

'So you didn't trust me either.' The one eye became faintly whimsical. 'We're not very sure of each other, are we?' he insisted.

'I couldn't have blamed you.'

'Was it such a shock to you?'

'Wasn't it to you?'

He shook his head. 'I always knew it could happen. I went into this with my eyes wide open. So don't blame yourself, crazy gal! And don't go jumping to conclusions. I'm not young and flighty like you, my duckling days are over.'

He was trying to smile, and she saw with a pang that his lip was bitten through. The least of his injuries, yet the one that hurt her most; she saw him harassed, gnawing his lip, and somebody's brutal fist under his jaw...she swallowed hard, and nodded, fixing her brimming eyes on the wall behind him. She touched the bandage and said lightly, 'Is this eye going to be all right?'

'I hope so, I can't see you properly like this.'

'Does it hurt much?'

'Not now. But my head aches.' He sighed and laid it in her lap. A log stirred in the grate and fell with an ashy whisper; firelight flickered up and fondled the room. Sam said drowsily, 'Sing something—sing me to sleep.'

'Sing...' She had never felt less like singing. It was so little to ask, and yet—'Sam—I can't...' Her voice cracked and failed her.

Sam's arm gripped her tightly as her grief broke through at last. 'That's better,' he said, 'that's better, let it all wash away...'

The forbidden sound reached Arthur in the adjoining room, and he started up angrily.

'I can't allow that, he's not fit for any kind of upset—'

'Now, Arthur, listen to me!' Maggie's usually gentle voice was so peremptory that he looked at her in surprise.

'He's not fit, Maggie,' he repeated. 'He wouldn't be out yet if he hadn't discharged himself, I really can't let that go on.' He moved towards the door.

'No, Arthur,' Maggie said sharply. 'Now look, my dear. You're a good doctor and you've done your best, but there's a hurt there that's beyond the reach of surgery. A few tears from the right eyes will do more to heal that than any medicine you can prescribe. Now, please trust me and don't interfere—they'll neither of them thank you for it.'

Her husband hesitated, his hand on the latch. He opened the door a fraction and listened: the disturbing sounds were diminishing. He closed the door again.

'It's against my better judgement,' he said gruffly, 'I hope you're right.'

Half an hour later when Maggie came to offer them tea they were both asleep in the firelight.

In the long reaches of the night Sam lay wakeful. He had flirted with sleep in the chair downstairs and now it eluded him. He looked longingly at the glass of water that stood on the bedside table, minute bubbles of air shining on the inside of the glass; but he could not drink lying on his back. It would have to wait until morning, and he pushed it out of sight behind the clock. Something fell to the floor and from a distant corner of the room Honey whispered, 'Are you all right?'

'Yes. Go to sleep.'

A pause. Then, 'Sure?'

'Sure. Go to sleep. Else I'll be over there with that hairbrush.'

'Bully.'

He smiled, remembering her scarlet-faced at twelve, shouting 'I won't! So come on, let's see you do it!' She

had called his bluff at last; yet when he summoned her she had come warily, her eyes on the brush upraised in his hand, trying to tuck her bottom out of reach. When he began to brush her hair her arms had choked him in a clumsy embrace—'Oh, I knew you'd never really hit me, you're too kind!'

'Not too kind, too big.' Hoisting her level with his face, 'When you get to be this tall, watch it!'

Her knees had been scabbed and knobbly, her teeth distressingly too large for her mouth, yet even then she had a quality that touched him, pushing even the loss of Georgia to the back of his memory. Georgia . . . her features were almost lost to him now, the living child obscured for ever behind the hideous death . . . it was not the train of thought for three a.m.

He tried again to compose himself to sleep. He could not get comfortable: the cast restricted his breathing, its raw edges galled his skin, and he itched unpredictably in inaccessible places. Already he had an accumulation of drinking straws which he had used as backscratchers and lost in his enthusiasm: he could feel them now, bent at angles and making their presence felt with every breath. If only he could turn over . . . he could not, pinned to the mattress by weakness and the weight of the plaster. He felt trapped in it, hot and helpless as a turtle on its back. Without the grip that had hung above his bed in the hospital he could do nothing, and after a few moments' futile sweating and straining he lay panting, wrestling with a rising claustrophobia. He knew he should have stayed there a little longer. But how could he, with that small wan figure at the far end of the ward, the cage supporting the bedclothes, the Brodniks passing his bed on their way to visit . . . he knew now why they had called him 'Murderer'. He wondered if they would have killed him that night if they had not been disturbed. And what about Honey, then—would they have left him for dead and then gone after her . . . suppose they tried again?

He wondered if she was sleeping. He needed to reach out and touch her, hear her breathing, feel her near. But here in the Colbys' guest-room she was on a divan behind a screen, a sacrifice on the altar of propriety. As if she must be protected, even now. He'd teased them about the arrangement—'See the gap underneath, bet I can limbo under there'—but only Honey had smiled, her sad eyes brightening.

Now he felt isolated, cut off from her by the disapproval of others, diminished and oppressed by their censure, unspoken though it was. He sighed. He had pitted his solitary strength not against a handful of village thugs, but against the full force of the world's condemnation. And Honey he could not protect because she had no wish to be spared; she would suffer everything there was. 'What hurts you, hurts me.' He could still hear the childish voice: she had flown her bright flag of defiance even then. She would go with songs to the battle, and singing she would fall. If there had ever been a time when he could save her, that time was gone. The die was cast, the battle joined...and this was only the beginning.

His head rolled again on the pillow, he shut his eyes to blot out the dark gulf of the future. His breath escaped him with a sound like a sob and he clamped his hand down hard across his mouth. The black waters of despair welled up and closed over his head.

'Sam...oh, Sam...darling.'

Her arms rescued him, her hair fell across his face. The tide of anguish receded; he drew his breath in a long tearing gasp and was still.

'What is it...can't you tell me?'

Dumbly, he shook his head. He could not tell her, dreaded that she had to hear. How could he say it? 'Remember that boy, the one with one foot? His mother died last week, a heart attack—the shock of the accident, they said. Well, she was never strong. They're saying that we killed her. You and me...'

After a while he took his hand from his mouth and pulled her close to him. 'I'm sorry,' he said hoarsely, 'I couldn't sleep.'

13

'I met Ellen on the stairs, she seemed to be crying.' She picked up the tray of used crockery. 'Look—she's left this behind.'

'Yes,' said Sam slowly. 'I'm afraid she's had a shock.'

'A shock—what about?'

'About us. I had to disillusion her. It was only fair.'

'You don't mean—she hadn't realised?' Honey was incredulous. Was it possible there was someone left who did not know?

'She hadn't believed it. In her tidy world decent people don't do such things.'

Honey forced a laugh. 'Poor Ellen, fifty years behind the times—why, you've only got to look at her clothes!' She sat down on the bed beside him, trying to cheer him. 'I'll look after this room from now on.' She was angry with Ellen for upsetting Sam. He was upset, she could tell from the way he smiled, as if he were trying to rise above something. Ellen should have no further opportunity, she would see to that. 'What did she say to you?'

'Nothing really.' He sat remembering behind closed eyelids. 'Nothing offensive.'

In her awkward, indiscreet way she had tried to sympathise.

'Oh, Mr Sam, I do hear tell there's the most dreadful talk in the village. People saying the most awful things!'

'What sort of things, Ellen?'

'Such things as I couldn't repeat, not to anyone, and wouldn't! That's what I wanted you to know—that I wouldn't repeat them. And whenever I hear anyone else, I always tell them it's not true.'

'Tell me what they're saying, Ellen. I'll tell you if it's true.'

Ellen looked embarrassed. 'They couldn't be true? Not things like that, not you'—she faltered, coloured uncomfortably—'with Miss Honey!'

'I know what they're saying about us, Ellen.' It had been difficult to speak the words. He would never have believed how difficult. He had said them quietly, lifting his head in defiance, 'It's all quite true.'

Ellen had stared at him, unbelieving; her chin began to quiver and her faded eyes filled.

'Oh, Mr Sam!' she said at last in a choking voice. 'And you always such a nice gentleman...' She had turned away and hurried from the room.

Now, he smiled for Honey. 'Where have you been all day?'

'Downstairs, helping Maggie.' She silenced him with the thermometer and avoided his eyes.

He took her hands in his and lay back contentedly. When she took the glass from his mouth he said, 'Arthur stop you coming?'

She nodded. He kissed her knuckles and said, 'Don't let it get to you. How am I doing?'

She twisted it this way and that under the bedside light, trying to find the mercury. He took it from her. 'Not cooked, let's try again.' When he looked again it was still showing subnormal. He said, 'Soon as this is steady we'll be out of here. I will anyway.' A hesitation. 'Whether you come is up to you.' She stared, and he added quickly, 'I don't want you to feel you have to. You could stay here with Arthur and Maggie, I'd understand. I mean, they'd have you any time, they said so...'

'Well, thank you,' said Honey crisply. 'I see you've discussed it already.' She got up and went over to the window, her back to him.

'I've spoken to Arthur,' he admitted. He thought he saw a tremor go through her. 'Look, it's rough and it could get rougher. I want you to know the door's open, any time you want out.'

'I do wish you'd stop trying to get rid of me!'

'I'm not trying to get rid of you, babe...Honey?'

She did not answer him. His head began to throb. 'Look, all I'm saying is you don't have to go through with this. We're not married, you're not tied to me in any way—'

'But I *am* tied to you—oh, Sam.' She turned towards him, her face in darkness. 'I nailed my shoes to your floor

when I was three, don't you know that yet? And as for not being married—what difference does a piece of paper make? Don't you see, I want to feel married to you. I need to feel secure, to know I belong, don't you feel that too?'

'You know how I feel.'

'Then stop talking about "you" and "me" and start thinking about "us". We will go back to Mango Walk and take whatever comes. We'll face it together, one person. Do you understand?'

Sam regarded her quizzically before the smile broke out. 'Well, suppose we come back over here and give us a kiss.' As they drew apart he chuckled. 'My old lady . . . Mrs McLeod. Hey, that means you have to honour and obey!'

'Oh, no!' Honey stood up, straightened the bedclothes. 'You're the patient, I tell you what to do.'

'It'll take you a little longer to do that!'

But when she had gone, his smile faded. Whatever his misgivings in future, he would keep them to himself.

He submitted to Arthur Colby's strictures as part of a tedious if necessary medical routine, and ignored them as often as he seemed to get away with it. But he noticed that Arthur's expression on observing him with Honey was by no means identical with his expression when he was caught out skipping treatment, and he saw that while Colby had been forced to accept their relationship as a *fait accompli* he was by no means won over to their point of view. It said much for him that he remained a loyal friend and made them free of his home even as they flew in the face of his household gods. There must be little more that friendship could ask. Yet he could not help wondering whether Arthur like the others would have found the situation less deplorable had his complexion been a good few shades lighter. Arthur paid him the compliment of treating him as an equal; it had clearly been a nasty jolt to see him behaving as though he were. Equal . . . but different. Equal . . . but non-interchangeable? There was a mental reservation there somewhere. It made him uneasy, impatient to take his black face home with him.

Maggie, he felt, neither approved nor disapproved with any continuity. She was easily shocked and as easily appeased, and her opinion was worth far less than her affection.

All this he turned over in his mind during the long

colourless hours in bed, while Honey fidgeted listlessly down below, irritating her host with her perpetual search for a pretext to dart upstairs.

'For God's sake!' he snapped. 'Let the man rest while he has the chance. He's not dying for lack of your company. They know far more about relaxation than we do.'

Stung, she retorted, 'They? We? Oh, Arthur, even you!' and flung away upstairs in defiance of him.

That night she dragged her divan to within a chaste three feet of Sam's. 'I'll be glad to get home,' she confided as she lay in bed, 'it's awful having to find excuses to come and speak to you. I don't know which is worse, Arthur's constant surveillance or Maggie's coyness. Makes me feel like the naughtiest girl in the dorm.'

Sam laughed. 'I know. I feel like a secret drinker. Maybe I should hide you in the wardrobe—'

'—and only take me out when the craving gets you—'

'I guess pretty soon you'd have me in there with you!'

They muffled their laughter for fear of being heard, and then in the darkness Sam stretched out a hand. Into the silence, Honey said, 'I miss you. No one to be foolish with...'

He answered very softly to the sadness in her voice, 'I know...I know.'

They held fast to each other's fingers for a long time before they slept.

As soon as Sam was able to stand upright without reeling he announced his intention of returning to Mango Walk.

'You're raving mad,' protested Arthur, 'at least wait until you're out of plaster.'

Sam shook his head. 'This is the best time to go, man. They won't touch me while I'm still encased.' He grinned. 'Not unless they're aiming to break their knuckles.'

Honey looked at him dubiously. 'Then let me go down tomorrow and start the fire, get the place warmed up a bit. I don't want to freeze if you do, even the beds will be damp after a fortnight with no one there.'

'Quite right,' said Arthur stoutly, on her side for once. 'Get the place properly aired and warm, we don't want to have to re-admit him with pneumonia.'

'All right, then.' She guessed that he was not really

feeling as strong as he made out. And while half of her longed to regain their privacy, the other half shivered apprehensively. 'But you're not going alone,' Sam added as if he had read her thoughts, 'I'll come with you.'

'Out of the question,' said Arthur, 'I'm sure Maggie can spare Ellen for an hour or two.'

'Of course, of course,' said Maggie and went away to organise it.

When they were alone, Sam said to Arthur, 'You wouldn't have an old golf club you don't use any more?'

Arthur looked up in surprise. 'You thinking of taking it up?'

Sam shook his head. 'I just want to borrow one club. It's safer than a gun. And it doesn't need a licence.'

At first glance Mango Walk looked to be just as they had left it. But as Honey attempted to open the door they knew; something seemed to be stopping it as she pushed, something soft, and—

'Oh, my Gawd, Miss Honey...what's that smell!'

Gagging, they stepped back as the full force hit them. 'The dirty disgusting animals!' raged Ellen. 'Who'd believe grown men could sink so low!'

Who indeed, thought Honey, shuddering as they shovelled and scraped and scrubbed, trying to eradicate with carbolic the smell that had permeated everything. Whose was it, she wondered? What had hated them enough to squat out there in the cold wet darkness, deliver into his hands and post his ordure through their letterbox... someone did. And she was responsible, she had brought this on Sam. Like a silly romantic schoolgirl she had imagined that she would be the one to come under fire, had seen herself as the heroine braving all for her beloved; only now did she understand what she had done.

'Ellen, please don't tell anyone about this, I'd rather Sam didn't know.'

'Don't fret, Miss Honey. I wouldn't soil my mouth—I wouldn't know how to find the words for such a thing. Shameful, it is, shameful...we'd best leave the windows open, get rid of the smell.'

'No, we daren't. There's no knowing what will happen if we do, we'll have to make everything fast before we leave. Perhaps the fire will help,' and she took the guitar down from above the bedplace and stowed it out of sight.

If they once realised what it meant to him they would move heaven and earth to destroy it.

Ellen picked up the hod and went out to fetch coal. A moment later she was back. 'Haven't you got any coal, then?'

'Yes...oh, no!' She followed Ellen out to look, but she had already guessed what she would find. 'Oh, Ellen.' She leaned her elbows on the rifled bunker and burst into tears.

At last they went home, with still a week to go before Sam was due to have his plaster off. The coal merchant had declined to deliver, on the pretext that stocks were low due to the time of year. But when Honey discovered that their driver was a cousin of David Bassett she was inclined to disbelieve him. Instead of arguing she went to town and brought back a fire to run on bottled gas. It took most of her savings, and necessitated bringing it and the heavy cylinder home by bus, since the small one they had used for boiling kettles on the gas-ring had long since been exhausted by their playmates; but it was something. She knew that Arthur, if asked, would have collected both for her; but she could not bring herself to ask him.

'Hey, what's this?' said Sam on seeing the strips of firewood roughly nailed across the letterbox.

'Oh...I thought we could do without anonymous letters to welcome us home.' She glanced up from making coffee. 'Don't take it off—'

But he had already stripped it, and she said nothing. Perhaps after all it would not happen again.

It did not happen again. For a time very little happened, except that Sam, predictably, again lost his job and this time for good. A letter of ultimatum from Haytons had been returned to them marked 'Gone away'. The next enclosed his cards, and they knew a moment of despair. Arthur, as always, caught them as they fell; there was a vacancy for a porter at the cottage hospital; the pay wasn't bad for a dead end job. It would mean shifts, of course. But it was only in Southcombe, much nearer, and for the night shifts he could use a bicycle—Vines had a bike he would probably lend him, the old chap never stirred abroad after six or so—

They expressed their gratitude and assured him they would manage.

'You're not staying here alone at night,' said Sam when

Arthur had left. 'I'll drop you up there on my way to work.'

Honey shook her head, though the thought chilled her with dread. 'I'll stay here and look after things. They won't touch a woman on her own.' She wished she believed it. 'Anyway it won't be yet. He said they'd keep the job open till you're fit.'

'I am fit,' he said.

But that night his head housed a steam-hammer and Honey, her eyes anxious, caught him taking codeine. He glanced up, the white tablets poised on his vivid tongue.

'What are you thinking?' He swallowed.

She swallowed too. 'Only that I love you.'

Sam gave a moan and pulled her into his arms. 'Tell me you love me, keep telling me, over and over. Never stop telling me...'

'Sam, oh, Sam...' She held him, her arms wound tightly about him, her face pressed to his, trying not to communicate her grief. Was there enough love in all the world to staunch a wound the depth of this, to neutralise the venom in the tide of hate that had risen up against him because of her...she could love him, oh yes. But she herself had loosed the black flood and could not undo it.

'I love you, Sam,' she whispered. 'Is it still enough?'

'It's enough, Honey. It has to be, it's all I have, all that saves me from believing what they think of me is true. Don't take your love from me, I'd go to pieces.'

'I couldn't...you know I couldn't.'

'Honey...' He held her tightly, awkwardly, pinning her painfully against the plaster cast. She welcomed the discomfort, feeling she was sharing it with him. 'The day will come when he'll be ashamed of you...' She wished she could lose those words.

Sam had his plaster removed, and although the cracked ribs were still tender and caught him with every breath they were lovers again for the first time in weeks. Afterwards he still held her desperately, as if he feared she might escape him.

'You still in love with me?' His eyes probed hers.

'My darling...'

'Say it! Swear it—'

'You know I love you—'

'No, I mean in love. There's a difference.'

'I know there is. Oh, Sam...what's the matter?'

'I had to come after you.'

'I wanted you to...' She smiled faintly, her lips against his skin.

His taut body relaxed a little, 'Why'd you want me to, you were never like that?'

'I had to. I had to be sure.'

'Sure of what?'

'That you really wanted me. That you weren't just being—compassionate.'

'Aw, Honey...'

She raised her eyes uncertainly and saw surprise, unbelief, finally laughter spread across the brown familiar face. 'Honey, Honey...' He wagged his head. There was nothing more to be said.

Honey, his sleeping head against her shoulder, wept soundlessly. It seemed to her that now the faintest ripple had the power to cast them both into a hell of doubt.

As a precaution against further stonings in the market place they brought out from the back of the pan-box the window shutters saved from the days of the blackout and fastened them in place. It gave them at least an illusion of security and helped to conserve the heat. The problem now was ventilation; the gas fire gave off noxious fumes and did not do the wholehearted job the stove had done. Every night they had to drag out the gas cylinder and lock it up for safety in the pan-box, every dark and bitter morning in the teeth of the wind, it must be brought in again before they could have warmth. The coal repeatedly ordered never came, and it seemed likely they had seen the last of their cosy firelit nights. Their daily milk no longer arrived; nothing came through their letterbox, not even mail, and water was suddenly no longer available at the farm.

The village lay doggo, aware of having attracted the unwelcome eye of the police. Certain questions had been asked, and breath had been held until it was clear that no one had been identified, no charges had been laid. But you couldn't be too careful, like. They Teddy boys from the city had had the blame this time. Been a bit in the local paper, there had, about 'windows smashed on the front in Southcombe and caravan dweller beaten up' as if it was all the same job. Well, that was a bit of luck! But that wasn't to say they'd swallow the same tale twice. Best lie low for a bit. Anyways, hadn't worked, had it,

still there he was, blast him! Only thing for the moment was see if you couldn't freeze 'em out...

So down at Mango Walk they drew their drinking water from the standpipe and boiled it laboriously in their slow, slow kettle on the gas ring. They eked out Sam's sick pay with what remained of their savings until he started work at the hospital, each of them secretly dreading the one week in four when he would be on nights. But the first turn came and went and nothing happened.

It was now well on into February. The winter rains overflowed the ditches in the lane and made long runnels down the dunes, early lambs lifted frail voices in the dusky afternoons, and one day Honey found the first snowdrop shining beside the dustbin. She waited for Sam's return to show it to him, and they walked to the edge of the cliff to watch the sun go down, a pale disc of rose drowning in a silver sea.

'Isn't it lovely?' she breathed, her hands tucked through his elbow against the cold. And Sam, remembering only dimly now the fiery deaths of the Caribbean sun, watched the mists dissolve and darken to lavender, the water bounce back the light, and said softly, 'Yes...it is.'

He could have loved England. If only it would let him.

It really began to look as though it might. They took the shutters down at last and Honey no longer sat up fully dressed throughout the nights when he was on duty at the hospital. He found a better atmosphere there than he had met at Haytons, the people he worked with more ready to accept him, and came home cheerful instead of already depressed. He found a means of obtaining coal by dint of humping it on his back, and the practice of buying it in penny numbers made it possible to store it where it could not be filched. Firelight came back to them, and slowly their spirits revived. They brought out the neglected guitar from its hiding place, and music stole furtively back into their lives.

'It'll soon be spring,' said Honey, beginning to breathe again.

And then in March, just as the savage gales came thrashing in off the sea, Norm was discharged from hospital, still awaiting the fitting of his National Health artificial foot, and moved in to live with the Brodnicks.

14

'I wish you wouldn't go to work with that cold,' said
Honey, helping him into his ancient duffel coat.

'I'll be fine.' He rummaged in the pockets, brought out
a crumpled white paper packet. 'I got my Fisherman's
Friends.' He tossed one of the brown tablets on to his
tongue and filled the caravan with its spicy fume.

'I can't remember you without those.'

'You know why they call them that? You just breathe
over the side and the fish jump out and give themselves
up. Ah, Honey,' he cupped her face between his hands,
'it's good to see you laughing again.'

'You're running a temperature, I can tell from your
hand. Please don't go, it's not as if it were day shift and
you could go on the bus. That bike ride—'

'It's good and warm at the hospital, not like Haytons,
back and forth across the yard. Now don't worry—and
don't come to the gate, it's blowing a gale out there. You
tuck up warm and I'll be back before you know it. Can't
afford to lose this job by going sick, Arthur must be running out of friends.'

Honey sighed. 'Good old Arthur. He must be a fine
person, I do wish I could like him more.'

'You worry too much about what he thinks of you. I
don't give a damn so we get along fine. Try wondering
what you think of him for a change. See you.' He pressed
a feverish kiss to her brow and was gone.

She sat listening to his footsteps on the path, the faint
clanking of the bicycle as he wheeled it beside him, the
sound of the gate closing. She could only just make out
the sounds above the wind. It roared and howled around
the caravan, rattled the gutters and fell upon the bulkheads like an animal, making the ageing timbers creak

in alarm. She was glad they had replaced the shutters. On the whole. They did protect her from spying eyes; on the other hand, she could not see out, and so much noise from the weather made her uneasy because she could neither see nor hear a prowler if he came.

She shivered, jumped as a slap of rain hit the caravan, wondering if Sam would make it to cover before he was soaked. He was unlikely to turn back. He was a vigorous cyclist and would be well on his way by now. But he was not well, she was sure of it; he had gone without his cigarettes and he had to be feeling rough not to want to smoke.

But sitting here brooding wasn't going to help him. Better to go to bed, get up early and be ready with a warm fire and a hot drink when he returned. She undressed slowly, doused the lamp and got into bed, but sleep did not come willingly. Anxiety and the boisterous night destroyed her peace and at last she drifted into an uneasy doze, half dreaming, half imagining herself storm-tossed on a towering sea. The bed seemed to roll with the breakers. She lay telling herself it was nonsense, confused between sleeping and waking, unsure which to choose.

She felt the jolt as something buffeted against the outside, heard the china rattle on the dresser. It was only the wind, she told herself sternly, wide awake now. Or . . . or maybe the cows had broken through the hedge as they did once before to strop their bony behinds against the wagon. Lucky he had built on, Sam had said: else they might have been rolled off the cliff edge on to the beach . . . Another jolt. Oh, please God let it be the wind . . . Then she heard the trampling of feet, a muffled cough. And now she knew.

Someone was trying to overturn the caravan.

Sam arrived at the hospital, wheeled the bike into the shed by the visitors' lavatories and hoisted it on to the stand. He took out the chain from the saddlebag and secured the front wheel to the frame, snapping the padlock shut. He always locked it when he left it outside, mindful that it was not his to take chances with. He suspected that Vines had been coerced into lending it; the least he could do was not lose it for him.

He straightened up with difficulty and went into the changing room. The heat in there instantly brought him out in a sweat. When he had changed his wet coat for

the freshly laundered overall he stood hugging the hot radiator while the green wall advanced and receded before his eyes. Presently it returned to normal behaviour, and he swallowed a couple of codeine tablets, sniffed hard on his benzedrine inhaler and went to report for duty.

For a full minute Honey sat motionless, hardly daring to breathe. She felt trapped and terrified without Sam, not knowing what to do, where to hide...She tried to be calm. Asked herself what Sam would do if he were here. He would send her for help. But how? There was no one now to create a diversion while she slipped out the back way. No one to absorb the fury—she wrenched her mind away.

Her only resort was to hide—but where? If they broke into the wagon, here in the bed-place was surely the first place they would look, panels notwithstanding they would be sure to find her there...she remembered the 'chavy-bed', the cupboard beneath the bed-place where she had slept as a baby, now used for storing brooms. If she could still fold herself up small enough—but she had no choice. A footfall on the steps—hammering on the front door—catcalls through the letterbox—and she was slithering boneless out between the panels, down into the cupboard among brushes and dusters on the chilling linoleum, thankful now for the noise of the storm to mask the sounds of her flight.

She pulled the door closed on her, crouched like a foetus in the dark womb of the wagon, holding her breath, wondering how long the air would last her, tainted as it was with choking vapour from the floor polish.

The banging on the door stopped. There was a scuffling on the porch, a clumping of boots down the steps—voices—another thud against the bulkhead—an ominous creak of timber from the direction of the washroom steps—dear God, if it tore loose! They could roll the wagon forward over the cliff—she would be trapped—helpless—a prey to the hungry tide! She wrenched open the cupboard door, struggled clear and fled like a rabbit down the threatened stairway to the washroom. For a moment she stood immobilised by terror—where?—where?—under the camp-bed in the doghouse! She scuttled underneath it, wriggled in behind the suitcases, let go her breath in a strangled sob.

Here they might find her, drag her out...but at least she would not be drowned in the caravan. She cowered shivering on the cold concrete, praying that Sam would come—that he would not come—not knowing how to pray, what to hope for. Listening in dread for the sounds of splintering wood she knew must come.

'Don't you know better than to come on duty in that condition?'

Sam focused with difficulty on the stern face confronting him. 'I'll be all right,' he reassured it, 'I can keep going.'

'It's not you, it's the patients. Do you think they need your troubles as well as their own? Go home and go to bed, we'll see you when you're better...' A brief smile to soften it—'And don't come back until you are clear.'

'OK, I'm sorry.' He had done his best, had shown willing; thankfuly he shuffled off to the changing-room, where he sank down on to a bench, his head in his hands. It throbbed, and there was a tightness in his chest that he remembered. He lurched to his feet as some one came in.

'All right, I'm going.'

It was one of the other porters. He peered at Sam. 'You don't look too good, do you want anything?'

Sam shook his head. 'I've got codeine. I'm going home anyway.'

'You'd better take some. Hang on a minute, I'll get you a hot drink. Then scat! You must have been mad to come in at all.'

He nodded, not wanting to make the effort of talking. Ten minutes later, his senses dulled by two more codeines and a mug of steaming tea, he went out to the bicycle shed and fumbled through his pockets for the key. Stupefied by medication and a mounting temperature, it took him several seconds to realise that he had left the bunch on the caravan table with his cigarettes. He stood still in the drizzle and tried to think. Then he turned automatically towards the gates and started to walk.

Honey had lain so long in one position that she had lost all count of time. That some had passed she had no doubt, because the wind was dropping and a steady fall of rain now drummed on the felted roof of the doghouse.

She stretched her ears for sounds of movement outside. Nothing. Perhaps the rain had come as a godsend, sending the would-be attackers in search of shelter. Slowly she flexed her cramped limbs. Carefully, making no noise, she emerged from under the bed. Still nothing. She edged her way to the window. Giving straight on to the dark hedge it told her nothing; she listened to the water steadily dripping from leaf to leaf and wondered what time it was. She dared not strike a light to look at the clock; it was still there ticking busily away up on the dresser as if nothing had happened.

But then nothing had; she scourged herself for a coward as she thankfully accepted the fact. Sam's solid carpentry had held: wagon and wash-house were still joined, still where they had always been. The siege had failed.

Or had it? Would they be back with reinforcements before morning...the new thought chilled her. Perhaps they had guessed there was no one at home, had retired to lie in wait for Sam on his return, an ambush concealed in the bushes along the lane...

She glanced again towards the window. It was dark as death out there. If she could go silently enough on unshod feet, could squeeze through the hedge as she had before, go up across the fields to the telephone in the village, ring the hospital, get a message through...It might not stop him coming home but at least he would be warned.

She had to try. But not through the window—that could not be fastened from the outside and would leave the place wide open. She would have to risk going by the door. She groped her way over to it and listened again. Only the rain, the soughing of the wind, the sullen crashing of the sea. She leaned against the woodwork, slowly turned the key, and realised that Sam must have oiled the lock recently. Now it moved smoothly, quietly; she opened the door a crack and stood back, flattened against the wall. And waited. She withdrew the key, stepped outside, shaking as she fumbled it back into the lock, turned it and made all fast. Then, clutching the key in her hand, she made her way round to the gap in the hedge and ran silently hell for leather up through the fields. She knew better than to stop at the farm or the policeman's cottage and made straight for the lighted beacon of the telephone booth.

There she stopped, catching sight of herself in the faint

scatter of light, clad only in a nylon nightdress plastered to her body by the rain and transparent as cellophane. Instinctively she shrank back into the shadows—but she had to warn Sam. With a quick glance about her she darted across the road and into the call-box, reached up to remove the bulb and burned her her fingers on the protective cage. How to put out the light, give herself decent cover of darkness, rendered anonymous instead of an illuminated target...She picked up the battered directory, struck out with it. The bulb blinked once and went on grinning gaudily. The key of the doghouse! She reached up above her and shielding her eyes, rammed it blindly between the slats of the cage. The glass shattered with a loud report and blessed darkness fell. She sighed in relief—and realised too late that she could not now see to look up the number of the hospital.

'Oh, no...' She drove her forehead against the evil-smelling metal of the window frame, wailing with inner dismay. Then she felt for the receiver and tried to calm herself. Arthur. She had no choice; it would have to be Arthur.

'Number, please.'

'I want Dr Arthur Colby, here in the village.'

'Number, please.' The voice was distinctly displeased.

'I'm sorry, I can't remember the number—'

'It will be in the directory.' A purring on the line told her she had been disconnected.

'Oh, God!' She slammed the receiver down. Waited. Picked it up again.

'Number, please.'

'Look, this is an emergency. I must speak to Dr Colby and I haven't got a directory—please, you must help!'

'Hold the line please, caller.' A pause. A different voice. 'Directory Enquiry, which town, please?'

Honey wanted to scream, tear out the telephone, smash the windows. But she had to make herself patiently spell out the name, the address, the initials. Wait for the number to be found. She could hear the pages being slowly turned, each rustle of paper raking talons through her nerves...

'F. A. Colby or A. W. Colby?'

'I don't know,' she said helplessly. 'Look, there's only one doctor in the village, Dr Colby, the Stone House.'

'Dr Colby,' repeated the placid voice. 'Ah, yes, the number you want is 206.'

'Thank you, put me back to the operator now.'

'Replace your receiver and then pick it up again. The operator will answer.'

'Can't you—'

The line had gone dead again. Despairingly, she obeyed.

'Number please.' Numbly, she repeated it. 'Have two pennies ready, please.'

'I haven't got any money, this is an emergency—'

'It's nine nine nine for Police, Fire or Ambulance. Which service do you require?'

Honey crashed down the receiver and burst into tears of frustration, leaned sobbing against the useless coinbox. At last she took a grip on herself, scrubbed the back of her hand across her face, rattled the phone on its cradle until she heard again the soulless, 'Number, please.'

'Look, I've got to get that number—'

Again, patiently. 'Number, please?' This was a new voice. A different operator. With what control she could muster she tried again.

'Please, I must speak to the doctor on 206. Only I've no money on me and they won't put me through. Oh, please, can't you help me, reverse the charge or something?'

'Hold on, caller. I'll ask if they'll accept the charge. Can I have your name, please?'

She gave it; there was a half-heard exchange on the other end, then a strange voice, thick with sleep.

'Dr Hartley speaking.'

'Dr Hartley?' she echoed stupidly. 'I want Dr. Colby, Dr Arthur Colby.'

'I'm Dr Colby's locum. Do you need a visit?'

'Not a visit, I need the number of the hospital—'

'Is it an accident?'

'No, no—look, put me through to Mrs Colby, you don't understand—this is terribly urgent—'

'Mrs Colby? Is this a medical emergency or is it not?'

'No, it's personal—please, oh, please!'

The voice at the other end was testy. 'My dear young lady! It is two a.m. and Mrs Colby is in Edinburgh with her husband, no doubt sensibly in bed. I suggest you ring again on Monday. Goodnight!'

A click, and she was left holding the lifeless telephone, a dead thing in her hand. She sank slowly to her knees in the draughty booth and gave way to her despair.

She was brought back to reality by a distant voice repeating with irritation, 'Number, please? Hello, caller. Number, please!'

She straightened up slowly, replaced the receiver and pushed her way out through the heavy door into the night. A squall hit her, soaking her afresh, making her teeth chatter. What now? She dared not go back to Mango Walk before daylight. She could think of no way of warning Sam. She could not wander the village throughout the night with no clothes...

She thought of the outbuildings of Bassett's Farm. With luck she might find a door unfastened. Weary and dispirited she trudged through the mire of the once familiar yard, walking barefoot through nettles, hardly noticing their sting; thinking that Sam at least, thank God, was warm and dry... At last she found the door to the loft unbolted, clambered up the ladder and curled shivering in the hay to wait for dawn.

Sam had not known that eight miles could be so long.

By the end of the first he was plodding head down against the wind in a travesty of his normal swinging stride. After five he was hardly moving, his breathing short and painful, shambling like an old man and making frequent stops for rest.

He reached Mango Walk at last and wondered briefly why the gate stood open. Then he hauled himself up the steps to thump feebly on the door.

'Honey...?'

No reply. She must be sleeping. He pushed open the letter-box and peered through. The place was in darkness; he could just make out the parting between the panels, a rumpled shape in the bedclothes that could be anything, dim and indistinct in the gloom. He called again, while his head buzzed and twittered and his body ached, went on knocking and calling it seemed for ever, until without knowing it he slumped into the angle of the porch, drifting, entangled in skeins of oblivion.

He had been there for some hours when Honey crept home from her hiding-place and found him in the early light.

15

Somehow she managed to get Sam inside, undressed and into bed. He sat limp and unresisting while she peeled off his clothes, his eyes bright and feverish, silent apart from an intermittent rasping cough. He seemed not to have noticed that she had come in from outside clad only in a nightdress, which alone was enough to tell her how ill he felt. But she was thankful to be able to spare him the details of the night's events.

The soaking and the chilling had not done her any good either; her own face was hot, her throat parched and stinging, and she knew she was succumbing to his cold. She swallowed four aspirins, filled both hot water bottles for Sam, and wrapped up warmly to walk to the telephone.

He struggled up as she opened the door, 'Where are you going?'

'Only to the telephone to call the doctor.'

'No,—don't go! I don't want you to go —'

It took all her strength to get him back to bed and she realised she would have to slip out while he slept. 'If I stay with you I want you to take some more codeine and go to sleep.'

He nodded, exhausted. 'Come sit with me...' It was late in the morning before she could extricate herself. She made up the fire as quietly as she could and slipped out, locking the door behind her.

This time, mercifully, it was Ellen who answered the phone.

'The doctor's already gone on his round, Miss Honey, but I'll tell him as soon as he comes in to lunch. I expect he'll call in this afternoon.'

This afternoon...but that was hours away. Her stom-

ach turned a somersault. 'Ellen, he's very bad. He was out all night in that rain—'

'There, there, Miss Honey, I'm sure it's not as bad as it seems, it never is. I'll tell the doctor when he comes in. Now, you mustn't worry, it's likely only a chill, you just go back and see he keeps warm. And you look after yourself, too, you sound as if you had a cold coming and all.'

At Mrs Figg's she bought a can of chicken soup, and one of mulligatawny, and a loaf of bread from the bakery next door. When she got home she opened a can of soup and set it to the heat on the top of the stove. But when it was ready she could not face the thought of food and Sam was still asleep.

Dr Hartley arrived about half past two, a tall elderly man with greying sideboards and the look of an ascetic. Sam had just woken from sleep and had lost something of his wild-eyed look. The codeine had taken his temperature down and he was sweating freely; he raised himself on an elbow, winced as the old man cracked his head on the low ceiling. 'Sorry about that.'

The doctor felt his racing pulse. 'Headache? Sore throat? Yes, influenza,' he said, backing away, 'there's a lot of it about.' He turned to Honey. 'Warmth, rest, plenty of fluids. Don't worry too much about food. I'm off tonight but I'll leave a message for Dr Colby, he may want to see him in a day or two. Good day to you.' And he was gone.

Honey's relief at the verdict was tempered by the fact that no treatment had been forthcoming. No prescription, not even a medical certificate...

'He wasn't much help,' she said doubtfully, 'I could have done as much myself.'

'I'll live,' croaked Sam, and was immediately racked by coughing. He tried a little of the soup to reassure Honey, but it was no good. He drank some water and with the aid of another dose of codeine drifted in and out of nightmares in which he saw the sea-green face of an old enemy. When he coughed up the rusty phlegm of pneumonia, he knew.

As darkness fell his fever mounted and he began to have to fight for breath. I could die, he thought, and terror flooded him. He could die on her hands, leaving her with the shame and the disgrace, to carry alone the burdens that had become too much for them both. He caught at

her arm as she passed, 'Honey ... hold on to me ... don't let me go ...'

All through the night she held on to him, her hands firm and calm in his, trying to give him her strength, drawing breath for breath with him throughout the numbing hours while he rambled or dozed, scarcely aware of her or of anything. Leaving him only to make the fire or to mop her own steaming cold, ready with a murmur of reassurance whenever the scorched eyes seemed to rest on her face. Her mind ached with bewilderment. How could such things be, if there was a God in Heaven how could such things be? In all her life she had not known Sam to do a spiteful thing; and yet he suffered and suffered and his tormentors were not diminished by so much as a hair. But even as she rebelled, something primitive within her was praying, praying while she held him in her arms and willed him to survive, while she tried to do the fighting for him; and her prayer made a bridge between the fear she could not look at and the hope she dared not touch.

By midnight he was delirious, tossing and muttering about a mongoose; it was all she could do to keep him in bed and she knew she would have to get help. She was pulling her second wellington when she heard a rap on the door. She froze. Not now ... oh, God, not now!

The rap was repeated more sharply and a familiar voice said, 'It's me, I got your message. Let me in, it's pouring out here.'

Swiftly she closed the panels against the draught from the door, opened up—and there was Arthur, hollow-eyed himself, salvation in a shabby tweed suit.

'Oh, Arthur!' And she burst into tears against his damp shoulder.

He put her aside and went straight over to Sam. 'How long has he been like this?'

'Since this morning—I tried to get you but they said you were away—the other doctor said it was 'flu—'

'Hold his arm while I inject. He ought to be in a hospital but I won't risk moving him, at this stage it could do more harm than good.' He glanced at her face. 'What the hell have you two been up to—no, don't tell me, just be thankful I decided to drive down tonight. I'll leave you some M & B, he should be able to take them by the time they're needed.' He produced the tablets from his

bag, dismantled the hypodermic and put it away. 'Go to bed and keep warm yourself. I'll drop by in the morning.'

Honey had to make herself say it.

'He . . . will be all right?'

Arthur pursed his lips before he said, 'You've been a nurse.'

When he had gone her confidence ebbed again. Sam did not look any different, he still moaned and tossed on the drenched bedclothes. She wrung out a cloth in cold water and bathed his face, turned his pillow and resumed her vigil.

Towards dawn his breathing eased a little; the fire in his skin died down and he sank at last into a natural sleep. She watched him for a long time before she dared to believe it, anxiously testing from time to time the heat of his face with her lips, until she was sure. She glanced at the time. In an hour she would have to wake him for the medication. Until then . . . she laid her own face down thankfully on his limp pillow, too weary and too overwrought to sleep.

Sam awoke in the grey dawn to find her sponging his hands. She smiled as he opened his eyes, and pillowed her cheek against his palm.

'We made it,' he whispered hoarsely. She nodded, and he felt her tears.

Arthur came soon after it was light. Honey made him coffee which he tossed off at a gulp as though he could hardly spare the time, and she guessed he had come without breakfast. She thought again how essentially good he was, how unfailing a source of help.

He gravely examined Sam and pronounced him provisionally on the mend. He would need good care, he told her sternly, warmth and rest and no more escapades when he was better. One more night out in the rain, and . . .

Anyone would think it had been due to some whim of hers, thought Honey. She quelled the rising tide of her resentment, biting her tongue; with Sam so ill she must not start an argument. She walked with Arthur to the car, determined to express the gratitude she felt whatever the cost. She tried not to hear while he reminded her sententiously that while she might be able to play ducks and drakes with her health at her age, Sam could not, such irresponsible behaviour . . .

He really blames me, she thought dully; he blames me for everything that's ever happened to Sam. Not those ignorant, bigoted people but me. For not giving in to them, for making him rebel, refuse to settle for only half a life. Perhaps if you go back far enough it is my fault. But where's the help—can we live at all without bringing down disaster somewhere along the line?

'I don't believe you've listened to a word I've said.'

'Yes, yes I have,' she said meekly, 'complete bed rest and the medicine strictly on time.'

He nodded. 'Better stay in the warm yourself. Maggie'll be down later to see if you need anything.'

She took a deep breath. 'Arthur, I can't tell you how grateful I am—'

To her amazement he snapped, 'I don't want your gratitude. If you'd kept your knickers on none of this would be happening.'

'Arthur!' Tears of indignation gathered in her throat, to be quelled almost instantly as the anger, the frustrations, the injustice of the past months rose in an overwhelming wave and swept her along with it. She hurried ahead and put herself between him and his car. 'What makes you think you have the right to despise me!'

'I have no feelings about you.'

'Oh, yes, you have!' She could feel her own face blazing as she challenged him. 'Your contempt shows whenever you look at me.'

'You're talking nonsense. Move, please. I want to get into the car.'

'I'm not talking nonsense and you know it. You hate me, you've always hated me, what you said just now only goes to show how much. I knew you were blunt and tactless, Arthur—I didn't know you could be spiteful. My God, how wrong can you be!'

Arthur regarded her coldly, apparently unmoved. The few who had tried conclusions with him would have recognised that look, which left his assailant effectively in mid-air, pounding angry fists into the clouds. Honey stood her ground, refusing to back down, to be abashed by his lack or retaliation. As he reached for the car door, keys in hand, she blocked him.

'You were nice to me once, kind and friendly when I was little—right up to the time when that woman came. You've never liked me since then, you've always been

290

hateful, ever since! I don't know what I ever did to make you so bitter towards me.' Her voice was low and her eyes ached with unshed tears. 'We both love Sam, that should have been a bond between us, a meeting point where we could work together for his happiness—'

Arthur rounded on her and his face at last was white around the mouth. 'We both love Sam!' The words were wrung from his tongue as though they tasted foul. 'What I feel for Sam and what you do are not to be mentioned in the same breath. I've always been a true friend to Sam, I wanted him to have a good life, to be liked and respected, a credit to his race; I wanted to see him push forward in the fight against racialism. And what did you do—you've disgraced and demoralised him, ruined everything. He's thrown away everything he could have become for you, a worthless chit of a girl with nothing to offer but the taste of forbidden fruit!'

Honey looked into the angry, tortured eyes for a long moment before she spoke. 'Oh, Arthur...If you really think that's all there is, I'm sad for you. And I may be worthless, but at least I'm real, not a walking prescription pad like you, prescribing what you think is best for people whether they want it or not. What you can't see is that Sam's a human being like me, with as much right to imperfection as the rest of us. You can't accept that because you want him to be perfect, to live by impossible standards so that you can be proud of him—never mind how lonely or unhappy he might be. I believe that's all you took up with him for, you wanted someone—anyone the right colour—to prove your rightness to the world. You'd swallow him alive if you could but I'm not going to let you! I won't let you do it to him, I won't...' Reaction overcame her and she began to weep.

Arthur gazed fixedly over her head into the middle distance. 'I think you've said enough.'

She pulled herself together and said quietly, 'No, not quite enough. We're out in the open at last, we understand each other. But whatever the hates or the jealousies, let's not show them in front of Sam. At least let's try to be friends for his sake, don't make things worse for him.'

'Friends. How can we be friends—we have nothing in common? As for jealousy...' His steely eye pierced her. 'If you were a boy, there'd be nothing in you to interest him.'

'Perhaps not,' said Honey, smarting. 'But he does need me just the same. He needs me for things you couldn't ever give him.' She gentled her voice because she knew that what she had to say must hurt him. 'You're a very good man, Arthur. But there's no love in you, only goodness. No warmth, only righteousness. And goodness and righteousness alone just aren't enough.'

She left him staring straight in front of him and went indoors to Sam.

He tugged at her skirt as she passed and she went and stretched out beside him, her hot face against his. He put an arm around her and said, 'You been talking to Arthur?'

'Mm-mm. What's the joke?'

'You two. Squaring up to each other—like two cats on a wall.'

She managed to say lightly, 'Don't worry about it. We understand each other,' which was true as far as it went.

The effort of speech tired him; after a pause for rest he said, 'Know what I am? Just an old bone of contention, that's what.'

What an unenviable position, she thought: even Arthur should be able to understand that. But Arthur never seemed to understand anything, it was as if he daren't try for fear of finding he was wrong...

'Darling...' She nuzzled her sympathetic face into his neck.

Sam closed his eyes. 'Get some sleep, baby.'

They set the alarm for the next dose and slept.

Arthur called again in the early afternoon. He asked Honey somewhat stiffy, 'How is the patient?'

She met his gaze levelly. 'As well as can be expected.'

Something that might have been amusement twitched at his mouth. 'You're learning,' he said.

He took a look at Sam, told him again absently that he was a bloody fool, and said he would look in again in the morning.

Maggie appeared as he was leaving, bearing gifts from her own rich kitchen, pies and jellies and fragrant soup. She had come down in the car with Arthur to see what she could do, she said, and just as well seeing Honey was looking so peaky herself. Was she not developing a cold too?

'I'll be all right,' said Honey, wishing she could feel

less weary. The small privations of fetching and boiling water, chopping wood to feed the fire, the carrying out of slops, had toughened into hardships now that Sam was ill; she had not realised how much he had been doing. Mercifully, the chemical lavatory was still being cleared by the Council: the men on the 'violet cart' came from disinterested Southcombe, and in any case had they refused would have had the health authority on their necks. But it was the sole service left to them; without drainage or main water everything had to be done the hard way, and for one sick girl it was too much. Now she tried to smile at Maggie.'It's Sam that's ill,' she said.

'That's as may be,' Maggie reproved her, 'but you need more rest than you're getting. I'll see about the District Nurse, maybe she can give you a hand.'

Honey thanked her politely, privately wishing the nurse would not come. She wanted no other woman's hands on Sam. And anyway, she couldn't imagine that village institution in this holocaust of sin. She laughed, so that Maggie went away thinking, There was always something odd about that child...

The pregnant spring dusk gathered under the burgeoning trees. Excited twitterings disturbed the hedgerows. Honey knelt by the dying fire, trying to make up her mind to go out and cut more wood. Finally she rose and put on one of Sam's heavy sweaters.

As she pulled it over her head there was a knocking on the door. Heavy and ominous, it shuddered the wagon and sent the shadows scurrying into corners. Honey moved uncertainly towards the door.

'Who is it?'

A man's voice answered, hard and unfriendly. 'Never you mind who 'tis. McLeod in there?'

'You can't see him.' She stood tense behind the door, not offering to open it.

'Ask him what he wants,' came Sam's harsh whisper from the bed.

'What do you want him for?'

A muttered conference. 'Never you mind. You send him out.'

'He can't come out,' she said desperately, 'he's ill—'

From behind her she could sense his struggle to rise. She went quickly and pushed him back.

'You stay where you are, I'll take care of this.' She drew the panels across the bed-place and made for the door.

Sam mustered what remained of his voice. 'Honey, no!' But his protest broke off as he was racked by coughing. The sound of it followed her through the open door as she went out, slamming it behind her, forcing the two men who had tried to crowd onto the porch to take a step down to make way for her.

'He's very ill,' she said defiantly, 'if you bring him out here you'll kill him. You'd better say what you want to say to me.'

'What's he got, then?' They eyed her suspiciously. Both were unknown to her; both wore rough farming clothes and one carried a sack.

'Pneumonia.'

They looked at each other, shuffled their feet. Plainly this was the unexpected and called for further deliberation.

'How do we know you'm not shamming?'

'Why should I be?'

They glowered, discomfited. She pressed home her small advantage.

'I'll tell him you were here.' She waited with sweating hands and a calm face for them to go. They hung on stubbornly for a moment, reluctant to abandon whatever it was they had come for. Then. 'Tell him we'll be waiting. You tell him that.'

'Who are you?'

'Never you mind. Just do's you'm told. You tell him.'

They departed sullenly, joined at the gate by a third man. She watched them out of sight, not trusting them enough to turn her back.

Sam had stopped coughing. She could hear him calling to her, exhaustedly. She stood silent, not wanting to answer him until they were out of earshot. The man with the sack had left it behind. She picked it up, started after him. Thought better of it. Something inside it seemed to be moving. She opened it, looked in...

She flung it from her in horror and fled shuddering indoors. Inside the sack was a very large adder.

In a few more days Sam was sitting up. Honey had got over the worst of her cold and was managing better; she had swept out the wagon and put clean sheets on the

bed, had taken a basin of water to Sam and helped him to wash and comb his hair. He raked the comb across his scalp and said, 'Doesn't look any different, it just feels better.'

'Why don't you let me shave you, you'd be much more comfortable?'

The old smile stirred among the stubble of beard, 'You don't get near me with that old cut-throat, that's for sure!'

She laughed and roughed him up a little. 'If you let it go much longer I'll have to use a scythe.'

He drew her down beside him, pushed back a straggle of hair from her tired eyes. 'Whatever happened to that nurse Maggie was going to send?'

'I don't know. She never came.'

'You should have some help, you're not getting any rest.' He stroked her cheek with fingers softened by idleness. She caught his hand and laid her head against it, closing her eyes against the grey-blue scars that still hit her like a blow over the heart.

'I'll manage. Funny she didn't come. Maybe she was scared of reprisals.'

'Pity the gang that waylaid her!'

Honey smiled. The nurse was a well-constructed lady, the saddle of whose bicycle mysteriously disappeared when she was riding it.

'A pillar of virtue,' she agreed. 'Maybe she was afraid of getting seduced.'

'Quit your devilling,' said Sam, and chuckled feebly at the picture the thought conjured up. Then he stopped laughing and thought of her resentfully, not as a figure of fun but as a woman who had failed his girl who was falling asleep where she sat, leaving her to struggle alone with work that was too much for her.

He got up sooner than he should have done and pretended to feel better than he did. Fortunately Arthur saw what he was up to and bullied him out of going back to work.

On his final professional visit he slipped an envelope into Honey's hand, having asked her to walk to the car with him when he left.

'Don't show this to Sam,' he said in some embarrassment, 'read it before you go back.'

She opened her mouth to say she didn't have secrets from Sam, but before she could utter he got into the car and drove off. She stood with it in her hand, debating

what to do about it; there was a promise of spring in the hot watery sunshine, and down the lane the whispering sea beckoned. No one would bother Sam for a few minutes, not in broad daylight. She strolled on down to the beach and read it there.

Honey,
Home truths are always painful but my behaviour the other morning was indefensible. I can only think I was more tired than I knew. Apologies are only words and I don't know how, or even if I can make amends. But I hope you will accept the enclosed as a small token of whatever it is I am making such a mess of trying to say.

Arthur

With it in the envelope were two tickets for a concert at the Festival Hall and a reservation for two at a London hotel. And a cheque made out to British Railways for the amount of their return fares.

Honey's eyes filled as she read it. She wanted to run after him, embrace him, weep...but she knew that was impossible. Impossible. Instead she hurried back to the caravan to tell Sam of the promised treat, trying en route to work out how not to tell him too much.

She found him with a paper in his hand, his face ashen under the dark skin. He looked around as she came in, hastily screwed it up and threw it into the stove.

'What's the matter?' she demanded.

He recovered himself quickly. Too quickly. 'Just one of the usual. It came while you were out.'

So soon, she thought. They must have been waiting, as they said. 'What did it say?'

'Just the usual, I told you. Forget it, I have...'

But he knew he would never forget it. It was subtly different from any of the others:

EVER SEE A FACE BEEN THROUGH A WINSCREEN A BROKEN BOTTLE DOES JUST AS GOOD YOU CANT BE THERE ALL THE TIME

A WELL WISHER

16

Arthur was discreetly delighted that his invitation was
accepted, although only he and Honey knew the full truth
of why. Sam took it with a sort of bewildered pleasure,
not understanding the why's and the wherefore's but glad
for Honey to have a break. Maggie beamed at what she
took for a noble gesture on her husband's part, and herself
insisted on treating Honey to a new dress.

They barricaded Mango Walk as best they could, and
with a prayer for the undefended garden went off in Arthur's car to the station.

At the other end things were not so simple. The desk
clerk at the hotel where they were booked in looked at
them coldly and insisted there had been a mistake. He
would be happy to refund their money, but alas, he could
not find them a room. He was very sorry...

After nine more attempts they found an hotel willing
to take them. It was a long way from the Festival Hall.
A long way in every sense from the one Arthur had
booked for them. The so-called double room was in fact
two communicating cubicles with windows that opened—
or failed to open—on to a roof valley in which two girly
magazines and a dead cat lay in the gutter. The wardrobe
opened to disclose dark patches of mildew and when
they went to the bar for a drink they saw a ratling scamper
long-legged across the floor.

'If you don't want the room, there's plenty that do,'
said the desk clerk crisply, 'lucky to get in anywhere if
you ask me.'

'No, no, it's fine,' they assured him hastily, and asked
what time there would be breakfast.

'We don't serve breakfast. There's a café across the
road.'

They exchanged wry smiles. But there was still the

Festival Hall, and they went back to their rooms to change. As they left they overheard, 'God, I hate to see that. A white girl with one of them...'

'Getting worse lately, too. One time they wouldn't have got in here but this place isn't what it was.'

'No...they say it's terrible round Brixton way, a white woman can't walk down the street alone, especially after dark...'

Honey tucked her arm through Sam's elbow and made for the lift. When it arrived the attendant glanced at them, stepped out and slammed the doors behind him.

'Not working,' he said, 'use the stairs.' And he left them standing there.

They climbed the four flights and when they reached their room Sam went over to the window and stood staring moodily out, his knuckles resting on the sill.

'Cheer up,' said Honey, leaning her face against his arm, and he turned too quickly.

'I am cheered up,' he said.

The concert was unsullied delight. The music took them into itself, the superb acoustics of the hall left no room in the mind for anything but the sound and the splendour, and when it ceased it left a hush that was almost tangible. In the interval they went to the bar with the rest of the audience, and like the rest they were served without hesitation.

'There, you see!' said Honey, pleased. 'One day it will be like this everywhere. We only have to wait, and not give in. You'll see.'

'You reckon?' said Sam.

'I reckon.' She reached up, kissed him lightly. Smiled as he drew back, disconcerted: 'Chicken,' she whispered, teasing him. Because coward was a word she could never use again.

At the end of the programme they hurried back to the hotel, albeit reluctantly, for fear of finding themselves locked out. But apparently the place was open all night and they plodded unchallenged up the threadbare stairs to their room. The door was provided with a cylinder lock of the sort usually fitted to street doors. Closing it, Honey paused to read a notice fixed to the inside:

> 'Please lock this door before retiring. Remember that London is a cosmopolitan city and we cannot guarantee your safety or that of your property.'

'A cosmopolitan city...' mused Honey, 'what do they mean by that?'

'They mean me,' said Sam. 'What they're saying is, "We let to scum like you, so watch out you don't get your throat cut."' For the first time there was an edge to his voice.

Honey pushed down the button with a snap. 'It works both ways,' she said, and tried to divert him by adding, 'like the double wrapping on those sweets that "keeps all the dirt out and all the flavour in".'

She was watching Sam, but he did not laugh.

For the first time in months they made love without having to listen for the sounds of danger. Afterwards they slept like spoons in the narrow bed, and awoke and smiled, black eyes into grey, grey into black. Glad to find life still good to them, after all.

In the morning Sam went down to settle the bill while Honey packed the last of their oddments into Maggie's weekend case. As she started down to join him she found her way blocked by the hotel manager.

'Going out, little girl?'

'Leaving, actually.' She mistrusted this man who eyed her like a tom-cat while ignoring Sam. 'May I pass, please.'

'So soon? Can't we persuade you to stay another night?' He edged closer, his inference unmistakable.

Honey sidestepped. He did the same. She backed up a stair to evade his encroaching arm. 'Please let me pass.' Her voice was shrill with nervousness. 'My husband will be waiting.'

'Oh, yes, your "husband"...' His smile was insolent. 'Let him wait.'

He knows, she thought angrily. He knows I've got to put up with this because I can't have Sam involved in a fight. The swine. The bastard. Patiently she tried to disengage herself. Through clenched teeth she said, 'Look—I told you I'm leaving. I meant it, so let me be!' Furious, she pushed at the hands that shamelessly explored her body. The face loomed unpleasantly close to hers, the pink moist mouth alien, repellent under the sandy moustache that smelled like shag tobacco.

'No need for a girl like you to sleep with a blackie, you can have a white man any time!'

She twisted her head backwards to avoid his mouth, biting back the words which came boiling to her tongue.

'Come on, come on...' he muttered thickly, impatient, showing the tip of his tongue between his discoloured teeth, thrusting his pelvis forward, banging against hers.

For the first time she was glad of her training as a nurse. She managed to free an arm and brace it horizontally across his chest. Unless he could remove it by force it kept her mouth effectively beyond his reach, and he could only remove it by releasing her. Baulked and frustrated, he glared at her across the deadlock.

'What's the matter, not good enough—I'm better looking than him.'

Honey glared back. 'That's a matter of opinion!' She braced a foot on the stair behind her and threw him off balance. His arms flew out to save himself, releasing her, and he went reeling down several stairs before he could arrest his fall. He picked himself up, glowering, and she did not wait to see more. With lightness and speed on her side, she ran back into her room and slammed the door behind her. She had left the lock on the button for the chambermaid and it did not catch, but she stood with her back against it, struggling for self-control. How dared he, how dared he...that loathsome little man. Her eye fell on the hairbrush she had left behind on the dressing-table and automatically she went over and picked it up. Then another wave of rage swamped her and she flung it with all her strength across the room. It landed with a satisfying crack in a corner, splitting the wooden back. It was then she remembered that Sam had given it to her.

She went over slowly and picked it up, sat nursing it on the shabby bed, her anger dispersed like a pricked balloon leaving her unutterably depressed. She looked up and there was Sam, standing tall and still in the doorway.

'Who was it?' he said quietly.

'Who was what?'

'Who tried to get fresh with you?'

She stared at him, wondering how he knew. 'You saw?'

'No, I didn't see. But it's in your face—and I was expecting it, it was bound to happen.'

He came and stood near her, his brown hands taut on the bedrail. She thought of those other hands and her clothing crawled against her skin.

'I don't understand,' she said, groping for his meaning. 'Why were you expecting it?'

'You're a coloured man's girl. A target for anything.

They think if you go with me you'd go with anyone.' He turned away abruptly and began to pace the room.

Honey watched him helplessly, not knowing what to say. 'Sam...'

He returned to her, grasping her shoulders roughly and shaking her to emphasise his words. 'Do you still want to be wretched with me, Honey...Do you—now you know everything it means?'

Honey knew there must be an answer to that but she could not find the words. All her life she had lost her way because she could not find the words. Her eyes filled as she looked at him, at his fingers bruising her arm. 'Darling...Sam...you're hurting me...'

He loosed his grip, reluctantly, and her head dropped on to his shoulder.

'Hold me a minute,' she whispered. 'Just till I feel safe again...'

He held her, broodingly and in silence, his face against her hair. But...you're not safe, he was thinking. You're not safe anywhere...with me

They stayed close to each other after that, even to waiting outside the doors of lavatories, their new-found freedom at an end. But they made the most of the few hours left to them, as though it might be all that there was. They booked out of the hotel and went to Regent's Park, ate sandwiches on a bench by the waterside and were entranced by the sparrows that fluttered about them, filching the bread from their fingers as they tried to eat, laughing at little things as though newly in love. The spring sunshine was hot on their faces, the water sparkled under the romping breeze; here and there the wan faces of Indians opened up like flowers in the sun.

'Look—there's a swallow!' cried Honey excitedly, pointing to the fine shape skimming across the grass. 'Wonder what it's doing in London—and so early in the year.'

'Trying to make a summer,' said Sam. He smiled with great tenderness, 'Like you.'

They went to Trafalgar Square and fed the pigeons from a tuppenny bag which they bought from a man with a tray. He was doing a brisk trade and the air was thick with churring and cooing. The birds settled on their arms, shoulders, heads, anywhere they could perch, generous with their favours in return for the food. 'It's supposed

to be lucky,' laughed Honey, watching the children dodging and giggling. But they were not blessed.

They chattered happily all the way to Paddington, holding hands openly, not caring who saw. Sam in particular was very bright, diverting his thoughts from the agonised conviction of his heart.

17

Back at Mango Walk they found pretty much what they expected. Shrubs hacked to the ground, flower-beds overturned, the caravan daubed with paint.

'What's this?' said Honey, scuffling a pile of ash on the porch, fingering the blistered woodwork on the front door.

'An old trick,' said Sam. 'Putting lighted paper through the letter-box. Good job I nailed it up before we left.' He wondered that they had not been burned out before now. But perhaps that was too audacious to be risked.

He applied himself patiently to the task of restoration. The garden alone took him most of Sunday and even then it still looked as if a hurricane had hit it. Honey was inclined to grieve over the martyred flowers.

'It's so unfair, why should they be punished—all they ask is to grow quietly in the sun?'

'It's all most of us want. A place in the sun.'

'Oh—just look at the poor little cherry tree! How could they...'

'It's the last time, babe. They won't do it again.'

'You've thought of a way to stop them?' Her eyes lightened unsuspectingly.

He kissed her quickly, unable to meet them. 'I've thought of a way.'

By the end of the week he had put his house in order. Now that he had reached a decision, was no longer tormented by doubts, he was conscious of a curious lightening of the spirit. As though he suddenly found the strength that was needed to carry it through. Small considerations ceased to worry him, dwarfed by the enormity of what he was about to face. In a strange way he felt free to breathe again. When the worst has been accepted, there is nothing more to fear. Perhaps there is a kind of victory in acknowledging defeat.

After this last ravage to their property they were left unmolested. To Sam it seemed that the village knew it had won: it was ceding him the freedom of the battleground for the privilege of bringing in his dead.

He went back to work, thankful that his duty turn was not for nights; they would hardly dare to touch her in broad daylight. Outside his working hours he spent every moment with Honey. Listening to her, talking with her, savouring the subtlest nuances of her voice. Stocking his memory against the years to come. Making love with a passionate tenderness that awakened in her a new, intenser sensitivity. And under the influence of his strange lightheartedness her crushed spirits began to revive; she laughed with him, bewildered, delighted in a way that wrung his heart.

He resisted the temptation to abandon his job and stay at home with her; that would have alerted her suspicions, and he wanted his last days with her unmarred by tears. It was selfishness, and he knew it. But he was too numb to care.

The week flashed by them and was lost. He spent the weekend in gathering together the shreds of their happiness, binding them about his love for a winding sheet.

Sunday they spent in tramping the beaches. The spring weather was hot and brilliant and when he suggested they should make the most of it she was glad to agree. They walked many miles, scarcely speaking, content to be together and feeling little need for words. When at last they were tired they turned inland and wandered up a little-used lane into a meadow. There they found a half-used haystack and climbed up on to it, finding in the harsh dry scent of clover a small and secret world under the high blue radiance of the sky.

There Honey turned to him a face tanned rosy by the

salt breeze and said softly, 'Sam...I love you and love you...don't ever leave me...'

He answered her only with kisses. Drawing her towards him, baring her breasts to his mouth so that she forgot all questioning, and at length they lay happy and a little out of breath, moist from the contact of skin upon skin, hot with their loving in the sun-warmed hay.

Sam drowsed for a while, her body his warm breathing pillow. Once she stirred murmuring, 'We ought to go.'

'Not yet...not yet...'

She did not know what she was bringing to a close. Only he knew, and sadness overwhelmed him as the sun went down. He pressed closer into the refuge of her arms. Honey shivered and reached for her clothes.

'Please adjust your dress before leaving,' he quoted softly, and their eyes met and laughed, perhaps for the very last time.

Late that night when she had gone to bed, he sat at the little table, writing letters. The first few were easy. One to Arthur, brief and to the point:

> Honey I entrust to your keeping because you are a good man, not because you are my friend. You always know the proper thing to do and though it gives me pain, I have to admit you were right.

One to the shipping company. One to Jane Fisher, addressed to her at the hospital in London. Surely, if she had left they would send it on...

One to Maggie, saying goodbye. And a few bills to be paid. It was the last letter of all that gave him pause.

He sat for a long time with the paper before him, watching her as she lay with her back towards him and the light: going back over the day behind them. Over the months, over the years, searching for the thing he had to say. For the first time, it was he who could not find the words.

'Honey...' he wrote. And then his thoughts dried like the ink on his pen, withered by the misery inside him. He went over and sat down on the edge of the bed, looking down into her sleeping face with a minute scrutiny that numbered the hairs of her curving eyebrow but did not find for him the words to say. She sighed and her fingers moved across the pillow, reaching unconsciously for him. Tomorrow they would make that errand in vain. He

caught the wandering hand and kissed it, unable to bear the sight.

She roused enough to gaze at him with sleep-filled eyes, 'Darling, come to bed...it's getting late...'

'One more letter to write.'

'Only one. Can't it wait?'

He shook his head, wretched beyond words, never to forget this hour.

'Only one, then. Promise...' She offered him her lips and he touched them briefly before burying his face in her neck.

'I promise,' he whispered hoarsely.

He went back to the table and began to write:

> Don't try to forgive me for what I'm going to do. Be angry, hate me, that way it will hurt you less. And when the anger is over and the memories come flooding back, remember too that in the end I deserted you like a coward lacking even the courage to say goodbye. Think any bad thing of me that will help. But never, never believe I didn't love you, if I loved you less I might have stayed longer. Come to think of it that's probably the first time I told you in so many words. Even now it feels like a forbidden thing to say.

> What I said to you years ago is true. I must give you a chance of happiness in the only way I can. You never could understand that, could you? But one day you will and then you may curse me for not living up to it better.

> The caravan is yours to burn, to live in, to give away. But don't stay in it, my dear love, to grieve for me. This thought of all the others haunts me the worst. I've stolen your watch to take with me, but you're allowed to forgive me for that. We have to be forgiven the small things or we couldn't live.

> When I have an address I will send it, so if any bad thing should come to you cable me, I'll come running wherever I am. And you'll be all right for money, I'll take care of that.

> Unless you do send for me you won't see me again. But when you are an old woman think of me. If I'm still on this earth I shall be then as always, ever your loving,

> Sam

He remained for a long time staring at what he had written, unable himself to believe in the irrevocable words. It could not be happening, after telling himself for so long that it had to be so, this could not be the moment of death, the point of no return. The fire still burned in the stove, the lamp with its familiar hiss still shed its uncertain light on the same homely things about the room. On the china hanging on the dresser shelves, a curtain moving in the breeze above the bed. And on Honey lying as she always did, curled like a kitten on her side, her fine hair falling across her face, obscuring it, gilded by the light. Everything was the same. It was just like any other night.

Only he knew that it was different, with a hideous and terrifying difference that marked it out from any other night he had known or would ever know.

He picked up the letters to Honey, to Maggie, to Arthur. Into the large envelope they went and it was over, the long ordeal of hope, the bittersweet joy, the despair. He would never feel anything as keenly again as in this hour, and it was past.

Honey stirred and murmured as he got into bed. He turned her over and took her in his arms, not speaking.

'Scratch my back...' she said drowsily, settling her face against his neck.

If she felt his tears she said nothing. It was not remarkable; sorrow had been their bedfellow too long.

The day dawned just like any other. The sky lightened, the clock shrilled its alarm. They rose and went about their usual preparations for the day. At breakfast he gave her the envelope. 'Take this up to Maggie for me, will you? I want her to get it before this evening.'

She took it and smiled. 'Secrets?'

'I want to explain why we didn't go up there yesterday.' A good lie always lay close to the truth. But uneasiness stirred in him. 'You'll take it early, before tonight? Promise...' He was filled with the thought that she might forget, might wait for him tonight... not knowing...

'I promise.' She was amused, surprised. Because she did not understand. He wrenched his face into a smile, 'I must get going—oh, wear my watch for me today. I don't want to take it with me.' He took it off and strapped it on her wrist, finding with some difficulty the hole he had punched so long ago to fit her.

'You did that when I was little and you were going away to sea,' she said, watching him.

'I did?' Dear God, he thought, lead her away... 'I must have thought you were a puppy.' Why had he not remembered!

'A puppy?'

'That's right. You take him from his mother you have to give him a clock to sleep with—then he won't keep you awake all night barking.'

She laughed. She thought he was fooling her.

'That's right.' He produced some semblance of a laugh. He was cold and trembling. How was it possible that she did not know?

Suddenly he wanted urgently to be away, not to have to see her unsuspecting face. He took down his coat from the peg. 'Bye, now.'

'Bye, then.' She scarcely glanced at him, busy with the morning chores.

On the steps he hesitated. For all his dreadful calm he could not go without a backward glance. He stood with a hand on the door, casting about for an excuse to linger. 'Don't forget that note.'

'I won't.' She came to the door, smiling, laid her arms along it over his. He stroked back the wayward hair from her eyes and before he could stop them the words had escaped him, 'Still love me, Honey?'

She rubbed her soft face still shabby with sleep against his. 'What is it,' she asked him tenderly, 'you want me to darn your socks?'

The ordinary words moved him unbearably, piercing the armour he had forged last night. He enfolded her, straining her body against him, as though in some way he could distil an essence of her to absorb into himself, to carry with him on his desperate journey. He closed his eyes. Past her shoulder he saw in his soul the vast bleak stretches of the sea.

'Honey...' he whispered. So faintly that she did not hear him.

He released her and stepped down, away from her.

'Love me a little longer...' He reached up to kiss her, swiftly. And made his escape.

Honey watched him down the path and through the gate, her heart disturbed with undefined misgiving. She strained her ears past the tinkling birds to catch the last

of his retreating footsteps fading into silence up the lane. They had reached vanishing point when she realised what was wrong.

He was carrying his sea-going case.

PART FOUR

❋❋❋

As Long as Songbirds Sing

'I'll give you back your letters, I'll give
    you back your ring,
But I'll remember you, my love, as long as
    songbirds sing.'

1
—

'He's gone,' said Honey, 'he's not here any more. He's
gone where you can't reach him, not you nor anyone else.
He left three years ago.' She looked calmly into the rad-
dled face before her, savouring her moment of triumph.

Nancy McLeod eased her spreading hindquarters on
to the caravan steps.

'Well, now. Who'd have thought it? Looks as if I've
had a long hot journey for nothing.' She pulled off her
headscarf and mopped her neck with it, ran her fingers
through hennaed hair that was greying at the roots. 'Ah,
well. I'll get you to give me his address before I go.'

'No, you won't,' said Honey with alacrity. 'I'll give you
a cup of tea and that's an end of it. I don't want you here.'
Her early training nudged her; she added, 'Sorry if that's
rude of me.'

Nancy shrugged, 'Ah well…it's understandable. It
wasn't exactly a social evening the last time I was here.'
She peered into Honey's face. 'It was you, the little thing?

Ah well, it's upsetting for kids, I wouldn't wonder, seeing the grown-ups squabbling. I well remember—' Her gaze shifted to something behind Honey and shock wiped all other expression from her face. 'Holy Mother of God!' she breathed, and hastily crossed herself.

Honey turned to see the cause of her alarm and met the round black eyes shyly peeping at the curtain's edge. She smiled, 'It's only Gaby,' and she opened the door and drew her daughter through.

The little girl came slowly, thumb buried in mouth, eyes enormous and shining like liquorice.

'Say hello,' Honey prompted, and the baby face was hidden against her skirt. 'She's shy—she doesn't see many people,' but she was thinking. Maybe she knows, senses something and is afraid. She curved her fingers about the tender nape, loving the soft hair.

Nancy looked deathly. 'I thought for a minute...'

Georgia, thought Honey. Poor little ghost, so long forgotten...If Nancy had had a bad moment it served her right. But she said, 'You'd better rest a minute. I'll make tea,' and went inside to do it.

When she came out with it Gaby was sitting on Nancy's knee, exploring with a pudgy finger a flamboyant plastic butterfly pinned on her green satin blouse.

'God, she's so like,' said Nancy wonderingly, 'it gave me quite a turn.' She looked up and added, 'He never did forgive me, you know. As if it was my fault.'

'Wasn't it?' Honey had not meant that to come out so sharply. But Nancy did not seem to have noticed it.

'No, God save us—how could I have stopped the bomb! Caught it in me own two hands and chucked it back up at them? No, I reckon it was because I was out when it happened. Out with a friend. Always jealous, he was; being coloured I suppose made it worse, I only had to look at a white fellow, he'd be going up the wall...But if I'd been there I couldn't have saved her, I'd just have been dead too. Maybe that was what he wanted,' she added broodingly, stirring sugar thickly into her tea. The child scrambled down from her knee and she said, 'So he left you with one as well, did he?'

'It wasn't like that,' said Honey. 'He didn't know. And doesn't. I don't want him told.'

Nancy stared. 'But you must tell him! It's his kid, make him come back and look after it—'

'No!'

'—but he would if you told him, he was always all right to the kid. Well, me too, most of the time, it was just—' she shook her head as though lost for words—'people. Friends, neighbours; couldn't mind their own business. And of course I could never take him home—well, you must know how it is. But then it's maybe not as bad as it was.'

'You mean it can be worse?' said Honey drily. They were both silent. Then she said, 'I don't want him dragged back. He's suffered enough.'

Nancy was pouring herself a second cup. She looked up in surprise. 'He suffered? Well... yes, I suppose. D'you know, I never thought of it like that.'

Honey said nothing. Thinking only how strange it was that they should be chatting companionably over tea, as if there had never been pain or bitterness between them. Perhaps it was because the barrier of Sam himself was no longer there. And then, Nancy was the only one in the world who had known him as she had known him.

Nancy looked at her watch. 'I'd better be going or I'll miss the train in Southcombe. Are you sure you won't give me his address, now? He ought to be told, you know, you're only a bit of a thing to be left to bring up a kid on your own.'

Honey shook her head. 'What was it you came for, by the way?'

'Oh—just the usual.' She rubbed her thumb and forefinger together and laughed, giving Honey a glimpse of the pretty vivacious girl she once had been. 'But I'll manage. You've got worse problems than mine.' She nodded to where Gaby splashed happily in the overflow bucket. 'They bring their troubles with them, God knows, I'll never forget when the midwife showed me mine.'

'Nor will I,' said Honey, her expression softening at the memory. That little wrinkled prune of a face had been the best thing she had ever seen, had brought the sunlight shafting back into the dark cell of her life. But she would not expect Nancy to understand that. Perhaps that was where Sam had gone wrong; he had looked for a greater depth in her than she had ever had to show.

She smiled and waved her goodbye, leaning on the gate.

'You'll be all right now, you're sure?' Nancy said surprisingly, to which she answered, 'Yes, I'm fine...' and laughed, shaking her head; and went back to Gaby.

'I still think you're a fool...' echoed faintly back down the lane.

Perhaps by Nancy's standards she was. But the village left her in peace now, as if it were satisfied to have got its way. Sam provided her with money from his pay on a Seaman's Allotment Note: twice a month she had to present it at the Post Office, where of all people David Bassett paid her in cash. But he was never other than coldly civil and she had learned to be thankful for small mercies. The Brodniks and their cousin had moved away to the city where the brighter pennies shone; the other lads had channeled their aggression into forming a football team. Water was once more available from the farm and the letters that came through her letterbox now promised nothing more sinister than visits from Jane in London.

Jane had come running when she heard the news; the only one who could begin to know how she felt. And it was Jane's hand she had wrung in the extremity of labour, Jane who descended from time to time to whisk her away for a weekend in London; but she resisted all attempts to persuade her to move away from Mango Walk. It was all she had of her life with Sam. She could not imagine living anywhere else.

It was the Colbys who made it possible, and she knew that without them she could not have managed. They were a never-failing source of strength, of protection, though whether for her sake or for Sam's she hardly knew. Maggie had watched and mothered her through pregnancy and confinement as though she were her own, and she in those early months had been in no state to resist. Only once had they come into conflict.

'Och, Arthur!' Maggie had protested, 'she cannot go back to that wretched caravan, not with a new-born baby. Make her see sense.'

Arthur had looked at them both over his newspaper, then at Honey alone, and the shrewd eyes under the shaggy brows had twinkled.

'I never managed to do that in the past. I don't know why you should expect it of me now.'

Honey's drawn face had begun to smile but Maggie had taken him seriously. 'Och, Arthur, don't be so hard on the child—she's surely enough to upset her.'

Arthur put down his paper. 'So you've had enough of us, eh? You think it's time to go home?'

Honey nodded, holding the warm moist bundle of her baby. 'Sam'—she still said his name with difficulty— 'wouldn't want me to give in.'

Arthur regarded her enigmatically. 'So that's settled,' he nodded as though in satisfaction, and disappeared again behind his newspaper. 'You know where to find us by now, I imagine.'

Ever since then he had passed Mango Walk morning and evening, regardless of the route of his visiting. He never came in but leaned his elbows on the gate or on the door. 'Everything all right? Good. Well, I'll be on my way.' The routine never varied; it was the most comforting thing in her life. That, and watching Gaby grow. And Sam's letters.

After three years he still wrote twice on every trip: once on the outward voyage, once on the return, jotting the oddments of his daily life, the titbits he thought would amuse her, leaving the letter to be added to from day to day, sealed and posted when he came into port. And after three years they were an unmixed joy; they had ceased to stir the longings that could tear her like wolves in the darkness. Well... almost ceased. Only in spring did the physical ache return. Spring, when the cherry tree bloomed and the children ran squealing to the beach; and the warm summer nights when she tossed and moaned with empty arms. But there was always Gaby to cuddle into them, Gaby with her African eyes, her round head and her soft, soft hair...

The first letter had been the worst, catching her off guard, because she was not expecting it. She had torn it open hoping—hoping—but no, he had not changed his mind. Neither had he known how to write to her, how to disguise the misery that stared hollow-eyed between the lines. Sober, stilted, barren, it had put a distance between them that had not been there before. Only when she reached the postscript had she found the Sam she knew: 'Must have left my sea legs under the caravan, I was sick all the way out.' She had not cried until she read that.

Nancy walked up to the bus stop in a mellow mood. Seeing that little mulatto had taken her back, indeed it had... poor little things, it was wicked bringing them into the world half-and-half, they didn't belong anywhere. Still, that was life. Not that she had much room to throw

stones—but at least she'd been married. Just. That little
thing, she thought again with amazement, so much like
Georgia—the spitten image! Shame in a way that he
couldn't have seen her, and him so gone on the first one.
But then, it was a hard old world to be sure, and he wasn't
the only one in it...

She glanced at her watch. Nearly half an hour to wait
before the bus. She could do with a cigarette. Maybe there
was a shop open somewhere in this godforsaken hole.
The Post Office. That might do...She pushed open the
door and walked in.

The man behind the counter was tallish and thin with
lank hair that fell across his eyes. She looked at him,
wondering where she had seen him before.

His pale eyes returned her curious stare. 'I know you,
don't I? You been here before?'

'Not for a long time,' she said, 'you'd have been a kiddy
then.'

'That's right, I would have been...about fourteen.
Yeah, now I got it! You come out from the caravan just
as I was going down the beach. I remember you come
out, then stood still, turned round and went back in again.
Don't see many like you round these parts,' he grinned,
'well, couldn't miss that hair.' He pushed the cigarettes
across the counter. 'One and six, now. Gone up, they
have. Well, fancy seeing you. Family, are you?'

Nosey, thought Nancy, all the same these yokels. 'In
a manner of speaking,' she said, 'more an old friend,
really. I came to look them up but there's no one home.
Somebody said they'd moved. I suppose you wouldn't
be having a forwarding address, you being a Post Office?
I'd like to have got in touch.'

The man pursed his lips; on such a long narrow face
the effect was extraordinary. 'Couldn't give it if I had.
Against the rules to do that. Did you want to write to
him?'

'Well,' she patted her hair, turned her best angle towards him, 'it'd have been nice to fill him in with the
family news. That's if I had an address for him, if you
get my meaning?'

'Told you,' he said stubbornly. 'Can't do that.'

'Not even,' Nancy hesitated, watching him, 'if I said
I was his wife?'

'That's where I seen you first!' He slammed a hand
down on the counter, making the gob-stoppers and the

jelly-beans dance. 'You come to the farm when I was a little nipper, right the beginning of the war. You come and raised cain with my ma for letting him have the caravan—you remember me, you must do? David—David Bassett.'

'Oh...yes,' said Nancy vaguely, although she did not. She recalled only the tawdry caravan and its smell, the shame of her predicament, her anger against the fat farm woman who had a safe, respectable home when she had not. 'I remember your mother,' she said.

'Oh-ah,' said David. 'Dead she is, now. And my auntie. Still, it's nice you remember her. Well, it's like I said, I can't give you no addresses. But then that's not to say I couldn't get it off a certain person's letters as she posts in the box here. And if you was to say write a letter and leave it with me, that's not to say I couldn't send it on for you. That's if it would help you, like.' He scratched his bony chin, looked her over appraisingly. 'Well, now. So you're his old woman, after all this time. Here,' he leaned across the counter, his manner confidential, 'what about his little love nest, then? Shacked up with his own daughter down the caravan—and then off and left her with a bun in the oven, what about that, eh?' He stopped, seeing her look of surprise, and coloured uncomfortably. 'I suppose she's your daughter, too. I didn't think about that.'

Nancy stared, 'Is that what he told you?'

David shuffled his feet, easing his corns in his winkle-picker shoes. 'Well...I dunno. He never said, not in so many words. Only he come down here in the Blitz, left her with us to be looked after like, said her mother had been killed—' He looked at Nancy in puzzlement. 'Now that's funny, come to think of it. She couldn't have been—well, could she? Not if it's you...'

Nancy shook her head slowly. 'I thought she was some girl he'd picked up in the village here.' She stood staring at the racks of onions and carrots, at the baking tins, the torch batteries, the packets of candles and of custard powder.

'Glory be to God,' she said at last, 'what a mess.'

2

'Next time you may go with your Mummy,' soothed Maggie, 'this time you stay with Auntie Mag and maybe if you're good she'll bring you sweeties.'

Gaby's lip trembled, and Honey felt herself weakening. She hated to be parted from Gaby, could not endure her tears; but she had promised for so long to spend a weekend with Jane, had put her off so many times. And Jane's tiny flat was shared with two other nurses, one of whom would inevitably be on nights; it was unfair to take a small lively child to disturb their sleeping arrangements. Besides, it was not good for Gaby to become inseparable. She smiled and said, 'I'll come back. I always come back, you know that, don't you?'

And Gaby nodded, and hid her face and tried not to wail out loud. She could never believe that Mummy had not gone for ever.

Maggie scooped her up and bore her indoors, and Honey escaped quickly down the gravelled drive and went to wait for the bus at the village stop.

Autumn had slipped in quietly, almost unnoticed. After weeks of rain there was no frosted blaze of colour on the trees, the leaves fell sadly, as though having waited for their destined glory they could wait no longer and dropped unrecognised on the waiting grass. Voices rang clearly through the distant lanes, strong voices, bred to carry across fields; the air sharpened with the perfumed tang of blackberries. Evening fell early and was violet blue, chilled by the departure of the south-bound sun; afternoon was filled with wood smoke, and pale grey scented rain swept the morning skies, dark as an elephant's back or pearly, shot through with shafts from a drowning sun.

Honey turned up her collar against the fine mist of rain that threatened. She pulled an unripe berry from the hedge, wondering again why she had not heard from Sam.

Since her encounter with Nancy in the spring she had received only one letter from him, posted in Aruba, telling her of the shore leave he had taken to visit his parents in Jamaica. He had found only his mother, wizened out of recognition, hardly knowing him. His father was long dead, his sisters married, his brothers scattered, one a doctor in Princetown, one an engineer in some distant place, two, émigrés like himself, living to his surprise in Birmingham. The ship would be coming in to Liverpool at the end of the trip... She knew the letter by heart. She had read it again and again in search of a clue to his sudden silence. She had half expected to hear that he had gone to look up the two brothers in Birmingham, not telling her until afterwards for fear she might follow him there... yet he had used up his shore leave in Jamaica. It was a mystery.

She sighed, and brought back her thoughts to Gaby; she had it in mind to take her blackberrying when she returned. But the berry she had pulled was pale and tasteless, lacking the warmth of sun to ripen it. As the bus came into sight she picked up her borrowed suitcase and turned her face from home.

When she alighted in Southcombe a fine drizzle was falling. As a watery sunbeam groped its way through a break in the clouds she looked for the rainbow she knew must be somewhere, and smiled, thinking of how he would tease her: You and your rainbows and your one swallow... There will be a summer one day, Sam... only not for us.

The down train had just come in and people were streaming off it, boiling towards her up the station approach, coats hugged tightly around them in the teeth of the wet wind that came gusting in off the sea. Nothing stopped them, not weather nor anything else, down they came in droves all summer long to shiver on the beach. Like lemmings, Sam once said, once they smelled the sea there was no holding them.

He was never far from her mind. She saw him everywhere, in shops, on trains. Still, if she half closed her eyes, she could fancy she saw his dark head bobbing among the crowd. There was even a man who looked like him—there at the back, duffel-bag and all. Even the same

height. The same way of walking—her heart gave a frightening lurch. And then she was standing transfixed, the sound of traffic receding, as slowly fantasy crystallised...into reality.

Hell-bent on meeting the train, George Draper swung his van smartly into the station approach and felt the hair rise on the nape of his neck. What was the stupid bitch doing here—right in his path! He punched the horn but she seemed not to hear, didn't move—was she deaf—he yelled at her—'Look out, you silly cow!'

He stood on the horn again—on the brakes—on everything—the road was wet, greasy—nothing happened—too late!

'Oh Christ!' he screamed, and hid his eyes as he felt the awful thump, the sliding of the wheels—

At the police station, in the ambulance post and in the fire station, alarm bells jangled people into action.

In faraway Stone House, Maggie Colby lifted a telephone.

'An accident...in Southcombe? The doctor's not here just now, he's out on his rounds, you'll need to ring for an ambulance...yes, straight to Casualty...The address was where? On what...on the suitcase...' Blindly she felt behind her for the arm of the chair, lowered herself into it as her knees dissolved. 'I see,' she said faintly, 'yes...thank you for ringing...goodbye.' She replaced the receiver with a hand that seemed to belong to someone else. Stunned, she stared through the open doorway to where a tiny figure stood, chin on windowsill, waiting for the rain to stop. 'Oh, no,' she whispered at last through stiff lips. 'Och, the poor little thing...'

Honey never fully understood what had happened to her. Only that by some miracle Sam was there, his hands sustained her in an obscure sea of pain, his eyes spoke reassurance as he bent above her, his beloved darkness blotting out the sky.

There was so much she wanted to tell him. That it was all right, everything...the morning dew...the laughing lovers in the sea...the good times, even the bad times...and Gaby, most of all about Gaby...but she could not say it, could not find the words...

She felt herself to be smiling but her face was no longer responding to her brain. Her lips only twitched, slid back from her teeth in a grimace so strange, so appalling that Sam in his ordeal could not watch but pressed his own mouth hard into her clammy palm.

He thought he felt a faint stirring of the fingers but when he looked her eyes were already glazing; she was dead long before the ambulance arrived.

He crouched there motionless for a time without dimensions. Helpless, useless. Yet lacking the initiative to move. It was as if his own life had drained out of him with hers. At length he became aware of the ticking of his watch, transmitted through her lifeless hand, the bones of his own skull. He unbuckled the strap from her wrist, fastened it on to his own. It still felt hot, as though her fugitive warmth had somehow ebbed into it and lingered in the metal. The fingers of his other hand closed over it and held it close.

'He's robbing the body!' A horrified whisper from a bystander. 'That man—he took a watch.'

Sam raised his head to stare uncomprehendingly at the circle of faces, not having realised that they were there. Nobody moved. Nobody spoke. Stunned by what they had seen, they stood and shivered in the feeble sunlight, waiting for something, anything, to release them from the mesh of his suffering into which they had been drawn. He stumbled as he got to his feet, stood swaying. Still no one moved, no one came forward to help. Rather they drew back a little, as if they feared a touch might send his agony pouring out to engulf them. With unseeing eyes he shambled away, moving numbly between the silent ranks that fell back to let him pass.

When he had gone they remained in silence, an audience still in the grip of tragedy. Then one by one they began to shuffle their feet, to utter indeterminate murmurs half to themselves; to explain to each other that after all there was nothing one could do. Someone remembered, apologetically, that he had a train to catch. Gradually, with sidelone glances lest they be thought unfeeling, they melted away.

Firemen with lifting gear came and jacked up the van; police and ambulance men carried out their gruesome duties virtually unobserved. The shattered driver was led away whimpering, to be treated for shock.

When at last the Council road cleaners arrived with their brooms, their buckets of sand and of water, there was no one left who could tell them what had happened.

'What in the world are we going to do about Gaby?' Maggie mopped her swelling eyes. 'I just don't know what to tell her.'

'Where is she now?' Arthur shovelled steak and kidney pie out of sight with even more speed than usual, the only outward sign of his agitation.

'Playing with the vicarage children, their mother said to send her over as soon as she heard the news. I didn't want her to see me upset, she'd only have started asking questions and how I'm going to break it to her I just don't know. Of only Sam were here! If only we had an address for him...'

'First things first,' said Arthur. 'Time enough for that after the funeral. You certainly don't want a child here with all that going on. What about your sister, wouldn't she have her for a few days?'

'Lucy? Well, her children are all grown but—yes, I'm sure she would. I'll give her a ring and explain.'

'Do it now. If they can have her I'll drive her up there tonight, get her out of the way before the news gets round. And you'd better get through to Hartley, see if he can do a locum for this evening.'

He swallowed his coffee at a gulp, and Maggie, glad to have been given something to do, took hers with her to the telephone to make the necessary calls. By teatime, Arthur and Gaby were on their way.

As dusk fell, Sam stood on the caravan porch. Fitted his key into the lock. He didn't know what he was doing there or where he had spent the intervening hours. It was as if, his course once set, his body had gone on mindlessly to complete the journey, moving legs, arms, hands without thought like those of a zombie. Except that a zombie could not feel...he wished he could not.

Now that he had arrived, whatever had motivated him switched off. He could only stand there staring at the door. Unable to grasp that if he pushed it open she would not be there within, head tilted...listening for him... He beat his clenched fists against the roof gable, drove his head down upon them. It was no good. He could not

even cry. At last he straightened up, opened the door and went inside.

The automaton wearing his clothes filled the kettle, set it on the gas ring; lit the lamp. He would have to do something about all this, he supposed. But not now...not now. It looked much the same as it always had, with a few exceptions. The mugs on the dresser, the threadbare rug before the fire. Even his guitar was where he had left it, and nearby a well-thumbed copy of the Clifford Essex Guitar Tutor. She must have been trying to teach herself to play. Whereas he had put music behind him, too evocative to be borne, not so Honey. There had always been that difference between them: he had run away from his past, while she had cherished hers. On the dresser he could see the record player they had bought one Saturday in Southcombe, beside a thin pile of records. He looked through the labels. Nat King Cole, Paul Robeson, Josh White...alone, she had filled her silence with black voices. Strange she had not told him any of this. He remembered the diaries of her school years, the barren letters of those days...she was still licking her wounds in private, still showing a brave face to the world. Even to him.

The kettle boiled and he turned off the gas. He didn't remember what he had boiled it for. Numbly, exhausted, he lay down on the unmade bed, turned off the lamp. He moved something knobbly from under him. Girl Sam, the ancient doll. Paint scratched, wig combed now to baldness, covered with a knotted handkerchief for a headscarf, one leg missing. Girl Sam...he rolled the hard body in his arms, turned his face into the pillow and wept.

Arthur had a difficult time with Gaby. She did not want to go to see Aunt Lucy. She did not know Aunt Lucy, had never seen her. A promised outing to the zoo fell on stony ground: she had never seen a zoo either. And Mummy had said she was to wait for her at Auntie Mags...His last vision of her was with quivering lip, small and tongue-tied on the step as he drove off. Her reluctant hand was engulfed in Lucy's, just as her wishes were engulfed by those of others. He found his thoughts echoing Maggie's...poor mite. But what in God's name was he going to do with her? If only to God they knew where to get hold of Sam—but there must be a way. There

had to be—he made a conscious effort to slow down as the needle of the speedometer touched ninety.

He reached home in the small hours to find Maggie already asleep. She looked tired and sad and he decided not to wake her; what he had to say could wait until morning. No point in asking her now to go down and search the caravan, tomorrow would do. But he was sure, now he had thought of it, there must be an address there somewhere. He tossed uneasily until dawn, listening to the whisper of rain on the windowpane. Telling himself he was just overtired.

All night the rain beat down. Tireless, ceaseless, relentless, like endless tears. In the morning the dawn came reluctantly, grey and unloving to a bitter shore. As the light grew along the horizon, an indigo bank of clouds wept ragged streamers into a leaden sea. Down in the caravan at Mango Walk, Sam woke to the knowledge that Honey was dead, and knew that he could not face such an awakening again.

3

Darkness and loss, Darkness and loss, and a groping down towards oblivion...

'Sam...Sam...'

Voices, not Honey's, trying to break through. Floating like bubbles on the surface. If he could stay down, he would be safe. The darkness inviting...silence a depth to be lost in, to be hidden in...

'Sam!' Arthur's voice, edged with anxiety. Pestering. No, Arthur, not this time...never again...not coming, never...ever...go away...

'Sam—come on, now—oh, no, you don't!' Arthur again, intrusive, impatient. And something striking his face. He barely felt it. Again. He tried to turn away. Aware of a pillow, bedding, hands...Hands mauling him, shaking him, trying to rouse him—to bring him back—he tried to twist free of them, suing for the mercy of sleep—

'Hold him, Maggie! I'll try giving him a shot.'

Hands on his arms, stripping back his sleeve—the cold sting of a needle—and his thoughts confused, agonised . . . shot...while trying to escape...

'Sam—pull yourself together!'

Shivering as the cold searched his bones and his stomach twisted with nausea, and then the awful breaking upwards towards the light—the cruel light—the hands without pity, drawing him on as he surfaced, vomiting, wretched...and now other hands, plump and motherly, trying to soothe him as he began to weep, weakly, despairingly, weeping for his loss, for his lost darkness, for his hope of escape.

'By God,' said Arthur, 'that was a near thing!' He had worked on him for what felt like a lifetime, pitting his skill, his experience, his sheer determination against Sam's own, and when the lifeless eyelids had flickered at last he leaned back, sweating with relief and satisfaction.

'Och, Arthur...' said Maggie faintly, not looking at him.

'He'll be all right, he'll pull through,' he said, misunderstanding her, 'he'll have to be watched for a bit, that's all.' He mopped his face, collected his gear, went through to the washroom to wash his hands.

Maggie followed him. 'It's not that. We've dragged him back, and he doesn't want to live. It seems so cruel, why couldn't you just have let him slip away!'

'You forget I took an oath,' said Arthur, his eyes like steel.

Maggie left him there, a stranger, and went back to comfort the still weeping Sam, who lay with distorted face pressed into the pillow, great sobs tearing through his helpless frame.

She did not know what to say, distressed beyond words by the sight of this dreadful grief. She tried to take him in her short plump arms but they would only encompass his head and one hulking shoulder; and there

he lay like some grotesque and awkward child. And there, like a child, he cried himself to sleep.

He recovered strength despite his effort to die. 'The knowledge that you are somewhere in the world,' Honey had written, 'makes it a better place for me to live in.' That had been true for him too, and he had cherished it: now there was not even that. And he could not rid himself of the conviction that he had caused her death. If she had not seen him...He sat on the edge of the bedplace and stared uncaringly before him...

'Time you pulled yourself together,' Arthur told him, 'behave like a man.'

Arthur always thought he could give you courage by bullying. He did not answer. Let Arthur have his say, it made no difference. There was always another time, and it was easier at sea. Slip over the side in darkness and there was nothing anyone could do—Next time there would be no frustration, no recriminations, no moralising; or if there were he wouldn't be there to listen.

Arthur was still talking. Making plans...he seemed to be waiting for an answer.

'Mm? What did you say?'

'I said,' repeated Arthur patiently, 'that you'll have to think about a job.'

'I don't want a job,' he said simply. 'I don't want a future.' As Arthur opened his mouth to speak, he added, 'Don't worry, I'll take myself off as soon as I can. You won't see me again.'

'And I know what that means,' Arthur's eyes flashed angrily. 'As soon as you're out of reach you're going to try again—all my work on you will be thrown away. I'm disappointed in you, Sam—I didn't think you were a coward!'

'No? Then for once Honey was right and you were wrong. She said I was a coward. But she had the right to say it and you don't. I've got nothing to live for. You don't know what that means.'

Listening to the flat toneless voice, for once in his life Arthur Colby was lost for a reply. At last he sighed. 'You'd better come up to us for a while. This place is no good for you.'

Sam followed him without argument out to the car. 'Don't stay in it, my dear love, to grieve for me...' No,

this place was no good to him. It held his own words like a sword to run him through.

A fortnight had passed since Gaby had been packed off to stay with Lucy, and still she had not been told that her mother was dead. Everyone wished the unenviable task on someone else, everyone hedged in the face of her pleading, 'Why can't I go home to Mummy?'

She whimpered unavailing day and night, refusing to eat or to be diverted, until Lucy in desperation wrote to Maggie that she really must come and take her away, she could bear it no longer.

In bed that night, Maggie showed the letter to Arthur. 'What are we going to do? She doesn't know Honey's gone. And there's Sam here forbye, not knowing she's been born—and he's only to take half a look at her, he's bound to guess.'

Arthur lay with closed eyes, considering. 'We'll just have to bring her home,' he said thoughtfully, 'and see what develops.'

'With him still here?' Maggie was dubious. 'But you know we promised never to tell him. It seems wrong somehow, the moment she's—gone.'

'He'll hardly need telling,' Arthur reminded her, 'and Honey wasn't to know what would happen to her. In the natural order of things she should have outlived him by many years.' He reached across her to set the alarm, and the suspicion of a twinkle lit his cool grey eyes. 'Who do you suppose she'd have wanted to inherit her child—a pair of old fossils like us?'

It was at moments like this that Maggie knew why she had married Arthur. She said nothing, but squeezed his arm through the wincyette pyjamas. Presently she said, 'Do you not think it'll be an awful shock to him to have the child thrown at him just this way, without warning?'

'Maybe a shock's what he needs,' mused Arthur. 'I don't know, he worries me. He eats when he's told, he shaves without trying to cut his throat. Yet he's totally apathetic. I can't move him to anything, not even to anger. His mind seems to be withdrawn to some place where I can't follow it.' He returned the pressure of her hand. 'You know, I'm fond of Sam—whatever young madam may have thought—fool though he is. I hate to watch him disintegrate knowing there's nothing I can do.'

'Is there really nothing?'

'Well...you see, there's nothing physically wrong with him, nothing I can treat. He's a perfectly normal efficient machine, but there's no—no motive power. Trying to give him the will to live is like trying to start a car with the ignition switched off.'

Maggie sighed. 'Aye,' she said sadly, 'I know just what you mean.' She too had tried in vain to strike a spark, however faint, from Sam.

Gaby sat on the lawn and wiggled her toes inside her sandals. She poked her big toe out of the open end as far as it would go and then drew it back again. It was like a snail putting its head out of a shell and going in again. She did it several times. The grass felt cool and tickly and she pretended that the snail was eating it. Then her toes began to ache and she had to stop.

She turned her attention back to the pile of daisies in her lap, big ones in pretty colours, not the little white ones that grew in the lawn. There weren't any left in the lawn but she had found these in one of the flowerbeds. She had picked them to make a daisy chain but now she couldn't do it. You had to do something with your thumb and she wasn't sure what it was. Mummy could do it...Mummy had long sharp thumbnails and she did something with them and all the daisies threaded up to make the chain.

Gaby took off her sandals and filled them with daisies, packing them carefully. When she was big she would have sharp thumbnails and soft pink hands like Mummy's. She was sure about this; all grown-ups had pink hands and one day hers would be the same. All except one...She had seen a picture once, of a man. He looked very dark in the picture, darker than Gaby; he was sitting on the beach and he was laughing, his white teeth made a gash across his face. But there was something she did not understand about this man, there was no one like that on the beach, she knew. And she did not want there to be. After showing her the picture, Mummy had cried, there was something vaguely frightening about a man who made Mummy cry...

Had she come home yet? She got up, spilling the daisies which were wilting now, and started across the lawn towards the house.

Up on the terrace where the grass was dry and crunchy

and came up prickling between her toes, she found Auntie Mag in a deckchair.

'Where's Mummy?'

Auntie Mag looked up from her knitting. 'Where are your shoes?'

Gaby looked at her feet, perplexed. She did not know about her shoes. They were not what she was looking for.

'I want Mummy.'

As if she hadn't heard, Auntie Mag said, 'Gaby, what have you done with your shoes?'

Why did Auntie Mag pretend not to hear—why wouldn't anyone tell her where Mummy was? 'I want Mummy!' she insisted shrilly, a scream of frustration and nameless fear building up inside her.

Auntie Mag stood up and took her by the arm. Her fingers felt fat and strong and unfamiliar.

'I want Mummy—I want Mummy!' Hysteria gripped her as she understood that Auntie Mag was not going to help her, was hindering her in her desperate quest, did not want her to go on looking... The scream broke loose at last, forcing its way up from her stomach and out between her teeth to burst full in the pale pink, startled, crinkly face. She lost all sense of reason or fitness, she bit and kicked and screamed, blind with rage and terror. If she screamed loudly enough Mummy would hear wherever she was hidden, would come as she had always come...

'Mummy—Mummy—Mummy!' she shrieked wildly, anguished, choking. She was still screaming as she was carried into the house.

In the quiet gloom of the library, Sam looked up and said, 'What was that?'

He was not reading as he sat there with Arthur in the stillness. The book between his hands was not even a pretence but merely a concession to Arthur's wishes: Arthur had decided it would be good for him to read. And so he sat there, silent, at the mercy of his thoughts.

Arthur looked up as he spoke. He too had heard Gaby's voice and was thinking rapidly.

'Mm-mm...what was what?' he said, playing for time while he assessed the situation. Sam was sitting upright, listening, showing the first glimmer of interest he had displayed since Honey's death; he knew he had to utilise that interest or see it die, perhaps for ever. Sam was in

a precarious mental state: a shock could undo him—or be his salvation. He was leaning forward now, his body not slumped in its habitual ennui but alert, attentive.

'I thought I heard a child.'

Arthur made his decision. He watched closely as he spoke, 'Your child, Sam.'

The listening eyes came slowly round to focus on his own. Clouded with trouble, with unbelief. But alive, not the dead eyes they had learned to expect in that face. The lips moved, saying nothing.

Arthur said quietly, 'Perhaps you didn't know that Honey was pregnant when you left her.'

The eyes held his a moment longer. Then the tension in them reached breaking point and they were wrenched away, he slumped back into his chair without a word in answer. Arthur, striving desperately to read his mind, could see in the shadows only the dark shape of his averted head, the long brown fingers like the slats of a blind dropped across his face.

It couldn't be true, Sam was thinking, oh, God, don't let it be true! Wincing at the picture of Honey, her elfin slightness distorted to the bearing of his child. In full sail; he remembered her saying that pregnant women looked like galleons in full sail. Honey...Honey—why didn't you tell me...

Distantly he heard Arthur's voice saying, 'This has been a shock to you. You had to know sometime.'

Sometime...sometime. I should have known from the beginning, and from you, Honey. Why didn't you tell me? Did you feel like Nancy towards the end, the way she lay there, thrashing, shrieking out her hate—

'Why didn't she tell me?' He had spoken his thoughts aloud.

Arthur seemed to hesitate before answering. 'She wanted to spare you. She didn't want you worried.'

'I'd have come back, she knew that—'

'Yes,' the word was spoken baldly, quietly. 'She knew.'

Sam stared at him, unspeakable things boiling up in the back of his mind.

'What you trying to tell me, Arthur, she didn't want me back, is that it?' He reared up suddenly as if on a spring, towering over Arthur who instinctively drew back.

'You know better than that,' he said evenly. 'Now calm down and listen sensibly. Feeling against you here was

running pretty high and you didn't improve matters by doing the vanishing act. Honey knew that. She wouldn't have you told about the baby for fear it might bring you running back into God knows what. Perhaps she wanted to have it in peace of mind, I don't know. But she said a funny thing at the time. She said you'd had your share of trouble and this was hers. She wanted to go through with it on her own. There was nothing I could do to persuade her.'

Sam did not answer. His hands unclenched and hung at his sides. He went slowly to the window and stood staring out. No, there was nothing Arthur could have done, he knew Honey and her wayward heart. It was so like her to spare him...him, of little faith...He closed his eyes and stood in merciful darkness.

'Did she suffer much—when it was born, I mean?'

'Hard to say.' Arthur's tone was guarded. 'They're generally rather tense with a first labour. She cried a bit towards the end of the second day.'

'The second day—Jesus, how long did it take?'

'About fifty hours. It was a normal birth.'

Sam turned away, unable to rationalise. Knowing only that Honey had spent fifty hours in pain and fear and he had not been there. All his love had been useless in the end. It had availed her nothing. He leaned his forehead against the cool still glass, desolate beyond words. They had buried her body somewhere, he supposed. He did not know where and he did not want to know. It was a part of the earth now, beyond his reach, of no more significance to him than it was to her. He did not want to kneel in the tearful grass and feel the cold stone harsh against his hands...Oh, Sam, look at all those things waiting for people...waiting for me...

'Would you like to see her now?'

He looked dazedly at Arthur. How could he see her, she was dead...

'See her?'

'Gaby—the little girl.'

'Oh, no!' He shook his head, instinctively warding off yet another threat to his ravaged emotions.

'Tomorrow, perhaps.'

'Not tomorrow.'

'Don't leave it too long. The longer you put it off the harder it will be.'

'Not tomorrow—not now, not anytime. I don't want

to see her. I'll go away, she needn't know I've been here.'

'But you must see her, Sam—you're all she has. She needs you, she's in a bad way—'

'She doesn't need me, she doesn't know me. You and Maggie, that's what she needs.'

Arthur regarded him indignantly, his sense of propriety outraged. 'You can't slide out of your responsibilities like that! You begot this child, you can't expect other people to bring her up.'

'Why not, it happens all the time?'

'Have you no conscience—'

'None. It's all worn out.'

'—no feelings—'

'All used up. I just don't care any more.'

'I shall never understand you!'

'No.'

Arthur glared impotently, unwilling to admit defeat. He got up from his chair and restlessly paced the length of the room. As if he had to force the words, he said, 'For Honey's sake—couldn't you do it for her?'

'Anything I do for her ends in disaster, you know that.'

'But—it's what she'd want.'

'She doesn't want anything. She doesn't know anything. She's dead...' It was the first time he had put it into words. It ached through his bones like the tolling of a bell.

Arthur returned to his chair, picked up his book, tossed it aside again, in an expression of nervous energy. 'What do you suppose is going to become of this child with her mother gone?'

'I don't know.' He added provocatively, 'There are places, aren't there?'

Arthur rose to the bait. 'You'd let her go into an orphanage!'

Sam's face shut like a trap. 'It's what you wanted for Honey.' His voice had an edge of flint.

Arthur floundered. 'That was different...'

'It's not different. One human being is worth the same as another.'

'It is different, it's always different when it's someone you know. You could let Gaby go because you haven't seen her, she's an unknown quantity. You know perfectly well I couldn't do it.'

'Yes, I know. So, you see, it's your turn now. You wanted Honey, you can have her daughter. Fair swops, isn't that what they say?'

'You can't be serious.'

'I am serious. Oh, you can do it, Arthur. You're so right—you're always so right! You won't make mistakes like I did, you'll be able to do the job yourself instead of only at second hand—you'll do it perfectly. And you'll have an advantage I didn't have, you'll be able to legally adopt. It'll all be plain sailing to you, just like rolling off a log.'

'But I don't want to adopt her—she's not mine.'

'Nor mine. A natural father has no rights, remember?'

Arthur slammed his book down on the floor. 'This is preposterous—I can't believe it's happening, it's fantastic—'

'No more fantastic for you than it was for me.' Sam's eyes were burning now. 'Or haven't you got what it takes to raise a child of another race, is that what gets to you after all? What's the matter, Arthur, lost the courage of your convictions now it comes to the point—Or are you just funking it? It's so much easier, isn't it, giving advice than doing the job; saying, This is the right thing, or You shouldn't be doing that—sitting comfortably out of the line of fire, not getting your feet wet or your hands dirty! It's different when it's you in there doing battle—well, it's not for me this time, someone else can have it all, someone else, not me. I've had enough, I'm finished, done, I'm a very tired old man. You do it, Arthur, and I wish you joy. You can dry the tears and foster the ambitions and wonder if you're loved—but in twenty years' time when you stumble and break your heart don't look to me for pity—I won't be there!'

Arthur was silent for so long that Sam felt himself slowly backing off like a dog who has changed his mind about picking a fight, moving away defensively while the angry fur subsides along his spine. At last Arthur said in a subdued voice, 'There's something I haven't asked you. What were you doing so close to home?'

Sam felt in his pockets and drew out the letter, flicked it across to Arthur. Without waiting for him to read it he said, 'Nancy's divorcing me at last. I came home to marry her,' and then, his eyes black pits of misery, he began to laugh.

Years afterwards, Arthur could still hear his terrible laughter in that room.

Maggie came in, perturbed, to see what was the matter. First the child, now him, she was thinking—if only coloured people were a little less excitable! But that was unfair, Honey had been as excitable as either of them and generally a great deal worse than Sam. That time she had nearly gone under the train...it still made her shiver to think of it. Take care of Sam for me, she had said, don't let him be lonely...Now she was dead and Sam sat laughing like a maniac, his eyes an abyss of agony nothing could assuage.

He stopped as she came into the room. The nerveracking noise subsided abruptly and he sat with his face in his hands, his body still shaking. She thought for a moment he was weeping but no tears came.

'Sam,' she coaxed gently, laid a hand on his arm. He shook her off angrily, roughly, coming to his feet.

'Keep away from me. I don't want you around me, any one of you. I'm going as far away from here as I can get and I'm never coming back, you hear me—never!'

Arthur said quickly, 'I've told him. He won't see her.'

'But you must,' cried Maggie, 'she needs you, you're all she's got—'

'No!' thundered Sam in desperate dread—if he saw her, if she looked like Honey—'No, no, no!' and he rushed past Maggie before they could restrain him and fled through the hallway and out of the house.

4

Sam marched unseeing down the drive in the first purposeful movement he had made for weeks. He was only peripherally aware of the sound of a car engine accelerating up the road outside, the running feet spattering the gravel behind him. Only habit made his hand shoot out involuntarily as the tiny figure hurtled by him on its way to the open gate—

'Wait!'

The child stood squirming, trying to free her arm. It felt fragile in his careful grasp, the skin like gold-brown satin. Crucified, he stared ... was he to be spared nothing?

'Child, you don't run into the road that way, you could be ...' He didn't finish that.

Gaby stopped wriggling and looked hard at the man who had arrested her. An uneasy memory stirred. She said accusingly, 'You made my mummy cry.'

Sam released her arm and took the sturdy little body between his hands. He studied her, searching her face for a shadow of his loss. But the eyes that looked back at him, unhappy, mistrustful, were his own. He knew then that he was trapped. He had turned away from Honey, from the unbearable pain of her. But how could he turn his back upon himself ...

'We all do it,' he told her gently, 'one day you'll understand.'

Gaby examined the thumbnail on the strong brown hand. 'Can you make daisy-chains?'

He shook his head. 'I can wiggle my ears,' he offered. She watched entranced, traced with a featherlight finger the scar on his cheekbone that had never quite disappeared.

'What's that?'

'What's that—what's that!' he teased her, tickling her until she squealed with delight. He tossed her up and caught her deftly, setting her down on the grass.

'What's your name?' she asked him, smiling up from where she swung from his trouser-leg.

'Sam. What's yours?' Although he knew.

'Gaby, like my daddy.' She stood up straight, enunciated carefully, 'Samson Gabriel, goes on a big ship. I can do head over heels,' and she broke away from him to demonstrate, rolling off the edge of the lawn on to gravel, sitting up nursing a grazed hand.

As he moved towards her she scuffled to her feet and trotted off towards the house.

'Mummy!' she called and then stopped, remembering. And turned back towards him, her round face puckered with distress. 'I want my Mummy,' she cried, her voice rising piteously in a thin reedy wail.

Sam closed his eyes in an agony of grief and loneliness. The child began to sob, her mouth contorted, tears that looked too large for her oozing slowly between the tightly squeezed lids. She stumbled blindly, aimlessly, over the grass, her inadequate knuckles scrubbing at her nose. He went down on his knees and drew her towards him. And then he was gripping her tightly, his own face hidden in her little heaving shoulder.

Maggie, hidden behind the curtain at the library window, held her breath. She watched in silence and after a while saw Sam dry the child's tears with his own large handkerchief. Distantly their voices reached her, 'Did your mummy ever tell you a story about a spider?'

Gaby nodded. And hiccuped.

He went on, 'I know all the stories your mummy used to know.' He stood up, 'Come on, Gaby. Time we went home.' He hoisted her up to sit astride his shoulders, his large hands gripping her tiny amber knees, and she went with him unquestioning, as children always had.

He moved off slowly down the gravelled drive, because he was weary and weakened by illness. Because he did not feel young any more and walked with more than the weight of a child on his shoulders. But his stride was lengthening as he turned into the road.

Maggie watched his head moving along above the hedge, saw the gait change after a few yards, heard the giggling as Gaby bounced and squealed and clutched at his hair.

She looked back at Arthur, still sitting disconsolate, his grey head bowed on his hands. She went over to him, laid a hand on his shapeless tweed shoulder.

'Arthur...my dear...'

He did not look up, depressed as she had never seen him.

'I made a mess of it, Maggie. And I tried so hard.' He shook his head, bewildered, still wondering where he had gone wrong.

The door burst open and there was Ellen, her face anxious. 'Oh, madam, I can't find Gaby—'

'Don't worry, Ellen. She's gone with her father.' As Ellen withdrew, she turned back to her husband, gently drawing his hands from before his face. 'You see, Arthur? It's all right after all.' She smiled into his eyes as he raised his head at last, 'I really think it's going to be all right.'

THE END

A SELECTED LIST OF
FINE NOVELS AVAILABLE
IN CORGI PAPERBACK

☐ 12142 8	A Woman of Two Continents		*Pixie Burger*	£1.95
☐ 11366 2	The Blind Miller		*Catherine Cookson*	£1.50
☐ 11160 0	The Cinder Path		*Catherine Cookson*	£1.25
☐ 11367 0	Colour Blind		*Catherine Cookson*	£1.75
☐ 12092 8	No Time for Tears		*Cynthia Freeman*	£1.95
☐ 11730 7	Portraits		*Cynthia Freeman*	£1.95
☐ 11776 5	Fairytales		*Cynthia Freeman*	£1.95
☐ 11140 6	Final Payments		*Mary Gordon*	£1.00
☐ 12001 4	The Company of Women		*Mary Gordon*	£1.75
☐ 11445 6	Mothers and Daughters		*Evan Hunter*	£1.75
☐ 11980 6	Love, Dad		*Evan Hunter*	£1.95
☐ 11963 6	Streets of Gold		*Evan Hunter*	£1.95
☐ 11446 4	Strangers When We Meet		*Evan Hunter*	£1.25
☐ 11944 X	The Wayward Winds		*Evelyn Kahn*	£1.95
☐ 10375 6	Csardas		*Diane Pearson*	£2.95
☐ 10414 0	Sarah Whitman		*Diane Pearson*	£1.75
☐ 10271 7	The Marigold Field		*Diane Pearson*	£1.75
☐ 10249 0	Bride of Tancred		*Diane Pearson*	£1.25
☐ 11981 4	Chasing Rainbows		*Esther Sager*	£1.50
☐ 10612 7	Six Weeks		*Fred Mustard Stewart*	£1.75
☐ 11575 4	A Necessary Woman		*Helen Van Slyke*	£1.95
☐ 11321 2	Sisters and Strangers		*Helen Van Slyke*	£1.95
☐ 11779 X	No Love Lost		*Helen Van Slyke*	£1.95

*All these books are available at your bookshop or newsagent, or can be ordered direct
from the publisher. Just tick the titles you want and fill in the form below.*